About the Editor

Makoto Ueda is Professor of Japanese, and Professor of Comparative Literature, at Stanford University. He has served as Chairman of the Department of Asian Languages and Director of the Center for East Asian Studies at the university. Professor Ueda's numerous publications in English and Japanese include *Nippon no bungaku riron* (Meiji Shoin), *Modern Japanese Writers and the Nature of Japanese Literature* (Stanford University Press), *Modern Japanese Poets and the Nature of Literature* (Stanford), *Art and Literary Theories of Japan* (University of Cincinnati Press), *Modern Haiku* (Princeton University/University of Tokyo), and *Matsuo Bashō* (Kodansha International).

The Mother of Dreams

and Other Short Stories

Portrayals of Women in
Modern Japanese Fiction

Edited by
Makoto Ueda

KODANSHA INTERNATIONAL
Tokyo • New York • London

NOTE: Japanese names follow the Japanese order, that is, family name followed by given name.

The editors wish to thank the following authors for allowing the publication of their stories: Harada Yasuko, Hiraiwa Yumie, Inoue Yasushi, Kaikō Takeshi, Matsumoto Seichō, Mori Yōko, Ōoka Shōhei, and Setouchi Harumi.

In addition, the estates of the following have granted permission for publication of their works: Ariyoshi Sawako, Dazai Osamu, Hirabayashi Taiko, Kawabata Yasunari, and Tsuboi Sakae.

"Shinda musume ga utatta..." (Song of a Dead Girl) by Abe Kōbō reprinted by permission of International Creative Management, Inc. Copyright © 1954 by Abe Kōbō. English translation © 1986 by Stuart A. Harrington.

"Mekura oni" (Blind Man's Buff) by Enchi Fumiko reprinted by permission of Orion Literary Agency. Copyright © 1962 by Fuke Motoko.

"Ratai" (Nude) by Nagai Kafū reprinted by permission of Orion Literary Agency. Copyright © 1954 by Nagai Hisamitsu.

Publication of this anthology was assisted by a grant from the Japan Foundation.

Distributed in the United States by Kodansha America, Inc., 114 Fifth Avenue, New York, N.Y. 10011, and in the United Kingdom and continental Europe by Kodansha Europe Ltd., Gillingham House, 38-44 Gillingham Street, London SW1V 1HU. Published by Kodansha International Ltd., 17-14 Otowa 1-chome, Bunkyo-ku, Tokyo 112, and Kodansha America, Inc. Copyright © 1989 by Kodansha International Ltd. All rights reserved. Printed in Japan.

First edition, 1986
First paperback edition, 1989
92 93 94 95 5 4 3

LCC 86-45069
ISBN 0-87011-926-5 (U.S.)
ISBN 4-7700-1426-0 (Japan)

CONTENTS

The Mother

The Working Woman

INTRODUCTION

"The most wonderful aesthetic products of Japan," Lafcadio Hearn wrote in 1904, "are not its ivories, nor its bronzes, nor its porcelains, nor its swords, nor any of its marvels in metal or lacquer—but its women." In equating women with precious objects, Hearn was restating the popular myth about Japanese women prevalent in the West during the second half of the nineteenth century. As global communication improved with time, the myth gradually waned, until, today, Japanese women are no longer the objets d'art they were once thought to be. Yet information regarding their lives and thoughts has not followed quickly. It is only recently that scholarly writings on women, as well as stories by Japanese women writers, have begun to appear in English.

This anthology of short stories is intended as a modest addition to the growing library of materials that shed light on Japanese women. All the stories in this volume, written by both men and women authors, are products of the era since the Second World War, and they show women living in a rapidly changing environment, as Japan rose from the ravages of war to become a prosperous industrial giant. The social transformation has inevitably wrought changes on women's lives, so that in many ways the women of today seem to be becoming radically different from the traditional stereotypes. Nonetheless, Japanese women do continue to play the traditional biological and social roles. The classification of the stories in this anthology into the five roles of the Maiden, the Wife, the Mistress, the Mother, and the Working Woman conforms to the traditional set. Obviously there are many other roles women can and do perform, but these five are at least a convenient starting point for an in-depth study of modern Japanese women, especially in regard to their

7

changing conception of themselves. To see the changes more clearly, we shall take a brief look at each of the five roles as traditionally conceived by the Japanese and depicted in literary works before the Second World War.

The Maiden

The image of a maiden in Japanese culture, as in many other cultures, has traditionally focused on purity, innocence, and virginal beauty. One of the earliest surviving works of fiction, *The Tale of the Bamboo Cutter* (*Taketori monogatari*, ninth century; trans. 1956), helped to create the prototype: the story revolves around a maiden of unearthly beauty, who eventually turns out to be a heavenly fairy in disguise. *The Tale of Genji* (*Genji monogatari*, eleventh century; trans. 1925-33) also features several lovely maidens, although some of them later marry. In modern literature, Higuchi Ichiyō's "Growing Up" (*Takekurabe*, 1895-96; trans. 1956) is especially famous for its portrayal of a radiant young girl, whose purity is all the more conspicuous against the backdrop of the Tokyo licensed quarters. A modern novelist most noted for his depiction of maidens is Kawabata Yasunari, to whom virginal beauty seemed to represent all that is precious on earth. Pure, innocent maidens appear and reappear throughout Kawabata's works, beginning with the celebrated story "The Izu Dancer" (*Izu no odoriko*, 1926; trans. 1955) and continuing through his postwar stories such as the three short ones included in this anthology.

Pure, innocent beauty is fragile, however. Recent writers have been more concerned with showing how it is destroyed or transformed into something less beautiful as the maiden grows up and enters the world of adults. Kawabata traced those two alternative courses of life for a maiden in his masterpiece, *Snow Country* (*Yukiguni*, 1937, 1948; trans. 1956), by portraying two women and the changes time brings to them. Another major modern novel, *The Setting Sun* (*Shayō*, 1947; trans. 1956) by Dazai Osamu, does the same against the background of the turbulent world of postwar Japan. Some stories present adults who, fascinated with the innocent beauty of a maiden, do their best to protect her or, at least, try to minimize the pain of her growth. In Tanizaki Jun'ichirō's novel *The Makioka Sisters* (*Sasameyuki*, 1943-48; trans. 1957), for example, the heroine is so naive and maidenly timid that she cannot even answer a phone call from a man she does not know well. The novel is mainly concerned with the efforts of relatives and friends to find a proper husband for this young woman who is totally incapable of finding one on her own. They would like to make sure that her maidenly beauty, which seems as pure and fragile as *sasameyuki* (thin snow), will be well guarded after her marriage.

In more recent writings, the traditional image of an innocent maiden seems to be changing. Already *The Makioka Sisters* shows something of a new type of woman by portraying the heroine's younger sister, who is more aggressive and independent. The social turmoil of the postwar era further accelerated the change. Many maidens—or young women, as they should now be called—no longer had the luxury of being protected by loving adults, who were too busy with their own affairs. Also, the Allied Forces that occupied Japan after the war helped to implement various measures that encouraged women's freedom and independence. For the first time in Japanese history, women obtained suffrage. They were given equal rights in inheritance, marriage, and child custody laws. The measure that affected young women most was the enforcement of co-education from elementary school through college. All the imperial universities used to be closed to women, but that changed after the war. The number of women going to college rapidly increased: in 1960, almost five times more women entered college than ten years earlier. In 1981, thirty-three percent of young women who graduated from high school proceeded to college (as against thirty-seven percent for young men). Such a change has to be reflected in literature, and it has been. Inoue Yasushi's "A Marriage Interview" and Harada Yasuko's "Evening Bells," included in this anthology, illustrate new images of the young, unmarried Japanese woman.

The Wife

In the creation myth as described in *Records of Ancient Matters* (*Kojiki*, 710; trans. 1882), the first divine attempt to procreate the islands of Japan fails because the goddess speaks before the god does. Traditionally in Japanese culture, as in most other cultures, the husband is the initiator and aggressor in the sexual act, in politics, and in business, while the wife is relegated to a more passive, submissive role. The stereotyped image of a virtuous wife has been a woman who fulfills that role with devotion, perseverance, and readiness for self-sacrifice. Such a model wife appears already in *Records of Ancient Matters*: in a famous episode, a princess throws herself into the ocean to pacify the sea god and thereby saves her husband from drowning in a storm. The image persists in numerous literary works in the following centuries: the loyalty and dedication of an obedient wife are highly commended, and in comic literature the shrew is repeatedly ridiculed.

Before the thirteenth century, a married woman of aristocratic birth in Japan at least enjoyed a degree of financial security because she normally had an estate of her own. Yet, living in a polygamous society, she still had to endure seeing her husband dallying with any number of other women. The agony of such a wife is given poignant expression in *The Gossamer Years* (*Kagerō nikki*, tenth century; trans. 1955). In later centuries a married woman had no financial independence, and, though polygamy was no longer sanctioned, she had to condone her husband's extramarital affairs. A good wife, in fact, was even expected to pawn off her wardrobe to finance her husband's amorous pursuits, as the hero's wife does in Chikamatsu Monzaemon's *Love Suicide at Amijima* (*Shinjū ten no Amijima*, 1720; trans. 1953). When a wife, somewhat awakened to the values of the modern age, refuses to do this in *The Family* (*Ie*, 1911; trans. 1976), by Shimazaki Tōson, she is beaten by her husband until she complies.

The beauty and pathos of an enduring wife are given artistic expression in a number of literary works, such as the nō play *The Silk Board* (*Kinuta*, fifteenth century; trans. 1914), "The House amid the Thickets" (*Asaji ga yado*, 1768; trans. 1974) by Ueda Akinari, and "The Thirteenth Night" (*Jūsanya*, 1895; trans. 1960–61) by Higuchi Ichiyō. Some wives, however, reach the limit of their endurance and turn into vindictive demonesses. Lady Rokujō in *The Tale of Genji*, for example, becomes so jealous of other consorts that her distraught soul leaves her body and haunts her rivals in love. In the nō play *The Crown of Iron Spikes* (*Kanawa*, fifteenth century; trans. 1912), a woman deserted by her husband becomes a demoness and tries to kill him and his second wife. In "The Caldron of Kibitsu" (*Kibitsu no kama*, 1768; trans. 1974) by Akinari and *The Ghost Story of Tōkaidō Yotsuya* (*Tōkaidō Yotsuya kaidan*, 1825; French trans. 1979) by Tsuruya Nanboku, the anger of the wives is all the greater because, until the time they discover they have been betrayed, they have served their husbands with the utmost love and devotion; subsequently they set out to take revenge in the most frightful way imaginable, and they succeed.

The image of an enduring wife still persists in a postwar story by Dazai Osamu included in this anthology under the title "The Lady Who Entertained." But the image is modified noticeably in other stories that follow Dazai's. They reflect the reality of postwar Japan, where wives became more self-confident and assertive. In 1948 married women formed a nationwide organization called the Housewives' Association and began various activities to protect their rights. Dressed in white aprons and carrying large wooden spoons, they would parade the streets in political demonstrations whenever the occasion called for it. Housewives also provided the main driving force for the latest wave of the women's liberation movement, which had its first national meeting in 1972. To what extent they have succeeded in changing men's attitudes is open to question. Yet it is unquestionable that the improved standard of living, with a washing machine, a vacuum cleaner, and an automobile in each household, has freed housewives from many of the chores that used to oppress their daily lives. The life of a Japanese wife has changed considerably in the last twenty years, and so has her image in literature. Two variations on the new image are seen in the stories by Mori Yōko included in this anthology.

The Mistress

What was called *onname*, a woman kept by a man for sexual service, existed from the earliest times in Japanese history, although a clear distinction between such a woman and a wife was often difficult to make during the centuries when polygamy was common. It seems that in the thirteenth century a man was legally allowed to have three wives, and any other spouse he had was considered a concubine. By the end of the sixteenth century, the second and third wives had lost their status and had come to be treated like concubines or even servants. In the upper class, a concubine was usually selected from a family socially lower than the man's. Rich merchants, on the other hand, often ransomed their favorite geisha and kept them in separate quarters. In general, a concubine's social status kept going down as centuries passed, until finally in 1882 keeping a mistress was prohibited by law. The law did little to eradicate the practice, however, and indeed had the effect of lowering the status of a kept woman still further.

The traditional Japanese metaphor for a mistress is "a flower in the shade." She is younger than the wife, more sensually attractive, and often more accomplished in music and dance. But, though she is beautiful, her beauty is touched by sadness and loneliness, reflecting the adverse circumstances under which she was brought up. Her current status as a mistress who is spurned by her neighbors and resented by the wife of the man who keeps her enhances the forlorn quality of her beauty. The mistress's capacity for perseverance has to be even greater than the wife's.

On the whole, Japanese literature has shown great sympathy for these hapless women. *The Tale of the Heike* (*Heike monogatari*, thirteenth century; trans. 1975) lyrically recounts the unfortunate demise of Lady Giō and Lady Buddha, two young professional dancers who had to serve a capricious tyrant. *Yoshitsune* (*Gikeiki*, fourteenth century; trans. 1966) portrays another beautiful dancer, Lady Shizuka, who had a more kindhearted master but who was forcibly separated from him and had to see her newborn baby executed by his political foe. Chikamatsu's *Love Suicides at Sonezaki* (*Sonezaki shinjū*, 1703; trans. 1955) relates the love and death of a young merchant and his courtesan, who kills herself out of genuine affection for the man she loves. The sad love of a professional entertainer is depicted less dramatically, but no less movingly, in several modern novels, including Kawabata's *Snow Country* and Nagai Kafū's *A Strange Tale from East of the River* (*Bokutō kidan*, 1937; trans. 1958). Understandably, some women try to resist, or even defy, the social stigma of being a mistress, although their attempt is usually doomed. *The Wild Geese* (*Gan*, 1911-13; trans. 1959) by Mori Ōgai and *A Certain Woman* (*Aru onna*, 1911-19; trans. 1978) by Arishima Takeo feature two such women.

The three stories categorized under "The Mistress" in this anthology portray more recent women victimized in a patriarchal society. The Anti-Prostitution Law of 1956 made all brothels and similar establishments illegal, but it did nothing to prevent women willingly utilizing their body for income. Call girls and kept women still exist in different guises. Some wealthy men continue to patronize young "hostesses" at high-class bars in the same way their grandfathers patronized geisha a few decades ago. In the last several years there have even been "lovers' banks," underground agencies that help their male customers to meet young women willing to become their part-time mistresses. One saving grace for recent mistresses is that they have learned to try finding some positive value for what they do. Though they know the pain of playing a kept woman's role, they are also aware that being a wife does not guarantee a happy life in the kind of society they live in.

The Mother

Throughout the history of Western culture the image of the mother has been ambivalent, ranging widely between positive and negative views. On the one hand she has been worshipped as the Virgin Mary, a holy giver of life. On the other she has been condemned as Eve, whose tempting of Adam brought death to mankind. For a child, the mother is an irreplaceable nurturer and protector and a source of pleasure and comfort, but she is also a disciplinarian who restricts the child's freedom and, if necessary, gives out severe punishment. By and large, traditional Japanese authors envisioned the mother in the former capacity, portraying her as tender and merciful and always ready to sacrifice herself for the child's welfare. Even a mother of the samurai class, who appears stern on the outside, is shown to be gentle and loving in her innermost heart.

Japan's earliest poetry collection, *Ten Thousand Leaves* (*Man'yōshū*, eighth century; trans. 1940), already includes a number of poems expressing motherly love with moving lyricism. One of the oldest collections of narrative prose, *Miraculous Stories of Japan* (*Nihon ryōiki*, ninth century; trans. 1973), contains a tale about a loving mother who, on discovering her son's intent to murder her, willingly offers her life to him, and when the Buddha intervenes, entreats forgiveness on her son's behalf. Japan's earliest surviving literary diary, *The Tosa Diary* (*Tosa nikki*, 934–35; trans. 1912), also has for one of its recurring themes the grief of a mother who has lost her child. With such beginnings, it was natural that Japanese literature of the following centuries came to produce many works featuring maternal love. The tradition reached a peak with the medieval nō drama, which, in such famous pieces as *The Sumida River* (*Sumidagawa*, fifteenth century; trans. 1920) and *Miidera* (fifteenth century; trans. 1921), showed the agony of a mother whose child has been kidnapped by a slave merchant.

The beauty and tenderness of a loving mother become more touching when envisioned in the mind of a child who has long been separated from her. Longing for a missing mother has been an important theme in Japanese literature even up to modern times. The amorous adventures of the hero of *The Tale of Genji* can be seen as manifestations of his unappeasable desire to find a substitute for his dead mother. The young heroine of the nō play *The Mirror of Pine Forest* (*Matsuyama kagami*, fifteenth century; trans. 1962) looks at her own image in a mirror whenever she misses her late mother. The hero of Tanizaki's *Arrowroot* (*Yoshino kuzu*, 1931; trans. 1982) pursues his search for his mother's relics until he finds her native village deep in the mountains and marries a remote relative of hers who lives there. In Dazai's *Return to Tsugaru* (*Tsugaru*, 1944; trans. 1985), the narrator's mother was too sickly to take care of him when he was a child, so that his search as a grown-up is for a nurse who served as a mother-substitute. Ōoka Shōhei's "The Mother of Dreams," included here, is a darker and more complex variation on this age-old theme.

The most significant change that took place in a Japanese mother's life after the Second World War has to do with a marked decrease in childbirth. In 1940 a married woman in Japan had an average of five children. That average steadily fell in the succeeding years, until it dropped below two in the 1970s. Compared with a woman in prewar days who had to spend almost all of her married life in bringing up children, a mother of today has a much easier time. Influenced at the same time by the rise of individualistic thinking, she has become more aware of her womanhood and of her right to pursue it for her own sake. Unfortunately, this awareness has sometimes led to a conflict with her maternal feelings. Our other two stories in this category, "Pheasant" by Setouchi Harumi and "A Woman to Call Mother" by Hirabayashi Taiko, study this fateful conflict between womanhood and motherhood.

The Working Woman

In Japan, as in many other countries, opportunities for women to work outside their homes have been very limited throughout the centuries. The few occupations open to women have been low-paying and usually subservient to men. In order to ensure this inferior position of women in professional life, one prominent eighteenth-century statesman even taught: "All women would better be illiterate. A learned woman does nothing but harm." Under Western influence, the situation began to change in the modern period. Still, as late as in 1908, a newspaper cartoon entitled "Professions for Women" shows only fifteen occupations as suitable. They were flower girl, telephone operator, drugstore attendant, babysitter, professional storyteller, wet nurse, woman gangster, concubine, prostitute, dancer, seamstress, masseuse, laundress, office secretary, and circus girl. The cartoonist, if he had reassessed the situation fifteen years later, would have added the factory girl, who rapidly multiplied in numbers as Japan's industrialization progressed. Factory girls suffered the most when the Great Depression came after the First World War.

Two types of working women dominate premodern Japanese literature: court ladies of the tenth and eleventh centuries, and courtesans of the seventeenth and eighteenth centuries. Their occupations were subservient to men's, yet they were accomplished in one or more of the arts, and their refined taste gave them the pride and self-confidence to compete with men on equal terms. A lady-in-waiting could laugh at a nobleman who might be much higher in court rank but who wrote mediocre poetry; a geisha could jeer at a merchant who might be much richer but who wore vulgar clothes. As characters in literary works, these women cut more lively, spirited figures than most other heroines.

Among modern authors, Nagai Kafū was particularly interested in depicting the lives of geisha and other women of similar professions, as in his novel Geisha in Rivalry (Udekurabe, 1916; trans. 1963), which deals with the lives of high-class Tokyo geisha. When the demimonde disappeared from Japanese cities after the Second World War, geisha were replaced by barmaids who entertained their guests not so much with music and dance as with witty conversation. Ariyoshi Sawako's "The Tomoshibi," included here, presents samples of such barmaids at work.

Another point of view is that of the humanitarian, who shows impoverished women struggling to survive at the bottom of modern industrial society. A particularly pessimistic example is A Case of Child Murder (Eiji goroshi, 1920; trans. 1930), a play by Yamamoto Yūzō, in which a woman laborer kills her baby because she is convinced that it would be better off dead than growing up in utter poverty. Proletarian writers, too, have shown women working in inhuman conditions, but they have often suggested a solution consistent with their Marxist beliefs. In Kobayashi Takiji's The Absentee Landlord (Fuzai jinushi, 1929; trans. 1973), for example, peasant women send their representatives to the landlord's wife to plead for relief in farm rent. Marxist implications are also found in Abe Kōbō's "Song of a Dead Girl," although elements of surrealism make the story distinctly different from most other proletarian works.

Professional women wanting greater freedom and independence began to appear in Japanese literature slowly but steadily in the twentieth century. One such woman is the talented musician featured in Tanizaki's *A Portrait of Shunkin* (*Shunkin shō*, 1933; trans. 1963); she demands and gets absolute subordination from her male student with whom she lives but whom she refuses to marry officially. Another example is a teacher of flower arrangement in Okamoto Kanoko's "Scarlet Flower" (*Hana wa tsuyoshi*, 1937; trans. 1963), who decides that she will not marry the man she loves but will use the experience to enrich her art. The last story in this anthology, "Lady of the Evening Faces" by Hiraiwa Yumie, features a woman who, though she has no artistic talent, still ends up deciding to "live just for herself." The decision is in sharp contrast with the action of her mother, who, like the "lady of the evening faces" in *The Tale of Genji*, gives unlimited love to a man who is already married.

Although the stories in this anthology represent only a tiny fraction of the contemporary Japanese literature that features women, they clearly suggest that Japanese women are breaking out of the types and roles traditionally assigned to them. Lafcadio Hearn would be saddened by what is happening, even though it was triggered and accelerated by his own countrymen who occupied Japan from 1945 to 1952. But there is no doubt that many Western observers, and certainly Japanese women themselves, welcome the change. Some regard it as long overdue, and they hope for even more change. Since literature not only records what has happened but also forecasts what will, and should, happen, we can be sure that Japanese writers, men and women both, will continue to play an important role in determining the kind of life that Japanese women lead.

I am indebted to a number of people in compiling this anthology. My thanks are due, above all, to the translators who gave me their best effort despite uncertain prospects for publication. I received valuable editorial help from Mrs. Shirley R. Taylor, who read this introduction, and from Ms. Sara Dillon, who looked through all the stories, as well as from Aoki-Brackin Associates, who worked on my draft translation of "Two Bedtime Stories." Mr. J. M. B. Edwards went over the entire manuscript for me and offered countless constructive suggestions, not only on matters of wording and style but on the contents and format of the anthology as well. Dr. Konishi Jin'ichi, Professor Emeritus of Tsukuba University in Japan, kindly answered my questions about women in classical Japanese literature. Lisa S. Oyama, an old friend of mine who is now with Kodansha International and who served as the supervising editor of this book, provided me with precisely the kind of encouragement I needed during the last stages of the project. I am also thankful to the Center for East Asian Studies and the Japan Fund at Stanford University for awarding me a research grant for this project over a two-year period, and to the East Asian Collection at Hoover Institution for securing source materials I needed. Gratitude is also extended to the copyright holders of the short stories.

Japanese names throughout this book (except those of the editor and translators) appear in the traditional Japanese order, with the surname preceding the given name. Diacritical marks are used for indicating long vowels in Japanese words, except in familiar place names such as Tokyo and Kyoto.

Makoto Ueda
Stanford, 1986

The Maiden

Kawabata Yasunari

In 1986, Kawabata Yasunari (1899–1972) was awarded the Nobel Prize for Literature for his "narrative mastery, which with great sensibility expresses the essence of the Japanese mind." One is tempted to insert a word and say "the essence of the Japanese woman's mind," for most of his works probe deep into the feminine psyche in an effort to discover an ideal type of beauty long cherished in traditional Japanese culture. Some psychoanalysts try to trace this penchant of Kawabata's to his lonely, motherless childhood, but his major novels reveal that the object of his longing was more often a maiden than a mother. He was irresistibly attracted to a young woman's romantic yearning for a distant lover, to her selfless effort to reach for the impossible ideal. In Kawabata's view, no beauty is purer or more innocent than a maiden's, and he tried to present it in his works throughout his career. His masterpieces, such as *Snow Country* (*Yukiguni*, 1937, 1948; trans. 1956), *Thousand Cranes* (*Senbazuru*, 1949–51; trans. 1958), *House of the Sleeping Beauties* (*Nemureru bijo*, 1960–61; trans. 1969), and *Beauty and Sadness* (*Utsukushisa to kanashimi to*, 1961–63; trans. 1975), all focus on maidenly beauty and its purifying power on men. It is the same even with *The Sound of the Mountain* (*Yama no oto*, 1949–54; trans. 1970), in which the heroine is married but still retains much of her virginal beauty.

The three stories translated here are selected from a book known as *Tanagokoro no shōsetsu* ("palm-sized stories"), a collection of over one hundred and thirty extra-short stories written by Kawabata at various stages of his career. The author considered them more poetry than prose pieces, as they depend more on suggestion than on explanation. Like *haiku*, they often have an open ending, too. "Autumn Rain" (*Aki no ame*, 1962) sketches the childhood of a typical Kawabata maiden—a lovely girl living next door to death, her fragility and her mistrust of grown-up men contributing to her unique beauty. The female narrator in "Socks" (*Tabi*, 1948) is a little older and has begun to show the kind of love she is capable of: both persons she loves die prematurely, and her longing is sealed in their coffins. In "Beyond Death" (*Fushi*, 1963) the maiden herself dies, and as a result her virginal love is eternally kept intact. The fact that she and her boyfriend enter a tree at the end is perhaps suggestive of Kawabata's ideal of love—pure, clean love devoid of animal passion.

THREE VERY SHORT STORIES
Tanagokoro no shōsetsu

Kawabata Yasunari

Autumn Rain (*Aki no ame*)

In my mind's eye I watched a shower of fire falling on mountains covered with crimson autumn leaves.

The mountains towered so high and so close on both sides of the stream that the valley seemed more like a gorge. I could see the sky only when I looked straight up. The sky was blue, but showed a tinge of approaching nightfall.

The white rocks on the riverbed seemed to have the same tinge. Perhaps I sensed the coming nightfall in the penetrating stillness of autumn leaves, which had descended from high above and was all around me. But on the deep blue water of the river there was no reflection of the leaves. I wondered why, and at that instant I began to see a vision of fire showering on the blue water.

What I saw were not sparks of fire raining in midair, but tiny fragments of light flickering on the water. There was no doubt, however, that the fragments were falling from the sky; they disappeared into the blue water one by one. I could not see them until they hit the water, because they fell against an iridescent background of leaves. I looked up above the mountains. Across the sky, innumerable sparks of fire were moving with surprising speed. As I watched, the narrow sky began to seem like a flowing river, a river carrying all those sparks of fire between the mountain tops.

That was a vision I saw aboard an express train bound for Kyoto. It was after nightfall, and I had begun to doze.

I was on my way to see a young woman at a hotel in Kyoto. She was one of the two girls I remembered from the days when I was hospitalized for a gallstone operation some fifteen years earlier.

One of the girls was a baby who had been born with no biliary duct. Because an infant like that would have only a year or so to live, she had just gone through an operation to insert a manmade duct between the liver and the gallbladder. I caught sight of her when she was in the hallway, held in her mother's arms. I drew close and peered down at her.

"Congratulations!" I said to the mother. "She looks lovely."

"Thank you," the mother replied quietly. "They say she will die today or tomorrow. I'm waiting for someone to come and take us home."

The baby was peacefully asleep. Her clothes, with their camellia design, looked a little swollen at the chest, probably because of the bandage that covered the surgical wounds.

It was really thoughtless of me to speak to the mother that way, but, being among fellow patients, I had been relaxed and offguard. The hospital specialized in surgery, and there were a number of children who had come for heart operations. They played around in the hallway and elevator before the day of their operation arrived, and I sometimes felt like speaking to them. They were from five to eight years old. Children born with heart malfunctions had to be operated on while they were still young. Without an operation, they would run the risk of early death.

One of those children especially attracted my attention. It was a girl I saw in the elevator almost every time I took it. About five years old, she would crouch alone in a corner of the elevator, her sulky face peeking out from among other people's legs. Her sharp eyes sparkled intensely, her defiant mouth was closed tight. According to my nurse, the girl rode the elevator for two or three hours every day. When I saw her seated on a bench in the hallway, she had the same sulky look. Once I tried to speak to her, but she did not even look at me.

"What a promising child!" I said to my nurse.

Then, one day, she was no longer to be seen.

"She had an operation, didn't she?" I asked the nurse. "Is she doing all right?"

"She went home without having an operation," answered the nurse. "She saw a child in the same room die. After that, she kept insisting she was going home, and there was no way to dissuade her."

"I see. But, if that's the case, isn't she going to die young?"

Now I was on my way to Kyoto to see that same girl, who had since grown into a young woman.

The sound of rain beating the window of the passenger train awakened me from my doze. My vision had vanished. I was aware of the rain hitting the window when I began to doze; apparently it had become so stormy that the patter could be heard inside the train. Raindrops that hit the window flowed diagonally across the glass, still keeping their shapes intact. Some of them flowed from one edge of the window all the way to the other edge. In the course of the flow, they would stop momentarily, move a little, stop again, then move again. Watching them move, I began to hear a rhythm. Some moving faster, some dropping lower, the raindrops drew all kinds of intricate lines on the window, and as they did so there sounded a rhythm, a music.

My vision of fire falling on the autumn mountains was not accompanied by any sound. There was no doubt, however, that the music of raindrops flowing across the window had become the vision.

At the invitation of a kimono merchant I knew, I was to attend a New Year's fashion show at a hotel in Kyoto two days later. On the list of models taking part, I recognized the name Beppu Ritsuko. I had not forgotten that little girl's name, although I did not know she had become a fashion model. I was traveling to Kyoto, not to see the fall colors, but to see Ritsuko.

The rain continued all next day as well. I spent the afternoon watching television in the fourth-floor lobby. Apparently there were two or three wedding receptions being held in the rooms nearby, and the lobby was crowded with guests who had come for them. I saw a bride pass by in a formal costume. Newlyweds who had just emerged from an earlier ceremony had their photograph taken behind me, and I turned to watch them, too.

My host, the kimono merchant, came up and greeted me. I asked him if Beppu Ritsuko was there. With his eyes, he indicated a spot right beside me. There she was, standing by a rain-misted window and casting her intense gaze on the bride and groom being photographed. Her lips were tightly closed. She had lived to become a tall, beautiful woman. I was tempted to walk up to her and ask if she remembered me, but I restrained myself.

"She is to wear a bridal kimono at tomorrow's show," the merchant whispered into my ear.

Socks (*Tabi*)

M y older sister had been such a gentle person. I did not understand why she had to die that way.

She passed out that evening, while lying in bed. Her body tensed, her arms reached upward, and her clenched fists shook convulsively. When the fit subsided, her head slumped to the left side of her pillow. It was then that a white tapeworm slowly crawled out of her half-open mouth.

The uncanny whiteness of the worm haunted my mind after that. Whenever I recalled the worm, I tried to remember about the white socks.

Mother was putting various things into my sister's coffin—the kind of things my sister would use in her afterlife. I called out to her.

"Mother, what about socks? Aren't you going to put them in, too?"

"That's right—I almost forgot. She had pretty feet."

"They should be size nine," I said emphatically. "Don't mistake the size for yours or mine."

The reason I spoke of socks was not just because my sister had small, pretty feet. It was because I had a special memory about socks.

It happened in December of the year I was eleven. In a nearby town a certain company that manufactured socks was showing movies as part of its promotional campaign. A band hired by the company, carrying red banners, paraded through all the neighboring villages, including mine. The band members tossed out a number of fliers and, according to a rumor I heard, some admission tickets to the movies were mixed in with them. Village children followed the band and picked up the fliers. Actually, the admission tickets were labels attached to the company's socks. Many villagers bought the socks, because in those days they were able to see movies only once or twice a year, when they were shown on festival days.

I too picked up a flier, which had a picture of a man who looked like an old townsman. Early in the evening I went into town and stood in line before the temporary theater. I was a little afraid that I might not be let in.

"What's this?" the man at the ticket box laughed at me. "It's just a flier."

Crestfallen, I trudged back home. I could not enter the house, however; I just stood outside, near the well. My heart was filled with sadness. My sister happened to come out, with a bucket in her hand. Putting the other hand on my shoulder, she asked me if something was wrong. I covered my face with both hands. She set down the bucket, went back in, and brought out some money.

"Now hurry," she said.

She was still standing there when I paused at the street corner and looked back. I ran as fast as I could. At a town store that sold socks, I was asked what my foot size was. I did not know.

"Let's see one of the socks you're wearing," the salesman suggested. It turned out to be size nine.

I showed the new socks to my sister when I returned home. She also wore size nine.

Two years later our family moved to Korea and settled down in Seoul. When I was in ninth grade, the school authorities warned my parents that I was too friendly with one of my teachers, Mr. Mihashi. They forbade me to pay him a visit. He had been ill, with a cold which continued to get worse. There were no final examinations for his courses.

A few days before Christmas, Mother and I went for to town shopping. I bought a top hat of red satin, intending to make it a gift for Mr. Mihashi. A sprig of holly, with deep green leaves and red berries, had been tucked under the ribbon. In the hat was a lump of chocolate wrapped in tin foil.

At a bookstore on the same street I came upon my sister. I showed my package to her.

"Guess what's inside!" I said. "It's a present for Mr. Mihashi."

"Oh, no!" she said in a low, reproachful tone. "You can't do that! Don't you remember the school said you mustn't?"

My happiness melted away. For the first time I realized she was different from me.

Christmas came and went, but the red hat remained on my desk. Two days before New Year, however, the hat was gone. I felt as if the last trace of my happiness had disappeared. I did not have enough courage to ask my sister about it.

On New Year's Eve, my sister took me out for a walk.

"That chocolate—," she began. "I offered it at Mr. Mihashi's funeral. It was beautiful, just like like a red ball against the white flowers. I asked for the hat to be put in his coffin."

Mr. Mihashi's death was news to me. I had not gone out after putting the red hat on my desk. Obviously my parents did not want me to know about it.

The red hat and the white socks. Only twice in my life had I put something into someone's coffin. I heard that Mr. Mihashi, lying on a thin futon, had died very painfully at his cheap apartment house, wheezing terribly, with his eyes almost coming out of their sockets.

I am still alive and keep pondering: What did the red hat and the white socks mean?

Beyond Death (*Fushi*)

An old man and a girl were walking.

The pair looked odd in several respects. There were probably sixty years between them, but they did not seem to mind it in the least, and walked close together like sweethearts. The old man was deaf. He could hardly catch what the girl said. She wore a purple kimono showing a pattern of small white arrows, although the lower part of it was hidden under a *hakama* of reddish purple. Her sleeves were a little too long. The old man was dressed in something like what a peasant woman would wear to go weeding in rice paddies. He did not wear working gloves or leggings, but his cotton shirt and pants looked like a woman's. The pants were too large around his bony waist.

On the lawn, and a short distance ahead of the pair, there stood a high fence of wire netting. Although it blocked their way, they seemed to pay it no attention. Without even slowing down, they walked straight through the fence, moving like a breeze.

The girl seemed to notice the fence after they were on the other side.

"My!" she stared at the old man with inquisitive eyes. "You were able to walk through the fence too, weren't you, Shintarō?"

The old man did not hear. But he grabbed the wire netting and began to shake it. "This damned thing! This damned thing!" he yelled.

He pushed the fence so hard that, to his surprise, it began to move away from him. He staggered and clung to the fence, his body leaning forward.

"Careful, Shintarō! What has happened?" cried the girl, dashing to hold his upper body from behind. "You can take your hands off the fence now." Then she added, "How light you've become!"

At last the old man was able to stand straight again. As he panted, his shoulders rose and fell.

"Thank you," he said and clasped the netting again, this time lightly with one hand. He then continued to speak in the loud voice characteristic of a deaf man. "Day in and day out I used to pick up golf balls on the other side of this fence. It was my job for seventeen long years."

"Only for seventeen years? That's not so very long!"

"They would hit balls any way they wanted. The balls made a sound when they hit the net. At each sound I ducked my head, until I got used to it. It was because of the sound that I lost my hearing. This damned thing!"

The wire fence, designed to protect caddies, had casters at its base and could be moved in any direction on the practice field. The field and the golf course were separated by a line of trees. The trees stood in an irregular line because they had grown there naturally and were left standing when the big grove was developed into a golf course.

The old man and the girl began to walk away from the fence.

"You can hear the same dear sound of the waves," the girl said. Wanting to make sure that the man heard her, she put her mouth to his ear and repeated, "You can hear the same dear sound of the waves."

"What?" The old man closed his eyes. "Misako, your breath is so sweet. Just like in the old days."

"Can't you hear the same dear sound of the waves?"

"The waves? Did you say the waves? And dear? How could the waves sound dear to you after you drowned yourself in them?"

"It's all so dear. I've come back to my old home after fifty-five years and found that you've come home, too. It's all so romantic." Although the words no longer reached him, she continued. "It was right for me to throw myself into the sea. Because of that, I have been and will be able to love you always, in the same way I loved you at the time I died. Besides, all my memories and recollections ended at the age of seventeen. As far as I'm concerned, you will be a young man forever. It's the same for you, too, Shintarō. If I hadn't killed myself at seventeen and if you had come back here to see me, you would have found an ugly old woman. How dreadful! I wouldn't have dared to see you."

"I went up to Tokyo," the old man began, in the mumbling tones of a deaf person. "But I couldn't make a go of it. I came home a frustrated old man. I got a job at a golf course. It was the course overlooking the sea, where a girl had drowned herself for grief after they wouldn't let her see me any more. I begged them to hire me there, and they took pity."

"We are now on the land that used to belong to your family, Shintarō."

"To pick up golf balls at the practice field—that was about all I could do. My back ached, but I carried on. There was one girl who threw herself into the sea, all on account of me. The rocky cliff where she jumped off is nearby, so even a senile old man like myself can get there and jump— so I kept thinking."

"Don't do it, Shintarō. Be sure to live on. When you are gone, there won't be a single person in this world to remember me. I'll truly be dead then." The girl clung to the old man as she said so, but he did not hear.

Just the same, he took her in his arms.

"Yes," he said. "Let's die together. You and me this time. You've come to take me with you, haven't you?"

"Together? No, you keep living on, please. Live for my sake." The girl raised her head from the man's shoulders and looked straight ahead. Her voice became animated. "Look! Those big trees are still there. All three of them look just as they were in the old days. How they remind me of those happy days!"

The old man turned his eyes toward the three big trees, too, as the girl pointed at them.

"Golfers are afraid of those trees," he said. "They want to cut them down. They say their balls always turn right, as if those trees were pulling them in with some magic power."

"Those golfers will die soon. Sooner than those trees, which have been standing there for centuries. They say those things because they don't know how short a human life is."

"My ancestors had taken good care of those trees for hundreds of years, so when I sold the land I got a promise that the three trees would not be cut down."

"Let's go over there," the girl urged and led the staggering old man by the hand toward the trees.

She passed through the trunk of one of the trees. So did the old man.

"Oh!" She gazed at the old man in amazement. "Are you dead, too? Are you, Shintarō? When did you die?" He did not answer.

"You're dead. You really are dead, aren't you? I wonder why we didn't meet in the land of the dead. Now, let's see if you are truly alive or dead. If you are dead, I'll enter the tree with you."

The old man and the girl disappeared into the tree trunk. They never came out of it.

The color of evening began to show over the bushes behind the three big trees. The horizon, from which the sound of the sea came, was hazed in faint red.

Translated by Makoto Ueda

Inoue Yasushi

Inoue Yasushi (b. 1907) is one of the most popular novelists among women readers, although his literary reputation is by no means limited to any specific group. It so happened that the most productive period of his literary career coincided with the years of Japan's rapid economic recovery. As living standards rose, women were freed from various household chores that had prevented them from reading novels and stories. Inoue's fictional works were especially appealing to them because, unlike the naturalist novels that had been the staple of modern Japanese fiction, they always had a well-constructed, intriguing plot, and a beautifully poetic prose style. Moreover, many of his novels with a contemporary setting, such as *The Hunting Gun* (*Ryōjū*, 1949; trans. 1961) and *Icy Crag* (*Hyōheki*, 1956; trans. 1967), were love stories featuring a handsome, masculine hero and a lovely, intelligent heroine futilely trying to wrest a meaning from life in the sterile modern world. Such historical novels of his as *The Roof Tile of Tempyō* (*Tempyō no iraka*, 1957; trans. 1975) and *Tun-huang* (*Tonkō*, 1959; trans. 1978) were large-scale romances that portrayed idealistic, intense men pursuing their hearts' desire in ancient China or Persia or some such exotic country. Many of these novels became bestsellers, and they contributed a great deal to narrowing the gap between "artistic" and "popular" fiction, a gap that had long existed in Japan.

"A Marriage Interview" (*Miai no hi*) was first published in a women's magazine in 1963. Written in a lighthearted manner, the story reveals changing attitudes toward a traditional Japanese institution known as the *miai*. Normally in old Japan a marriage was arranged through negotiation between the two families with the help of a go-between, sometimes even before the prospective bride and groom had met. The *miai* was a formal occasion to introduce the two young candidates. Inevitably, people of the younger generations grew increasingly reluctant to accept a custom reminiscent of feudal times. Some insist, however, that the *miai* is not without its merit in a modern society, where marriage from passion and impulse too often ends in conflict, estrangement, and divorce. The time-honored custom still survives, with some modifications, in today's Japan.

A MARRIAGE INTERVIEW
Miai no hi

Inoue Yasushi

On the morning of the day she was to first meet young Minato Yaichi, Keiko slept until nine o'clock. This was a rare occurrence, since Keiko, even at her latest, never stayed in bed much past seven. From where she lay, she could hear her mother and younger sister chatting away in voices far more animated than usual. It occurred to Keiko that her mother had probably left her undisturbed to sleep her fill in the hope of presenting at the marriage interview a daughter glowing fresh and lovely.

Keiko left her bed just long enough to go and draw back the window curtain, then returned to her covers. The bright blue of a totally cloudless sky filled the window. Autumn leaves, having passed from red to brown, still clung to most of the oak and zelkova trees; it would still be some time before those waving branches near the window were completely bare. Along with the sunlight, these leaves took on a luster of their own. Even lying on her side in bed, Keiko knew that it would be one of those splendidly clear days of late autumn.

"Keiko!" Her younger sister Hisako called to her from the staircase. "Mother says it's time to get up! Remember, it's the day of your *miai!*"

Hisako had said it again. For the past ten days, her mother and sister had talked of nothing else. Keiko was hardly surprised that her mother should keep mentioning the meeting, impelled as she was by a parent's instinct to settle a daughter's marriage prospects before that daughter should pass the proper marriageable age. However, Keiko was quite at a loss to understand seventeen-year old Hisako's behavior. Evidently in high spirits over her elder sister's *miai*, Hisako was sporting about impishly.

For her own part, Keiko found the entire matter of the day's *miai* nothing

31

more than a nuisance, and not just as far as her feelings were concerned. It seemed that this resistance to the *miai* extended right down into the lower part of her body, which was listless and languid—sufficient proof that neither her heart nor her body had any sense of joy in anticipation of it. In fact, Keiko had no real expectations at all from this arranged meeting with Minato Yaichi, a young man who, having graduated from the medical school of K University, had stayed on there as an aspiring medical researcher. Yet, since her entire family had made such a fuss over this *miai*, she had agreed to it out of reluctance to dampen their spirits. This would, in fact, be her very first *miai*. There had been talk of a number of possible matches prior to this, but she had managed to let them all pass. Each time, she had invented a plausible excuse and evaded going through with the *miai* in question.

This meeting with young Minato was not in itself particularly objectionable; it was just that Keiko felt it impossible to work up any enthusiasm toward a *miai*. She had given in this time purely because those around her had shown such persistence, but she had also decided in advance that she would later turn down the offer.

When she was twenty, Keiko had known a young man about whom she had decided, then and there, that were she ever to marry, he would surely be the one. When this young painter died of a sudden and totally unexpected overnight illness, Keiko had believed that, in all the world, there was no other man she would ever marry. She had not arrived at this conclusion by any conscious means; rather, the impression left on her heart by the painter was just too strong to admit of any other. Keiko simply could not bring herself to wish for marriage with anyone else. No one in her family was aware of what her feeling toward the young painter had been. Before she had either opportunity or occasion to tell them, her painter departed this world without warning. Keiko said nothing of her disinclination to marry any other man. The only person who knew of that was her closest friend, Sagawa Keiko.

Thus, this day's marriage interview with the promising young medical doctor simply held no meaning for Keiko. In a few days' time, she would dream up the sort of excuse which would inflict no pain or loss of pride on the young man, and decline any further consideration of the match. In that sense, it would amount to no more than a sort of nonsensical one-act play, witnessed by a handful of spectators.

Keiko at last descended the staircase. Although their plan was to set out for the agreed-upon location at one o'clock, her mother was as flustered as if the *miai* were her very own; indeed, she had already made up her face and laid out several choices of clothing from her own and Keiko's wardrobe.

"It's not a wedding ceremony, Mother. It's a *miai*," Keiko said.

"But this first meeting is even more important! It's the *miai* that decides everything. Hurry, now, hurry!"

Keiko could hardly see any reason to rush, but her mother's urging was not to be gainsaid. Still, in the spirit of hoping to thwart her mother, Keiko said, "I'm not going to put on any makeup for this. I'd rather have him see my true face."

Leaving such preparations aside, she went outdoors to pat her dog. A pale autumn sunlight was scattered across the grass of the yard.

The elevation on which the restaurant stood commanded a wide view of the Tama River, which flowed away far in the distance. The restaurant served refreshments prepared in a spare, but painfully elaborate, tea-house style. When all the trays had been cleared away, Keiko, at her mother's side, sat gazing out into the tiny courtyard.

A small grove of perhaps ten bamboo grew just beyond the veranda of the formal parlor. The quiet sunlight, as it fell on the green leaves, seemed more a thing of early winter than late autumn.

Keiko's *miai* partner, Minato Yaichi, was seated next to his mother, in such a way that they faced Keiko and hers. The elderly Mr. Senuma, vice-president of an insurance company, was seated next to his wife, their backs to the alcove. Mr. Senuma had originally been responsible for broaching this *miai* to both sides.

"Well, Keiko, how do you like physicians?" Mrs. Senuma asked, perhaps in the hope of making Keiko speak up. Throughout the meal, a lively conversation had proceeded along lines totally unrelated to the young pair, but this shift seemed to indicate that it was time to bring them center stage.

"I don't particularly like or dislike physicians. But I can't really say I'm very fond of them." That was, in fact, Keiko's unembellished estimation of doctors.

"Young people these days all seem to say that. It must be because one only sees the doctor when one is sick!" put in Yaichi's mother. A youthful fifty years old, plump and glowing, she spoke without altering her pose whatsoever. Inappropriate as it was felt to be for a woman, she was reputedly an avid student of the nō theater, and it was perhaps from that that her fine posture came.

"But my son says he will not go into private practice—he'd rather spend his life in the research laboratory. Of course, whether that's a good thing or a bad thing, we really can't say." One could hear in her words a mother's desire to shield her son.

"Yaichi is a fine student," replied Mr. Senuma, "so it's best for him to go on with his research. A scholar's is the greatest path; he'll certainly gain the respect of others, in any case!"

"I'm not sure a scholar gains any respect!" retorted Yaichi, but in a cheerful, relaxed tone. "A scholar lives his whole life in poverty, wearing threadbare clothes and toting around a tattered old bookbag! He gets tossed about on the train every single morning. Then at school, he's harassed by his students; when he comes home, he gets it from his wife! It's a wretched existence! I don't relish such a fate, but, unfortunately, I'm not suited for anything else."

"In that case, maybe private practice would be better," suggested Mrs. Senuma.

"I'm just not cut out for private practice. I'm so careless, I'd probably botch my diagnoses; and I'm too timid for surgery. When I hold a scalpel, my hand shakes like mad, and I can't get it to stop!"

"Oh, my!" Keiko laughed in spite of herself. At the same time, she felt a nudge from her mother.

Keiko looked across at the young man. He appeared to be neither nervous nor timid. Indeed, he was of so fine a physique, it seemed a shame for him to be locked away in a laboratory. By any estimation, he was very solidly built.

"You've always said you prefer the slender type, so this young lady should be just the thing," said Mrs. Senuma, attempting to change the subject.

"Did I really say I liked slender women? I once heard that slender types are almost always clumsy. From that time on, I began to think that plump girls are better after all. They say that plump girls are usually lively and a little scatterbrained—like my mother, for instance!"

"What a fresh thing to say! And what about you?" his mother exclaimed. Keiko quite agreed with her.

"Oh, men should be a little on the fat side, too. That's why all the nurses make such a fuss over me," the young man continued in a flippant tone.

His mother frowned. "You stop that, now! What's gotten into you today?" She then turned to Keiko. "You must be appalled. He's always like this; as far as he's concerned, this is no *miai*!"

This time it was Keiko who spoke up in a rebellious vein. "Oh, it's the same with me. It was my mother who was so keen on coming, not me. Come to think of it, isn't it strange? I mean, seeing someone for the first time, how can you tell if he's good or bad?"

"Now what's gotten into *you* today?" It was her mother's turn to ask.

"I'm not against such meetings," said Yaichi. "Just a glance at your partner's face, and you can make a fairly good guess at what the future would hold. It's a kind of game, isn't it? That's fine with me. Actually, these things ought to be more natural. I suppose the ideal is really a love match."

"That's what you say, but you're hardly the type for that!" his mother replied.

"I mean it! Anyone who's reached our age has had at least a couple of love affairs. It's just that the family doesn't know about it. Isn't that so?" Yaichi turned to Keiko for collaboration.

"I really don't know about such things," she answered.

But Yaichi persisted in his argument. "I mean, is there anyone who hasn't been through something of the sort?"

"I suppose it's only human," said Keiko.

"But you haven't done anything like that!" Keiko's mother scolded.

"Oh, Mother, you know all about it, don't you?"

"No, I don't!"

"Of course you do! Remember—in grade school, I was madly in love with my homeroom teacher."

"Oh, if we start including those, my list goes on and on," declared Yaichi. Though this was supposed to be a peaceful gathering, it was threatening to become chaotic.

"Let's save the true confessions! This is a *miai*, after all!" said Mr. Senuma. "But never mind; a little candor's good for the soul! You two just go right ahead and get things out in the open!" He seemed to be trying to prevent the discussion from getting so far out of hand that the party would be spoiled. "We're just going to stay behind here and have another cup of tea," he went on. "Why don't you two young people go out and have a stroll along the river?"

"Let's do that, then!" Yaichi leaped to his feet. Keiko felt relieved as well. Anything was better than being cooped up in that narrow room with a young man who was undeniably ill-mannered, along with the two mothers as witnesses to the duel.

Going toward the veranda, Yaichi took care to bend over as he passed out of the room, but ended up grazing his head on the lintel nonetheless. When at last he stood up straight, he proved to be incredibly tall. He stood head and shoulders above the average person.

As instructed by Mr. Senuma, the two made their way out onto the road that ran along the river embankment, but what with the steady stream of cars, they could hardly enjoy a leisurely stroll.

"How about going on down to the water's edge?" Yaichi suggested.

"All right."

"What shall we do? As far as I'm concerned, we might just as well say goodbye here and now. For the sake of the families, though, we should at least be able to say we walked together for an hour or so. Otherwise, the Senumas would be hurt, wouldn't they?"

"Well, then, mightn't we continue on for a bit? That's the most natural thing to do."

The two climbed down close to the water's edge. They could see pairs of young lovers sitting here and there in the wild grass that lined the river. Just beyond these overgrown fields, the Tama River flowed past like a blue-green obi. The opposite bank had been turned into a practice ground for student drivers, and dozens of cars crawled about in the distance like toys.

"What a relief!" Yaichi exclaimed. "You know, it was the Senumas who first mentioned you to us; they were terribly enthused about the whole affair. My parents got caught up in the excitement, and, before I knew it, they were all carried away, too. And here we are! So, as far as we're concerned, isn't this where we cut our losses and call it quits?"

Depending on one's point of view, his remarks were in fairly bad taste.

"I intended to refuse right from the time it was first discussed," Keiko said.

"Of course, I thought so. That was my plan as well."

"You're to blame, though, since your side agreed first. I had no choice, then, but to go along with it."

"You're quite right. I'm really sorry. In fact, I want to postpone marriage for a while. My research isn't much, but I'm quite preoccupied with it. I even sleep about half of every month in the laboratory! It takes up so much of my time that I wouldn't know what to do with a wife and family right now. If I had enough time to spend with my wife, I'd just as soon spend it with a guinea pig."

"That's just splendid," Keiko said, thoroughly irritated with him by now. If she allowed him to go on talking, there was no telling what might come out. "Then I was simply wasting my time today, wasn't I?"

"Not only you!" the young man replied. "In fact," he went on, "from the beginning, you had no real interest in getting married, either. Isn't that so? I heard as much directly from someone who says she's your best friend."

"Who do you mean?"

"Sagawa Keiko."

"Oh, Keiko!" Of course, there had been no way she could fool her. "Then you know her?"

"Not really; I was just introduced to her by chance at a friend's house. Since she mentioned having gone to the school you were from, I brought up your name. Then I found out that she knew you well. Of course, she spoke without knowing that we had this *miai* coming up, but what she had to say really surprised me! I thought that I had gotten myself quite a partner for a *miai*!"

"What was it she said?"

"That someone you loved had died, and that you had refused all the *miai* ever suggested to you; and that if you ever did accept one, you'd decide in advance to refuse the offer. She said that's just the sort of person you are. Well, anyone would have been surprised—not just me! On the other hand, though, I was relieved too. I went along with the *miai* knowing I didn't want to get married, either. All right, so my partner has no intention of really getting married—we suit each other perfectly, then. I figured there'd be no hard feelings on either side. That being the case, no one was really tricked into wasting their time, were they?"

Hearing it put that way, Keiko found herself thinking that, after all, he could be right.

"I see. I was wondering why you started right in saying those nasty things!"

"Oh, no—you're the one who got nasty first. You started it, then I got angry and paid you back."

"Oh, really? But I simply took my cue from you! I thought, 'Fine! If that's the way he wants to be!'"

"Everyone must have been surprised!"

"No question about that! And it certainly wasn't very considerate toward the Senumas."

"Oh, I don't think they mind. Playing the go-between is one of their hobbies. Anyway, they can't expect people to get married just because they happen to set up a meeting."

The two cut across a field of wild grass and came out on the very edge of the river. Then they followed a path leading upstream. Here and there in the far distance they could just make out groups of small children, as well as pairs of young lovers. They saw the sleeping figure of a woman, a handkerchief across her face to ward off the autumn sun.

Suddenly, a voice called out, "Keiko! Oh, Keiko!"

Keiko stopped in her tracks and looked around her. From the midst of the group of small children playing in the grassy field to her right, Utsuki Nobuko came forward to greet her.

"It's been such a long time! I've been wanting to see you!"

"Utsuki Nobuko!"

"I have a new family name, you know. No more Utsuki—I'm Kaneko now!"

"I completely forgot—I'm sorry. Are these your children?" Keiko gestured toward two small ones nearby. The older looked to be about four or five; the other was just leaving the toddler stage.

"Yes, they really keep me busy."

"You look so happy!"

"I'm doing pretty well."

"That's wonderful. I envy you."

Nobuko lowered her voice a little and said, "You two seem very friendly. Is he your husband?"

"No!"

"Well, then, your boyfriend?"

"Hmm. . . ." Keiko gave a vague reply and laughed. It seemed a shame to deny it.

"He's quite something!"

"What do you mean?"

"He's so handsome! He looks like a foreign movie actor."

"He does research—in a university."

"Is he an athlete?"

"Well. . . ."

"What a physique!"

"He's just big, that's all."

"You really shouldn't show him around too much. Everyone will be jealous."

"Don't be silly!"

"No, I mean it! Won't you introduce us?"

"Not quite yet. Sometime later."

"How mean of you! He'll hardly disappear just from being introduced to someone!"

"After we're married."

"Before that you'd be worried?"

"Maybe a little."

"You're terrible! Will you invite me to the wedding?"

"Of course."

"You can get my address from our class register, but let me give it to you now, anyway."

Nobuko returned to the group of children, and came back immediately with her handbag. She took out a namecard and handed it to Keiko.

"You must come to our place, too," she said. "I'll introduce you to my husband. Mine isn't as handsome as yours, but he's very kind."

Keiko bid Nobuko a hurried farewell, then turned to find that Yaichi had gone off to chat with some children who were fishing from the river bank. As she approached him, Keiko said, "Sorry to keep you waiting like that."

As she spoke, she looked this young man over once again. Perhaps he did indeed bear some resemblance to a foreign movie actor. Even so, why did he have to be so very large?

"Now, now, let me do a bit of the fishing for you," he was insisting to the children, speaking from far above their heads.

"No, leave it alone!" The children were being most ungracious about it.

"Let me try it just once."

"No!"

"Don't be so selfish. Hand over the pole. You know," Yaichi went on, beginning to walk away as if he had quite given up on being allowed to try his hand at fishing, "if you let me use your fishing pole, I'll catch all kinds of fish for you!" He then turned to Keiko. "Oh," he said, "it feels good to walk like this! This is what they call a clear-sky *miai*, isn't that it?"

"My friend back there was complimenting you—she said you were very handsome."

"Who, me? That's the first time I've ever had compliments from a woman."

"But you said all the nurses make a fuss over you."

"Oh, that! You've got me there. I just said that to be sociable."

"You chose a strange way of being sociable." After a pause, she added, "Are you going to keep on walking?"

"It *is* pleasant, walking along this way. Why don't we have a *miai* every once in a while? In any case, let's head back for today. I don't see any need for us to return to that restaurant."

"I agree."

"We can go by train together as far as Shibuya, then go our separate ways from there," said Yaichi.

Arriving at Tamagawaen Station, Yaichi bought two tickets for Shibuya and handed one over to Keiko. She thanked him politely as she took it from him. Just as they were heading for the platform gates, an elderly man of about seventy came hurrying towards them from the opposite direction.

"Well, if it isn't young Mr. Minato!" the old man cried out, drawing to a halt right in Yaichi's path. Yaichi hadn't even noticed the old fellow until he heard his own name being called out.

"Oh, Sensei, it's you!" He halted abruptly. Keiko stood a little apart from the two.

"So, you're still alive, I see!" the energetic little man cried out at the top of his voice.

"I'm sorry for not having stayed in touch with you," Yaichi said.

"If you're so sorry, why haven't you come to see me?"

"I will come, one of these days."

"When is one of these days? Next year or the year after? It seems that once you graduated from college and started doing pretty well for yourself, you forgot all about your old high school teacher!"

The old man's manner was decidedly blunt.

"No, I'll really come to see you very soon." Yaichi's large frame seemed to grow smaller right before Keiko's eyes.

"All right, then—come and have at least a cup of tea with me now. My house is right close by. You can't have forgotten where I live, can you?"

"No, of course not!" Yaichi was certainly showing that he had a diffident side.

"Do you have something else to do?"

"No, not at all."

"Come on over, then!" The old teacher paused. "Is that your bride over there?" he asked, referring, of course, to Keiko.

"No, not my wife."

"Not married? What's the story, then?"

"She's my fiancée."

"Oh, so you're getting married!"

"It looks that way." Yaichi took out a handkerchief and wiped his face.

"In that case, you two must come along together. I'm going to buy some fruit, so you go on ahead of me."

"Fine, we'll do that."

"See you later, then!" The old man parted company with Yaichi and walked off across the square in front of the station. Even after he had disappeared, Yaichi stayed for a while rooted to the spot. It was several moments before he returned to where Keiko was waiting for him.

"What a person to run into here!" Yaichi exclaimed. "He was my high school teacher, notorious for his strictness. Actually, he's wonderful— very kind-hearted and all that, but I just can't seem to relax in front of him. When I see him face to face, I get all tongue-tied."

"You did seem to stiffen up quite a bit!"

"I told you, didn't I? Actually, it was rather embarrassing—I haven't been in touch with him for over a year now. In fact, he's just invited me to drop over to his house before I go home."

"And are you going?"

"I suppose so. I have to, actually. I hate to ask you this—I know it'll be a bother, but do you think you might come along with me? I just went and told him that we were engaged!"

"Did you really?"

"As long as it slipped out like that, though, we really ought to go together."

"I don't mind at all. Of course, let's go! I'll just think of it as a sequel to our *miai*. As a matter of fact, I told my friend back there that we were engaged, too. So we're even." Keiko said. "But shouldn't we bring along some sort of gift?"

"You're right, we should."

"Let's buy some sweets or something."

They stopped at the pastry shop in front of the station and selected a box of cakes. It was Keiko who paid for the purchase. They walked a short way along the side of the station building, then climbed a road which led up the slope of a hill.

"I'll warn you now. Whenever I see that old teacher of mine, I start shaking in my boots. And there's nothing I can do about it!"

"I know that much already—I had a look at you back in the station."

"I can't understand it myself, but that's the way I always get. I guess I'll always see him as my teacher." He seemed to be trying to justify his timidity. "Anyway, help me out somehow, won't you?" he asked.

They stopped before the gate. The signpost read, 'Ōnuki Shūzō.'

"I used to be terrified just looking at his nameplate!" said Yaichi. "I remember how he used to send for me and shout at me."

"What did he call you in for?"

"Oh, sometimes I'd be caught smoking, sometimes I got bad marks, skipped school, you know. . . ."

"What a bad boy! But I thought you were such a brilliant student!"

"That's a bit of an overstatement. It's true that after I started at the university, my grades improved quite a lot, but I was hopeless in high school."

As they approached the hallway of Mr. Ōnuki's house, a voice greeted them from inside, "Come right on through!"

"Let's go," Yaichi murmured to Keiko, stepping over the threshold ahead of her. A narrow corridor led directly into a sitting room which appeared to serve as both the teacher's study and a guest room. This house, like the restaurant, commanded a view out over the Tama River where it flowed in the distance. In the teacher's tiny garden, white chrysanthemums were in bloom. The room was a peaceful and pleasant one. The old teacher himself was seated on the opposite side of a low rectangular table. Yaichi and Keiko took their places facing him.

"So what is your name?" the old man asked Keiko.

"Keiko—written with the characters 'laurel' and 'child.'" She seemed to be as nervous in the old man's presence as Yaichi.

"That's a fine name. Hmm—Keiko. You're far too good for young Mr. Minato here."

Yaichi lowered his head a little.

"Yes, that's true."

"See that you take good care of her!"

"I will."

"You can always tell a good person at a glance. She's a fine young lady." The old man poured hot water from a thermos bottle into a small teapot, in front of which he laid out three teacups. To judge from his manner of arranging the tea things, the old teacher seemed to have lost his wife some time ago.

"Shall I pour for you?" Keiko took over for the old man and poured out the tea into the cups.

"There's some fruit in the kitchen. Could you take it out for me? Plates, knives, forks—you'll find everything you need in the cupboard," the old man said to Keiko. She rose instantly and went to do exactly as he had directed her. Peeling the fruit, she set it out before them on dessert plates. After waiting a little while, she also set out the pastry they had brought with them, and made some black tea to go with it. During all this time, Yaichi had not relaxed his formal posture, but seemed to be chatting cheerfully enough with his old teacher. Although he had said he just couldn't face this old man, he wasn't doing so badly after all.

The pair stayed talking for about an hour before taking their leave of the old teacher. At the door, he said to them, "I want to be invited to the ceremony. I'll give a little speech."

"Yes, we'd like that," Yaichi answered.

"You know," the old man continued to Yaichi, "in high school, you hadn't much to show for yourself, but there are two things you've done right since then, and they deserve a little praise. The first is that you studied hard at the university; the second is that you found Keiko."

"Yes."

"That's what I'll say at your reception."

"I'd appreciate that." Bowing several times to his teacher, Yaichi led Keiko out through the front door. It seemed to be about four-thirty; already, darkness was falling. They walked side by side down the same hill they had come up. The temperature had dropped suddenly and they felt chilled.

"Was I wrong when I agreed to invite him to the wedding?" Yaichi asked. "Anyway, you can understand why I did, can't you?"

"Especially since I promised my friend exactly the same thing!"

"To invite her to the wedding?"

"Yes! But, anyway, no matter how much we might want to invite them, if there's no real ceremony, there's nothing to invite them to!"

"That's true, I guess," said Yaichi. "But if there should be a ceremony, we could invite them, couldn't we?"

"I suppose so."

"If we must invite Mr. Ōnuki and that friend of yours, there's nothing for it but to go all out and have the ceremony."

"We'll just be forced to, won't we?"

"Right."

"Maybe that will make for an interesting wedding," Keiko laughed.

"Marriage by coercion from beginning to end! Nothing to do with what the bride and groom might like." Yaichi also laughed as he said this.

"That's the way it has to be," said Keiko.

"As you say, it might prove to be pretty interesting. The natural outcome of a forced *miai* is a forced wedding." Yaichi slackened his pace a little. "How about having dinner together on the Ginza?" he asked.

"I'd be happy to accompany you."

"Western food or Japanese—which do you prefer?"

"I'd rather have Western, but what about you?"

"Well, if I had my druthers, I'd like Japanese—but I'll go along with you tonight. Next time it'll be my choice."

"That's fine with me." Then she continued, "The people at home must be worried. I'd like to give them a call from somewhere."

"What will you say?"

"Hmm. . . ." As a matter of fact, she really was at a loss what to tell them.

"How about this?" Yaichi seemed to have come up with something. "Since I have to call home as well, here's a story we can tell both sides. You tell your family that you were against it, and I'll tell mine that I was against it—but, in the end, we each had marriage proposed to us so persistently that we couldn't give no as an answer. For the time being, then, we plan to meet every once in a while. If that goes well, we'll go ahead and get married at some future date!" Yaichi evidently found his own idea fairly amusing and laughed unabashedly.

"That's a pretty weird tale," Keiko protested. "But, anyway, that's what I'll say, too. I can tell any crazy story if I really put my mind to it, you know." Then Keiko joined in with Yaichi's laughter. At that instant, an image of the young painter rose up in her mind's eye, but to Keiko as she was at that moment it seemed very small and extremely far away.

She and Yaichi walked back toward the station together. She had never walked along with a man in quite this way before. Yaichi took such long strides that she found herself every now and again having to run along to keep up with him. If I were to marry this young man after all, she wondered, would I always have to walk along with him just like this?

Translated by Sara Dillon

Harada Yasuko

Harada Yasuko (b. 1928) grew up on the northern island of Hokkaido, which was later to provide the setting for many of her stories. After finishing high school she worked as a reporter for a local newspaper, until she married one of her colleagues. Around this time she began writing stories and had them published in local magazines. One of them, a novel called *Elegy* (*Banka*, 1955–56; trans. 1957), attracted the attention of an editor in Tokyo, who subsequently arranged its publication in book form. It immediately became a bestseller, with a sale of some seven hundred thousand copies in 1957 alone. Later the novel was made into a movie, which also was so popular that Hokkaido began to attract many more tourists than before. Harada has since written a number of novels and stories, still keeping her residence in Hokkaido.

Many of Harada's works are love stories, often featuring a young woman and a middle-aged man. Although her characters live in spacious, ruggedly beautiful Hokkaido, the social upheaval and moral chaos of postwar Japan have not spared them. While older folks have lost confidence in themselves and in the society they live in, younger people, especially women, have gained the courage to defy traditional morality and behave as freely as they like. They seek love, but they have few or no romantic expectations of it. They want to live, but they know the world of adults looming before them is a spiritual wasteland. Harada's stories have introduced a new type of women to Japanese literature, and the heroine of "Evening Bells" (*Banshō*, 1960) is an example.

EVENING BELLS
Banshō

Harada Yasuko

I was just about to leave the house when Father called and asked me to put off going out for a while. Since Father hardly ever telephoned me, I was dying to find out what it was he wanted. He just laughed, though, and said, "I'll tell you when I get home," before he hung up.

I felt a bit irritated at this, as I was supposed to be at the local broadcasting station by seven o'clock. As a member of the station's choral group, I rehearsed there in the studio twice a week. Of course, I loved to sing; but, as I waited for Father, it seemed to me that missing just one rehearsal wouldn't make that much difference. Part of the reason I enjoyed going to the studio was that it was one of the few places where I could socialize.

It was past eight o'clock and still Father hadn't returned. Not having the slightest idea what was on his mind, I got tired of waiting around for him. I thought I might pick out a tune on the piano, and slipped quietly into the parlor without bothering to turn on the lights. I was afraid that if I went striding across the carpet, I might send the dust flying all over.

No guests had appeared at the Kuki residence in quite some time. That was why I had not been cleaning the parlor as often as I should. I didn't invite any friends to my house and they, for their part, never came to visit me at home. Father also seemed to have made it a rule to receive guests only at his office. It wasn't just the parlor I neglected, but, giving myself up to laziness, I also left several unused rooms completely untouched. I limited my cleaning to the living room, kitchen, bathroom, and the two bedrooms Father and I used. Since the two of us were living alone in the house, there was no need to keep the other rooms tidy.

I drew open the heavy window drapes to let in the starlight and seated myself at the piano. The unkempt garden beyond the window lay in darkness. There were wild grape vines clinging as they do to the side of the house; their withered leaves tapped lightly on the window pane.

In the dark, my fingers ran softly over the cold, faintly whitish keys of the piano. My tune was neither an elegant etude, an enchanting chanson, nor a lively jazz piece. Rather, I played an impromptu which took as its motifs everything around me: the withered leaves scattered across the garden, the cracked walls of the house, its sagging floor, the smell of dust mixed with a faint odor of mold, forgotten books resting in the middle of the bookcase, a one-armed Negro doll lying on its face in our display cabinet; also, those people who had died and those who had simply disappeared; and last but not least, Father with his affectations and I myself, Father's pet, twenty-two-year-old homemaker and young lady of the Kuki family.

Father arrived home shortly after I had entered the parlor. I didn't hear him come in and, while I was still playing, he quietly approached me from behind, laying his hands on my shoulders. I whirled around in surprise. There was Father, still wearing his white duster, smiling at me.

"Sorry to keep you waiting like this."

"I won't forgive you," I replied, a little put out at having been taken by surprise.

"Let's go into the other room," Father said, pushing softly against my back.

The living room was bright and tranquil. Our cat, Clotilde, sat crouched beneath the dining table. Father drew back the white cloth I had spread over the evening meal. Tiny plates and bowls heaped with dried fish and Chinese cabbage glittered up at him.

"As usual, an unspectacular repast," Father said, replacing the cover. "You haven't eaten yet, either?"

"Well, I've been waiting for you."

"That's just perfect, then."

"What do you mean?" I asked. Then I suddenly remembered Father's telephone call. "What was it you wanted to speak to me about, anyway?"

"Have there been any love letters for me?"

I decided to play along with him. "Why would you get any love letters?"

I noticed that Father was more voluble than usual, and very persistent. His words had the distinct aura of alcohol about them. His broad forehead, still tanned from the summer sun, was faintly reddish. There was nothing extraordinary about Father taking a few drinks on the way home, but at such times he was most apt to grow reticent and sink into a kind of melancholy.

Without even taking off his coat, he sat down on the sofa and lit up a cigarette.

"Are you sure there haven't been any love letters? I don't mean today—maybe four or five days ago."

"Ah!" At last I had remembered something.

Four days before, a special delivery letter addressed to Father had arrived. Far from being a woman's letter, it was no more than an undistinguished, brown paper envelope from the office of a local town magistrate. It was also stamped with the name of the sender, a man I had never heard of. Since it certainly didn't look like anything important, I stuck it into the drawer of the cabinet and forgot about it. The only reason I had not mentioned it to Father was that during the week since it had arrived, Father and I had hardly run into each other at all. He would come back home after I had gone to bed, and, since I liked to sleep late in the morning, he would be gone before I was up and about.

I hunted around in the cabinet for the letter and, as I handed it over to Father, I noticed for the first time that the sender's name bore the title of bailiff. Father, cigarette still dangling from his mouth, carelessly cut open the envelope. I sat down beside him and peeped over his shoulder at the letter which was typed on thin Japanese paper. I was struck by the very first line: Notification of Distress.

"What is that?" I asked impatiently. I could feel my heart beating faster. "Has something happened?"

"I've tried everything I can. The debt's too big. I just can't handle it," Father answered in a surprisingly calm tone of voice, folding the letter back up. "This house, the land, and all the valuable furniture are going to be seized."

"When?"

"Probably tomorrow."

Totally taken aback, I stared at Father. He smiled at me tenderly. I knew that Father's company had fallen on hard times, but I had never really taken any interest in its actual management. Since it hadn't once occurred to me that our very house might be seized as a result of Father's business failure, it seemed incredible that we would be forced to give up all our property within the next few days.

"This house will be gone?" I asked, still watching Father nervously. "We can't stay here after tomorrow?"

"Well, there is something of a grace period."

"But we can't go on living here, isn't that right?"

"We can't stay here, no."

"But where will we go?"

"We'll find a place somehow."

"Oh, no!" Unwittingly, I let out a low cry. "No, I'm not moving! You go without me; I'll stay here and kill myself!"

I grew more and more excited as I spoke, until at last I burst into tears. Clotilde came over and jumped onto my lap. As I stroked her cold nose, I pressed my face into the back of the sofa. The velvet was warm against my tear-wet cheeks. I felt the bitter pain of being forced to part even with this sofa. So I would really have to leave them—these chairs and old pieces of furniture so familiar to me that I had never bothered to handle them with loving care. As the sadness grew more intense, I sobbed all the harder, while Father gently stroked my head.

"Come, dry your tears," he said, smiling faintly. "Papa will take you out."

Father had surprised me once again. I lifted my face and he looked down at me teasingly.

"I came back especially to take you out for a good time."

"Do you have enough money?"

"Oh, sure," Father laughed.

"Where shall we go?"

"Wherever your little heart desires."

"I don't want to go," I said hoarsely. "How can you think about having a good time, when after tomorrow everything will be gone!"

"Tonight, I want to have a nice time with my little girl. You can humor me once in a while, can't you? You must admit, you've pretty much neglected me lately."

I silently bit my fingernail. I knew only too well how much affection for me lay behind Father's words. I was certain that he was genuinely sorry for me. Perhaps he wanted to be kind to me tonight, show me a good time, and let the future take care of itself. Or perhaps he was hoping, if only for tonight, to bury his agony by doting on me.

Looking at things in that light, I felt my pain and sadness melt into something sweet and comforting. Of course, my sitting in the house wouldn't bring about any miracles. It seemed best simply to go out with him as he had suggested and, forgetting about tomorrow, bask in his kindness like a little girl. I pushed Clotilde off my lap and smiled at Father for the first time that evening.

"Wait for me, okay? I'll just run and put on some makeup."

As Father smiled back at me, I could make out deep crinkles at the outer corners of his eyes. Father was forty-nine years old; the white hair at his temples, more than one might expect in a man of his age, gleamed silver.

I hurried over to my bedroom and changed into a wool dress I hadn't yet worn since making it in the spring. It was close-fitting and of a bluish-purple color. It seemed to me, as I put on my makeup and a pair of crystal earrings, that the dress had been specially made for this very evening. So soon after tears, my eyes glittered feverishly. Then I suddenly felt as though, just behind this stately three-way mirror in which they had so often been reflected, stood Mother and her entourage, smiling at me. It made me want to start sobbing again.

Father and I went out into the street together. The dense, cold night air of mid-October was a reminder of the approaching early winter.

Our family house stood on the edge of a rise. From between the trees of our garden, we could see fanning out below us the downtown area, overflowing with lights. From deep within those lights, there arose the faint stirrings of the town. The harbor, too, was bright with the lights of several ships at anchor. Yet the reality of what was clustered all about me—the red-tinted evening sky, the dark and distant sea, the noise of automobile horns and neighborhood radios—all these intimate traces seemed terribly far away, quite beyond my reach. I felt, rather, that even now it was the distant days gone by which were my only reality.

As we stepped out through the front gate, I turned to look back at our house. Only the living room was lit. The one-story, wooden Kuki home stood imposingly in the hushed darkness like a lovely medieval manor.

Only during Mother's lifetime did lamps burn in nearly every room and guests pass back and forth over our threshold. Father had never entertained his friends or business associates at home, so nearly all our guests had been Mother's.

However, despite the many visitors, our house was a quiet one, and we rarely held large, ostentatious gatherings. Mother's guests were not the sort to burst into unrestrained laughter or converse noisily. Most of them were either elderly people or women near Mother's own age. The elderly guests had been friends of my great-grandparents and grandparents, all of whom had died before I was born. These old people talked about the ambition and flair for business which had marked the careers of my great-grandfather and grandfather, coming as they had to settle in eastern Hokkaido at the beginning of the Meiji period in 1872. One could see on the faces of these guests a nostalgia for the dramatic days of their youth, before the town had been developed, as well as the awe and respect they felt toward my forefathers. When they spoke of my father, though, one could faintly detect in their tone a certain disapproval of what he had done. This was because Father, having abandoned much of the work handed down to him by my grandfather, had become a civil engineer and devoted himself to the management of the Kuki family enterprises. Our family fortune, built up by the older generations, had gradually begun to disappear after I was born. When the elderly guests had said all they wanted to say, they would go off into the altar room and spend long hours chanting Buddhist sutras before returning home with a sense of satisfaction. As for the ladies who came to visit Mother, they were our town's well-to-do women, those who took special care to conduct themselves according to the high-society manners of Tokyo. But the serenity which prevailed in the parlor, despite this throng, was due above all to the composure of Mother's character.

Mother was by nature a quiet person, always the listener rather than the talker. When she spoke with her guests, a smile would play about her eyes and lips. When she laughed her quiet laugh, the corners of her soft, lovely mouth always tilted upwards. Her hair and eyes were also beautiful, but I especially liked her hands. She nearly always wore one particular ring on her smooth, delicate finger—a large, glittering jade ring, the deep green of which set off the fairness of her hands. Her lady guests, with all their high-society affectations, invariably stared at Mother with a mixture of admiration and animosity in their eyes. For that reason, I didn't like them. I often felt irritated at Mother for not brushing off these women who talked of nothing but the most tedious sort of gossip.

There were, however, two young guests whose arrival I always awaited:

a young man called Komatsu Shūichi and a girl, much younger than Mother, called Wajima Jun. They were the two callers who appeared most frequently at the Kuki house while Mother was still alive.

Komatsu Shūichi was a young man who began giving me private piano lessons the spring after I turned eight years old. At that time, the wars on the Chinese continent and in Europe were just escalating.

Komatsu Shūichi came to our house twice a week. However, giving lessons was only a side job for him; perhaps he was really a music instructor at some junior high school or at a school for girls, or just an unrecognized musician with nothing to show for himself but his ambitions. Even after I was a bit older, I couldn't find out from Mother anything more about Komatsu's past.

This young piano teacher of mine had a defective leg. His face was narrow, his eyes and eyebrows betrayed a certain intensity and his complexion was poor. Only his Cupid-like, softly curling hair gave his appearance a touch of youthfulness.

Even walking along our hallway, Komatsu Shūichi never let go of his heavy, curved walking stick. At its tip, this lustrous black stick was streaked with traces of dry white mud. Whenever I caught sight of that slender body of his, leaning as always on the cane and moving among the garden trees, or heard the sound of his cane as he came down the hallway, my heart began to throb as if something were just about to happen. To my ears, the sound of that cane had the same uncanny, mysterious quality as a magician's wand. Komatsu Shūichi's deformity cast a deeply romantic shadow over his whole person.

I awaited Komatsu's coming not because I enjoyed my piano lessons, but because I was enchanted with his very aura. In learning to play the piano from him, I was merely following Mother's instructions. As a matter of fact, I found piano lessons much more of a trial than a pleasure. At my young age, I found it difficult to memorize the music, and my fingers never did manage to run freely over the keys. On top of that, Komatsu Shūichi was very strict with me, refusing to indulge me at all. During all the time I had lessons with him, even toward the end, I never did master the art of playing the piano. And I never felt anything but hostility toward Beyer's exercises.

During our private lessons, we had the parlor all to ourselves, just this young man with the defective leg and I. Under Komatsu's merciless instruction, I was either so frightened or peevish that he, too, often lost his patience. He would push me down off the piano bench and start to strike out a piece himself. With me, he never chose a sweet melody from his repertory, but instead played only rigid, fast-paced tunes that demanded much technical skill.

His playing sounded lovely to me, full of a tension which would leap out at anyone who might draw too near. As he played, the bluish blood vessels that rose up along his forehead were in perfect keeping with the sounds he drew forth from the piano. Resting my chin on the top of the piano, I watched in amazement the dizzying speed of his fingers and the expression on his face. Although I despised the very existence of our parlor piano, I loved both his music and Komatsu Shūichi as he played it.

Each of my lessons ended with Komatsu Shūichi taking over at the piano. As soon as he began to play, Mother would prepare some refreshments, which she carried in to us there in the parlor. I always ran and clung joyfully to Mother, but Komatsu would not leave his place at the piano, even after Mother had entered the room.

As long as Mother was there, I felt no fear whatsoever of Komatsu Shūichi. Dragging her over to the piano, I would try everything to make him stop playing. As Mother approached him, the color gradually rose into his pale cheeks. At that instant, the faintest shadow of fear would also pass across Mother's face.

Komatsu Shūichi and my mother were in love. No doubt it was for the sake of their love that I was made to take piano lessons for five long years. But I merely provided an impetus for their affair; what really drew them together was in all probability Komatsu's handicapped leg. There was never anything aggressive about my mother. She was invariable gentle and graceful; discreet towards one and all. My mother certainly had much with which to captivate this undoubtedly stubborn young man. It seems to me that at first Mother displayed an affectionate concern for Komatsu; then, by the time she realized he had fallen in love with her, she, in her excessive gentleness, couldn't bear to wound him. It was this very gentleness which led Mother into that perilous liaison to begin with.

Of course, I was too young to realize all this at the time. All I was aware of then was that in the air between Komatsu and my mother were intimations of something out of the ordinary. That this something was love I didn't know until much later.

I occasionally saw Komatsu and my mother alone. Except for the cold-est winter days, I would go flying out the front door right after my piano lesson, for all the world as if I had been uncaged. Sometimes even after I had played about along the evening shore and in the garden, Komatsu Shūichi's shoes were still set out on the veranda when I returned. I would go racing down the hallway and throw open the parlor door. Komatsu and Mother were invariably seated in armchairs facing each other. Even when I entered the room, Komatsu did not so much as spare a glance for me, his pupil. Instead, he was staring fretfully at, first, Mother's chin, then her throat and ears in turn. Sometimes he sat tapping the end of his stick against the floor or wall. Once he abruptly tossed his half-smoked cigarette onto the carpet and rubbed it out with his foot. At such moments, the look in his eyes was just like that when he played the piano. Watch-ing the two of them together like that, I felt as if the parlor were overflowing with the sound of Komatsu's music. For her part, Mother would smile timidly, as if trying her best to pacify the tense, strained Komatsu. See-ing me there, Mother's smile grew all the more gentle. Although dinner would be ready soon, she would begin to peel some fruit, until I just didn't know what to think.

Whenever I came upon these two together, I became strangely excited, for I saw that there was something between Mother and Komatsu Shū-ichi which did not exist between Mother and me, Father and me, Father and Mother, or between Komatsu and me. I realized gradually that Koma-tsu and Mother shared something which was theirs alone.

My first clear perception that this relationship of theirs was somehow peculiar came about three years after I had begun piano lessons with Komatsu, when I was eleven.

It was a day in early summer. As usual, I was off to play by the shore as soon as my lesson had finished. Heavy and milk-white, the evening fog which hung over the sea seemed to bubble up from its very depths. I was absorbed in gathering shells up and down the damp sand dunes until sunset, returning home at last with my sweater quite drenched in fog. Passing through the front gate, I trotted across our front garden, where lilac flowers gave off their fragrance into the fog. The lamps of our dining room, kitchen, and living room shone forth from among the trees. I crossed in front of the parlor. It was dark as a cave, its windows left wide open.

It was the very first time I sensed Komatsu's presence without having seen his shoes left by the door. What told me that he was still in the house with Mother was, rather, the eerie darkness of the parlor.

As I entered the house and tiptoed along the corridor, my chest grew so tight I could hardly breathe. In my sweaty palms the shells I had collected were wet and clammy. I came to a halt before the parlor door. Dead silence within; the rough-grained door shut tight. In fear and trembling, I reached out my hand for the doorknob. Perhaps because I was so frightened, the door seemed dreadfully heavy, almost like the great rock gateway to Ali Baba's cave. Biting my lip and pulling at the door with all my might, I was greeted by a rush of sea fog as it finally opened.

The parlor was aswirl with a cold fog and sea wind, mixed with the smells of lilac flowers and seawater. A noisy wind shook the wall hangings, the curtains, and the wide-open window. Mother and Komatsu stood side by side near the windowsill, with that pitiless sea wind blowing in on them. They stood close together, facing each other in silence. Those motionless silhouettes of Mother and Komatsu loomed up in the faint white fog like a rigid pair of statues. With my gaze still fixed upon them, I drew up short in the center of the room. There was a severity about their statue-like profiles which would allow no one else to approach. It was then that I felt that I was nothing but a nuisance to them. Even so, I couldn't turn back; were I to do so, I felt, Mother would be lost to me forevermore. It was this vague terror which kept me rooted to the floor in the middle of that room.

"Mama," I called out at last in a hoarse voice, "I brought you some seashells."

Mother still did not move.

"Mama, don't you want them? Mama, I'm asking you!" At the instant my sentence rose up into something like a shriek, the statues by the window gave way. Mother rushed over to my side. I threw my arms tightly around her soft body. At that moment, Komatsu wrenched the shells from my hand, threw them onto the floor, and stalked from the room without uttering a word. As the sound of his walking stick receded into the distance, Mother tried to cradle my head firmly in her arms. I twisted out of her grasp and looked up at her. There were tears in her eyes.

From that time forward, Komatsu Shūichi grew harsher still during our piano lessons. Small as I was, he acted with the sort of severity a master craftsman might use in training a gifted apprentice. No doubt his harshness grew from the hopelessness of his love and from his hatred toward me, since I had guessed the nature of the secret he shared with Mother.

Yet, being over eleven years old at that time, I learned how to deal with Komatsu's merciless treatment. It wasn't that I came to enjoy piano any more than before; it was just that I was attracted to Komatsu's face when he was most severe with me. When he scolded me, he was not an ugly young man; his became a face lovely in both its pain and fastidiousness. Darting a glance at that face of his, I often simply lost control of my fingers on the keyboard. Although Komatsu took no notice of what had distracted me, he would hardly let my faulty playing pass by unchastised. A few false notes, and he would make as if to strike me. I, giving a start, would instantly turn my full attention back to the music sheet before me.

But I was a child, after all. While I was certainly charmed by Komatsu's face, I couldn't be entirely insensible to his cruel manner. Once, to punish me for my poor memory, he even rapped me on the forehead with some rolled-up sheet music. My hands faltered and, in a fit of anger, I slammed the piano shut. The humming of strings reverberated out across the room.

"If you don't want to play any more, that's fine with me," he hissed. "You can drop dead as far as I'm concerned!"

I went pale at his words. It wasn't a passing rage that drove him to say such things. No, rather, I saw that he despised my very existence from the bottom of his heart. Yet there in his eyes as he glared at me was the same lovely, yet indescribable suffering as before. Then I began to hate him as he hated me, still downcast under that clear, hard gaze of his. Growing more agitated, I glared up at him.

"Cripple!" I let out a low cry and retreated a step backward.

His fingers closed around the top of the walking stick that was leaning against a small table.

"Cripple!" I shrieked once more.

At that moment, someone flew like a small wind into the room, but it wasn't Mother. It was Wajima Jun, the young woman who was a special favorite of Mother's.

"What do you think you're doing? And to a little child like this!" she scolded Komatsu in her resonant voice. Then she ran off down the corridor, dragging me along behind her.

To have appeared out of the blue at just the right moment, Wajima Jun must have been eavesdropping from outside the door. In fact, she seemed to be always alert to what Komatsu Shūichi was up to. Whenever she caught Komatsu in one of his nastier moods, she would chuckle softly, her large eyes sparkling with merriment.

Wajima Jun was the daughter of one of father's business associates, so I suppose she was first introduced into our family by either her own parents or my father. I can't recall her very first appearance among us, but, in any case, her visits began long after Komatsu Shūichi's. At that time, she must have just graduated from a girl's high school. She was a lovely girl, with long hair and a neat, boyish figure.

Unlike Komatsu, she visited our house only irregularly. Around the time the war was drawing to an end, Jun went to work at her father's office, although it seems she took time off whenever it suited her. She might well appear at our house without warning at any time of the day or night. Instead of entering through the front door, Jun always crept stealthily in through either the kitchen door or the balcony of the sunroom. She would sneak up behind Mother or me, startle us by covering our eyes, and proceed to chatter about something. Playing up to Mother, Jun would toy with Mother's white fingers as she spoke. Of course, I was put out by Jun's manner of playing up to Mother—Jun was, after all, a good deal older than I. But Mother, for her part, was also very sweet to Jun. Mother always seemed to be watching over this young girl with a look of both tenderness and fatigue. I recall certain moments when Jun, gazing at this expression of Mother's, would suddenly go pale, the usual bloom fading all at once from her cheeks.

I knew exactly what Jun, cheerful and chatty as a little bird, was always afraid of: more than anything, she dreaded meeting my father while she was at our house. Although the hour of her visit was totally unpredictable, she never appeared when Father was at home. When she did come to visit, she would grow increasingly uneasy toward nightfall, watching the front of the house, and even asking me to keep a lookout for Father's return.

Father had always come home late in the evening; he also travelled quite frequently on business. His trips to distant factories might last for days, or even weeks. Even when he was home, he hadn't much to say to his family, but spent most of the time alone in his study. I can't say we were very intimate. He seemed to me like a steep and inaccessible mountain. That doesn't mean I didn't love him. I could feel the warmth in his eyes when he looked at me. And I liked the way he was in his study— quiet, thoughtful, with a faint bitterness traced along his brow.

I was also fond of Wajima Jun. Her stories about all the different places around the world were so vivid, it seemed she had visited all those places herself. When she played with me on the beach, she was as lively and energetic as a boy. And she always took care of my unfinished homework for me. This was different from the attraction I felt toward Komatsu Shūichi and his particular aura; Jun I valued as an elder companion.

I could not understand why Jun should be so frightened by my father. First of all, unlike Komatsu Shūichi and my mother who were so often alone together, I had never once seen Jun with Father. I could hardly imagine mild-mannered Father posing any threat to a young girl like Jun. Each time she had me stand guard for Father's possible return, I wanted to know just what it was she was afraid of. On those occasions when I did ask her, though, she would grow very cross. Glaring at me, she warned that if I so much as breathed her name to Father, she would make me pay dearly for it. At such times, should Mother and Komatsu Shūichi be within earshot, Mother would look away and smile weakly, while Komatsu would have an icy smile on his face. Holding back her tears, Jun would begin showering Komatsu with abuse. Flustered, Mother would try to calm Jun down, while Komatsu's teasing grew all the nastier. I was totally forgotten in the midst of all this.

I felt suffocated by this strange blend of tension and ennui that surrounded the trio. I detested them, I envied them. In the end, I couldn't help regretting my hasty, thoughtless question.

But it did not take me long to find out why Jun was so afraid of Father.

While Father was away on business trips, Jun was constantly at our house, sometimes even staying overnight. It wasn't that Mother encouraged her to stay; on the contrary, as soon as Mother, concerned about the hour, suggested that Jun head for home, Jun would put up a fuss about having to leave.

I looked forward to those nights when Jun would stay over at our house. Instead of sleeping in the guest room, she always slept in mine. We would nestle down together like two kittens in my narrow little bed. For me, accustomed as I was to long and dreadfully dark nights, nights alive with witches, goblins, and reptiles, the presence of Jun, whom I liked so well, was naturally quite a treat.

One particular night in early winter, while Father was away on a business trip that was to last three weeks, Jun had come to sleep in my room. With our hair entangled and the tips of our noses nearly touching, we whispered together far into the night. As we talked, Jun stroked my back and bottom with her cold hand. Through our pajamas, my breasts which had at last begun to fill out and Jun's own soft ones were touching each other. Unlike Mother's eau de cologne, the fresh scent given off by Jun's body reminded me of gooseberries and almonds. I drifted toward sleep, wrapped round in a faint sense of shame and a gentle joy.

When I awoke in the middle of the night, Jun was not at my side. And I heard a man and woman talking in low voices in the next room. It was probably their voices that had awakened me. Listening hard, I realized that the man's voice indeed belonged to Father. At the same instant, I knew that the girl must be Jun. Startled, I immediately sat upright in bed. It wasn't Father's unexpected return that surprised me so much; rather, I was shocked that Jun, ordinarily so frightened of Father, should be in there talking to him.

The room next to mine was only used to store useless, worn-out furniture. Still in my pajamas, I slid down off my bed, far too surprised and curious to sleep any longer. I could see that snow was just beginning to fall out beyond the window, and the floor of our silent house felt cold under my feet. Pressing myself up against the wall, I clenched my teeth to keep them from chattering in the cold. Try as I might, though, I couldn't make out what the two were talking about; I could only tell that Father was scolding Jun for something. As low as he was speaking, I could still detect a certain sharpness in his tone. I was trembling as much from the severity of his voice as from the cold. I wanted to go and call Mother, but felt reluctant to tell her how very angry Father was. I was certain that this harshness, a harshness I had never heard before from Father, was meant for Jun's ears and hers alone. Deep within Father's scolding voice were sweet, dark hints that neither Mother nor I should by any means ever hear. How striking was the resemblance, I thought, between the atmosphere escaping from that room piled with old furniture and the air about Mother and Komatsu Shūichi as they stood together in the fog-white parlor. After a little while, Jun managed to say a few words, followed by the sharp sound of something being struck.

Some twenty or thirty minutes later, Jun returned to my bed and, lying down, took me in her arms once again. She was chilled to the bone and trembling slightly. As she sobbed, I felt her wet cheek against my ear. Shocked as I was, I was sorrowful at the same time; I knew that my lovely night had been spoiled. I felt the tears rising in me and, in my confusion, thrust my face against Jun's shoulder to prevent her from seeing I wasn't asleep. I vowed to myself that I would never divulge what I had heard that night.

Just as I grew weary of feigning sleep, I did in fact fall asleep. When I awoke early the next morning, Jun had already gone home. The snow that had fallen during the night lay in a thin cover over the dead leaves in the garden. I went running out into the yard to look at it. In the hard, cold air of early dawn, the Kuki home stood utterly silent. Not even the maid was up and about, and each window was firmly shut. A heavy shade had been drawn down over the window in Mother and Father's room. It almost appeared that some tranquil, pre-dawn slumber prevailed in Mother and Father's room, quite as if nothing at all had happened. But this tranquility only served to exude a menacing loveliness. Forming a snowball in my bare hands, I crept up beneath the window and crushed my snowball against the wall.

Father and I climbed the stairs to a restaurant on a busy downtown street. Burnt out during the war, the restaurant had been rebuilt in such a clean, tidy style that a good deal of its former charm had been lost.

This not being the dinner hour, the place had but a handful of customers—four or five small groups of men talking about business and drinking beer. We chose a table by the window. Every bar on the street sent its own music blaring out into the cold night air; perhaps because it was nearly winter, the crowd on the pavement just below us was unusually large.

Father ordered a brandy and a high ball, saying, "We can eat something if you like, but let's have a little drink too."

"Sure."

"What would you like to have for dinner?"

I read over the menu. After I had gone ahead and ordered some shrimp and chicken dishes, I almost regretted having done so.

"You don't mind my being a little extravagant?"

"I invited you out, didn't I?" Father laughed. "Don't you worry about it."

"I'm sorry, Papa." Batting my eyes at him, I gave Father a clownish apology. Alone with him like this, I had decided to enjoy myself to the full and spoke as I did quite without thinking. It wasn't as if I were simply forcing myself to have a good time; I was responding, rather, to an impetus from within my heart itself. It was rare for me to either walk the streets alone with Father or go to dinner with him. The luxury of ordering such a dinner, the sort of luxury I had nearly forgotten, also did much to lift my spirits.

In the old days, Mother's home cooking had been very elaborate. Mother and I frequently went out for meals together, too. On those occasions, Wajima Jun often came along. I never remember once going to a restaurant with either Komatsu Shūichi or Father. Even when the war had entered its most critical phase, we knew a place which would serve us French food on the sly. In a small back room of some restaurant, undisturbed by either music or other people, Mother, Jun, and I would spend long, lazy afternoons chatting and laughing quietly together.

As I reflect on it now, it seems clear that the reason Mother was so kind to Jun was that she knew well that Jun loved Father. By the same token, Jun would play up to Mother because, while aware of Mother's affair with Komatsu Shūichi, she herself was in love with Father. Of course, Father too must have have been aware of the relationship between Mother and Komatsu, and so turned his affections toward Jun.

One peculiar thing is that I never once witnessed a quarrel between Mother and Father. For that matter, I never saw either of them even irritated or cross. Whatever their true emotional state might have been, once they were face to face, they were as quiet as could be. I saw nothing to indicate that somewhere else, in some place known only to them and forbidden to me, this tranquility was lost or violated. Mother was by nature reticent and Father was certainly not what one could call frank or open. Perhaps their naturally restrained characters prevented them from arguing. Or perhaps, because of their unconscious contempt for the reckless ways of my great-grandfather and grandfather, both Mother and Father sought to preserve at least the outward appearance of gentility. It is also possible that the only way left for each to apologize to the other was to leave the other's love affair undisturbed.

After Mother died, the memory of the peaceful days Mother and Father had spent together never failed to amaze me. This amazement also had a certain sensual joy in it, of the sort one might feel when suddenly embraced by a man with whom one has long been infatuated.

Mother died of angina in the autumn of the same year we lost the war. A small unit of American soldiers had just taken up quarters in our town at the time, and Mother's funeral turned out to be a pitiful, poorly attended affair. Nearly all the mourners consisted of those affected middle-aged ladies who used to bore me so when I was a little girl. There were hardly any elderly people present, as most of those old guests who used to visit our house had passed away during the war. Neither Komatsu Shū-ichi nor Wajima Jun appeared at Mother's funeral. As I looked about at the mourners in their dark clothes that day, I kept thinking to myself that the only people to feel any real grief at Mother's death were probably just Father and I, Komatsu Shūichi, and Wajima Jun.

However, even after the funeral, neither Komatsu Shūichi nor Wajima Jun ever appeared at the Kuki home again. Of course, it was natural for Komatsu to avoid our house, and after Mother's death, he could no doubt see no point in continuing to give me piano lessons. For my part, I had no desire to go on learning piano from him, either. I knew that my role was finished. I never so much as opened my practice books again.

I didn't expect to ever see Wajima Jun again, either. Perhaps her love affair came to an end with Mother's death as well. Thinking it over afterwards, I wondered if perhaps Jun's passion disappeared as soon as she lost her rival in love. With the image of Mother fading from memory, Jun had no more hopes of finding happiness with Father. Perhaps Father and Jun continued to see each other outside somewhere. Of course, it was hard for me to really know what was going on between Father and Jun, but I couldn't help feeling that after Mother's death the two simply followed each other quietly offstage. I made no attempt to ask Father what had become of either Komatsu Shūichi or Wajima Jun, and I never ran into them around town.

Thus Father and I settled down into this quiet life of ours. When I finished my schooling, I let our maid go. I felt that I could certainly look after Father's needs by myself, and I had no desire to leave him to move out on my own. Without any constraints, I wanted only to go on being good to Father and spoiled a little by him in return. He was good to me, too—the gulf that had always separated us quite disappeared. We became so friendly that we often laughed and joked together.

Even after we began to live alone like this, though, Father continued to spend a good deal of his time outside the house. I was left alone, then, in this house which was far too big. Free from any and all prying eyes, I would get up at whatever hour I pleased, neglect the housekeeping, nibble on whatever I felt like eating, tease the cat, or just lie in bed reading newspapers and books. If the mood should strike me, I might do a little pruning in the garden; that was about the extent of my activities. There were many days when I spoke not a word to anyone, and I became thoroughly lazy.

But I wasn't totally confined to the house. I loved to have fun and enjoy myself as other girls my age. I joined the choral group of our local broadcasting station. Shutting the door behind me, I would go out to movies or coffee houses; I also enjoyed dressing up. I became friends with a number of young men, and thought some of them especially attractive.

When I found myself with a young man I liked, though, I never got very serious. I was merry and talkative, and loved to banter back and forth. My companions were as light-hearted and cheerful as I and they were good-natured. I enjoyed going out with them to coffee shops or taking a stroll through town in the evening. At such times, I was completely free of Mother and Komatsu Shūichi and Wajima Jun; then they had no chance to get hold of me. At moments like that, should I happen to recall those three, they seemed to me like strangers living out lives in some foreign city. Late at night, though, with only Clotilde for company, I felt these three coming back to seek me out. I could hear the sound of Komatsu Shūichi's walking stick and of Father's hand striking Jun across the face. Then, what had seemed real until just a few minutes before would in its turn seem but an exotic tale, and my past would take over as my true, continuing reality. Compared to these scenes from the past, my budding feelings of love seemed unbearably silly.

I never felt any repulsion toward the everyday life I knew as a child. Yet I couldn't but find hateful the sort of lovely tension in the air about those now dead and their accomplices—a tension which both stimulated my passions and stood in the way of my achieving real love.

I most longed for Father's return in the evening when a certain love of mine ended before it could become real love. Alone and dejected, full of fury, I felt that with the love between Father and Mother, and my own love, having amounted to no more than a pack of lies, the only truth for me was in my life alone with Father. I waited for his return from trips with the greatest anticipation. What a shame, I felt, that we had never begun the habit of kissing one another on the cheek or forehead in greeting. But Father would pat me gently on the back and I would welcome him home by linking my arm in his. I would act out in comical fashion the things that had happened while he'd been away; Father, in turn, would tell me about the slow progress of his latest construction project. I even told Father the sad story of my lost love. He gazed down at me, smiling— there was, after all, between Father and me a certain tender feeling not unlike that between real lovers.

We grew closer not only because we had lost Mother, but also because we had so few chances to see each other. After the war, Father was increasingly preoccupied with business matters. Perhaps the government and the big investors, having been deprived of their colonies, at last saw fit to turn their attention to the development of Hokkaido. Father was constantly harried by the construction of roads, bridges, and factories.

I'm sure that Father's bankruptcy resulted from one of these road-building projects. I knew that two years before, Father had been awarded a contract to build a road through a remote area at a ridiculously low price that did not even cover the construction costs. Once, when I was visiting his office, I had heard the young workers there criticizing Father's recklessness. I had no idea why Father involved himself in such a risky project. At heart, he had always been an engineer, and his business sense didn't come to one tenth of grandfather's. That was why, right from his youth, Father had always been much more keen on actual construction-site work than on managing the company itself.

I couldn't help thinking, though, that after Mother's death, Father went out into remote areas because he really wanted to. Even if it was partly attributable to a technical man's contempt for business, it seems that Father also longed to devote himself to some dangerous, challenging work. Perhaps he hoped to bury the memory of his wife and his lover out in the far depths of the forest, or in the marshes, the gorges, and ravines. Or perhaps single-minded concentration on such work was the only way left to Father of confirming his own existence.

Perhaps my interpretation of Father's behavior has been influenced too much by a daughter's love. It does seem to me, though, that Father, too, in some place unknown to me, was held in thrall by the events of the past. If not, I can't understand why he didn't either remarry or interfere in the slightest with our household affairs. The very fact that he was so overly kind to me seems proof that he wasn't really thinking about me at all. I imagined my father as he must have been on those trips of his: surrounded by wind and sunlight, rocks and tree stumps, the smell of sweat from the laborers and the whirring of machines, Father so engrossed in his work that he hadn't a single thought for me. My eyes would fill with tears at that vision, and I found myself longing to cry out to Father in my sorrow and bring him back. When I discovered that he had embarked on that hopeless project of his, I gave a secret name to his road. I called it "Dreamway."

Father's "Dreamway" was completed only recently. Perhaps in that drained sense of satisfaction which follows the end of a work project, Father wasn't too unnerved even by the financial ruin facing him.

It was ten o'clock by the hourglass on the restaurant stove when Father and I left for home. There were now more drunks on the street than earlier. We looked at the display windows of shops and walked by a little park.

"Just what will happen at this property seizure?" I asked, troubled anew by Father's bankruptcy.

"They'll put seals on all the furniture."

"Seals?"

"They'll put up pieces of paper saying 'These things are no longer yours.'"

"What sort of paper?"

"I guess it's red paper," Father said, and began to laugh. "I want you to be there for all that. I've been so busy lately."

"No, I'm scared!" I shuddered, but I did want to witness that moment, so close now, when all the furniture of the Kuki house was declared to be no longer mine. I imagined the scene in which the bailiff would go around to all our furniture and, in a firm, business-like manner, hang each piece with a red sign. All the furniture I had loved so well that I hadn't even known I loved it—the furniture covered with the handprints of those I had loved! At the moment the bailiff laid his hand upon those things, perhaps there would be a red seal on all the people I had loved too. My lips began to tremble at the very thought of it, but the pain which rose up in me was strangely refreshing.

"Papa, why don't we go somewhere and have a drink?" I invited him suddenly. "You said we could have fun in whatever way I wanted."

"Are you up to it? I think you're a little tipsy as it is."

Without answering, I trotted off toward the little back streets lined with bars. I was a bit unsteady on my feet, but I could feel joy opening out inside me, a joy which was at one with my refreshing sense of pain. I opened one bar door after another to have a look inside. I wanted to go someplace without too many customers. Dodging the drunken men and bar girls, I went on opening door after door in high spirits. When I found just the sort of bar I had been looking for, I motioned to Father, who had fallen way behind me, and went on in. It was a charming little stand-up bar.

Father ordered a brandy for himself and a liqueur for me. The cold sweetness of the liqueur soaked into the tip of my tongue.

"When things settle down a bit, how about going for a trip?" Father asked. I stared at him in surprise. Though he had drunk a good deal more than I, he was certainly the steadier of the two. He wasn't even much more flushed in the face than when we had left the house.

"We've got to enjoy ourselves once in a while. When we come back from the trip, we can worry about what happens after this."

"Where do you want to go?"

"You make the plans, Noriko."

"Wonderful!" I clapped my hands together and started to laugh. Perhaps Father and I were just hopeless romantics; in any event, we weren't rationalists. We had lived without regard to social norms and decorum. And now, even though we were coming to the end of the line, here we were planning a trip! In any case, the way we had come was far lovelier than any norms and decorum.

"Well, Papa, cheers!" I said, raising my small glass. "To our yesterdays!"

"No, this is for our tomorrows!" said Father.

"What a big talker you are!" I said mischievously, and seized Father by the hand that held his glass, jarring him so that the brandy spilled out over both our hands and onto the counter. We left that bar after about an hour.

We walked slowly along the now nearly deserted streets. The cold night air was so crisp and clear it almost seemed to vibrate; I welcomed this cold which felt so good against my cheeks and neck, warm as they were from drinking.

Uptown, all was dark, as if already deep in midnight slumber. As if to announce the end of choral practice, and the end of the broadcasting day, the station tower stood straight and silent against the night sky.

Humming quietly, I drew closer to Father as we walked along. From time to time, Father would stop to light a cigarette. I would then cup my hands skillfully around the flame to shield it from the wind. Looking up at the crinkles at the outer corners of Father's eyes, I would laugh lightly, as if I were Father's young lover.

As we neared home, my steps grew a little shakier. Both my joy and that refreshing pain took on a heavy quality.

As I passed through the gate, my legs felt weak underneath me and I took hold of Father's arm. The dead leaves that covered the path rustled about our feet. There was a faint smell of asters, and we heard the deep, eerie sound of the sea.

"Papa, I love you," I said, burying my face in the sleeve of Father's coat. "Do you love me, too, Papa?"

"You really did have too much to drink. What a little pest!" Father laughed quietly and gave me a hug. With Father's arm lying heavily across my shoulders, I felt the strength drain slowly from my body. I suspected that Father was drawing from my shoulders the same sensation he had drawn from those of the women he used to love. At the same time, I felt course through my body a desire to be held this way by somebody else, someone who was not my father.

Leaning still closer to Father, my mind raced on: perhaps Father would never rebuke or strike a woman again. But I would have to love someone, love someone with all my might, in joy, in conflict, fear and sorrow—even should I myself be struck, I would have to love. Set free from the languid days I had passed, I would have to confirm and lay hold of my own existence. That's what I would use my tomorrow for.

The sudden urgency of these thoughts and the dark building now visible among the trees made me uneasy. In my wavering field of vision, the

Kuki house looked as much the lovely, deep black medieval manor as ever. My heart had begun to beat fast. I stood still and stared before me at our house.

"Are you all right? What happened?" Father's voice sounded gentler to my ears than ever before.

"I love you." I repeated it again in a low cry, these words I should have been saying to someone else. Then I lay my forehead softly against Father's shoulder and moved my head slowly from side to side.

Translated by Chia-ning Chang and Sara Dillon

The Wife

Dazai Osamu

Dazai Osamu (1909–48) attempted suicide several times—and finally succeeded—during his eventful life, each time accompanied by a different woman who was willing to die with him. He created many moving portraits of women, beginning with that of a wood-cutter's abused daughter in "Metamorphosis" (*Gyofukuki*, 1933; trans. 1970) and ending with that of a cartoonist's trusting wife in *No Longer Human* (*Ningen shikkaku*, 1948; trans. 1958). He also wrote a number of stories using a female narrator, and in 1942 published a collection of nine such stories under the title *Women* (*Josei*). Several of his later works in the same category, such as "Villon's Wife" (*Viyon no tsuma*, 1947; trans. 1955), "Osan" (1947; trans. 1958), and *The Setting Sun*, are among his finest works. Dazai himself was modest about his understanding of the female psyche: he once said, "A man and a woman are different from each other. They differ as a horse and a charcoal brazier do." But one is tempted to agree with the critic Yanagita Tomotsune, who observed that "Dazai was at his best when he wrote in the form of a woman's monologue."

"The Lady Who Entertained" (*Kyōō fujin*), published five months before the author's death, is also written from a woman's viewpoint. The lady of the title is a typical Dazai character who appears time and again in his works in different guises. Dazai prized "tenderness," a natural capacity to sympathize with human weakness, as the highest moral principle, and he saw more of it in women than in men. His portraits of married women, such as the lady featured in the following story, add a new dimension to the traditional Japanese image of a long-suffering wife.

THE LADY WHO ENTERTAINED
Kyōō Fujin

Dazai Osamu

The mistress was rather fond of entertaining and had always been the type to fuss over her guests. But in her case, it wasn't that she enjoyed having guests. In fact, I'm tempted to say that she was actually frightened by them. Whenever the doorbell rang, I would answer it and then go to the mistress's room to give the names of the guests. Already, the mistress would be wearing a strangely tense look, like that of a small bird which had heard the sound of an eagle's wings and is about to take flight at any moment. Brushing back her stray locks and straightening her kimono, the mistress would fidget nervously, and before hearing even half of what I had to say, she would rise, go out into the hall, and hurry to the entrance with small, quick steps. Suddenly, in a strange, half-crying, half-laughing voice like the trilling of a flute, the mistress would welcome the guests. Then, with the expression on her face changing continually like that of a person gone insane, the mistress would run madly between the parlor and kitchen, upsetting pots and breaking dishes. "Excuse me, Ume, I'm sorry," she would apologize to me, the maid. After the guests left, the mistress would sit slumped in the parlor all alone, utterly exhausted and in a daze, not cleaning up, not doing anything. There were even times when the mistress's eyes would fill with tears.

The master of the house had been a professor at Tokyo University, and I hear he came from a well-to-do family. The mistress too, I am told, came from a family of wealthy landlords from Fukushima prefecture. These circumstances—and surely the fact too that they hadn't any children—made it possible for the couple to retain something childlike and carefree in their manner.

I first came here to work as a maid four years ago, while the war was still going on. Because he was rather weak physically, the master was to have fulfilled his military obligation in the home reserves. But about half a year after I started working here, the master was suddenly called to active duty and immediately sent to the South Sea Islands. The war ended shortly thereafter, and yet, his whereabouts are still unknown. The information we received was vague and incomplete. Then, the mistress received a simple note from the commanding officer suggesting that it might be best to resign herself to the loss of her husband. From that point on, the mistress threw herself more and more frantically into entertainment of her guests. I felt so sorry for her, I couldn't bear to watch.

Before that Professor Sasajima began to call, the mistress's contact did not go beyond her husband's relatives and her own family. Even after the master was sent away to the South Sea Islands, the mistress's family sent an ample allowance, so things were quite comfortable for her. Life was peaceful and, one might even say, elegant. But ever since that Professor Sasajima started to call, life here has became a confused and disorderly mess.

This area is a suburb of Tokyo, and luckily, we were able to escape ruin during the war. But since we're not very far from the heart of the city, the people left homeless after the bombings came pouring into this area like a flood. Walking through the town's shopping district, I would feel as though the whole crowd of passers-by had changed completely.

It must have been. . . let's see now. . . toward the end of last year that the mistress ran into her husband's friend, Professor Sasajima, at the market. Since she hadn't seen him for about ten years, she invited him over to the house. That was how all this trouble began.

Professor Sasajima is about forty years old, which is also about how old the master would be. I understand they were classmates in middle school. Professor Sasajima teaches at Tokyo University, too, I hear, but while the master was a scholar of literature, Professor Sasajima teaches medicine. Before the master built this house, he and the mistress lived for a short while in an apartment in Komagome. At that time, since Professor Sasajima was still single and lived in the same apartment building, they were friendly with one another. But after the master moved out this way—and I guess the fact that their research was in different fields had something to do with it too—the master and Professor Sasajima never called on one another. So they'd been friends for only a short while, and casual ones at that.

Some ten-odd years had passed since then when, quite by chance, Professor Sasajima happened to catch sight of the mistress in the market one day and called out to her. Having been called out to in that way, the mistress should have simply said her hellos and parted with the professor. Really, she ought to have let it go at that. Instead, her inherent graciousness getting the better of her, the mistress went on, "The house is right over there, so please won't you come over?" The mistress didn't really want to entertain the professor, but she was all aflutter and so afraid of offending him, that without meaning to, she went quite overboard. And so, cutting an odd figure in his inverness and with a shopping basket over his arm, Professor Sasajima came to this house.

"Well, well! What a splendid house! And no war damage? You must've had the luck of the devil on your side. And you're living alone, are you? How very extravagant of you. But of course it must be difficult to find someone to live in an all-female household, especially such an immaculate and meticulously tended house as this. Surely a boarder would find it uncomfortable. But, madam, I had no idea you lived so close by. I had heard that your home was in M Town, but well, people certainly are stupid creatures, aren't they? It's been almost a year since I moved out this way, and not once have I noticed the nameplate on this house. You know, I often pass in front of your house. In particular, whenever I go to the market, I invariably take this road. Ah, but I too met with my share of suffering during this war. Right after I got married, I was called away to active duty. When I finally returned, I found my home burned to the ground, and discovered that my wife had taken the boy she had given birth to while I was away and fled to her parents' home in Chiba prefecture. I want to send for them, but since there is no house here for them to live in, I have no choice but to stay in Tokyo by myself. I'm renting a three-mat room in back of that general store over there. I do my own cooking, you know. Tonight I thought I'd make myself some chicken stew or something and then drink the night away. And so there I was, toting around this shopping basket and wandering about in the market. It's hell, you know, when a person gets to be this way. I don't even know myself whether I'm dead or alive." Sitting cross-legged in the parlor, the professor rattled on only about himself.

"You poor thing," offered the mistress. Her habitual hospitality already astir, she came scurrying into the kitchen with a changed expression on her face.

"Ume, I'm sorry, but. . . ." Apologizing, she then asked me to prepare some chicken stew and warm some saké. Then, whirling around, she hurried back to the parlor. Or so it seemed, for suddenly she came dashing back into the kitchen to get the fire going and take out the tea service. Although the scene is the same every time we have guests, the way she carried on in her excitement, tension, and confusion was more than pitiable; it was disgusting.

Speaking in a loud voice, once again Professor Sasajima let forth in his brazen manner, "Ah, chicken stew, eh? Excuse me for saying so, but whenever I make chicken stew I always add *konnyaku* noodles, so if you don't mind. . . . And while you're at it, if you added some broiled *tōfu*, that would make it even better. If you don't add anything more than green onions, the dish is rather bland."

Even before he had finished, the mistress was on her feet and flying into the kitchen. "Excuse me, Ume, but. . . ." Looking like a discomfited baby in tears, the mistress timidly asked me to prepare the dish.

Saying that it would be too much of a bother to keep refilling a tiny saké cup, Professor Sasajima drank greedily from a glass instead and soon became quite drunk. "So, your husband is one of the missing too, is he? There's an eighty to ninety percent chance he's been killed, you know. There's really nothing you can do about it, so don't feel so bad. After all, you're not the only one to have suffered, you know."

Professor Sasajima dismissed the matter with appalling tactlessness and started to talk about himself again. "Take me, for example. I have no home and I've been separated from my beloved wife and child. Our furniture, clothing, bedding, and mosquito nets were all destroyed by fire, and we haven't a single thing left. You know, before I took up residence in that three-mat room in back of the general store, I used to sleep in the hallways of the university hospital. What a sight that was—the doctor worse off than his patients! I even used to wish I were a patient instead. It's been no fun at all, I tell you. It's miserable. You know, you're actually one of the lucky ones."

"Yes, that's true," the mistress quickly conceded. "I agree. Compared with everyone else, I've really been much too fortunate."

"Indeed you have, indeed you have. The next time I come, I'm going to bring along some of my friends. They're all such miserable fellows, I really must beg your indulgence."

Tittering as though this pleased her greatly, the mistress said, "Of course. . ." and added earnestly, "I'd be honored."

Ever since that day, our house has been in a state of utter chaos. He might have been drunk, but the professor hadn't been joking when he said that he was going to bring along some of his friends on his next visit. Indeed, about four or five days later, he actually had the nerve to show up at our house with three of them.

"Today the hospital had its year-end party, and now we're going to hold our second round of partying at your house. Madam, we shall begin now, and drink all night long. You know, these days it's really hard to find a suitable house for holding a second round of partying. Hey, everyone! No need to be shy at this house. Come on in, come on in! The parlor's this way. You may keep your overcoats on; it's unbearably cold in here!"

The professor shouted noisily and carried on as though this were now his very own house. On top of that, one of the professor's companions was a woman—apparently a nurse—and the two of them flirted openly in front of everyone.

By now, the mistress was quite rattled, but all she did was force a nervous laugh. Professor Sasajima ordered her around unrelentingly, as though she were a servant or something. "Excuse me, Madam, light a fire in the brazier, will you? And take care of the drinks again, like you did the last time. If there's no saké, grain alcohol or whiskey will do. And as for something to eat. . . oh yes, that's right. Tonight, Madam, I've brought along a fine gift for you. Eat up, it's broiled eel. When the night's as cold as this, there's nothing like broiled eel. One skewer for you, Madam, and one skewer for each of us. Now let's eat, shall we? And hey, didn't one of you guys have an apple? Offer it to the mistress, come on now. Madam, this is what they call an Indian apple, and it's exceptionally fragrant."

When I brought the tea into the parlor, a small apple which had fallen out of someone's pocket rolled along and came to a stop at my feet. I felt like kicking it away. One apple! He had the gall to flaunt it as a gift.

And even the eel—I took a look at it later and saw that it was a pitiful, flattened and half-dried thing that looked like a piece of jerky.

That night, forcing the mistress to drink along with them, Professor Sasajima and his friends carried on boisterously until close to dawn. Then, at daybreak, they assembled themselves around the brazier and went to sleep. They made the mistress bed down with them too. I'm sure she didn't sleep a wink, but the rest of them slept soundly until past noon.

After they woke up, they ate some rice gruel. No longer drunk, naturally they were a little out of sorts. I made it clear to them that I was losing my temper, so they all avoided me, as I did them. Eventually, worn out and looking as dejected as dead fish, they trooped wearily out of here and returned home.

"Madam, how can you sleep among such people? That kind of behavior is too much for me."

"Forgive me. I just can't say 'no'." Her face was pale with exhaustion from lack of sleep and there were tears in her eyes. When I saw this, I could say no more.

The raids on us by this pack of wolves got worse and worse. Before long, it was as though we were running a boarding house for Professor Sasajima and his friends. If the professor wasn't here, then his friends were. And whenever they came over and spent the night, they'd always make the mistress bed down with them. Although everyone else was able to fall asleep like this, the mistress was not. Eventually, whenever she wasn't entertaining guests, the mistress—who hadn't been very healthy to begin with—had to stay in bed.

"Madam, you've become terribly thin and haggard. Stop bothering with those people."

"I'm sorry, but I can't. They're all so unfortunate. Coming here to relax is probably their only pleasure in life."

It was ridiculous. By now, the mistress's estate had dwindled considerably. At this rate, it appeared as though she would have to sell the house in half a year. Yet she never allowed her guests to catch even a glimpse of her impoverished condition. And though she was not at all well, whenever guests came to call, the mistress would spring out of bed, dress quickly, and hurry to the front door, where she would welcome them in her strange, half-laughing, half-crying manner.

One evening in early spring, we were, as usual, entertaining a group of drunken guests. Since it was bound to be an all-night affair, I suggested to the mistress that the two of us have a quick bite to eat before it got too late. So, without even sitting down, the two of us ate dumplings in the kitchen. Although the mistress would lavish any amount of delicious food on her guests, she herself would always make do with very meager fare. Suddenly, a burst of vulgar laughter erupted from one of the drunken guests in the parlor.

"Oh, come on now, something must be going on between you two! Even she. . . ." He used medical jargon, but what he said was filthy and intolerably rude.

A youthful voice—it sounded like a certain Professor Imai's—retorted angrily, "What do you mean? I don't come here for love. As far as I'm concerned, this is just a boarding house."

I raised my head in indignation. Patient as the mistress was, tears were glistening in her downcast eyes this time, as she stood there beneath the dim light, silently eating a dumpling.

I felt so sorry for her, I couldn't speak. But the mistress said softly, "Ume, if you don't mind, would you heat the bath tomorrow morning? Professor Imai enjoys a morning bath."

That was the only time I ever saw the mistress display any chagrin. After that, laughing brightly for her guests, once again she dashed wildly between the parlor and the kitchen, as though nothing had happened.

I was well aware of the mistress's deteriorating health, but, since she never betrayed the slightest hint of fatigue to company, not one of those guests—though all were supposedly distinguished doctors—seemed to notice that she was unwell.

One peaceful spring morning, when, fortunately, we hadn't been burdened with a single overnight guest, I was leisurely doing the wash at the well when the mistress came tottering unsteadily down to the garden in her bare feet. Then, crouching alongside a hedge of blossoming yellow roses, she vomited a considerable amount of blood. I screamed and ran to her. Holding her from behind and using my shoulder to support her, I led the mistress to her room and laid her gently on the bed. Then, crying, I said to her,

"You see. . . that's why I hated having those guests! Look what they've done to you! Well, now that you're so ill, and since they're all doctors, I'm going to insist that they act like doctors and restore your health to you."

"Stop it now. You mustn't say such things to our guests. They'll feel responsible, and that will only dampen their spirits."

"But look at yourself, and tell me, what do you intend to do from now on? Will you stay up all night to entertain as usual? You'd make quite a spectacle vomiting blood in the middle of a circle of sleeping guests."

The mistress closed her eyes and thought it over for awhile. "I'll go to my parents' home and rest there for some time. Please look after the house and put up the guests that come to call—they've no place else to go and relax. And please don't let them know that I'm sick." She smiled gently.

Since we had no guests that day, I took advantage of the situation and immediately started packing. Then, thinking I should at least see the mistress safely to Fukushima, I purchased two train tickets. Two days later, the mistress seemed to be much better, and happily, there still wasn't any sign of bothersome guests coming to call. Hurrying the mistress along as though we were fleeing from something, I closed the rain shutters and locked up the house. We had just stepped out the front door when. . . .

Good Lord! Along came Professor Sasajima—drunk, in the middle of the day—accompanied by two young women, apparently nurses.

"Hey, going out?"

"No, no. It's all right. Ume, excuse me. . . will you please open the rain shutters in the parlor? Please, Professor, do come in. Really, it's all right."

Welcoming the professor and the two young women in her peculiar, half-crying, half-laughing voice, the mistress ran round and round like a little mouse. The frantic entertaining of guests had begun again.

I was sent off to the market. In her confusion, the mistress handed me her travel bag instead of her purse. Opening it up at the market to pay for the groceries, I was surprised to find her train ticket in there, torn in half. When I realized that the mistress must have quietly torn it up as soon as she saw Professor Sasajima standing at her door, I was struck with amazement at her infinite kindness. It was then that I realized, for the first time in my life, that in man there exists, as in no other animal, a special, very precious quality.

I reached into my kimono sash and pulled out my own ticket. I tore it in half quietly. Thinking that I would like to pick up a few more treats to take home to our guests, I turned back around to do just a bit more shopping.

Translated by Karen Kaya Shimizu

Tsuboi Sakae

Before she turned to creative writing in middle life, Tsuboi Sakae (1900–67) had been a housewife, mother, and friend of people who were engaged in the proletarian literary movement. Born in a humble family on a small island in the Seto Inland Sea, she began earning money for her parents at the age of nine. Her school education ended in the eighth grade, after which she did all kinds of work to help with the family finances. In 1925 she married a young leftist poet in Tokyo, and through him she came to know a number of proletarian writers. Her new life in the capital was not easy, not only because she had to look after an adopted child and two of her younger sisters, but because her husband was twice imprisoned for his left-wing activities. She barely managed to support her family by doing chores at a small publishing house. Encouraged by authors she met at the publisher's, she gradually became interested in fiction writing and began publishing stories around 1938. Her first short-story collection, which appeared in 1940, won her the Shinchō Literature Prize and helped launch her literary career. But, partly because of government censorship, she turned her creative energy toward juvenile literature in subsequent years. "Under the Persimmon Tree" (*Kaki no ki no aru ie*, 1948; trans. 1965) is representative of her work in this genre. Her name became well known to children and adults alike when her novel describing a rural schoolteacher's life, *Twenty-Four Eyes* (*Nijūshi no hitomi*, 1952; trans. 1957), was awarded the Education Minister's Prize. The success of a movie based on the novel further contributed to her fame.

"What is juvenile literature?" Tsuboi once asked. "Is there such a thing as juvenile literature as distinct from literature at large?" Her answer to the second question was definitely in the negative. Her stories for children carry serious messages for adults, while her works for adults often criticize contemporary society from the viewpoint of a child. "Umbrella on a Moonlit Night" (*Tsukiyo no kasa*, 1953) is written from the viewpoint of a mother who sides with her children in criticizing the ways of their father, who is more representative of the adults' world than she is.

UMBRELLA ON A MOONLIT NIGHT
Tsukiyo no kasa

Tsuboi Sakae

There were people who wondered whether our group wasn't some sort of gathering of women of leisure or ill repute, but this was far from the truth. We were housewives who, for some twenty years, had relied solely on our husbands' pocketbooks. Like tame dogs, we had, without even knowing it, lost what little rebelliousness we once had. We were, in short, faithful wives who took comfort in being ordinary mothers. That is the sort of women we all were. Our purpose, if you can call it that, was simply to get together and pass the time gossiping when our husbands weren't home.

It is only recently that we have adopted such fashionable terms as the English word "group," but not out of vanity. Looking back—has it been that long?—well, anyway, we first got together during that period around the end of the war, a season our generation was forced to endure in place of life's springtime. Back then we thought nobody's lives could be harder than ours, and we complained freely among ourselves of how unfair and frustrating everything was.

Even after the war, when democracy was coming into vogue, we would still mope around with gloomy faces. As I recall, we were envious of the merry-looking gatherings that young single people had at book clubs, dance parties, and what not. I'm sure some people would say that it was too bad we just didn't go on out and have fun. But how could a woman do this when she had children, a mother-in-law, or even worse, a husband not yet back from the war? We had also taken a jaundiced view of women's liberation and democracy, as if these had somehow passed us by. Whenever two of us were together, we would talk about selling off our best kimonos to raise some money. If there were three of us, the discussion would turn to getting food from the countryside. Strange as it seems, I recall that though we tended to be melancholy, whenever four of us got together we would burst into laughter.

"Hey, look here, if we're not to be outdone by youngsters, shouldn't we start a club of our own? A club just for our enjoyment." It was Mrs. Ono, the only war widow in our group, who first proposed the idea to us.

"Of course! It could be our club that meets by the well. Every week, on Monday at noon, a weekly well-side gossip meeting!"

When Mrs. Kurata, a mother of two, said this, everyone immediately burst out laughing. It just so happened that that day was a Monday, and Monday was usually the day we all got together. For us housewives with working husbands and children going to school, there was no time at which we felt so drawn together as Monday at noon. Usually we would all end up visiting one another's houses without even planning for it in advance. The easiest house for us to visit belonged to Murai Kaneko, who had been called by her nickname, Kāchan, since childhood. Only Kāchan's house had not suffered any direct war damage and was still the big, old home it had always been.

"If it's going to be a well-side club, then we'll have to meet at my place, right? The rest of you only have covered wells. None of you have open well-sides, do you?"

Kāchan said this because only her house still had in use an old well with a large drainboard. After being burned out of their own homes, both Mrs. Kurata and Mrs. Ono had had some bittersweet experiences by that well-side. Hearing that certain wild plants were edible, they would go pick them and wash them at the well. Then, after soaking some black rice, they would boil all this into a kind of porridge. They had, in fact, looked to Kāchan when they were seeking refuge. It was through Kāchan's efforts that they were able to rent rooms, and later to find inexpensive houses to buy. It was also Kāchan who assisted those of us who had been evacuated to the countryside to obtain land that, in retrospect, seemed ridiculously cheap.

We had all gone to the same girls' school, and the war forced us into the same neighborhood. If we derived any benefit at all from the war, I guess it was this new friendship we developed.

"But calling it 'The Well-Side Club'—isn't that expression a bit old-fashioned? I mean, I think it would be nice if we had something a little more. . . well, the kind of club where we seemed to dominate our husbands once in a while."

Everyone cheered heartily when I said this. As it turned out, though, we lacked the ability to conclude a debate and ended up settling for a well-side club, one in which at least we wouldn't speak ill of others.

Our membership was made up of us four. All in our thirties, we felt a rivalry toward the younger women in the neighborhood, who had formed the Young Cedar Club. Obviously, we were not satisfied with the name "The Well-Side Club." We would, after all, occasionally discuss politics and also read popular books.

"Since there are four of us, how about 'The Four-Leaf Club'?"

When Mrs. Kurata said this, the widowed Mrs. Ono rejected it, complaining that it was too silly. "We're not a bunch of schoolgirls. And a name like 'Four-Leaf' would be laughed at by the Young Cedars. 'The Well-Side Club' is still better."

"Well, how about 'The Monday Club'?" Kāchan suggested.

Mrs. Ono folded her arms like a man and replied, "Well now, are we all going to meet every single Monday? If we do that, I'll go broke. And besides, doesn't 'The Monday Club' sound like a meeting for professors or politicians or businessmen? It just doesn't suit us very well. What do you think?"

At this point, I murmured as if to myself, "A name like 'The Social Club' is just too ordinary; I wonder if there's a word that means we share each other's joy and anger, pleasure and grief?"

"Huh? What? Joy and what?"

"I said joy and anger, pleasure and grief. We do share with one another the things we're happy about or sad about, don't we? Well, I was wondering if there's a word that means that."

"Well then, what's wrong with 'The Joy and Grief Club'? Let's go with that."

From the very beginning, Mrs. Ono had emerged quite naturally as our leader. Thinking back on it, this group of young women barely in their thirties was rather pathetic, but even so, our gatherings were certainly enjoyable. We all got together once a month. Being poor, each of us took turns at treating the others to a meal. True to our name, there were, in succession, times of joy and times of grief.

My story is jumping back and forth. But if I remember correctly, it was around the time of our club's third meeting that Mrs. Ono became a widow. She had received a letter from one of her husband's soldier-friends telling her of his death in the war. She brought it with her to our meeting and, without saying a word, laid it in front of us. For the longest time Mrs. Ono didn't raise her head. I'll never forget that day's meeting, which happened to be at my house. I had made sweet dumplings with saccharin, but no one touched them. Instead, they each took some and went home.

For us, happiness meant getting hold of a few cups of polished rice; but we sure got angry when the clerks at city hall were rude. From among these emotions of our everyday life, there was nothing which could begin to compare with the tremendous sorrow and anger caused by a person's death. And yet—shall we call it the power of human adaptability?—Mrs. Ono seemed to recover quickly, which made us all feel very relieved. As if she had quite forgotten that only Mrs. Ono was a widow, Mrs. Kurata once remarked, "Hey, do you know what? My husband has been secretly keeping money from me. Have you ever heard of such a thing? For a man, he sure is stingy."

Encouraged by these comments, Kāchan quickly added, "That's the way it is, all right. Used to be that hiding money was something only women did. They say that since the war men and women have equal rights in that department. As far as stashing away money is concerned, though, a woman still has the upper hand, seeing how she's in charge of the household expenses. The stingier a husband gets, the more a wife will stash away for herself. That's only natural! And sometimes a wife is going to want to go see a good movie or something, isn't she? Even if a husband doesn't forbid her to go to a single movie, a lady might want to just pop out to a movie when her husband is gone, without having to get permission each time."

No sooner had I thought that I'd go on to make a little speech against my husband than Mrs. Ono commented with a smile, "My husband this, my husband that! You'd think they were a terrible bother. Considering how lost you'd be without them, I wouldn't complain too much. What about me?"

Startled, I looked into Mrs. Ono's face, but couldn't see into the depths behind her expression. Making full use of her sewing machine, Mrs. Ono has struggled all these years to support herself and her child. Yet, even now, she's the most cheerful of us four, and even looks the youngest.

Whenever I notice these qualities in Mrs. Ono, I suddenly wonder just what it is that makes women grow old.

Another housewife in the neighborhood found out about our club and wanted to join in with us. She was envious of all the fun we seemed to be sharing. Once she happened to come by where we were meeting. After her unexpected visit, we discussed the problem.

"What should we do?"

"If we don't let her in, she'll think badly of us. We've got to tell her something. . . ."

"Ah! I've got it! What if we said it's a gathering of former schoolmates?"

"That's it! That's it!"

Without knowing it, we had shown what typically narrow-minded females we were. But this incident brought the four of us that much closer together.

"What do you think? Will 'The Four-Leaf Club' really not do? 'The Joy and Grief Club' is too complicated; little kids would never understand it. Besides, it's too gloomy," Mrs. Kurata remarked somewhat obstinately. She had been the first to suggest "The Four-Leaf Club." This time even Mrs. Ono simply nodded in assent, "Sure, that would be fine. 'The Four-Leaf Club' or 'The Group' or something like that. Let's set up a challenge to that Young Cedar Club and make ourselves young again."

As a result of all this, the name "The Joy and Grief Club" more or less disappeared. This doesn't mean that we always used the name "The Four-Leaf Club." Instead, we started calling ourselves simply "The Group." Compared to the Young Cedar Club, which made a great beginning but soon started to fizzle out, we flourished more and more as time went on. Even the boundaries of our adventuring slowly widened.

"Shouldn't we be a little rowdy sometimes? It's not right to leave all the drinking to our husbands. And we might learn a little something by playing pachinko at the game parlors."

We were able to start talking like this mostly because we had gotten a little free time. Since rice was finally available at the distribution center, a housewife could take a little more time to amuse herself. But we were, after all, housewives on fixed allowances. No matter how carefully one saved up pin money, there wasn't enough for a whole day's entertainment. In a family like mine, with no more than the income of a junior high school teacher, it was all one could do to save away, at most, ten yen a day. Even to hang onto five-yen coins or one-yen bills was an exacting task. Even so, never a month went by that, when payday arrived, I didn't borrow some spending money for myself from the family budget. It was amazing that I could in this way save up five or six hundred, or sometimes even a thousand yen, without my husband ever knowing about it. This was my very own money to use without worrying about the other family members.

After we became the Four-Leaf Club, our monthly expenses rose drastically. No longer satisfied with just meeting at home, drinking tea, and nibbling at sweets, we started taking three to five hundred yen and going out on the town. It wasn't enough any more to meet only when our husbands and children were not at home. We would clear out of the house on a Sunday or holiday without apology and spend all day enjoying ourselves here and there. We had two approaches. One was to leave in the morning and not come back until it was time to start preparing dinner. The other was to leave at noon, eat dinner out, and even take time to see a movie before returning home. On those days when we would be returning before dinner, we wouldn't give much thought to leaving our families. If we were going to be eating out, though, we'd have to worry about our children and husbands left behind at home. With that in mind, we'd start humoring them the day before. At such times, I was very grateful to my children.

"Mother, don't you worry about it; just go out and have fun! Take your time. It's only once a month, isn't it? If it's just a Sunday, we can take care of things at home."

When my oldest boy, a high school senior, made that offer, my daughter—a year younger and not to be outdone—volunteered, "That's right. I can take care of dinner. I'm great at making curry rice."

Dinner on those nights was almost always curry rice. It was the only meal my daughter really knew how to make. My third child, a boy, was in the sixth grade. All of them acted as if they were full-fledged adults. In fact, it was my husband I always had to worry about. Whenever I had plans to go out, he would openly display a sullen, unhappy expression.

"Do I have a white shirt to wear tomorrow?"

"Yes, you do."

"I had planned for everyone to clean the garden today, but never mind."

"Well, let's postpone it then. All right?"

Whenever we had this kind of conversation, the children would all side against their father and come to my assistance.

"Daddy, you're mean. How can you say such nasty things when Mom's just about to go for her Four-Leaf Club meeting? You're feudal."

My daughter had a habit of calling "feudal" anything a male did—even her father or brother—that she felt was a little unreasonable. But it was surprising how much this word "feudal" of hers actually contributed to the peaceful atmosphere of our home by making us think over just how feudal we were. It was a word which almost never crossed my lips but which the children used boldly. Such was the case on Mother's Day one May.

"It's unfair that there's a Mother's Day, but no Father's Day, don't you think?"

My husband had only been joking, but my daughter quickly turned on him.

"That's a lie! I don't think so at all! Having Mother's Day once a year isn't enough. Daddy, you have Father's Day every day. You're feudal!"

It was probably just my being old-fashioned, but I would get a kind of heavy, sinking feeling in my heart before our group was to get together. Sometimes I even thought of leaving the group. But when I attended the meeting after all, I was always happy I hadn't said anything to my husband. Still, I would quietly look around at the others' faces, wondering if they had had thoughts like mine.

For our meeting in July, we went out in Western clothes. I left the house wearing new canvas sandals and looking youthful for the first time in a very long while. Grinning at me, my oldest boy quipped, "Hey, Mom, we're gonna have a present waiting for you when you get back. Oh my, it's all inside. Yes! Yes! Isn't that right, Jirō?"

As if enjoying a secret, the two boys looked at each other and laughed.

"Oh my, it's all inside" was the password my family used when referring to a secret matter. It had all started with my husband, who, when he was drunk, would sing a popular old song which began, "I wanted that woman so bad I could die, good thing she finally became my wife." There was a certain verse in it he would sing in a secretive tone of voice, "Oh my, it's all inside. Yes, it's all inside." My daughter and oldest boy found this line amusing and started using it themselves. It was the sort of song that even now I'd turn red all over if I heard it in front of others. At the time I was in fact very upset at my husband, thinking to myself, "How could he, in front of our children?" But our children, of course, are from a new generation. With childlike innocence, they simply mimicked the verse they found pleasing. But children will drink from dirty water as well as clean and still not poison themselves. I guess we parents are out of date and there's nothing to worry about.

Our schedule for that day was to window-shop in the morning, see a fashion show, and then have a simple lunch of noodles. In the afternoon we were going to see an Italian movie, and for dinner we had decided that, even if we could only afford one à la carte item, we would go to a certain European restaurant. In the evening, we planned to relish the atmosphere along the Ginza, even trying a little pachinko, before returning home. We ended up heading for home without having set foot in a pachinko parlor, but this was the only activity we had to put off until our next meeting. We had put a five hundred-yen ceiling on our spending that day, and, as expected, had used it all up. It was an unusually extravagant meeting.

"Next time, let's set a strict spending policy," Kāchan said. But Mrs. Ono objected, saying, "What do you mean? If anyone, I should be saying that. Don't you want to play sometimes as much as the men do, and spend everything you've got? But we can't go that far, so at least don't talk about running out of money! All your husbands got mid-year bonuses, didn't they?"

Mrs. Ono pulled out a lighter and lit up a cigarette, puffing out smoke like a real smoker. Mrs. Ono had only recently started smoking, but she moved her hands as if she had been at it a long time.

"Hey, will you give me one too?"

Mrs. Ono handed the whole pack over to Kāchan, who had stuck her hand out rather awkwardly to receive it. Looking me right in the face, Mrs. Ono said, "After Kāchan, Mrs. Kurata will probably start. It'll be a while before you're smoking, huh?"

"That's not so!" I said. "I'm the one who first suggested a club where we can dominate our husbands. I can at least smoke cigarettes. Give me one, give me one!"

"What?" Kāchan responded, "Does smoking cigarettes and dominating one's husband have that much in common? That's crazy!"

At that, everyone burst out laughing, while I choked on my first puff and, with the tears streaming down, coughed violently. Right in the middle of the Ginza, flooded by neon lights, Mrs. Ono gently patted my back and said, "You idiot. You were trying to act like a widow or a lady hounded by her mother-in-law."

"Now, *that's* crazy!" I said, still coughing and not willing to admit defeat. At the same time, though, for no particular reason I suddenly thought of my husband.

Premonitions. . . it's probably only old-fashioned women like us who speak of such things, but these premonitions are surprisingly accurate.

Even after getting on the train at Shinbashi, I felt terribly anxious about my family. It was a feeling of something depressing waiting for me. My anxiety must have shown in the look on my face. When we sat down together after changing to the Chūō line at Tokyo Station, the first thing Kāchan asked me was, "What's the matter? You're awfully quiet."

"I'm a little tired."

"I bet it's because we walked all eight blocks of the Ginza. But wasn't it interesting?"

"It was."

Because I gave such an unenthusiastic answer, Kāchan quickly turned toward Mrs. Kurata. I closed my eyes and silently began to think. I recalled how I left the house that day.

". . . Highly inward. Yes, yes."

". . . It's bad luck if you tell anyone."

It was "our present for you" that my sons had jokingly sung about, and apparently they were even being "on the inside" toward their father. I had guessed, from the fact that for some time they had been all on their own, saving up their allowances and then buying and collecting empty apple boxes, bamboo, and wire netting, that it was a henhouse they were making. As I tried to imagine where on earth they might have been building it, I became very uneasy. Had it been a day when my husband was at home the problem would have been simple, but I remembered that today, unfortunately, he had said he was going over to his friend's place to play *go*.

"You know, all of a sudden I feel worried about my husband."

Unable to stay silent, I disclosed this to Kāchan. She grinned and responded half-teasingly, "That must be because it's getting late. It's the same for anyone. I've realized lately that at times like this it's better to take things in stride. If we start getting nervous about whether we've annoyed our families, we've lost, haven't we? But, when we go out on the town like this, don't you feel like you sort of understand what goes on in your husband's mind when he comes home from having his fun? Doesn't he try to butter you up by bringing home a gift? And then doesn't that make you feel more like being hostile? Wouldn't you much rather he was honest and open? So, let's be honest and open."

"Honest and open. Just talking like that shows you're dishonest and sneaky. Let's go home with dignity."

As Mrs. Kurata said this, I thought to myself that she was also probably dishonest and sneaky.

At Asagaya we made the last bus going to Nakamura Bridge. Getting off at the second block of Saginomiya we parted with Mrs. Ono, and the three of us headed in the same direction, turning left along the main road. As we walked along side by side, Mrs. Kurata said in a dejected voice, "Women are pathetic."

"It's only because we say things like that that we become pathetic. Don't talk like that!"

Just as Kāchan was telling her off, we arrived at the corner where I had to part from the other two.

"Good night. Thanks a lot."

I ran along a path that wound through the wide fields, taking short brisk steps at a pace far quicker than I could manage in the daytime. The lights were on in my house, and seeing it there underneath the starlit sky, I felt a sharp pang of nostalgia.

"I'm home!"

The instant I opened the front door my built-in radar sensed that something was wrong. "I knew it," I thought to myself. The children came out to greet me as I was untying my shoe laces. I had to force myself to sound cheerful.

"I had a delightful time today. Thank you."

Looking over the children's faces, I handed my daughter a package of candy I had brought home as a gift.

"For us, today wasn't delightful at all. Daddy was totally unreasonable."

My daughter whined softly. "Just now we were all complaining about him, weren't we?" She went on, turning to her elder brother.

From the gloomy look on her face it was obvious that she had a lot to complain about.

"What on earth's the matter? Don't you understand your Daddy's personality?" I scolded her.

"But it wasn't just his personality today. He was absolutely feudal. Tell her," she said, looking over at my elder son.

"I can't even talk about it. He may be our father, but this is too much!"

My oldest boy was even starting to cry. Led by my children, I went into the boys' room, which was next to the front porch. One by one the three children told their story. As I thought, they had built a henhouse in the front yard. My daughter vented her indignation, saying, "As soon as Daddy got home he got furious, and before we could say anything he kicked it with his foot. We'd worked hard on that henhouse, and he smashed it all apart. He broke up the poles. The wire is so tangled up it'll never be usable again."

"You built it without permission, right? You never consulted with him. If you had handled it better, your father would never have done such a thing."

"But we thought he'd be really happy," my oldest son said. "We could have eaten the eggs the hen laid, so we wouldn't have had to buy them. We were sure you'd both be really happy. Isn't that so?" he asked his sister.

Right down to my youngest boy, they all stood firm. As usual, it was my oldest son who, reconsidering things a little, was the calmest.

"But, Mom," he said, "even if it was wrong not to consult with Dad first, he didn't have to smash it up with no warning. We started the whole thing with completely good intentions. And just because Dad didn't like it, he smashed it all to pieces without even consulting with us a bit."

"Now, you know your father's temper."

"Well, then, just because he's the father, it's O.K. for him to lose his temper? That's why he's feudal."

"But, anyway, leave everything to your mother. You mustn't oppose your father too much."

"We're not giving in! Even if we act like we're trying to make up with him, our feelings won't change. From today on, we'll never feel the same way about him."

"That's right! I don't see how you could have lived with that stubborn man for twenty years, Mommy. You've been so submissive—you act as if it's O.K. to just let him be so bossy. Mommy, you're as bad as he is!"

"I hate Dad."

These condemnations were very noisy. My husband had never heard such talk. I was the one who made sure he never heard it.

My daughter had said, "Mommy, you're as bad as he is!"—but I realized that "Mommy" was even worse than he was.

"Well, what can we do? How about if your father apologizes? I'll say something to get him to apologize."

"That's no good! Dad would never apologize," my younger boy declared resolutely.

I responded with a laugh, "Now, you don't know that for sure. All right, then, I'll get him to apologize. In exchange, you will all apologize for the bad things you've done."

"We haven't done anything bad. Isn't that right?" he asked his sister.

"That's not so," she answered. "We dug up the moss Daddy was trying so hard to grow."

My daughter was finally showing a more subdued attitude. However, she went on, "But is moss all that important? I think eggs are better, right?"

"That's right," her older brother agreed. "Moss—it's a lousy hobby."

I held my tongue and listened to all this. There was no reason why the children should comprehend the pleasure my husband got out of that garden moss, never forgetting to sprinkle it with water every day, and taking such good care of it. Indeed, it would have been unnatural if they had comprehended this even a little bit.

I let the children talk as much as they liked. After that, they were easy to deal with. I gave them candy and they quickly went off to sleep. Afterwards, their anger apparently having infected me, I had to control my temper while talking to my husband. "Even though you're their father, this is too much. You may think they're only children, but they still understand everything that's happening."

Completely indifferent, he remained silent. I thought his silence was a sign of penitence, but the next morning my husband left the house without saying anything, still unyielding.

Poor man!

I spent that whole day reflecting on my husband, from the time he was young until the present. Because of my outdated way of looking at things, I had never said this to anybody, but ours was a marriage of love. Even though there had been stormy times, it was with feelings of joy that we had had children and raised them. How could I keep silent when my husband was alienated from his children?

That night, without saying anything to the children, I left the house for the train station. It had been a long time since I had gone to meet my husband there. Even if it was raining, one could always rent an umbrella, so I almost never went out to meet him. When I was younger, I used to go boldly up by the ticket taker to wait for him, but this time I hid by a telephone pole near the front of the station and watched the passengers. My husband worked late on Mondays, so by this time the train wasn't very crowded, and I could pick out the passengers as they emerged one by one. I must have waited about fifteen minutes. My husband came out of the train car at the very front. He was holding an umbrella, and his shoulders were stooped in a posture so I could even imagine his facial expressions. He headed for the ticket taker face down. I don't know why, but while I watched him take one step after another I felt the blood rush to my head. Leaving the ticket taker, he stopped at a fruit stand, and, after having something wrapped up into a bundle, he finally headed in my direction. I don't know what he was thinking of, but, as he neared the railway crossing, he opened up his umbrella. Having no way of knowing that I was secretly waiting for him, he walked calmly toward me. I let him pass on by me, while trying to keep myself from laughing. It wasn't raining. In fact, the moon was out. My husband seemed not to notice that. He also didn't notice me a few moments later when I came out and walked along behind him. After we turned into the big road leading toward our home, I even quickened my steps, but my husband—who was convinced that one carried an umbrella in order to use it—never once turned around. I followed quietly behind this strange figure holding an umbrella in the moonlit night.

Translated by Chris Heftel

Matsumoto Seichō

Matsumoto Seichō (b. 1909) began writing fiction at around forty years of age, having worked mostly at a newspaper press before then. He established his literary reputation in 1952, when one of his early stories was awarded the Akutagawa Prize. His interest in analyzing motives of human behavior, as well as his talent for constructing a dramatic plot, soon induced him to try his hand at detective fiction. Many of the novels he wrote in this genre in the subsequent years, starting with *Points and Lines* (*Ten to sen*, 1957–58; trans. 1970), became great bestsellers. Japanese detective fiction of earlier times had tended to be unrealistic stories of ratiocination. Matsumoto wove contemporary issues into his plots and so provided stimulating, socially relevant reading. Many younger writers followed his lead until today the majority of Japanese detective stories make use of current social issues. It would not be an exaggeration to say that Matsumoto singlehandedly changed the course of detective fiction in Japan.

"Wait a Year and a Half " (*Ichinenhan mate*, 1957) is also a detective story about a social issue—the problem of battered wives. The problem had been prevalent in Japan until recently, partly because many wives were willing to take abuse rather than get a divorce. Divorce was legally allowed, but not socially sanctioned. One survey shows that, in 1954, the divorce rate was less than one per thousand marriages. It further reveals that 95 percent of divorces were by mutual agreement and involved no legal or government agency. The Japanese in general were reluctant to go to court on any matter in the 1950s; it was unthinkable for an ordinary housewife to sue her husband for divorce, even though she fully had the right to do so under the Civil Code.

WAIT A YEAR AND A HALF
Ichinenhan mate

Matsumoto Seichō

1

I will begin with the facts of the case.

The defendant was a twenty-nine-year-old woman by the name of Sumura Satoko. She was charged with the murder of her husband. Satoko had graduated from a certain women's college during the war. Upon graduation, she had become an employee of a certain company. During the war, there was a time when companies were shorthanded, with their men summoned to active service, and women were hired in great numbers as substitutes.

When the war ended, the men who had been drafted began to return, a few at a time, and the need for substitute female employees gradually subsided. Two years later, the women who had been hired during the war were dismissed all at once. Sumura Satoko was one of them.

Immediately after, she married a man with whom she had fallen in love while at the office. This man was Sumura Yōkichi. He was three years older than she. Because he had only been to middle school, he felt a kind of romantic admiration for Satoko, a college graduate, and it was he who proposed to her. From this fact alone, one can see that he was a somewhat timid young man. As for Satoko, it was this timidity that had attracted her.

Eight years passed without incident for the couple. They had two children, a boy and a girl. Yōkichi was not a college graduate, and so he remained an ordinary office employee without much of a future. Nevertheless, he worked conscientiously. His pay was low, but he was able to make a living, even managing to save a little along the way.

Then, in the year of 195-, because business had fallen off, the company decided on a personnel cut. Yōkichi, never regarded as particularly capable, was discharged along with the superannuated group.

Yōkichi panicked. Relying on connections, he drifted in and out of several companies: either the job was unsuitable or the pay was too low. Satoko was now forced to work to supplement their income.

At first, she worked as a bill-collector for a finance company. But the job was so physically exhausting and the pay so low that, through the introduction of a woman she had met on one of her business calls, she became a sales representative for a certain insurance company.

Though she had to struggle in the beginning, her sales record gradually improved. She learned the essentials from the woman who had introduced her to the company. Satoko was not particularly beautiful, but she had large eyes, and there was something charming in the curve of her lips when she smiled and revealed her nicely-shaped teeth. Moreover, being a college graduate, she was on the intellectual side as a sales representative. In her manner of persuading customers as well, she gave an impression of intelligence. She soon came to be well thought of by her clients, and her work became easier. The essentials of selling insurance were pluck, charm, and verbal skill.

In time, she was earning twelve to thirteen thousand yen a month. As often happens in such cases, her husband Yōkichi became totally unemployed. Unable to hold down a job, he had nothing to do. Now, he had no alternative but to rely on Satoko's income. Apologizing to his wife again and again, he remained at home, lying about in idleness.

Satoko's income was, of course, not based on monthly pay but on a meager fixed minimum, and for the most part, on commission. There were months when sales were so poor that her income was pathetically low.

The competition was fierce among sales representatives of every insurance company. In the vast city, the flood of rival concerns left each solicitor with scarcely a toehold. By now, some were resigned to the idea that opening new territory was impossible. Satoko wondered whether, the prospects in the city being so bad, there might not be a good outlet elsewhere.

What Satoko turned her attention to were the dam construction sites. At the time, dam construction was in urgent demand by any electric power company developing power resources. Such construction was contracted by huge civil engineering and construction companies, like X Constructors or Y and Company. There could be several thousand, perhaps over ten thousand, workers at each site. All these workers, involved either in building high embankments or in blasting, were constantly exposed to the danger of death or injury. The sites in most cases, were located deep in mountain areas which were not readily accessible. Even the shrewdest solicitor had not ventured that far. In fact, such territories had escaped notice.

It occurred to Satoko that surely this was virgin soil. Together with a close female colleague, she set out to a dam construction site deep in the mountains of a neighboring prefecture. Naturally, they had to bear all the travelling expenses themselves.

Excluding the seasonal laborers who drifted from one place to another, Satoko concentrated on regular employees of the construction companies such as the engineers, technicians, machinery supervisors, and operations managers whom she felt would be reliable clients.

This new territory turned out extremely well. The men were already part of a group insurance plan, but well aware of the dangers surrounding them, they responded readily when approached. Satoko's sales soared to an almost giddy level. Anticipating the inconvenience of collecting payments, she had everything arranged on yearly installments.

Her discovery was a success. Her monthly income nearly doubled, and for many months exceeded thirty thousand yen.

As their life was finally becoming comfortable, her husband Yōkichi grew lazier. Extremely dependent by nature, Yōkichi was now in the position of relying on Satoko for everything. He lost all desire to look for a job, and with each day that passed, become more and more accustomed to a feeling of security.

What was more, Yōkichi, who had until then refrained from drinking, began to frequent bars. Satoko, who was always out, had entrusted her husband with her income so that he could pay the household expenses. From this, Yōkichi stole his drinking money. Though at first he took in small amounts, he became bolder and bolder as the income increased.

Satoko understood the frustrations of her husband who kept house while she was out working, and more or less overlooked the matter. She loathed the childish, degrading way he furtively stole his drinking money, and so, sometimes when she returned home, she even encouraged him to go out for a drink. At such times, he would leave the house, looking greatly relieved.

The fact was that Yōkichi had taken up with a woman.

2

In view of what occurred later, Satoko was probably responsible to some extent for what happened. For it was Satoko who actually introduced the woman to Yōkichi. The woman was an old friend of hers.

Wakita Shizuyo had been a classmate from Satoko's schooldays. One day, they had run into each other by chance on the street. Shizuyo's husband had passed away, and she had just opened a bar in Shibuya, she said. She had given Satoko her business card at the time. Shizuyo, who had been pretty in her school days, was now almost unrecognizably thin and haggard, and her face resembled that of a fox. Looking at her, Satoko could well imagine the appearance of her bar.

"I'll drop by for a visit one of these days," Satoko said, and took her leave of Shizuyo. On hearing Satoko's income, Shizuyo had said how envious she was.

When Satoko returned home, she told Yōkichi about the meeting.

"Maybe I ought to go there for a drink sometime. Since she's your friend, she'll probably charge me less," Yōkichi had said with a sidelong glance at Satoko.

Satoko thought that if Yōkichi were to drink anyway, so much the better at an inexpensive place. Since it would be helping Shizuyo's business as well, she had replied, "That might be a good idea. Why don't you go and take a look?"

Soon after, Yōkichi did in fact go to Shizuyo's bar and came back with his report.

"It's such a small place that if you cram five or six people in there, it's packed. For a dingy place, though, it's got some fairly good liquor. Thanks to you, she charged me less."

"Is that so? Well, that was nice," Satoko had said at the time.

Every month for about a week, Satoko went to the dam construction sites. Once she became a familiar face, people would introduce her to other sites. Making the rounds from Dam A to Dam B to Dam C, she had no rest from her work. Her income held steady.

Satoko handed over all the money to Yōkichi and had him take care of household matters. In this home, the roles of husband and wife were completely reversed. That was what had been wrong, she later said in retrospect.

Yōkichi's laziness grew steadily worse, while in pilfering money to go drinking he became craftier and bolder with each day. Coming home after work, Satoko would find her two children crying with empty stomachs. Out since noon, Yōkichi would come home late at night reeking of wine. To Satoko's reproaches, which she could not hold back, Yōkichi began more often to shout back in an intimidating manner. He would roar, "I'm the master here, don't take me for a maid! Drinking's a part of being a man. Who do you think you are just because you're making a little money?"

At first Satoko sympathized with his anger, which she thought grew out of his degradation, but she gradually began to lose her temper. As a result, quarrels became more frequent. Obstinately clutching his drinking money, Yōkichi would leave the house and come home drunk late at night. Returning from work, Satoko would be pressed with preparing dinner and taking care of the children. During her business trips to the dams, she now had to ask their next-door neighbor to look after the children.

It was incredible that the rage Yōkichi was capable of displaying should be hidden deep in the person of one so timid. Every day, depending on his whim, he either beat or kicked her. Worst of all, Yōkichi's squandering was driving the family into poverty. Even with an income of thirty thousand yen, there were times when they had problems paying for the rice ration. Unpaid PTA fees and lunch money for the children were accumulating. Satoko could not even buy new clothes for the children. Not only that, Yōkichi developed the nasty habit, when drunk, of waking up his children and physically abusing them.

An acquaintance, unable to overlook the matter, secretly informed Satoko about Yōkichi's woman. When Satoko learned that the woman was Wakita Shizuyo, she was completely taken aback and beside herself with anger. I don't believe it, she told the informant. Fully aware of how foolish she must have looked, she nevertheless listened to reason and suppressed her emotions. That she neither charged over to the woman's place nor quarreled with her husband in a loud voice that could be overheard by the neighbors, was also due to her own reasonableness and restraint.

When she rebuked him in a low voice, Yōkichi replied boldly, "Shizuyo's got it all over you. One of these days, I'm going to give you the boot and marry that woman."

Since that day, each time they argued, Yōkichi would throw these same words at her.

Yōkichi cleared out all the clothes in the dressers from end to end and pawned them. While Satoko was away, he was free to do as he wished. Not a single piece of Satoko's clothing was left, and she had nothing to change into. As for the money from the pawns, he handed it all, down to the last penny, to his woman. Within the half year since Yōkichi had met Shizuyo, Satoko's life had fallen into such straits.

Satoko wept often, feeling that no one in the world could be as unfortunate as herself. When she thought about the future of her children, she could not sleep at night. And yet, in the morning, she would cool her swollen eyelids, and, wearing a smile, go out and make her sales calls.

One cold night in February of 195-, Satoko was crying by the side of her sleeping children. There had been no sight of Yōkichi since she came home. When she asked her children about him they replied that Daddy had been out since early evening.

It was past midnight and almost one o'clock when Yōkichi returned and rapped on the front door. Theirs was a small, four-and-a-half mat, two-room house. The floor mats were torn, and she had patched them by padding them here and there with cardboard. Walking along those mats, she stepped down onto the entrance way and opened the door.

As to what took place after this, it would be faster to read her testimony.

3

"My husband was dead drunk. His eyes were fixed in a stare, and his face looked pale. When he saw that I was crying, he sat down cross-legged by the children's pillows, and began to yell at me, 'What are you crying for? Since I've come home drunk, you're deliberately crying to spite me, aren't you?'

"In retaliation, I said, 'How dare you come home every night drunk! How dare you take away more than half of my hard-earned money every night and spend it on drink, when we can't even pay for the children's school bills, and when we're having trouble paying for our rice ration?'

"It was the same old quarrel we always had. My husband, that night, seemed wilder than ever.

"In a threatening manner, he said, 'Don't be so stuck-up, just because you think you're making a little money. Because I'm unemployed, you take me for a fool, don't you? I'm no parasite!—you'd better believe it!'

"Then he went on, 'You're jealous, aren't you? You idiot, with your face you don't even have a right to be jealous! Just the sight of it makes me sick!'

"With this, he suddenly struck me on the cheek.

"He's getting violent again, I thought, and, as I recoiled, he said, laughing as if amused, 'It's all over between us now. I'm going with Shizuyo now—you understand?'

"In spite of this, I swallowed the insult. Strange to say, I had no feelings of jealousy. I didn't know what sort of woman Shizuyo had become, but she couldn't possibly have had any intention of marrying this good-for-nothing. In the end, I could only feel furious with my husband for having been taken in by the sweet talk of a gold digger.

"Then my husband shouted, 'What kind of a look is that? Is that the kind of face a wife should make?'

"Then yelling, 'I've had enough of this!' he stood up and kicked me on my back and on my side. Seeing that I was gasping and unable to move, he now flipped aside the children's covers with his foot.

"When the children awoke, he took them abruptly by their collars and began to beat them, as he always did in his drunken fits. The children were crying and calling out, 'Mommy, Mommy!' In a daze, I got up and ran towards the front door.

"Beyond the thought of my children's miserable future and of my own wretchedness, it was terror which first arose in me. I became truly frightened. I took hold of the wooden door bolt.

"My husband was still beating the children. The older one, the seven-year-old boy, had pulled himself free and was crying, but the younger one, the five-year-old girl, whining and sobbing hoarsely, her eyes turned up and face flushed as if on fire, was still being beaten.

"Suddenly I raised the bolt and, with all my strength, dropped it onto my husband's head. He staggered under this first blow, and seemed to be turning around towards me. I became frightened and, in a panic, hit him again with the bolt.

"With this, my husband, as if crumbling, collapsed on his face. Even after he had collapsed, I felt as if he were going to get up again, and, in my fright, I dropped the third blow on his head.

"My husband coughed up blood onto the mat. Though it was only a matter of five or six seconds, I felt as if I had undergone a long period of hard labor. Exhausted, I sank weakly to the floor and sat down. . . ."

These were, more or less, the facts constituting the crime of Sumura Satoko's murder of her husband.

Upon turning herself in to the police, she was arrested. Based on her testimony, a detailed investigation was made by the Criminal Investigation Bureau of Metropolitan Police Headquarters, and it was confirmed that the facts were exactly as testified. The cause of Sumura Yōkichi's death was fracture of the lower cranium from severe blows with a wooden bar.

Now, ever since the newspapers had reported the crime, the public was in sympathy with Sumura Satoko. Letters of consolation to the prisoner from total strangers flooded Metropolitan Police Headquarters. Needless to say, most of them were from women.

When the case came to trial, public sympathy mounted even more. Women's magazines, especially, treated this case as a major issue. Articles including the views of social commentators were published. Naturally, these were views sympathetic to Sumura Satoko.

Among the commentators, the one who took the deepest interest in the case and voiced her opinions most ardently was Takamori Takiko, a noted feminist writer. Ever since the crime had appeared in the news, she had been expressing her views on the matter in various magazines, especially in those oriented towards women. A summary of her articles would consist essentially of the following points:

"This case is a perfect illustration of the violent husband in the Japanese home. Despite the fact that he had no earning power, he neglected his family, went out to spend money on drink, then found himself a lover. Such a man is completely oblivious to the happiness of his wife and to the future of their children. Furthermore, the money he spent was the family living expenses which his wife, woman that she is, had worked hard to provide.

"Middle-aged men, bored with their worn-out wives, are apt to get carried way by their interest in other women. This immoral conduct cannot be tolerated. The unique position of the husband in the Japanese family system produces such selfish egocentrism. A certain segment of society, it appears, continues to look with indulgence on these perverse folkways. In the eradication of such indulgence no pains should be spared.

"This case is especially outrageous. A husband who comes home dead drunk from his lover's place, then physically abuses the wife who is supporting the family single-handedly, even going so far as to beat their own children, has not a speck of humanity in him.

"That Sumura Satoko allowed her husband to be so high-handed reveals again the mistaken traditional concept of the virtuous wife. Despite her higher education, she became a victim of this concept. However, looking beyond this weakness of hers, I feel, as a woman, indignation and rage towards her husband. It is understandable that, after being abused and seeing her dear children being beaten right before her eyes, she was overcome by her anxieties towards the future and by her fear.

"I believe that her action, from a psychological point of view, ought to be taken as legitimate self-defense. I don't believe there can be anyone who is unable to understand her state of mind and her situation at the time. She should receive the minimum sentence. As far as I am concerned, I would advocate that she be pronounced not guilty."

Takamori's opinion won the sympathy of all women. Every day, letters expressing total agreement with her opinion were forwarded to her place by the bundle. Among them, there were not a few which requested that Takamori herself stand in court as a special counsel to the defendant.

As a result of this, Takamori's name became even more highly regarded by society. She personally mobilized those of her fellow feminist writers with leadership potential and sent to the Chief Justice a jointly signed petition to reduce Sumura Satoko's sentence. Indeed, she even volunteered to act as special counsel to the defendant. Photographs of her overweight kimono-clad figure together with the downcast figure of the defendant appeared prominently in the newspapers. Like a blaze which had been lit, petitions from across the nation converged on the court.

The sentence which was three years at hard labor, was suspended on condition of two years' probation. After one trial, Sumura Satoko accepted the sentence without appeal.

4

One day, Takamori received a visit from a stranger. She had declined once, saying she was busy, but when the man indicated that he wished some kind instructions from the writer concerning Sumura Satoko, she decided, at any rate, to invite him into the house and meet with him. On the card was the name Okajima Hisao, but for some reason, the address on the left side had been blotted out with black ink.

Judging from his appearance, Okajima was around thirty. He was heavy-set, and he had a healthy tan on his face. Despite the vigor in his bushy brows, high nose, and thick lips, his eyes were as limpid as those of a young boy's. Takamori was impressed with those clear eyes.

"What might this inquiry be that you have concerning Sumura Satoko?" she asked, the man's calling card pinched between her babylike, fat fingers.

In a guileless manner, Okajima apologized for his rudeness in disturbing Takamori from her busy schedule and expressed his high regard for all of her esteemed views on Sumura Satoko's case, which he had had the honor of reading in magazines and elsewhere.

"It was just marvelous, wasn't it, that she was granted probation!" said Takamori, nodding her head as she narrowed her small eyes in her round face even more.

"That was due to your efforts, Miss Takamori, entirely due to your support," said Okajima.

"Oh no, it was not so much my efforts," replied Takamori, smiling and wrinkling up her flat nose, "as it was social justice and public opinion."

"However, it was you, Miss Takamori, who promoted those forces, so it was after all, due to your efforts."

Takamori smiled without resisting. Her double chin was childlike. Her thin lips opened and her white teeth showed her satisfaction at hearing a familiar compliment. Her smile exuded the self-confident, magnanimous air befitting a celebrity.

But what on earth had this man come to inquire about? Judging from his manner of speaking, he seemed awfully sympathetic to Sumura Satoko, she thought. She turned her eyes away nonchalantly and gazed at the spring sunlight falling through the living room window.

"I know Mrs. Sumura slightly," said Okajima, as if he had guessed Takamori's thoughts. "You see, at her solicitation, I joined her company's life insurance plan. That's why I could not feel entirely disinterested in this matter."

"Oh, I see." Takamori lowered her chin, as though she had understood everything. Double-layered grooves appeared on her neck.

"She was a kind and charming woman. I could hardly believe that such a woman would murder her husband." Okajima stated his impressions.

"When such a woman is overcome by extreme emotions, she is bound to do something drastic. As you know, she had been holding herself back for a long while. Placed in such a situation, even I would be liable to do the same thing." Takamori narrowed her eyes in her usual manner.

"You would?" Okajima raised his eyes as if slightly surprised. He looked doubtfully at her, wondering whether this level-headed woman writer would act in as reckless a manner as an ordinary housewife, if her husband ran off with a lover.

"Certainly. When one flies into a rage, there's no room for reason to function. This is true even for a woman like Mrs. Sumura who graduated from college."

"As for such fits of anger," Okajima's clear eyes peered out, "were they related in any way to Mrs. Sumura's physiological condition?"

Because the word physiological had slipped out so suddenly through Okajima's thick lips, Takamori was slightly disconcerted. Then she remembered having read in the trial record that, at the time of the crime, Satoko was not having her menstrual period.

"I don't believe so."

"No, no," Okajima said, looking a bit embarrassed. "I don't mean physiology in that sense. What I mean is the usual physical relation between husband and wife."

Takamori's smile vanished. This man seemed to know something, but what was it he wanted to find out?

"Do you mean to say that there was some physical deficiency on the part of her husband, Sumura Yōkichi?"

"No, the other way around. I feel that there might have been such a problem on the part of Sumura Satoko."

Takamori fell silent for a while. Then, as if to fill in the gap, she took a sip from the tea that had grown cold, and faced Okajima once again.

"Do you have any evidence?" Just as when she was facing an opponent in debate, she tried to locate her opponent's weakness by asking for proof in a level-headed manner.

"No, nothing as substantial as evidence." Because Takamori had fixed her eyes on him, Okajima suddenly became timid. "You see, it's like this. I know a friend of Mr. Sumura. According to this friend, Yōkichi had been complaining from a long time back—yes, from about a year and a half ago—that his wife wasn't complying with his physical needs. That is why I wondered whether Satoko may have had a physiological problem which prevented such relations between husband and wife."

"I wouldn't know," replied Takamori, looking rather out of humor. "As a special counsel to the defendant, I was obligated to read the records of the trial, but there was no mention of any such thing. I assume that such a matter would have been investigated during the pre-trial hearing. Judging from the fact that it wasn't mentioned in the records, I believe Satoko did not in fact have any physiological problem. Wasn't it because Yōkichi was visiting his lover that Satoko refused her husband?"

"No, that couldn't be, because all this began before Yōkichi became intimate with Wakita Shizuyo. That's why it's so strange. Hmm. . . is that so? If, in fact, Satoko did not have any physical problems, then it's a bit odd."

Okajima looked as if he were thinking something over.

5

Takamori drew her brows together into a faint wrinkle. Those brows were narrow, like her eyes, and thin.

"Odd? What do you mean by that?"

"I cannot understand why she refused her husband."

"You see, women," replied Takamori, as if scornful of men, "are apt, at times, to experience an intense aversion to married life. This kind of subtle physiological psychology may be a bit difficult for a man to understand."

"I see." Okajima nodded, but the look on his face showed that he didn't follow her quite so completely. "Now, it appears that Satoko began to act this way about half a year before her husband became intimate with Wakita Shizuyo. In other words, it was after Satoko had continuously refused him for about half a year that things began to develop between Yōkichi and Shizuyo. I feel that there's a causal relation between these two facts."

Though Okajima deliberately used the difficult term "causal relation," Takamori was aware of its meaning.

"I would think there is," she said, drawing her thin brows ever closer together. "That is to say, Yōkichi found an outlet for his frustrations in Shizuyo, isn't that right?"

"Well, yes." Okajima pulled out a cigarette before continuing. "This Wakita Shizuyo is an old friend of Satoko's. It was Satoko who first sent Yōkichi to Shizuyo's bar. She may not have intended it, but it was Satoko, after all, who created the conditions that brought her husband and Shizuyo together."

As Okajima lighted his cigarette, Takamori's narrow eyes flashed.

"Are you trying to say that Satoko deliberately acted as a go-between for her husband and Shizuyo?"

"No, I cannot make such an assertion. However, if you look at the result, it would seem that she, at least, performed the role of bringing them together."

"If we concern ourselves with results, there will be no end to it!" replied Takamori, a bit sharply. "Results are apt to be completely contrary to one's intentions."

"Yes, of course," Okajima meekly agreed. Blue smoke puffed out of his thick lips and wafted brightly across the sun rays streaming through the window. "However, there are also cases in which the results do turn out as expected," he added.

"Oh, no!" thought Takamori. She felt the conviction behind Okajima's manner of speaking. "Do you mean to say, then, that Satoko did in fact have that intention from the beginning?"

"A person's thoughts can only be known by the person himself. I can only make presumptions."

"In that case, what are the data upon which you base your presumptions?"

"The fact that Satoko had been providing Yōkichi with money to go drink at Shizuyo's. Though this was only in the beginning."

"But, that was out of Satoko's kindness," argued Takamori, flickering her narrow eyes. "Her husband is jobless and lying around idly in the house, while she, the wife, is often out because of her work. Knowing how depressed her husband must be, she did it out of kindness. The reason she let him go to Shizuyo's bar was presumably because she thought that Shizuyo would no doubt charge less for his drinks. Besides, if he were to drink anyway, she wanted to help out a friend in trouble. She never thought, even in her wildest dreams, that her kindness would prove to be her ruin and produce such a result. I don't approve of your way of making judgments by twisting the facts around."

"If so, let us say that it did begin from her generosity." Again, Okajima nodded in compliance before continuing. "In spite of her kind arrangement, Yōkichi betrayed Satoko and became totally involved with Shizuyo.

He used up his wife's hard-earned money on the woman and on drinks. He ran off with articles for pawning. Heedless of the poverty they were fast falling into, he enjoyed himself at the woman's place and came home late every night. Once home, raving drunk, he physically abused his wife and children. Satoko, through her generosity, had invited disaster. Because of Shizuyo, her life was now in ruins. To her, Shizuyo had become an enemy who was more than detestable; she was dangerous. Yet in spite of all this, Satoko didn't go to Shizuyo's even once to protest? Why not? It would at least seem reasonable that she go and plead with Shizuyo before letting things turn into such a mess. It wasn't as if they were strangers. They had been friends."

"It often happens," Takamori responded quietly, "that in society, there are wives who charge furiously over to the other woman's place. A foolish thing, which only harms the woman herself. Women with education will not take such disreputable and embarrassing action. A husband's disgrace is a wife's disgrace. She thinks of her responsibility and dignity as a wife. Since Satoko is an intellectual and a college graduate, she would have been incapable of such crudity."

"I see, that may be true." As usual, Okajima first expressed his assent. "However," he continued in the same vein, "Satoko, without reason, continued to refuse her husband for half a year. When he was in this state, she brought him together with Shizuyo, a widow and a bar owner. Her husband, who loves to drink, had also been kept in a state of sexual frustration. All the dangerous conditions were present. Naturally, things developed between the two. Satoko stood by, though, without raising any objections against the other woman. If the facts are laid out this way, one can sense a chain of thought running through them."

6

A hostile gleam appeared in Takamori Takiko's sleepy-looking, narrow eyes. Her living room had been decorated in a subdued and harmonious style. The color of the walls, the framed picture, the living room set, the furniture pieces, all bespoke her polished taste.

The lady of the house, however, had suddenly stood out from this subdued background. Her face was trembling with irritation.

"By extension, then, do you mean to say that Sumura Satoko had set up such a plan?" Takamori asked, speaking a bit more rapidly.

"It's a presumption. A guess based on only these data. . . ."

"A presumption based on extremely poor data, isn't it?" said Takamori promptly. "I can tell the character of just about anyone by a glance. Ever since I became involved in this case, I've not only read an enormous number of transcripts, but, moreover, as special counsel, I've met with Sumura Satoko on many occasions. There was no place anywhere in the records which gave rise to suspicions of the kind you raise. Moreover, when I met Satoko, I was struck by her mature intelligence. Her crystal clear eyes were purity itself. Once again I was overcome by indignation towards her husband, asking myself why such a woman should have to submit to her husband's violent abuse. Such a marvelous and educated woman is not to be met with everywhere. I trust my intuition."

"I share your view about Satoko's fine education," said Okajima, moving his thick lips. "I couldn't agree with you more."

"Where on earth did you get to know Satoko?" Takamori questioned him.

"As I mentioned to you before, I was solicited by Sumura Satoko to join her life insurance plan. I forgot to say that I work at X Dam construction site up in the mountains in the northeast. I am an assistant engineer for Y & Co." For the first time, Okajima spoke about himself.

"Other than our work, our life in the mountains is plain dull," he continued. "As it is, we're up in the mountains where we have to be jostled in a truck for one and a half hours in order to get to the nearest town with a train station. When our work ends and night approaches, there isn't a single thing we can do for fun. Our life consists only of eating and sleeping.

"Of course, there are some who study, but the monotony of the environment soon gets them down. At night, gambling at chess and mahjong are popular. During the two days of vacation each month, the best we can do is to go to a small town at the foot of the mountain about two and a half miles away and release our frustrations at disreputable houses which were quickly set up with the dams as their aim. At such places, a man can spend as much as ten thousand yen or twenty thousand yen at one time.

"After this, we trudge back up the mountain, but no one feels any satisfaction. Though we took up this work after graduation because we wanted to, it's only natural as we cross mountain after mountain, that we should become homesick for the city. The majestic mountains all by themselves leave something to be desired after all."

Somewhere along the way, Okajima had lapsed into a confidential tone.

"Of course, it isn't that no one falls in love. However, the women are all daughters of nearby farmers. They have no intelligence, no education, nothing. They were chosen as partners for no other reason than that they were women. It couldn't be helped since there were no other women around. Considering the environment, the men had no choice. But a sense of dissatisfaction remains. These fellows feel regret, then resign themselves to the fact. They are a sad lot."

Takamori listened in silence. She moved her plump body slightly, and the chair gave a faint creak.

"It was to such a place that two women, Sumura Satoko and a Miss Fujii, came all the way from Tokyo to sell insurance. Since Miss Fujii was close to forty, she wasn't so popular, but Sumura Satoko was popular with everyone. She wasn't beautiful, but she had a face which men found attractive. Plus, when she spoke, she showed intelligence. It wasn't that she flaunted that intelligence, but it felt like something which emanated from inside her. It was strange how even her face began to look beautiful. No, deep in the mountains, she was definitely a beauty. Her speech, intonation, and gestures were all those of a Tokyo woman, a type we had not encountered for so long. It was no wonder that she drew the attention of everyone. Besides, she seemed to be kind and friendly to everyone. Of course, it must have been part of her work. Even though they knew this, everyone was delighted. Needless to say, everyone joined the insurance plan, and furthermore, introduced their friends and acquaintances. I believe her sales record rose beyond expectation. She appeared once every month or two months, and everyone welcomed her arrival. As though in response to that, she sometimes brought presents of taffy candies. They were just trifles, but everyone was delighted. There were even some who felt homesick just looking at the wrapping paper from a Tokyo department store."

At this point, Okajima paused briefly and drank the rest of the tea, which had by then turned cold.

"There was still another reason why Mrs. Sumura drew everyone's interest. This was the fact that she had been saying she was a widow."

Takamori's eyes, which had been only half open and on the verge of closing, opened wide as she looked into Okajima's face.

"This was probably unavoidable, since in selling insurance one depends largely on one's charm. To put it drastically, it's the same as the bar girls who all say they're single. Sumura Satoko claimed, with a smile, that she had to work because she was single. No one doubted what she said. That was why some even began sending her love letters."

Relighting his cigarette, which had gone out, Okajima continued.

"Naturally, Satoko didn't give anyone her home address. All the letters were mailed to her office. This sort of small deception is perhaps forgivable. From the point of view of her business, it was unavoidable. But, this clearly encouraged a number of men to make advances to her. Among these men, there were some who suggested that the women come not together, but alone. The women stayed over at the only available lodging used for those who came to inspect the site. Some of the men would barge over and plant themselves at the lodging until very late. However, Satoko always evaded these temptations with a smile. She was well versed in the art of escaping skillfully and gently, without evoking the displeasure of her business clients. On no account was she unfaithful to her husband. I know this for a fact. However. . ." From the word "however," Okajima's tone seemed to change a little. He seemed to speak in a meditative murmur.

"However, at the dam site, there are many other men of fine character. These are men who are devoting their entire lives to their work. To put it in poetic language, they are men challenging the might of nature in the towering mountain ranges. Their work is to change the face of the mountains through human strength. They are, truly, the most masculine of men. No doubt, when she saw these men, Satoko must have begun to detest her good-for-nothing husband. The contrast must have grown sharper with each day that passed. As one side appeared more and more powerful and admirable, the other side grew more and more wretched and repulsive."

"I realize this is in the middle of your talk," the woman writer, who had been listening until then, interrupted with undisguised displeasure, "but are you imagining all this?"

"Yes, I am."

"If it's just a figment of your imagination, then there's no need for me to listen to it at length. I do have some work left to do."

"I'm sorry," said Okajima, bowing his head once. "I will explain the rest in brief. It wouldn't be unnatural to imagine that Sumura Satoko took an interest in one of the men in the mountains. Let us suppose that this man, too, felt more than an interest in her. It would only be natural, since he had been under the impression that she was a widow. Besides, he must have felt that there could not be a woman as intelligent as she in the world. Satoko must have been troubled. She had a husband called Yōkichi—a husband whom she abhorred beyond hope. As her feelings leaned in another direction, she longed to free herself from her husband. Since her husband would never let her go, she couldn't possibly contemplate divorce. Only her husband's death would free her. She would have to be a widow as she had said she was. Unfortunately, Yōkichi was in robust health. If a premature death didn't seem likely, then there was no other way than to lure him to his death."

Takamori Takiko turned pale and was unable to utter a word.

"However, to murder one's husband is a serious crime." Okajima moved on. "Even if she killed her husband, if she were to get capital punishment or be imprisoned for a long time, the whole thing would be pointless. Being a smart woman, she wondered if there was any way in which she could kill her husband and avoid the death penalty. There was only one way: to be granted probation. In this way, as long as she didn't commit an offense again, she would be physically free. This would be her best choice. However, for this to be possible she would need the mitigating circumstances required for a reduced sentence. At the time, Yōkichi didn't even have the means to earn a living, but this wouldn't fit in as a mitigating circumstance. Thus, she must create the circumstance. In a level-headed way, she produced that circumstance, after a thorough calculation of Yōkichi's character. Following this, all she had to do was to draw the water correctly into the ditch that she had dug, and lure Yōkichi into it. She set to work on her one-and-a-half-year plan. To begin with, during the first six months, she consistently refused Yōkichi, placing him in a state of frustration. With this, she laid the groundwork. Next, she sent him to the widow's bar. She calculated that her frustrated husband would inevitably seek out the woman. Had she failed with Wakita Shizuyo, she probably would have come up with another woman, since there are, no doubt, many women of this type, However, Shizuyo was a woman made to Satoko's order. Yōkichi fell for her like someone in a trance. His self-destructive character, together with his heavy drinking habit, proceeded to destroy their life together. It happened exactly according to her testimony. The only thing is, since there were no witnesess at each point, it's possible that there may be exaggerations in her account. This second stage took about half a year. Within half a year, Yōkichi had turned into the type of person Satoko had anticipated, and behaved exactly as hoped for. In other words, the condition for a reduced sentence was completely ready. Her plan and Yōkichi's character couldn't have coincided more perfectly. Following this, she executed her business. The trial followed. The sentence tallied beautifully with the answer to her calculation. It took half a year to arrive at the sentence. In other words, her plan was completed a year and a half after she set out to establish her initial mitigating circumstance. Oh yes, speaking of how her calculations added up, even what you called public opinion. . . ." As he started to say this, Okajima looked at the woman writer's face.

Takamori Takiko had turned ghastly pale. Her round face was drained of all color, and her thin lips were trembling.

"Are you imagining this?" Takamori's nostrils quivered as she breathed heavily, "Or do you have some solid evidence?"

"I am not just imagining it," replied the sun-tanned Okajima Hisao, "since, to my marriage proposal, Sumura Satoko asked me to wait a year and a half."

Having thus finished speaking, he put his pack of cigarettes into his pocket and prepared to rise from his chair.

Then, before he walked away, he turned around once more to look at the woman writer, and said, "However, no matter how many claims I make of this sort, it won't affect Satoko's probation at all. You needn't worry. Even if such evidences were confirmed, she cannot be subject to double jeopardy. Once a decision is made on the sentence, a retrial that is to the disadvantage of the person in question is not recognized by law. Satoko's calculation seems to have extended this far. The only thing is. . . ."

He turned his childlike eyes intently on Takamori.

"The only thing is, she made one miscalculation. That is, the man she had wait a year and a half has gotten away."

Having finished, he lowered his head and left the room.

Translated by Wei-ming Chen

Mori Yōko

Mori Yōko (b. 1940) is definitely a writer who grew up in a Westernized Japan. She once wrote that she was "a complete devotee of things Western who, even as a child, never went to see a Japanese movie." All the literary works she read in her youth were translations from Western writers—Sartre, Camus, Françoise Sagan, Simone de Beauvoir. She was also fond of Western music and specialized in classical violin at Tokyo College of Arts. After graduation, she married an Englishman living in Japan. She began writing stories at the age of thirty-five, and, naturally enough, a number of Westerners appear in them. The first of those stories, entitled "An Affair" (*Jōji*, 1978), won the Subaru Literary Prize.

In most of Mori's works, however, the central character is not a foreigner but a Japanese—usually a mature Japanese woman. "I have no interest in women," she once said, "who are in their teens or twenties and who do not know what to do except to say 'I did this and that' and push themselves forward all the time. When I talk of women, they are always grown-up women." To Mori, most younger Japanese women seem too dependent on their families, employers, or friends. Thus the heroines of her stories are usually women who have outgrown their youth, mentally if not physically. *Bedtime Stories* (*Beddo no otogibanashi*, 1984–85) is no exception, as can be seen in the two examples that follow. "Be It Ever So Humble" (*Sasayakana kōfuku*) and "Spring Storm" (*Haru no arashi*) were both published in a popular weekly magazine.

TWO BEDTIME STORIES
Beddo no otogibanashi

Mori Yōko

Be It Ever So Humble *Sasayakana kōfuku*

I t was slightly past lunchtime in the restaurant. Most of the customers had finished eating and were now sitting cosily behind their cups of coffee.

Through the window facing the main street the leafless branches of a maple, the image of a tree on a Bernard Buffet canvas, pointed at a cloudy winter sky. Apparently there was wind outside, for its naked twigs shifted uncomfortably in the chill of the afternoon.

Inside the restaurant, however, it was warm and restful. No music flowed; only the chimes of teaspoons on china accompanied the low melody of female conversation. Vases of bright flowers stood around like colorful islands among aromatic currents of espresso.

For some time now, Akiko had been gazing at the bare branches outside the window. The casual onlooker might have guessed her to be absorbed in admiring the wintery view; but, in fact, her expression was molded not from admiration but from bewilderment.

"Now I've told you the reasons," Aono said to her, fiddling with an empty wineglass. "I'm sorry."

He raised his eyes and stole a glance at her.

I'll be perfectly all right without him, Akiko persuaded herself. Until two months ago, I didn't even know this man Aono existed. It didn't inconvenience or depress me then, not knowing him. So I'm simply going back to the way it used to be—that's all.

The way it used to be. The thought rushed in with a flood of insufferable anxiety. She flicked her eyes up at Aono. No, she could never

117

go back to the way it used to be. How could she return to the deathly boredom of that daily routine?

"I'm going to die," she groaned.

"Stop it! Don't make jokes like that," Aono did not try to hide his irritation. "We had our agreement, didn't we?"

"I wasn't serious. I only wanted to see how it would sound when I said it."

Aono looked relieved. Akiko averted her eyes from him. He is not what I really need, she thought. All I need is something to take me away from the kitchen and the TV once in a while. Anything that forces me out of the stifling comforts of my home just for a couple of hours. It doesn't have to be Aono. Heck, there isn't a single reason why it should be him. Except that he was interested in me.

An ache gripped Akiko's chest whenever she wondered why she had agreed to follow this stranger who had accosted her at a supermarket. Aono was precisely the type of man who would accost a housewife with a yellow shopping basket on her arm. That was Akiko's first impression of him.

In truth Akiko's pride was hurt when it happened. The man's once white shirt showed grubby cuffs from under his suit, and his hair was mousy.

A mousy kind of man, she thought. However, when he said he would like to treat her to a cup of tea, she accepted the invitation almost automatically because she was ashamed of herself for having been spoken to by that kind of man. There were a number of other women shoppers around her.

If she turned him down, and if he still went on propositioning her, the two would surely attract attention. Her only thought was to leave the spot as soon as she could.

Because she accepted his proposition so readily—although she was boiling inside—the man seemed momentarily flustered. Looking as if he could not believe his ears, he followed Akiko toward the exit.

In the end, she went to bed with him on that same day. As to why she should have done anything of the sort, she had no logical explanation. It was probably related to the same impulse that had made her act as she had at the supermarket earlier.

In the coffee shop they entered the man looked uneasy, but unable to hide what he had in mind.

"Uh—ma'am—you'll, er—come with me, won't you?" he said falteringly, avoiding her eyes. "Won't you please?"

There was no reason why Akiko should go with him. Everything about him irritated and repelled her. She felt insulted by his attentions; she could not forgive him for assuming her to be so cheap.

She couldn't help noticing the suspicious glances being cast in her direction from tables nearby—from a couple of housewives of about her own age, and from several girls, probably office secretaries taking extra-long coffee breaks. The glances disturbed her, urged her into action and so she ended up whispering "All right" to the man.

Even at that point, Akiko had no doubt there would be a chance to free herself from him once they left the coffee shop. All she had to do was tell him she had changed her mind.

She stepped outside while the man was paying for their coffee. The sun was beginning to set. The evening glow over the metropolis was filtered by dust. A piece of plastic whirled by her in an eddy of wind that also carried with it the smell of sizzling beef from a nearby restaurant. Akiko wondered what she would prepare for dinner.

She thought of the small kitchen at home, of the lunch dishes left unwashed in the sink. She could even visualize the lipstick stain on the rim of her coffee cup above the dried coffee dregs.

As the last blur of the tired sunset struggled through the gritty haze the temperature seemed to plunge. Akiko shivered. At that instant she was struck by the desperate feeling that nothing mattered any more. In that cosy home of hers was there anything she really cherished? She was overcome by a terrible sense of futility.

The man came out of the coffee shop. When he saw Akiko, he blinked a few times and forced out a grin. "I was afraid you might have left," he explained almost apologetically. Obviously he had expected her to be gone by now.

"Why a lady like you? I still can't believe it. I'm mystified." He kept shaking his head as they started to walk together.

Despite his thin shoulders, he had a pair of stout hands. At least, they looked clean. Akiko knew she would not recoil from those hands if they touched her. And, for that sole reason, she went to bed with this stranger, who said he was a salesman.

She had not expected any fireworks in bed. And she was right. Aono was clumsy, and his palms were oddly warm. The elastic in his black socks was worn and they hung limply on his ankles. Afterwards he muttered that he might be short of money to pay the hotel and with an embarrassed look accepted two thousand yen from Akiko.

"Well, then. . . ," Aono stammered as they were about to part. It was at that moment that Akiko clearly saw that he had been taken unawares by the turn of events just as much as she, and had been just as scared. Her tenseness dissipated. For the first time she felt some warmth, something akin to a tender affection, beginning to rise within her.

"Shall we meet again?" she suggested.

Aono's eyes opened wide. Then a smile appeared and spread over his face. There was a touch of boyishness in his expression.

"How?" he asked.

"Like today," Akiko answered softly. "That is, by accident."

They parted in front of the railway station. The sun was long gone. The wind of early winter chilled the gloom.

Akiko, however, had a comfortable refuge. After the bleakness of their clandestine lovemaking, it was a pleasant thought to know a husband and home awaited her, no matter how small and humble that home was. She even saw herself as a happy woman.

Despite her promise to Aono that day, Akiko was distressed over the prospect of his reappearing at the supermarket. As she looked back, what she had done seemed incredibly imprudent. She tried to think of it all as an accident. For the next three days, she did not go to the supermarket.

On the fourth day she went there to do her shopping, deliberately choosing a time different from the usual. To her dismay, she found herself restlessly scanning around as soon as she had set foot inside the store. Aono was not there. She felt relieved, yet somehow let down. From the following day, she began going to the supermarket at her usual time—the time she had met Aono.

As days passed with no sight of him, her sense of relief gradually turned to disappointment; she felt as a woman who had been jilted by her lover after a one-night stand, her relationship cut short before anything worthwhile had developed.

On the ninth day, Aono showed up. He was standing behind a pillar near the cashier, looking as if he were trying to hide himself. As she walked toward him, Akiko knew her face was breaking into a blissful smile and was irritated with herself.

"What a coincidence!" he said.

"It certainly is," she responded, her eyes instantly reconfirming the sad memory of a thin-shouldered, shabby-looking man.

As anticipated, Akiko once more went to bed with him and, also as she had anticipated, she was once again disappointed. As before, he took two thousand yen from her—a transaction that was to be repeated in their subsequent meetings.

As they parted, Akiko felt a relief that swelled from the bottom of her heart. She resolved never to see him again. When she arrived back home she was so happy that she hopped around the rooms, lightly touching every piece of furniture; the cushions, the sofa, the drapery—everything looked fresh. When her husband came home, she was tempted to jump at him like a dog and lick his face all over. Of course she didn't, but in comparison with the frigid-looking hotel room she had entered with that wretched man, her home was a paradise. I must love my husband more than ever, she thought. I must protect my home more than ever! She experienced an attachment to her husband and home as never before.

Inexplicably, she continued to see Aono. He came to the supermarket once every five days or so, and whenever Akiko pondered on the continuing affair she felt sick at heart. But she also knew she would be crushed with despair if Aono should stop appearing.

She did not even know whether he was married. She did not care. Aono as a person did not interest her in the least. Sometimes she would wonder why it was him she had responded to. A number of men had accosted her before. Most were definitely more handsome and better dressed than Aono; some of them youthful college students in blue jeans. But she had never entertained any idea of responding to a single one of them. With pride, she had turned her back on them, assuring herself she was not that kind of woman.

After she became acquainted with Aono, too, some men who saw her in the crowded street or at the railway station tried to invite her out for a cup of tea. Each time she resolutely shook her head and ignored the invitation.

As time passed, Akiko's irritation grew whenever she found Aono leaning against his usual pillar in the supermarket. He seemed completely without shame.

But she became even more upset when he did not show up and several more days would pass, in which she would repeatedly curse him for having such a nerve. Yet, as soon as he reappeared she felt her body grow heavy with a gentle numbness; her heart quietly surrendered to affection, and she was ready to follow him as if manipulated by invisible strings. Not once did Aono wear a new pair of socks.

"Well, I'll be going then," mumbled Aono from the other side of the table.

Akiko stared at his face, which looked more ashy than ever. I've learnt almost nothing about him, she thought. Have I ever tried to study that pale face seriously?

Aono reached for the bill and started to rise from his chair. At that instant Akiko felt a choking sensation in her throat.

"What will become of me?" The words spilled from her mouth involuntarily.

Startled, the man's mouth dropped open. "What? What do you mean?"

"It's intolerable," she stuttered. "Without any discussion, you go ahead and announce that we'd better not meet again. I won't accept it!"

Behind him, the leafless branches were now swaying wildly. The lead sky had dropped into an even gloomier mood. At any moment, it would begin to snow or sleet.

"I suggested it because I thought it would be better for both of us," Aono meekly looked down.

"Don't decide by yourself what's best for us. How can you tell what's on my mind?"

Like a man pained by the cold, he contracted his body further.

"There'll be nothing left for me—absolutely nothing," Akiko groaned in a small, pathetic voice. "If you walk out on me like this, and if I can't see you again, there'll be nothing left for me."

She was well aware of the utter falsity of all this, for she still had a husband and home. The lie, however, expressed precisely her feelings at that instant; reason had been confused, the circumstances out of her control by the thought that this man was about to desert her.

"You say there'll be nothing left, but. . . ," Aono searched desperately for the words to a way out. "You say there's nothing left, but you still have a husband, don't you?"

Her answer was ready without preparation. "It's because of you that I manage to get along with my husband. Because I have you, I can go on living in my house." Once again, truth and untruth became confused. Tears came to her eyes. "I'm not making any big demand. I'm not asking you to marry me. If you can keep seeing me as before—once every five days or so, even once every ten days—that's all I ask."

"You can say what you want, but . . . ," he paused, unconsciously crumpling the bill in his hand. "I don't think I can go on with it."

"Why not? Am I being unreasonable?"

The restaurant was now a sea of empty tables. Its lunch period ended at two o'clock and the shop was to be closed until five. It was a few minutes past two. Waiters were clearing away the last dishes.

"I feel uneasy," Aono looked around the room as if seeking help, "because I don't understand all this. I'm sure you're a good person, but. . ."

Suddenly it was as if Akiko had awakened from a spell; something freed itself inside her. Gone was the numb feeling she always had when she was with Aono. It was replaced by an unaccountable impulse to burst out laughing. Soundlessly she began to chuckle.

Dumbfounded, Aono stared at the giggling woman. His stupified face was so funny that she laughed and laughed, until her eyes were brimming over with tears.

As she continued to laugh, though, she felt a coldness growing in her chest. Deep inside her, she sensed the opening of a dark abyss.

Aono rose hurriedly from his chair, an awkward twist on his face. "Well, I've got to go." He hovered for a second, his eyes still warily on Akiko. Her gaze was fixed, not on him, but on the barren branches outside the window. He turned and started to walk away. From behind, Akiko's low voice murmured something after him.

As soon as the man had disappeared from her sight, her face regained its normal composure.

A waiter came to tell her that the restaurant was closing for the afternoon. With a bright nod she stood up and walked toward the door, the subdued sound of her heels echoing through the empty room. This is the way it should be, she thought. What a relief! Good thing I was able to end the affair so easily. One little problem, and the man might have kept pestering me until I had a marital crisis. I wasn't in love with him anyway—I didn't even like him. Thank goodness he's gone, that's a load off my mind! Akiko opened the glass door. A cold wind, funneled up by the spiral stairway, blew right at her face. It swept away her sense of relief, and in its place left a devastating loneliness.

Just as she had feared, she was overwhelmed with the prospect of having nothing left, that the man had taken everything away with him. She felt abandoned by the entire human race.

With the greatest effort she climbed down the steel stairway, placing her feet with deliberate care. Her body seemed out of gear. Barely managing to steer herself, she at last stepped on the ground.

If she were to head for home right away, she would reach there at around three. She could visualize herself seated in her usual corner of the sofa with a cup of coffee. She could even see the automatic movement of her hand turning on the TV switch. No doubt she would gaze at the television screen as usual—with no enjoyment whatsoever.

Akiko started to walk aimlessly in the opposite direction from home. Several people brushed past her. One of them, a young woman, glared at her and said, "Watch where you're going!" Akiko was taken aback—had she been staggering?

The dark blanket of the sky was so low it seemed about to settle over the leafless branches. If it was going to be a snowy end to the afternoon Akiko wanted it to start right away. With her chin buried into the collar of her overcoat, she stopped at an intersection to wait for the traffic signal.

A number of other people were waiting there, some of the more impatient men already standing in the road. Because Akiko had no reason to hurry, she lingered on the sidewalk after the signal had turned green.

Then it happened.

"Won't you have a cup of tea with me?" A man's voice breathed closely in her ear. It was so close, indeed, that she could feel his warm breath on her neck.

Suppressing an impulse to jump back, she looked at the man. Her first impression of him was of the color gray. Perhaps it was because of his gray suit. The next instant, her eyes were on his hands.

"All right," she said with a faint nod.

By the time they had crossed the road, Akiko found herself intimately walking with him shoulder to shoulder.

Spring Storm *Haru no arashi*

The small orange light on the lobby wall showed the elevator was still at the seventh floor. Natsuo's eyes were fixed on it.

From time to time her heart pounded furiously, so furiously that it seemed to begin skipping beats. For some time now she had been wild with excitement.

Intense joy is somewhat like pain, she thought. Or like a dizzy spell. Strangely, it was not unlike grief. The suffocating feeling in her chest was almost unbearable.

The elevator still had not moved from the seventh floor.

The emergency stairway was located alongside the outer walls of the building, completely exposed to the elements. Unfortunately for Natsuo, it was raining outside. There was a wind, too.

A spring storm. The words, perhaps romantic, well described the heavy, slanting rain, driven by a wind that had retained the rawness of winter. If Natsuo were to climb the stairs to the sixth floor, she would be soaked to the skin.

She took a cigarette from her handbag and lit it.

This is unusual for me, she thought. She had never smoked while waiting for the elevator. Indeed, she had not smoked anywhere while standing up.

Exhaling the smoke from the depths of her throat, she fell to thinking. I'll be experiencing all kinds of new things from now on, I've just come a big step up the ladder. No, not just one, I've jumped as many as ten steps in one leap. There were thirty-four rivals, and I beat them all.

All thirty-four people were well-experienced performers. There was a dancer with considerably more skill than hers. Physically also the odds were against her: there were a sizable number of women with long, stylish legs and tight, shapely waists. One Eurasian woman had such alluring looks that everyone admired her. There were professional actresses currently active on the stage, too.

In spite of everything, Natsuo was the one selected for the role.

When the agency called to tell her the news, she at first thought she was being teased.

"You must be kidding me," she said, a little irritated. She had indeed taken it for a bad joke. "You can't trick me like this. I don't believe you."

"Let me ask you a question, then," responded the man who had been acting as her manager. In a teasing voice, he continued, "Were you just kidding when you auditioned for that musical?"

"Of course not!" she retorted. She had been quite serious and, although she would not admit it, she had wanted the role desperately. At the audition, she had done her very best.

"But I'm sure I didn't make it," she said to her manager. "At the interview, I blushed terribly."

Whenever she tried to express herself in front of other people, blood would rush to her face, turning it scarlet.

"You're a bashful person, aren't you?" one of her examiners had commented to her at the interview. His tone carried an objective observation rather than sympathetic inquiry.

"Do you think you're an introvert?" another examiner asked.

"I'm probably on the shy side," Natsuo answered, painfully aware that her earlobes had turned embarrassingly red and her palms were moist.

"The heroine of this drama," added the third examiner, "is a spirited woman with strong willpower. Do you know that?"

Natsuo had sensed the skepticism that was running through the panel of examiners. Without doubt she was going to fail the test, unless she did something right now. She looked up.

"It's true that I'm not very good at expressing myself, or speaking up for myself, in front of other people. But playing a dramatic role is something different. It's very different." She was getting desperate. "I'm very bashful about myself. But I'm perfectly all right when I play someone else."

If I am to express someone else's emotion, I have no reason to be shy, she confirmed to herself. I can calmly go about doing the job.

"Well, then, would you please play someone else?" the chief examiner said, with a nod toward the stage.

Natsuo retired to the wings of the stage and tried to calm herself. When she trotted out onto the stage and confidently faced them, she was no longer a timid, blushing woman.

It was impossible to guess, though, how the examiners appraised her performance. They showed little, if any, emotion. When the test was over there was a chorus of murmured "Thank you's." That was all.

Her manager was still speaking on the phone. "I don't know about the third-raters. But I can tell you that most good actors and actresses are introverted, naive, and always feeling nervous inside."

He then added, "If you don't believe me, why don't you go to the office of that production company and find out for yourself?"

Natsuo decided to do just that.

At the end of a dimly lit hallway, a small group of men and women were looking at a large blackboard. Most of the board was powdered with half-obliterated previous scribblings, but at the top was written the cast of the new musical, with the names of the actors and actresses selected for the roles.

Natsuo's name was second from the top. It was scrawled in a large, carefree hand. The name at the top was her co-star, a well-known actor in musicals.

Natsuo stood immobile for ten seconds or so, staring at her name on the blackboard. It was her own name, but she felt as if it belonged to someone else. Her eyes still fixed on the name, she moved a few steps backwards. Then she turned around and hurried out of the building. It never occurred to her to stop by the office and thank the staff.

Sheer joy hit her a little later.

It was raining, and there was wind, too. She had an umbrella with her, but she walked without opening it. Finally realizing the fact, she stopped to unfold the umbrella.

"I did it!" she cried aloud. That was the moment. An incomparable joy began to rise up inside her, like the bubbles crowding to exit from a champagne bottle; and not just joy, pain as well, accompanied by the flow and ebb of some new irritation. That was how she experienced her moment of victory.

When she came to, she found herself standing in the lobby of her apartment building. The first person she wanted to tell the news to was, naturally, her husband Yūsuke.

The elevator seemed to be out of order. It was not moving at all. How long had she been waiting there? Ten minutes? A couple of minutes? Natsuo had no idea. Her senses had been numbed. A round clock on the wall showed 9:25. Natsuo gave up and walked away.

The emergency stairway that zigzagged upwards was quite steep and barely wide enough for one person, so Natsuo could not open her umbrella. She climbed up the stairs at a dash.

By the time she reached the sixth floor, her hair was dripping wet and, with no raincoat on, her dress, too, was heavy with rain.

But Natsuo was smiling. Drenched and panting, she was still beaming with an excess of happiness when she pushed the intercom buzzer of their apartment.

"Why are you grinning? You make me nervous," Yūsuke said as he let her in. "You're soaking wet, too."

"The elevator never came."

"Who would have considered using the emergency stairs in this rain!"

"This apartment is no good, with a stairway like that," Natsuo said with a grin. "Let's move to a better place."

"You talk as if that were something very simple," Yūsuke laughed wryly and tossed a terry robe to her.

"But it is simple."

"Where would we find the money?"

"Just be patient. We'll get the money very soon," Natsuo said cheerfully, taking off her wet clothes.

"You passed the audition, didn't you?" Yūsuke asked, staring intently at her face. "Didn't you?"

The young man had a strangely intense expression on his face. It was almost like despair.

Natsuo stared back at him. He looked nervous, holding his breath and waiting for her answer.

"Natsuo, did you pass the audition?" As he asked again, his face collapsed, his shoulders fell. He looked utterly forlorn.

"How. . . ," she answered impulsively, "how could I have passed? I was just kidding."

Yūsuke frowned. "You failed?"

"I was competing with professionals, you know—actresses with real stage experience. How could I have beaten them?" Natsuo named several contending actresses.

"You didn't pass?" Yūsuke repeated, his frown deepening. "Answer me clearly, please. You still haven't told me whether you passed."

"What a mean person you are!" Natsuo stuttered. "You must have guessed by now, but you're forcing me to spell it out." Her eyes met his for a moment. "I didn't make it," she said, averting her eyes. "I failed with flying colors."

There was silence. Wiping her wet hair with a towel, Natsuo was aghast and mystified at her lie.

"No kidding?" said Yūsuke, starting to walk toward the kitchen. "I was in a state of shock for a minute, really."

"How come? Were you so sure I wouldn't make it?" Natsuo spoke to him from behind, her tone a test of his sincerity.

"You were competing with professionals." There was now a trace of consolation in his voice. "It couldn't be helped. You'll have another chance."

Although Yūsuke was showing sympathy, happiness hung in the air about him.

"You sound as if you were pleased to see me fail and lose my chance."

Combing her hair, Natsuo inspected her facial expression in the small mirror on the wall. You're a liar, she told her image. How are you going to unravel this mess you've got yourself into?

"How could I be happy to see you fail?" Yūsuke responded, placing a kettle on the gas range. His words carried with them the tarnish of guilt. "But, you know, it's not that great for you to get chosen for a major role all of a sudden."

"Why not?"

"Because you'd be a star. A big new star."

"You are being a bit too dramatic." Natsuo's voice sank low.

"When that happens, your husband would become like a Mr. Judy Garland. Asai Yūsuke would disappear completely, and in his place there would be just the husband of Midori Natsuo. I wouldn't like that."

"You're inventing problems for yourself," she said. "You are what you are. You are a script writer named Asai Yūsuke."

"A script writer who might soon be forced to write a musical."

"But hasn't that been your dream, to write a musical?" Natsuo's voice was tender. "Suppose, just suppose, that I make a successful debut as an actress in a musical. As soon as I become influential enough and people begin to listen to what I say, I'll let you write a script for a musical."

"Let you write, huh?" Yūsuke picked on Natsuo's phrasing. "If you talk like that even when you're making it up, I wonder how it'd be for real."

The kettle began to erupt steam. Yūsuke flicked off the flame, dropped instant coffee into two cups, and splashed in the hot water.

"Did you hear that story about Ingrid Bergman?" Yūsuke asked, his eyes looking into the distance. "Her third husband was a famous theatrical producer. A talented producer, too." Passing one of the cups to Natsuo, he continued. "One day Bergman asked her producer-husband, 'Why don't you ever try to get me a good play to act in?' He answered, 'Because you're a goose that lays golden eggs. Any play that features you is going to be a success. It will be a sellout for sure. For me, that's too easy.'" Yūsuke sipped the coffee slowly. Then, across the rising steam, he added, "I perfectly understand how he felt."

"Does this mean that I'll have to be a minor actress all my life?" Natsuo mused.

"Who knows? I may become famous one of these days," Yūsuke sighed. "Or maybe you first."

"And what would you do in the latter case?"

"Well," Yūsuke stared at the coffee. "If that happens, we'll get a divorce. That will be the best solution. Then, neither of us will be bothered by all the petty problems."

Natsuo walked toward the window. "Are you serious?" she asked.

"Yes." Yūsuke came and stood next to her. "That's the only way to handle the situation. That way, I'll be able to feel happy for you from the bottom of my heart."

"Can't a husband be happy for his wife's success?"

"Ingrid Bergman's second husband was Roberto Rosselini. Do you know the last words he said to her? He said, 'I'm tired of living as Mr. Ingrid Bergman.' Even Rosselini felt that way."

"You are not a Rosselini, nor I a Bergman."

"Our situation would be even worse."

From time to time, gusts of rain slapped at the window.

"When this spring storm is over, I expect the cherry blossoms will suddenly be bursting out," Yūsuke whispered.

"There'll be another storm in no time. The blossoms will be gone, and summer will be here." Brushing back her still moist hair with her fingers, Natsuo turned and looked over the apartment she knew so well.

"You've been standing all this time. Aren't you getting tired?" Her husband asked in a gentle voice. She shook her head.

"You're looking over the apartment as though it were for the first time," Yūsuke said, gazing at his wife's profile. "Or, is it for the last time?"

Startled by his last words, Natsuo impulsively reached into her handbag for a cigarette and put it in her mouth. Yūsuke produced a lighter from his pocket and lit it for her.

"Aren't you going to continue with your work this evening?" she asked.

"No. No more work tonight."

"What's the matter?"

"I can't concentrate when someone else is in the apartment. You know that, don't you?"

Natsuo nodded.

"Won't you sit down?" Yūsuke said.

"Why?"

"I have an uneasy feeling when you stand there and smoke like that."

Natsuo cast her eyes on the cigarette held between her fingers. "This is the second time today I've been smoking without sitting down." The words seemed to flow from her mouth at their own volition. His back towards her, Yūsuke was collecting some sheets of writing paper scattered on his desk.

"You passed the audition. Right?" he said. His voice was so low that the last word was almost inaudible.

"How did you know?"

"I knew it from the beginning."

"From the beginning?"

"From the moment you came in. You were shouting with your whole body—'I've made it, I'm the winner!' You were trembling like a drenched cat, but your face was lit up like a Christmas tree."

Natsuo did not respond.

"The clearest evidence is the way you're smoking right now."

"Did you notice it?"

"Yes."

"Me, too. It first happened when I was waiting for the elevator down in the lobby. I was so impatient, I smoked a cigarette while standing. I've got the strangest feeling about myself."

"You feel like a celebrity?"

"I feel I've outreached myself."

"But the way you look now, it's not you."

"No, it's not me."

"You'd better not smoke standing up."

"Right. I won't do it again."

There was silence.

"You don't at all feel like congratulating me?" Natsuo asked.

Yūsuke did not answer.

"Somehow I knew it might be like this," Natsuo continued. "I knew this moment was coming."

Now she knew why her joy had felt like pain, a pain almost indistinguishable from grief. Now she knew the source of the suffocating presence in her chest.

"That Rosselini, you know. . ." Yūsuke began again.

"Can't we drop the topic?"

"Please listen to me, dear. Rosselini was a jealous person and didn't want to see his wife working for any director other than himself. He would say to her, 'Don't get yourself involved in that play. It'll be a disaster.' One time, Bergman ignored the warning and took a part in a play. It was a big success. Rosselini was watching the stage from the wings. At the curtain call, Bergman glanced at him while bowing to the audience. Their eyes met. That instant, they both knew their love was over, with the thundering applause of the audience ringing in their ears. . ." Yūsuke paused, and then added, "I'll go and see your musical on the opening day."

Natsuo contemplated her husband's face from the wings of the room. He looked across.

Their eyes met.

Translated by Makoto Ueda

The Mistress

Nagai Kafū

Among leading novelists of modern Japan, no one has written more about the lives of geisha, prostitutes, mistresses, and other downtrodden women than Nagai Kafū (1879–1959). One of his major novels is indeed entitled *Flowers in the Shade* (*Hikage no hana*, 1920), alluding to its main character, an unlicensed prostitute, and to the people around her who are living similarly shady lives. Other important works by him, such as "The River Sumida" (*Sumidagawa*, 1909; trans. 1956), *Geisha in Rivalry*, and *A Strange Tale from East of the River*, also include portraits of young women who are, or are destined to be, "flowers in the shade." His interest in such hapless women was derived partly from his sympathy for them, but it also had a good deal to do with his admiration for European Naturalist literature on the one hand and for the popular fiction of premodern Japan on the other. Having made his literary debut as a follower of Maupassant and Zola, he was ever aware of the power of sexual passion as an all-important determinant of human behavior. However, having spent four years of his youth in the United States and France, he also knew that Japanese sensibilities could never be completely Westernized. To him, Japan's attempt to Westernize herself seemed disgustingly superficial. As time passed, he became increasingly attracted to the demimonde, whose inhabitants he thought retained much of the lifestyle of premodern townspeople. In story after story he wrote about women of the town, and when criticism arose regarding his personal life he resigned, without regret, from his prestigious teaching position at Keiō University. He married twice, each marriage lasting only for a few months. It seems that he felt at ease only when he was in the demimonde.

"Nude" (*Ratai*, 1950) depicts a young office girl against the backdrop of postwar Japanese society, a chaotic society just liberated from a prolonged period of wartime repression. The story's focus, however, is on the biological forces that work on the heroine from within and eventually change her into an almost different person. In some basic way, Kafū was a Naturalist to the end of his career.

NUDE
Ratai

Nagai Kafū

Okamura Sakiko was the daughter of a public bathhouse owner in the town of Funabashi in Chiba Prefecture.

At the end of last year, during which she turned eighteen, she started working in an office in the Ginza district of Tokyo for a certified public accountant by the name of Sasaki.

One day, as always when it was finally time to go home, Sakiko had hastily gotten her things together, exchanged perfunctory goodbyes with the other women, and was about to leave the office with her friend Kimiko.

"Hey, wait a minute. There's something I want to ask you about." Called back just as they were about to walk out the door, the two women turned and looked at Sasaki's face.

Sasaki's broad shoulders and stocky build suited his bald head and square face, with its jutting lower jaw, making him appear to be a superbly powerful man. But in the light at the window, reflecting the rays of the setting sun, it was the whiteness of his closely cropped moustache that caught the eye. He must have been past fifty. Sasaki rose from his chair and, pressing his pot belly against the edge of his desk, leaned toward them.

"Just you, Sakiko. I don't need you, Kimiko. Go on home."

The accountant watched Kimiko lower her eyes in a silent bow and go out the door alone and then, in a somewhat lower voice, said, "Come over here, a little closer."

"Yes, sir."

"There's no one around now, so I thought I'd just go ahead and ask you about this today."

"Yes, sir, what is it?"

"It's because you and Kojima are the only ones in and out of my office

135

all the time. Kimiko's just the telephone receptionist after all, and besides, she's just started working here. And so. . . well, I just thought I'd start with you first. Mind you, if it's my mistake, I intend to apologize. This morning, that customer who always comes in—you know, Mr. Kanbara—left a bundle of money on that table. But when I checked it later it was a little short. This isn't the first time it's happened either. Somehow lately, money just seems to keep disappearing from time to time. I'm not saying you're the only one I want to check up on. Sooner or later, I intend to get around to everybody. But you're the one I feel most comfortable with, so I thought I'd start with you. Don't take it the wrong way, but could I take a look at your handbag?"

"Sure, take a look. I'm not the kind of woman who steals money. Not me. You can look anywhere you want as far as I'm concerned."

"I know, I know. I just thought I'd ask to make sure. Don't get mad."

After the accountant had lined up the things from Sakiko's handbag one by one on the table, he moved closer and, as if to placate her, began to stroke her arms lightly with his fingertips. It was one of those days when the lingering heat of late summer had still not dissipated, and the sleeves of Sakiko's dress were as short as could be, just barely covering her shoulders and underarms. The vaccination scars on both her arms were clearly visible.

"Just as I thought, it was all my mistake. Here, I'll put everything back."

"Satisfied already? Here, sir, check inside my lunch box if you want to."

Sakiko did not appear to be particularly angry. Pressing the handkerchief she was holding against her sweaty forehead, she was gazing at the man with a dimple in one of her full, round cheeks. Ever since the end of the war, hardly a day passed when she did not hear about something disappearing or being stolen, if not on the train, then when she came to the office in this building, or when she got home. Money disappeared from people's wallets and they could never figure out whether they had dropped it somewhere or had had their pockets picked. She had heard of umbrellas disappearing from the stands they were left in and of a raincoat that had disappeared almost as soon as it was hung on the wall. There was even a story about someone who had opened her lunch box at noon only to discover that the food packed that morning was no longer there. None of this was of any concern to Sakiko, as long as her own things did not disappear. And she seemed to think that if a person were going to worry or get angry every time someone cast a little suspicion upon them there would be no end to it.

The woman's attitude was so contrary to his expectations that Sasaki, who had been secretly afraid that Sakiko would be mortified and get angry, or even cry, began to feel sorry for her. But in complete opposition to that feeling, her manner made him remember hearing somewhere that it was precisely those women who are kleptomaniacs by nature who are able to remain completely calm and affect an air of serene innocence in a situation like this. Without really meaning to, he found himself staring at the woman. Sakiko—what was she thinking?—suddenly jumped up from the chair she had just sat down on and, slapping her dress with her palms, said, "Sir, search me, anywhere you like. Here, I don't even mind taking off what I'm wearing." She tilted her head back slightly and vigorously shaking it to the left and right two or three times to loosen her hair, reached back and began quickly unfastening the hooks of her dress.

Ever since she was a little girl, Sakiko had sat in the high attendant's seat between the men's and women's baths in her father's public bathhouse, and she had become thoroughly accustomed to seeing men and women taking off their clothes and walking around nude. In a situation like this, alone with her boss and no one else around, she thought nothing at all of standing there in just her chemise.

"See? I'm not hiding a thing."

"All right, all right. . . . I understand. That's enough." But even as he said this, Sasaki was overcome by curiosity, instantly aroused by Sakiko's body. He could not keep his hands from touching her breasts and her hips, covered now only by the sheer fabric of her chemise.

The way the woman's muscles expanded and contracted, squirming in her body as she writhed and twisted under his touch. The man's face reddened, as if he had suddenly become intoxicated. Sweat began to pour down his face.

"I was wrong. I apologize. I'll buy you something to show you how sorry I am. Come with me to Ginza."

Sakiko smiled at him in a manner that was almost affectedly seductive and said, "Sir, the things I want to buy. . . there are so many I wouldn't even know where to begin."

Taking advantage of the fact that everyone else in the office had left for home, Sasaki took Sakiko's hand and got into the same elevator with her. Typical of a man past fifty, and one who had always enjoyed a little self-indulgence, Sasaki had often thought that if only the opportunity presented itself he would like to have a fling with one of these office girls—or perhaps one of the salesgirls in the department stores—who all appeared to have become more and more licentious since the end of the war. But up to now he had never had a good chance. Oh, he had begun to entertain certain ambitions toward Sakiko as early as that first day at the end of last year, when she appeared to answer his help-wanted advertisement in the newspaper. The way she had looked that day in her red sweater and boyish dark blue trousers—the way her breasts and hips swelled so deliciously, so much more than most girls. And her air of sophistication, far beyond her years. But it had turned out that it was even more difficult to make advances to a girl he used in his own office, and the thrill he had felt on that first day gradually faded as he got used to seeing her everyday. He had just let things go on as they were until somehow, without really meaning to, he had forgotten all about it. But the body he had felt beneath the sheer material of her chemise! The way she was acting! Sasaki was quite beside himself.

First an open-air stall on Sukiyabashi Avenue—a ring with a red glass setting for eight hundred yen. Then out to the main boulevard, where he bought her a pair of sandals for two thousand yen. As they walked through the crowded streets, Sasaki put his arm around her waist and drew her hip against his own. He even tried taking her hand. But Sakiko did not appear to be the least bit averse to what he was doing, and Sasaki concluded that since things were going so well it couldn't hurt to go one step further. He began trying to think of a place where he could take her clothes off.

Before the war, he would have known where to go without even stopping to think about it, but now everything had changed and he did not have the slightest idea where he could take her. Struck suddenly by an idea, he turned back to the pedicab drivers who were loitering around the Sukiyabashi Bridge waiting for passengers.

"Hey, you guys, isn't there an inn around here? Doesn't have to be overnight. . . ." He stole a glance at Sakiko as he said this, but she didn't appear to be particularly suspicious, so he turned to her and said, "Come on, let's have a bite to eat. I'll send you home in an hour or so."

The two pedicabs went through the intersection at Owari-chō, over the Mihara Bridge, and finally turned into a dark side street off the road that runs along the streetcar tracks in Tsukiji. They stopped at the door of what appeared to be a private residence, and the pedicab drivers received two hundred yen apiece.

A woman of about forty, whose face suggested that she understood perfectly what Sasaki required, led them upstairs. It was an eight-mat tatami room in which *futon* had been spread neatly over the floor. When he saw the bedding, Sasaki was overcome once again by fears that Sakiko would be shocked and try to escape and, without giving her a chance to protest, or even to sit down, he threw his arms around her and attempted to throw her down right where they stood. But, again, Sasaki's fears were needless. Sakiko quietly placed the things he had bought for her beside her pillow, as if to say that they were more important than her body, and fell back onto the *futon*, spreading her legs as she rolled onto her back.

Three days after that evening, Sakiko quit her job at the office and moved into a rented room in the Nakano-Kōenji area.

Sakiko had achieved a status that required nothing of her on days when Sasaki did not visit but to go out to the movies, or to her dance lesson, or perhaps to spend half the day polishing her nails. But all too quickly the affair was nearly half a year old, and her patron's visits—so frequent at first that she was surprised he did not get tired of seeing her everyday— gradually became further and further apart. Finally he failed to show up at the end of the month when she was supposed to receive her allowance. She sent him a letter, but there was no reply.

One day, Sakiko went to the accountant's office, intending to find out what was going on, and was surprised to find that while the number of the office was the same, the gold lettering on the glass door had been changed, and now spelled out "M. M. Trading Company." When she inquired about this to the building superintendent, she was told that Sasaki had vacated the office about a month ago and turned over his rights to it to the firm that was there now. He didn't know the details, he said, but Sasaki's business seemed to have fallen off considerably lately, so much that it probably no longer justified paying so much rent to maintain an office.

Sakiko did not know Sasaki's address, only that he lived in Kawasaki, but even had she known she could not very well have called on him at home. Suddenly she felt forlorn and hopeless. She did not even look back at the theater marquees along the way as she slowly started for home. It was on that day that Sakiko ran into her dance instructor, a certain Tsuda, on Sukiyabashi Bridge. Tsuda, who could have been slightly under or slightly over forty, pomaded his hair and wore suits in the latest fashion with expensive-looking ties. He spoke to Sakiko in languid, wheedling tones.

"I'm so sorry I was out. I had a little business to attend to."

"Oh, I hadn't called on you yet today. I had something to do, too."

"Uh, Miss Okamura, I have a good proposition for you. Come over here a minute."

"A good proposition? What kind of proposition? . . ."

"Miss Okamura, ah. . . say, wouldn't you like to make a little money? I have a deal where you can make a thousand yen for only an hour or two's work."

Sakiko had no idea what Tsuda might have in mind, but having just discovered that she might well be without a patron, she could not bring herself to brush him off.

"What kind of work is it, Mr. Tsuda?"

"There's going to be a dance party tonight at a certain place I know. You just go to the party and dance."

"Do you think I could do it? Didn't you say I still can't dance at all yet?"

"No, no. . . that doesn't matter. You'll do fine. But there is one little condition. You can hide your face with a mask, but you have to dance with nothing else on."

"So, it's nude. . . ."

"Uh-hmmm. You're game, aren't you?" The dance instructor answered Sakiko with a deliberately casual air and then added, "The place is in Meguro, a big mansion. We have these parties once in a while for the members of a certain club. You know, we can't take girls from dance halls or places like that. We want girls with a little more class, and better bodies. It's from eight to ten tonight."

"But is it safe? The police . . ."

"This place is absolutely safe. It's not a cafe or a dance hall, you know."

"Will there be a lot of people?"

"Probably twelve or thirteen, tonight."

In the nearly six months since she had become the mistress of a fifty-year-old man, Sakiko had thoroughly mastered a great variety of ways to have sex, and as a result she was often tortured by an irrepressible lust that seemed to well up from within herself. Already, she entertained ample desire to peer into the bizarre world about which she had heard so many rumors. And, indeed, given her nature, her physical constitution, and her upbringing, the path this woman would take may well have been largely determined from the very beginning. She had graduated from junior high school during the war and was immediately conscripted to work in a factory. But unlike most of the other girls, she had not minded being conscripted. Going to the factory, a production site for war supplies in name only, had been easier than being at home, where she was worked all day long, a baby strapped to her back while she helped clean up in the kitchen or the bathhouse. The work was not that hard at the factory, and it had been fun flirting with the "peace soldiers" during lunch breaks or on the way home.

Sakiko had been used to seeing the nude bodies of men and women in the bathhouse since she was a child. She had seen the men who sometimes came to peek into the women's side of the bath, and she had seen the bath attendants douse them with water or grab them and drag them off to the police box. And at some point these scenes had deeply engraved on Sakiko's mind the fact that men like to look at naked female bodies. One day, she was accosted by one of the boys on the way home and she had taken off her clothes quite willingly. And on Sundays, when they went to swim at the beach nearby, she had astonished the boys by stripping naked. Their surprise had given her a feeling of triumph. After the war, the general mood of society, and the things she saw and heard every day, only made that consciousness more and more unshakable.

The illustrations in magazines and novels, which one could never have seen during the war . . . The photographs in the newspapers . . . The sketches on the advertisements displayed at street corners . . . Handbooks on birth control . . . The lively activity of the prostitutes that one could see at every train station . . . And the rumors and gossip that people talked about tirelessly whenever they came together. They never failed to make Sakiko's skin crawl, as if a sultry, unpleasantly warm breeze were blowing over her body.

Sakiko consented easily to the dance instructor's proposal and that evening was taken to a mansion in Meguro.

Until the day of defeat it had been the residence of an army general, but its owner had been purged, and the former mistress of a tea house in the Tsukiji area had bought it and made it over into an inn. Inside the gate, a two-story Western-style building was concealed behind a deep, densely wooded grove. The spacious drawing room—a place where generals with close-cropped hair had once proudly displayed their swords and medals as they plotted military strategies for uniting the eight corners of the earth in universal harmony—had become the dining room. The neatly arranged tables were spread with white cloth, setting off vases of beautiful flowers. The rooms on the second floor had become guest rooms, furnished with double beds and closets for Western-style clothing. The tatami rooms that continued on from the rear of the main building were furnished with round, red-lacquer tables. In the *tokonoma* alcoves hung *ukiyo-e* prints of beautiful women, and behind sliding panels in each room were stored *futon* with red covers dyed in the Yūzen style. At the end of the gallery connecting the tatami rooms to the main building was a door. This door opened onto a large underground room. Once the vault in which the military had stored its most secret documents, the room had been constructed in such a way as to eliminate any fear of damage from air raids. Now it had been transformed into a bizarre secret world of gambling and illicit sexual pleasures.

When the dance instructor ushered Sakiko up to the second-story room that had been chosen as the changing room, three of the other girls who would be dancing that night had already come and were busily repairing their makeup before hand mirrors. Just as they had completed their greetings, and the conversation had shifted to small talk, the rest of the women began arriving in groups of two or three. Finally, when it appeared that everyone was there, the dance instructor gave a brief explanation of the order of the evening's performances.

When all the guests were comfortably settled in the underground chamber, the mistress of the hotel would put on a record. By this time, the women were to have taken off whatever they were wearing and changed into the black stockings he had brought for them. There were also masks for those who did not want to show their faces. Silver and red shoes had been provided, and they were to wear them for the performance. Now, when the record began, they were to join hands and skip down the stairs two or three at a time from the connecting gallery to the underground room. Once all the women were assembled there, and an appropriate amount of time had elapsed, a really sexy Western film would be shown. And on top of that, tonight's entertainment would be made even more interesting by some people who were going to stage a live sex performance. This was the way the evening had been planned, and now they should all know what to expect.

Chattering noisily among themselves, and without the slightest sign of hesitation or shyness, they all took off their clothes and picked up their masks. But among them were two or three women who did not cover their faces at all, and went scampering off to the underground chamber as if they could hardly wait for the phonograph record to give the signal. Sakiko was one of them.

The pale red lighting in the underground room was hazy, obscuring the spaciousness of the chamber as well as the people seated in the chairs and couches arranged against the walls. It was impossible to discern how many guests were present. But there seemed to be a fireplace burning somewhere in the room, for though it was an October evening, the room felt too warm even before she began dancing.

Gradually, the glasses of cold, tasty punch and well-chilled beer that she gulped down each time she had a break from dancing began to take effect. And the Western movie and the live sex performance for which she had waited so impatiently stimulated her excitement to the extreme limit. When the party finally ended and the men and women were preparing to leave, three of the girls were quietly called aside by the mistress of the mansion, who told them that if they could stay for the night she would very much like to have them do so. Sakiko, of course, was among them.

Perhaps never before that night had Sakiko been so enraptured by the pleasures and the delights of having been born a woman. Again and again she had shaken the man awake when he was on the verge of falling asleep—so many times, in fact, that even in her elated mood she had felt a little embarrassed to have him see her face in the morning. It was near-ly noon when she finally returned to her second-floor apartment, still floating in feelings of conquest and good fortune. No sooner was Sakiko through her door than she pulled a stack of money out of her handbag and went out again to pay her overdue rent and the money a friend had spent to buy her rationing for her. After paying back every single yen that she owed people, she went off to the neighborhood public path to wash her sweaty body. When she took off the clothes she was wearing, that body, which had been completely uncovered from the previous eve-ning until she had left for home that morning, stood before her in the dressing room mirror. For a little while, Sakiko could not remove her eyes from it—as if she were gazing at the form of another person.

The public accountant Sasaki, who had paid her only three thousand a month in the beginning, had let her quit her job in the office and without begrudging any of it, had rented an apartment for her and given her ten thousand yen every month to live on. And why had he been so generous? Hadn't it all started from the time she had taken her clothes off in the office and shown him her naked body? And even after that, Sasaki was never satisfied until he had made her spread her *futon* before the big full-length mirror and had watched her writhing body as she twisted it into various poses for him.

The man she had slept with the night before had begun his lavish praise of her nude form even while she was still dancing. There are very few women like you. Your whole body is possessed of a classical balance of proportions. Sure, we say that plump women are best, but that doesn't mean that she should have a short neck, broad, jutting shoulders, and a long, flabby torso. The most beautiful women are those who, viewed from behind, make one wonder if they aren't in fact a little skinny. One should still be just able to see the line of her spine. The ones whose tor-sos are merely fat are called "Zundō vases," because their waists are not tapered even slightly above the hips. Their figures are ugly, and they are not pleasant to embrace. Women with flat, grossly large buttocks are no good either. A woman's flesh must have a firm plumpness, and a resilient spring. The best breasts are those that do not sag limply from the chest but rather are round and firm, like a tea bowl turned upside down, so the ideal bottom is the same. It must protrude from the hips with a taut roundness. Only the thighs may be stout and powerful—the more so the better, in fact, when it comes to titillating a man's eye. But the legs must be long and slender below the knees. And the underside of the foot—the arch must be deep, indented to the utmost. The big toe should curve back on itself and be elegantly long and pliant. As Sakiko recalled these points one by one, and how the man had lavished praise on her, saying that her body was flawless in every respect, she studied the bodies of the four or five women squatting in the soaping area before the big tub, comparing them to her own. And ever since she had gotten into the hot tub, she had not been able to stop stroking her naked body with her own hands.

When she awoke, after returning to her walkup apartment and flopping herself down for a short nap, scenes from the foreign movie and the live sex show she had seen the night before came floating up before her eyes again, and Sakiko began to feel that she could not stand just sitting at home by herself—that she wanted desperately for someone to embrace her as tightly as he could. Already, the short autumn day was coming to an end, and when she looked toward the window, the evening sun fell on the translucent paper of the *shōji* screen at a sharp angle. Still sprawled out on the floor, Sakiko stretched out her hand, reaching for the skirt she had flung off earlier. She hastily dabbed on a little makeup and went out. She boarded the train and after a short ride got off at Shinjuku Station.

For no particular reason, Sakiko had suddenly wanted to see the bustling streets of Shinjuku, men and women pressing against each other as they walked to and fro before the glass display windows full of gaudy merchandise. It was not the first time she had felt this way. Even when she was an office girl, Sakiko had liked to loiter on the busy street corners, mingling among women who appeared to be prostitutes and eavesdropping on their conversations while gazing at their figures and mannerisms. As she had experienced more and more extreme sexual acts as the mistress of an elderly patron, the conduct of these women, and of the men who approached them, had made her feel all the more intensely a kind of mystery and longing.

The lights had been turned on at the station and in the shop windows. In the fading sunlight, the streets in the far distance were wrapped in dust and a leaden haze. But all around her it was as bright as afternoon. Stopping for a moment at one of the open-air stands to look at the obscene pictures on the covers of the novels and magazines lined up on the counter, it occurred to her to enter one of the movie theaters around the station and wait for nightfall.

She crossed an intersection through which cars and trucks barreled past at an even more reckless pace than usual, and just when she had gotten a little tired of walking, her eye was caught by a theater marquee. Without a second glance, she walked up to the ticket window. It was then that she realized that the ad poster was not for a movie. Pictured instead was a large group of nude women, all dancing in various poses. Among the other passersby who had stopped to look, someone was loudly reading off the titles written on the poster. *Horror at Midnight. Ero-Grotesque No. 1. Melody in Curves.* Others were nervously waiting to buy tickets.

Sakiko had grown up during the war years, a period in which revues had been banned, and so there was something strange and marvelous about the pictures on the poster. And they also reminded her of the women who just the night before had come to the mansion in Meguro to dance in its secret, underground chamber. Without a thought for the one hundred yen entrance fee, Sakiko bought a ticket, still reliving in her mind the experiences of the previous evening.

The darkened theater was so crowded that she could not find an empty seat. She pushed her way into the throng of customers standing against the walls and somehow managed finally to at least peer through them to the brightly illuminated stage.

On the stage, a backdrop had been lowered that made it seem that she was looking at a flower garden, and from the garden she could see a clear, blue sea through the surrounding forest. Three women wearing costumes that revealed their bodies beneath some white, gauzy material were dancing in time to a musical accompaniment. They held old-fashioned water jars over their heads. Presently, a heavily bearded male actor entered the stage, his body below the waist transformed into that of an animal. A horse or perhaps a goat. This half-man-half-beast chased the dancers around the stage trying to throw his hairy arms around them or raise their skirts. The women fled in feigned panic and finally ran off stage. Suddenly, the music became soft and gentle. A single woman appeared in a dazzling costume that reflected the stage lighting. As she danced, she became a maiden picking flowers. The satyr appeared again and gave her flowers from a narcotic plant. In an instant, her dancing became languid and uncertain, as if she had suddenly become intoxicated. The satyr followed her movements, clinging to her body and tearing at her costume. But even as he ripped her clothing off—first her blouse, then her brassiere, and finally even her skirt—stripped her naked, the woman did not awaken from the trance induced by the perfume of the poisonous flower. She sank slowly to the ground, and the stage darkened. Now, a woman in white entered and left the stage with cards upon which something—apparently the names of foreign artists—had been written in *katakana* script. Each time she appeared with a new card, a brilliant spotlight illuminated a large picture frame within which nude women struck various standing or reclining poses.

During these performances, a kind of strained stillness had blanketed the dimly lit theater, a hushed silence in which not even the sound of a cough could be heard. But as soon as the curtain began to come down, people noisily got up to leave, and others were pushing and shoving to get to the empty seats after them—and in the midst of this confused commotion she began to hear the voices of the hawkers calling out as they moved through the audience with their baskets of candy and cider.

It seemed about time for the curtain to open again, but Sakiko had been caught up in the crowd of people who were pushing and shoving to get outside, as if there could be nothing more of interest now that they had seen nude bodies. She could do nothing but allow herself to be pushed outside with the others. Night had already fallen in the street outside, and the scene was animated by the blare of radios, the lights, and the people milling around her.

For reasons that even she did not understand, Sakiko was overcome by a wonderful feeling of exhilaration. She wanted to eat recklessly—to eat her fill of something really delicious, no matter how much the cost. When she was still an office girl, she had passed by coffee shops after gazing wistfully at the prices on the dishes displayed in the glass cases— even coffee shops. But now there was nothing she could not eat if she felt like it, and this thought made her recklessly, excruciatingly happy. And that wasn't all. It seemed to her that all the people milling about her must be people on their way home from seeing the nude revue. Either that or they were on their way to see it. When she thought of the amazing popularity that focused on the nude female body, Sakiko naturally could not help feeling a profound sense of security toward life, and pride and confidence in her own body.

She had not eaten breakfast or lunch and just as she was once again counting in her head the money she had received the night before at the mansion in Meguro, her eye was caught by the gaily decorated wreaths of flowers lined up before a Chinese restaurant that had just opened. She went in and took a table near the door.

The interior of the shop seemed deserted, not at all like the hustle and bustle outside on the sidewalks. There was a couple at a corner table, and a young man in a suit sitting near the counter. He read a newspaper as he ate. The three waitresses were leaning against the wall gazing dreamily at the people passing by outside.

Sakiko had a bowl of noodles and steamed dumplings and then went outside again. It was already that time in the evening when the street walkers and cafe waitresses were beginning to come out to look for customers. One really could not tell them apart as they began to appear in all the side streets. Feeling a little frightened, she stood at the street corner watching them. Just then, someone rushed up beside her, so suddenly that she thought he was going to crash into her, and grabbed her hand. She whirled around in astonishment and alarm, but it was the young man she had just seen reading his paper and eating alone in the Chinese noodle shop. With his long, oval face, a lock of hair falling over his forehead, and his slender physique, he had looked not altogether unattractive when she saw him in the restaurant, and Sakiko allowed the hand she had started to pull away to be held.

"Walk with me a little ways, will you? This isn't my turf."

"Hmmm? You from Ueno then?"

"Come on, let's have a drink."

"Uh. . . you a waitress? I'm not going to any cafe."

"I'm no waitress. I just asked you because I can't go into a bar by myself. Don't worry, I'll pay."

"Doing pretty well, huh?" He was looking at her face dubiously. "How about it. . . uh. . . how about it tonight?"

"For goodness sakes, why are you making such a face? Don't I look like a whore?"

"If I say you do, you'll get mad, and. . . What am I supposed to say now?"

"Look, I'm feeling lonely tonight, that's all. I don't want your money." Taking advantage of the bustling crowd around them, Sakiko kissed the young man on the cheek and gave him a hug. His look of stunned astonishment was so funny she couldn't stand it, and shaking all over, she laughed and laughed and laughed.

Translated by Mark A. Harbison

Kaikō Takeshi

Kaikō Takeshi (b. 1931) belongs to the generation of Japanese whose youthful prime coincided with the period of social turmoil that immediately followed the end of the Second World War. His college days were spent in war-ravaged Osaka, where he struggled to survive by taking any job that came his way: he worked at a factory, sold lottery tickets, taught English, even dealt in black-market goods. Although he was a law student, he did a great amount of reading in literature—especially modern French literature. After graduation, he began working in the sales promotion department of a whiskey maker and for many years edited a highly successful PR magazine for the company. His reputation as a writer was established in 1958, when one of his early stories, "The Naked King" (*Hadaka no ōsama*, 1957; trans. 1977), won the Akutagawa Prize. The story, a critical comment on the current state of education in Japan, is already indicative of his deep commitment to social reform, a commitment that has also motivated him to write most of his later stories. In these stories he seems to take a liberal leftist stand, but his basic faith is not so much in a specific ideology or political system as in the potentially explosive power of the masses. The harrowing experiences of his youth also made him an ardent pacifist, and he was one of the most vocal antiwar writers during the Vietnam War. His trips to Southeast Asia were sometimes overly adventurous—once he was almost killed on the front line—but they resulted in several novels, including *Darkness in Summer* (*Natsu no yami*, 1971; trans. 1973) and *Into a Black Sun* (*Kagayakeru yami*, 1968; trans. 1980).

"A Certain Voice" (*Aru koe*, 1955), one of his earliest stories, also deals with an important social issue of the time. During the Korean War, certain Japanese cities teemed with American soldiers on furlough, thereby attracting a number of young Japanese women who wanted to become their "companions." The story centers on one such woman, but its implications go well beyond political protest.

A CERTAIN VOICE
Aru koe

Kaikō Takeshi

Let me tell you about my room. I am living outside the city in a farmer's storehouse. I have a small room on the second floor, like an attic. The building, once a granary, was reconstructed during the war to house evacuees. There is a young woman living in the room below me. The U.S. Army has a hospital and barracks in the next town and American soldiers often come to visit her. She still seems very girlish. Whenever she smiles the tip of her small pink tongue appears in the space between her front teeth. She has no friends and seldom speaks to anyone. When she is alone she shuts herself up in her room. When she goes out to shop she walks timidly along the edge of the road, her eyes downcast. As soon as her errands are finished she hurries back. Two or three times I've written a letter for her to an American soldier named Henry, but I know next to nothing about her.

The farmyard is quite large. In one corner is the storehouse where I live. It is hidden from view of the main house by the animal shed and a cluster of sycamore trees. I can come and go through the nearby garden gate rather than using the gate to the farmhouse. Behind the storehouse is a bamboo grove. No one passes through there, except for an occasional chicken or rabbit which has strayed from its pen in the wheat threshing area near the main house. The wind whistles softly through the bamboo. In the distance the sound of a bucket being raised and lowered into the well can be heard. In such seclusion one could, if he wished, pass his days never speaking to a soul.

When I look down from the little window of my room on a summer afternoon, the fragrance of straw, the smells of barnyard manure and fresh grass, all waft silently through the area bounded by the bamboo grove and the cluster of sycamores. The heat is intense. It is so quiet that I imagine I hear the sunlight bubbling like boiling liquid. A thicket ablaze with red and gold canna and sunflowers adds a touch of brilliance to this sunny enclave, like a single clash of cymbals breaking the silence of an air pocket.

Sometimes a lizard makes its way up the thick, ivy-covered wall, its small, dry claws clicking as it flickers across my window like a green-gold flame. Not an inch of wall is visible through the dense ivy. Countless leaves and vines tangle and twine, covering even the window. They bury the wall, crawl up over the eaves, scale the roof, and stretch even beyond, toward the sky. It was winter when I moved here with a friend, and only dead vines, like the network of blood vessels in an old man's hand, covered the entire surface of the rough gray wall. When I first entered the farmyard through the garden gate, the wall in the distance looked as if it were covered by a rusty wire netting. Right now if one were to pluck off some leaves and tear away the surrounding vines, for two or three days that bare patch would stand out like a gaping white wound. But in no time at all the vines would be back coiling around, the leaves as luxuriantly thick as before. Such resilience!

So one could say that I am living in the shade of the ivy leaves, peeping at life through the meshes of a vine net. But during the day I lower the blinds and sleep. I am working as a proofreader for a second-rate newspaper company. It's a temporary position. These days I work only the night shift. I return from the office at eight or nine in the morning, eat a quick breakfast, sleep until four in the afternoon, get up at dusk, and go back to the city, where in that dimly lit, disorderly proofreading room I wander through a jungle of words until the dawn. After two or three months of this schedule I began feeling utterly run down. But my boss has never offered to make me a regular employee. My eyesight has deteriorated, so I have managed to scrape together enough money for a pair of glasses.

Lately I haven't been sleeping well during the day. I sweat profusely, and my underwear is drenched. The lethargy I feel upon awakening makes it briefly impossible for me to move my limbs. The window blinds are so hot they nearly burn to the touch. When I raise them even a crack, the summer sunlight, like molten metal, floods the room. My room faces south, and since there are no eaves or awnings over the windows, there is no respite from the light. My only defense is to keep the blinds lowered and sit motionless facing the wall in the semidarkness. I futilely wonder what would become of me if my body ceased to function properly except in the gloom.

On Sundays I occasionally take a stroll through the city. The sunlight reflecting off the pavement and the walls of the buildings stings my eyes like a hypodermic needle until the tears begin to flow. At times I am driven to take refuge in one of those back-street cafes that play music by candlelight even in the daytime. I grow nostalgic just thinking of that part of town where symphonies reverberate in rooms behind gold-lettered doors, where through the chinks of windows under red and white striped awnings the aroma of freshly brewed coffee seeps out and winds through the narrow cobblestone streets. Be that as it may, the thought of trudging along the country paths into town, the sunlight reflecting brilliantly off the tile roofs, leaves me limp with fatigue. So usually, even on Sunday, I lie prostrate in my room beneath the roof, like one of the animals in the shed outside. No one comes to visit and no one writes to me here.

When evening comes I raise the blinds, switch on my hot plate, and prepare a meager meal. I toast bread and put jam on it. Sometimes, on a day when the rain has just stopped, I glance up to see a little frog stuck to the window pane like a green splash of rain water. It has come waddling up the wall through the thick ivy toward the light outside my window, intent on the mosquitoes and birdlice which gather there. Blinking its eyes encircled by thin gold rims, it opens and shuts its mouth with imperceptible speed and engulfs a victim. Then it leaps suddenly away from the window and vanishes from sight. Even after it has grown completely dark, if I shine a light from above I may see it still clinging stubbornly out there, its small, white belly amazingly bloated.

After dinner I either take a walk into town or I open up an atlas. My roommate often tried to cure me of this habit by bringing home various novels and magazines, but I would delve into the travel accounts and guides without so much as a glance at the rest. Not that I am planning to travel. I am perfectly content with a map of any place, even if I know nothing about it. When I am in a bookstore it is only the set of atlases that inspires me with a desire to collect every volume. I can pore over a single map for an entire day without losing interest. I tried any number of times to explain this to my baffled roommate. Although to him a map depicting mountain ranges and their elevations was nothing but a conglomeration of curving lines, to my eyes those curves delineate luminous shapes of splendid mass and volume. No matter how exhausted I feel, when I look at a map someplace inside me responds immediately, like light-sensitive paper that retains an image when exposed. My friend never did understand. He saw in me simply an escapist tendency combined with an attraction to the exotic. Any discussion of the matter would end with his declaring in exasperation, "What it comes down to is surrogate satisfaction. You're a prisoner gazing through bars at the blue sky."

Opening the window wide to let in the evening breeze, I stretch out on the worn and prickly straw-matted floor and smoke one cigarette after another, surrounded by an electric heater and a rice cooker, tea cups and medicine bottles, neckties and a wristwatch, all jumbled together and strewn around me. It is Saturday and I am free until Sunday night. I open up the world atlas, now tattered and soiled from so much handling.

In the past a certain American soldier used to visit the girl downstairs on Sunday evenings. Sometimes he just came and spent the night, and at other times the two of them went out for the evening. As I lay there absorbed in my maps I would hear him enter the garden gate, run to the place beneath the girl's window, and begin to whistle. I don't remember him very clearly any more except for his slight frame, blond hair, and boyish cheeks. The girl would rush across her room, peer through the darkness, and answer his calls. Her voice was short and clear, and it resounded with emotion. She would wait all day for him, cooped up in her stuffy room. The soldier would call cheerfully to her, then he would begin a thin, high-pitched whistle that pierced the air as clearly as the song of a little bird. Whenever I heard that sound I felt as though the vibrating column of air was scratching like a metal tip against the thin window pane and boring into it.

That whistle often revived my memories of the previous war. At the time of the labor mobilization I was a high school student working at a shipbuilding yard in Kobe. Four or five American air force men who were prisoners of war were also working there. When evening came they were handcuffed and escorted back to solitary confinement cells. When we students passed beneath their windows on our way home they would always be whistling the same piece of jazz. The sound of that whistling, too, lingered clearly on the air, like a stream of pure, sparkling liquid. Even at the time I did not know the name of the song, and when the war ended I completely forgot about it. But once in Kyoto's Kamo River area a friend and I were making the rounds of the *yakitori* shops, drinking cheap saké, when he suddenly began to whistle and my memory revived. "What's that song?" I asked. "You don't know? 'St. Louis Blues,' of course," he answered, as if annoyed. I later learned that the piece had originally been a Negro gospel song. I remembered all that whenever the American soldier who visited the girl downstairs began whistling in the dark garden below.

The girl downstairs certainly lives quietly. Since I work the night shift I leave the house at dusk. In the daytime I lower the blinds and sleep like a log, so I have no idea how she spends her time. It was usually only on Sunday evenings, when that particular American soldier used to come, that I would be reminded of her existence. Occasionally I did run into her—on the stairs, in the garden, on a path in the field, or on one of the village roads. In town I might spot her in front of a bean curd shop or grocery store where she had been shopping. At those times she would pretend not to notice me. Or if she was simply unable to avert her glance, she would greet me with a timid smile, the tip of her tongue showing through the space between her white teeth. She is terribly shy and seems to be a loner.

She is thin, her coloring poor. She wears shoes with run-down heels or worn-out wooden clogs whose red straps have faded from many washings. She seems very fastidious; not a day passes that her fresh laundry isn't hanging out to dry in the corner of the garden. And how discreetly she dries it. In a sunny corner of the bamboo grove that is plunged into shade when the sun moves, she hangs two or three pairs of underwear, carefully hiding them from public view.

At times I strain my ears. Particularly since I witnessed a certain scene, I am alert to any sound which may be coming from the room below me, but in vain. The walls and floor of the storehouse are too thick. I try to go out on evenings when she has a man staying with her. She and I live side by side, so we try to stifle all the warm and vibrant, soft and spontaneous things that betray our presence: the scent of a body, the sound of breathing, footsteps across the room, someone turning over in bed, a sigh. I am vaguely aware of her unhappiness and misfortune, but am helpless to do anything about it. Sometimes I picture myself descending from my loft, entering her room, and starting to speak with her. But I cannot imagine having the power to effect a positive, organic change deep inside another person by means of my words and voice. My life has been a series of failures. Each time I have tried to crystallize my feelings in some way, or to seize the moment at hand, my efforts have fallen short. I am unable to make her aware of horizons and lights, warm currents and whirling eddies. I could perhaps find words to describe the quiet process of disintegration and decay that is taking place inside me, invisible to anyone. But that would only make matters worse for her.

When my friend and I lived here together, we used to pick up a little money by writing letters to American soldiers for their girlfriends who lived in the town. Neither of us had prospects for a job after graduation, so we felt unmotivated to begin our senior theses. We ran around presenting ourselves to various companies here and there, but while our fellow students were being snatched up all around us, we were invariable passed over, like fallen leaves left to wither on the ground. By translating the prostitutes' letters we at least made enough money to drink cheap saké.

Once my friend caught a stray cat, picked it up as if it were a log or a sandbag, and flung it against a rock in the garden. The corpse stayed in a corner of the grove, and after a while gangrene set into its lungs and it began to emit a foul odor. Finally the carcass dried up in the sun, leaving a small pile of white bones. After my friend had been drinking for a few hours he would look at me and inquire bitterly, "Each time you stumble and fall, do you really think you're getting fatter as you roll, like a snowman?"

Sometimes we translated the letters which the women received from the soldiers into Japanese, too. We took care to translate those parts which were sure to please the women. But the bad news—a man's change of heart, his return to the States, a transfer brought about by a shift in the battle front or a change in his rank—we would either omit or render ambiguously. Most of the women, with the unfailing instinct of wild animals, grasped the real situation, shrugged off their disappointment and went after a new man. But there were others whose man had long been dead or had returned permanently to the States who persisted in believing that he was still out in the front lines. They continued to write their letters, attach the translation fee, and bring them over to us. This was at the height of the Korean War.

My friend, too, was sometimes asked by the girl downstairs to translate letters for her. They were all addressed to a Henry Fairchild who was living in the barracks in the next town. In her letters she lamented their plight of being engaged but unable to marry while the confusion of wartime lasted. The soldier's letters were written in unusually correct and refined English. The girl, unable to read or write any English, would approach one of us in the garden or the hall with her request, hand over the letter, and disappear as if she were escaping. Since I became familiar with her personal circumstances through the letters, I tried to devise ways of striking up a conversation with her the next time I delivered her translation. But when that time came she would invariably lower her gaze shyly, her fragile body would stiffen like a schoolgirl's, and she would be gone.

On his free days Henry came to visit his small, timid fiancée. I would look down at him as he entered the garden, his blond hair shining like silk under the rays of the sun. His slender build and boyish face gave a wholesome impression. When the weather was fine they went out together. I watched them walk away, the girl in her plain, sturdy clothes looking more like a bank teller than what she actually was. And when Henry changed into civilian clothes, he didn't come wearing those Aloha shirts like the other American soldiers. They were economizing, putting away money for their marriage. He began teaching her some English and she taught him some Japanese, in faltering tones.

My roommate finally gave up on finding regular employment here and resigned himself to returning to his home town. When we parted at the station there was a rare seriousness in his voice as he murmured, "I hope things go well for that Fairchild pair." But things did not go as we had hoped.

In Korea the war effort was intensifying by the day. The town around the next station had grown boisterous. Soldiers moved in and out of the barracks and hospital more frequently, and the women who lived in the town changed accordingly. It was said that on an evening when a new group of American soldiers arrived, a great number of women carrying suitcases would alight at the station, having come from the town near the base that the soldiers had just left. Posters on which roman letters had been carelessly splashed in paint sprang up by the dozen around the station. They advertised bars, cabarets, teashops offering "special services," "love hotels," souvenir shops, camera shops with developing and printing facilities. Violent incidents perpetrated by American soldiers were common.

Just after my friend had gone home I learned from a letter brought to me by the girl downstairs that Henry had been sent to Korea. I saw the weariness and dejection in the girl's eyes, her plans having gone awry. Fatigue had made her skin dry and left dark circles under her eyes. I silently translated the letter and waited until she was out to slip it through the paper screen doors to her room.

About a week later I learned by chance that Henry had died. Since there is no mail box on the garden gate, the farmer's children bring our mail to our rooms. When we are out they slide it through our doors. One day I picked up a letter lying on my floor which had been sent from a friend of Henry's to the girl downstairs. I read it and learned of the blond youth's death. Henry must have given his girlfriend's address to this friend. With that blue stationery spread out in front of me, I laid down and got up, started to stand but sat down again, my mind in turmoil. I opened up the world atlas but could focus on nothing. I recalled how my roommate and I had made a practice of always concealing any bad news, and I decided not to take the letter downstairs to the girl. Instead, I placed it in my ashtray and carefully burned it. I had become acutely sensitive to any sound from the room below, but on that evening there was total silence. I glanced down into the garden from my window, but her light was not on. As I smoked one cigarette after another, I pictured the frail young girl sitting there in the darkness, her eyes shut tight, listening to the sounds of life inside her.

One evening I went to the office as usual, but realizing that I was too exhausted to work, I found someone to substitute for me and left early. I got off the train at the next town intending to pick up some bread and butter. It was around eleven o'clock at night. Dozens of fishy-eyed prostitutes loitered around the ticket collector's gate waiting for American soldiers. Their painted eyebrows and thick applications of lipstick and eyeshadow made their cheeks and mouths glisten as if smeared with raw animal fat. Impish, brazen children with shoeshine kits, vying with each other for business, rushed up to long-legged soldiers, grabbed their feet, and tried to force them up on their own shoe stands. Even when a child was hit or kicked away, the light that gleamed from his eyes like the blade of a knife continued to shine undaunted. One exasperated soldier peeled away a boy who was clinging to his trousers and threw him like a sand-bag across the pavement. Fragile bones and meager flesh thudded as the ragged lump of a child rolled along and landed in a ditch. He jumped out nimbly, snatched up his nearby shoeshine box, faced the soldier and spat at him. "You goddamn fucking bastard. . . !" By the time the soldier noticed him and made a move, the boy had vanished.

The street in front of the station overflowed with drunken American soldiers and prostitutes. After finishing my grocery shopping I stopped to look in two or three book stores, then I returned to the station. As I walked past the ticket gate, I noticed a girl leaning against the gray wall, staring out blankly. There was something familiar about the hair with its unhealthy reddish cast, the weak chin, the delicate neckline, and the sunken shoulders, so I went back. She was resting against the wall as if tired from walking, and gazing at the brightly lit ticket gate. Her vacantly parted lips revealed, as ever, the small tongue peeping through the space between her teeth.

Her clothes were terribly shabby and rather soiled, the area around her eyes and cheeks gaunt and wasted; her appearance had totally changed. Yet I recognized without a doubt the girl who lived in the room below me. The red polish on her nails had been carelessly applied. She squinted incessantly, perhaps because of the bright lights. A clump of false eyelashes, too big for her, trembled on each of the delicate eyelids and seemed ready to drop off at any moment. Just then she made a clumsy attempt to adjust them, and on her raised hand I could see even at a distance white patches of fingernail beneath the peeling red nail polish. So at last. . . . I was overtaken by fatigue and I left.

Two or three days later, on a Sunday evening, I saw her again. It was in a little field some distance from the village. I had gone out for a walk and was passing by there on my way home. A crowd had gathered and was making quite a clamor, so I approached to have a look. I peered over the shoulders of the onlookers and saw that five or six women, obviously prostitutes, had formed a circle around a young girl and were abusing her. The girl was lying face down on the ground, her arms and feet smeared with mud. Pieces of straw and grass poked through her hair, and her thin dress was badly torn.

"You already have a man, don't you? Do you think you can fool around with someone else's and get away with it?"

"Just a young thing but she can't get enough of it, eh?"

"She's trying to make fools of us."

The older prostitutes were all calling her names and tormenting her. They kicked her with their clogs and slapped her face. One of them grabbed the object of their contempt roughly by the hair and twisted her head back and forth while the others shouted insults at her and slapped her small face without restraint. The girl was pinned down and she writhed desperately, but she kept her mouth shut tight and never uttered a sound.

"Tougher than you'd expect, isn't she?"

"She hasn't had enough yet."

"Never mind. Here's one way to make her cry."

Suddenly one of the women crouched down and shoved her hand under the girl's dress. Her claw-like nails were on that secret, soft place. I smelled something that reminded me of a rain-soaked bitch. The girl's face was distorted, her lips trembled, her head moved violently from side to side. A little cry escaped from between her clenched teeth.

"That's enough, isn't it? Even guys wouldn't be so rough. . . ."

The remark had come from someone in the crowd of spectators. A woman watching the scene with folded arms whirled around, glared fiercely in our direction and barked, "You shut up!" The man closed his mouth, grinned sheepishly and withdrew from the crowd.

The girl kept trying to escape those sharp, probing claws. She began to roll over and over on the ground, twisting her skirt but desperately holding it down to keep the others from tearing it off. Each time her face approached the feet of one of the women, her chin would be kicked or her face slapped. They taunted her mercilessly.

"Don't you ever fool around with Joe again. If you're after a man, you'd better look for him in another town."

When the women had gone, the lingering smells of their bodies and perfumes pervaded the entire area. The spectators drifted away one by one, as if bored, leaving the girl lying there on the ground. When she sat up she was panting, her shoulders heaving. Through dishevelled hair she looked around in my direction and I saw that her eyes were dry. They were like two burnt holes. She lifted her body up slowly, brushed the dirt from her slender elbows and knees and pulled down her skirt. A delicate network of blood vessels was visible on her long white calves. She picked up her worn-out pair of clogs by their torn red straps, and began gingerly walking home barefoot on the path through the field.

I decided not to go back to my room and instead went to the next town. I wandered here and there, drank some strong liquor at an outdoor stand, and finally, after about three hours, I went home. I opened the garden gate. There was no light on in the girl's room. I thought of the letter that I had burned, but went straight to my own room on tiptoe. I opened the window. In the dark the ivy leaves rustled constantly in the night breeze. To my drunken ears the sound was like the feet of millions of tiny crabs scuttling around the roof. After a while I realized that I was waiting for the dark garden to reverberate with that bird-like whistle that used to summon the girl.

There was no let-up in my busy schedule. I dragged my weary body through my nightly routine, then withdrew to my room beneath the roof and slept until dusk, like a lobster in its shell. Thus my solitary existence continued. The money that the soldier used to send had long since stopped, so the girl downstairs was forced to join the other women in the street at night. Whenever I looked, the light in her room was off. I never knew whether she was in there or not. Even if she was, she did not make a sound. I pictured her frail, thin body as she nibbled like a mouse at a portion of suffering too great for her, trying to digest it bit by bit. Since the day I witnessed her being attacked by the prostitutes in the field, I tried to ignore any sound that came from the thick, old, crumbling storehouse walls. Anyway, there was no sign of life from her room.

I was anemic, and one evening a couple of weeks after that incident I blacked out in the men's room at the newspaper office and came home early. A dissolute-looking youth was playing a guitar in front of the village grocery store. The smell of warm soap rose from the dark ditch outside the public bath. The wind was whistling through the grove of bamboo behind the storehouse. As I walked past the farmhouse, I heard the dull sound of a cow's hoof kick against the side of its wooden stall in the animal shed.

I started to open the garden gate, then stopped short. There was a light on in the girl's room and I could see a person's shadow moving. Someone had apparently just passed by, because the smell of cheap cigar smoke floated on the air. I hid in the clump of bushes near the gate. The girl left her room and came out to the garden. Her footsteps clicked along the stone path, then she softly opened the gate. She leaned against it and stood facing the darkness. After a few moments I heard her soft, low voice begin to call, "Henry. . . ." A wide, hazy halo of light spread out from the lamp above her head. Her face was startlingly close to me. If I were just to stretch out my arm I could probably touch that distraught little cheek, shining now with a peculiar light, and feel its warmth.

"Henry, come back," I heard her whisper in a hesitant, childlike voice. She spoke slowly, in English, saying each word deliberately, as if attempting the correct pronunciation. It had a strange effect on my ears.

"I want you."

She spoke in a husky, warm murmur, heedless of her surroundings now, and her words had changed to a daring and urgent appeal.

"I want you!"

She practically shouted it out. It seemed to me the words had acquired the physical density of wood or stone. The girl's appearance was totally transformed. Beside her mouth a deep, scar-like crease had formed. Her nose stood out sharply from her gaunt face and her dark eyes were suffused with a passionate light. She stared unblinkingly toward the dark road where an American soldier had just gone, puffing on his cigar, having absorbed the warmth of her body. I felt overwhelmed. She had stopped speaking and simply stood under the light with her head lowered. I sensed in her bowed neck and the line of her shoulders a ripeness and a raw power that excessive suffering must have yielded. It was that power which had torn those ardent words from deep within her body where the blood ran warm and dark. (Could my own voice ever resonate with such fervor?!)

The girl, her head still bowed, finally laughed softly. She shut the gate behind her and left the lamplight. She continued to laugh as she rushed back across the garden toward her room. Her voice caught in her throat, its shrill echo pierced the darkness and slowly died away. Was she crying?

I came out from the bushes, practically kicked open the gate, and raced across the garden in the direction of the light coming from her room. As I ran I tried desperately to recapture the exact timbre of those clear, newly-learned words, spoken to no one at all. Again and again I forced my mouth to shape them: "I want you! I want you!"

Translated by Maryellen Toman Mori

Enchi Fumiko

Daughter of a Tokyo University professor, Enchi Fumiko (b. 1905) grew up in a scholarly family environment that encouraged her to read works of literature and go to the *kabuki* theater. She herself began writing plays as a young woman and continued doing so after she married a journalist in 1930. Two years later she gave birth to a daughter. After this her creative urge seemed to intensify, and she sought a new outlet in writing novels and short stories. The war, however, brought a drastic change in her life. In 1945, her home was destroyed in an air raid. The following year she was operated on for cancer of the uterus and was on the verge of death several times because of post-surgical complications. The long period of illness and poverty gave a new dimension to her works when she finally resumed writing in 1949. The novel she began to write that year, entitled *The Waiting Years* (*Onnazaka*, 1957; trans. 1971), won the Noma Literary Prize in 1957. She has been one of the most prolific writers in Japan ever since, publishing a number of prize-winning novels and stories that have received high critical acclaim. She has also found time to translate *The Tale of Genji* into modern Japanese; the result, an excellent work, is now known as "Enchi Genji." In November of 1985, Enchi was decorated with the Bunka Kunshō (Cultural Medal), the highest award an individual can receive, by Emperor Hirohito.

Although Enchi has written many types of stories, her main aim always seems to have been to pursue the basic nature of womanhood, both in its social context and in its relation to fundamental human instincts. In *The Waiting Years*, for example, she studied the plights of several women who had no alternative but to accept the demeaning roles that contemporary society had assigned to them. In such works as "A Bond for Two Lifetimes—Gleanings" (*Nisei no en shūi*, 1957; trans. 1982), *The Mask* (*Onnamen*, 1958; trans. 1983), and "Boxcar of Chrysanthemums" (*Kikuguruma*, 1967; trans. 1982), the focus of her study is more on female sexuality and its powerful and sometimes enigmatic manifestations. "Blind Man's Buff" (*Mekura oni*, 1962) is a story that combines both categories, as it portrays a mistress's daughter who, partly because of her environment and partly because of her own inclinations, follows in her mother's footsteps when she grows up.

BLIND MAN'S BUFF
(*Mekura oni*)

Enchi Fumiko

A light rain was falling that late November night when I got a telephone call from my sister's house in Kyoto. The mistress of the house—Ichiko, my younger sister by another mother—had left two days earlier, saying that she was going to Osaka, and hadn't yet returned home.

It just happened that our former maid Kinu, who had known Ichiko from childhood, had come for an overnight visit at my place. So after I hung up the phone, it was only natural to tell her what the call was about.

"Oh, Miss Ichiko in Kyoto," Kinu said, and paused. Then she started to laugh. "She should be past the age of running away from home."

"That's true, . . . but that's what Mr. Kajita's afraid she's done."

Mr. Kajita was the chief priest of the temple from which Ichiko leased the land for her Buddhist-style vegetarian restaurant. Ichiko was his common-law wife. Her name wasn't entered in his family register, but all the families that were members of the temple accepted the situation. She once told me why she wasn't entered in the register. It wasn't that religious doctrine forbade Kajita to marry. He was hesitant about it, feeling that his parishioners might not accept Ichiko because she had been a geisha; and Ichiko herself didn't want to join the temple and be known as the priest's wife.

"But Miss Ichiko is only one year younger than you, Ma'am. She must be fifty-two." Kinu continued to be preoccupied with Ichiko's age.

"Whether they're fifty-two or fifty-three, people now are different from before. There aren't many women who don't mind being single and shriveled up, like me," I said.

"Of course I know, Ma'am, that you and Miss Ichiko are different. But there couldn't be any reason for her to run away from home. They say her restaurant is very popular."

"Exactly. Just now on the phone, Mr. Kajita said that he had no idea what could have happened. He said she left the house two days ago, saying she was going to spend the night with a friend in Osaka. So they didn't think anything of it when she didn't return yesterday. When she still hadn't come back this morning, they sent a telegram—her friend doesn't seem to have a telephone—and found out that she'd never shown up there at all. That's when they started to worry and called here wondering if she might have come to Tokyo."

"Well, it does sound a bit odd."

For the first time, Kinu began to express some doubt.

Though Ichiko and I were born in different years, our birthdays are within six months of each other's, mine in November and hers the following May. This showed that we couldn't have been born to the same mother. I was one of the children of my politician father and his legal wife, while Ichiko's mother was a geisha in Yoshi-chō.

I don't know what the circumstances were, but as far back as I can remember, Ichiko had always lived with us in Ichigaya as part of our family, and was raised as my sister. Together we advanced from the primary to the middle school attached to Ochanomizu Higher Normal School for Girls. I was an average-looking girl, and on the way to school no one paid much attention to my freshly scrubbed face. Although people said we looked alike, from the time Ichiko was twelve or thirteen her face already glowed like the bud of a brightly colored flower. There was an indescribable charm in the look that played around her eyes and mouth.

While she was riding the train to and from school, boys sometimes slipped love letters into her kimono sleeve. She showed me one or two of them. This kind of attention was probably one of the things that encouraged Ichiko's precocious sensuality. The spring that she started ninth grade, she fell headlong in love with a friend of my brother's who was a student at T University and ran off with him.

The affair was brought abruptly to an end. After this, because of the effect it might have had on the other children, Ichiko was sent back to her real mother's house to live. Father died a year or two later. By this time Ichiko's mother had become one of the area's top independent geisha, employing several younger geisha. She was a clever woman and on the surface got along well with my mother.

Even after being sent away from our house, Ichiko still wanted to be close to me. Sometimes she sent letters and invited me over to her part of town. At that time, I was a student at Tsuda College of English. Rather than feeling resentful, Ichiko was proud of me. When I think about it now it seems strange, but I would lie to my mother and tell her that I was going to a friend's house. Instead, I would meet Ichiko at the base of Azuma Bridge. From there we would take a steam launch to Hyakkaen Garden or Shirahige Shrine and stroll through the grounds.

Ichiko hadn't yet become a geisha, but she had her hair done up in the traditional apprentice-geisha style and wore bright, striped kimono and various red-patterned obi. The contrast between her appearance and my own upper-middle-class one—hair parted at the side—must have seemed incredibly odd. We were often teased by crewmen on cargo boats and workmen taking smoking breaks. We walked along the Sumida because I was an avid reader of Nagai Kafū at the time and was absorbed by *The River Sumida, The Peony Garden, Night Tales of Shinbashi,* and his other stories which were set in the pleasure quarters. It was a source of some pride to me that I had such a beautiful half-sister from that old, romantic part of Tokyo.

When I graduated from college, I married a man who was soon sent to America to work as a bank officer, and we moved to New York. Four years later, our son died of an illness. We weren't compatible anyway, and I used that as an excuse to divorce my husband and returned to Tokyo. Since I had no desire to remarry, I moved back in with my mother and lived with her until recently, when she died.

I led a routine life teaching English. If there was any occasional, unexpected brightness to color the monotony, it was brought by Ichiko. Even my mother, who had considered Ichiko a nuisance when she was young and had sent her back to her real mother, came to love her far more than she loved my brothers' wives. Whenever Ichiko came to visit, Mother would listen intently to Ichiko describe the transformations in her own and her friends' lives.

While I was abroad, Ichiko became a young geisha in her mother's establishment and began entertaining at banquets. She had a vivid beauty and a talent for repartee. She was also fortunate enough to have her mother's guidance in everything. Nothing about her suggested that she might be a geisha of loose morals, even though her training in the art of entertainment hadn't begun in childhood. After three or four years as a top-level geisha, Ichiko became the mistress of Katsuyama Kijūrō, a well-known art dealer. He established her in a house in Takagi-chō in the Aoyama district. Since I lived in Zaimoku-chō in nearby Azabu, Ichiko could visit frequently. It was during this time that Mother and Kinu came to know Ichiko as an adult.

Katsuyama was an art dealer who traded mainly in Japanese paintings. His family was said to have been money lenders during the Edo period, so an instinct for being a patron may have been in his blood. He was fond of supporting the families of young painters and those with unrecognized talent, almost as if it were a gambling habit, and he squandered a good deal of money on this hobby.

These artists gathered at Ichiko's house and, since Ichiko understood Katsuyama so well, she looked after them with care. At Ichiko's house the bath would always be ready, even in the morning, and at meal times delicious food would be served together with a bottle of beer. It was no wonder that many artists congregated there.

"It's amazing that he doesn't mind sending those unkempt young men to you to take care of. Usually men who keep women don't even like to have their mistresses' own family members wandering around the place."

In those times I listened with amusement to my mother's comments. Mother had learned what she knew about men from my father, who engaged in dalliances with geisha while pretending to be faithful to her. Since I had been married for only three or four years while living abroad, I would never have dreamed of making such a comment.

But Ichiko smiled, revealing the slight dimple on the curve of her cheek. In those days, I felt, whenever I saw Ichiko's face, that the skin of her cheeks, so soft and supple, was as sensuous to the touch as ripe fruit. Intellectual women, who make their living using their minds, were never blessed with such sensuality.

"Mother," Ichiko said (by then Mother didn't mind Ichiko addressing her that way), "that's no problem. Katsuyama trusts me. He says I'm not the type of woman to go wild over men. The artists who gather at my house are attracted to me in one way or another. Katsuyama seems to take pleasure in seeing them sublimate their attraction to me into a passion for their work. I once got angry and accused him of using me to arouse that passion. But I can't argue with Katsuyama. He thinks of everyone as material for good paintings. I heard that his former mistress ran off with an artist."

"And what happened to that artist? Has he become successful?" I asked.

Ichiko shook her head, "No, he never made it. It seems he's now somewhere in Kyushu painting for restaurants and inns."

"So Mr. Katsuyama failed completely with that artist. His mistress was stolen, and if the paintings weren't any good, he lost on both counts."

"No, on the contrary, one result of losing his mistress was outstanding," Ichiko said, laughing. "There's an artist who's become really well-known through the Nitten Exhibition and even serves as one of its jurors now—the Japanese-style painter named Hirade Shūsai. They say he's the most promising of Katsuyama's protégés. Well, he was in love with Katsuyama's mistress. He doesn't talk about it, but she rejected him and ran off with that other artist. You can't see into people's hearts, but Mr. Hirade's style developed tremendously after that incident. You know, it's close to impossible to buy his paintings unless you go through Katsuyama. They've become very profitable items. . . . So you can't say that Katsuyama lost."

There was some truth in what she said. Katsuyama did use Ichiko as a decoy in his business. Ichiko said that she allowed herself to live the life she did because she was intrigued by the way Katsuyama used people as dice in this strange gambling game. That a woman of only twenty-seven or twenty-eight would take up this kind of life seemed a bit too calculated to me. It was oddly nihilistic. How could Ichiko, in the prime of her beauty, be comfortable living in a world where people's fates were being juggled about like that? Even if this manipulation appeared to be only in the interest of art, it still seemed strange and unnatural. And, although we were related, I felt I couldn't question her more closely.

Mother and I met Katsuyama during this period. In order to raise money for renovating part of our house, we asked Katsuyama, through Ichiko, if he would like to buy some scrolls painted by Hōitsu and Bunchō. He invited us to a formal Japanese dinner in Azabu to thank us for selling him these valuable pieces. Naturally, Ichiko joined us.

On our way home, Mother said with a rueful smile, "Mr. Katsuyama loves Ichiko, but he loves his business more. Many politicians are like that. They may lavish attention on a woman, but if it's necessary for their own work, they can easily give that precious woman to someone else."

I didn't fully understand what Mother meant when she said that. But when I thought it over later, I realized that she must have been reflecting on what she had learned from her experience with Father. From this perspective, I could understand that Ichiko might not have disliked living with the much older Katsuyama because of her subconscious longing for a father figure.

During the more than ten years that Ichiko was Katsuyama's mistress and the mistress of the house that served as the gathering place for his obscure, young Japanese-style painters, I never heard any rumors that she was involved in a romantic scandal with any of them. Neither did I hear of any trouble between Ichiko and Katsuyama.

Katsuyama died of stomach cancer two or three years after the war ended. In his will, Ichiko was left the house in Takagi-chō, and she continued to run the art dealership. During the time she had spent with him, she had learned the business thoroughly. Quite a few artists had become successful under Katsuyama's patronage, and most of them continued to benefit from Ichiko's influence. It was natural that, although the connection with Katsuyama's main household was severed, the business in Takagi-chō was still supported through Ichiko's personal connections. Just as she did when Katsuyama was alive, Ichiko had young artists in and out of her house without forming an intimate relationship with any of them. She seemed to have adopted completely Katsuyama's style of manipulation and was still using these artists as pawns in her business.

Ichiko was now past forty. She had ripened into a mature, physically well-endowed woman, with a taut fullness of shoulder and bosom that showed no signs of middle age. She preferred to wear stiff-woven Yūki or Shiozawa kimono made of fabrics that didn't cling to her body. She seemed unaware that such fabrics made her even more alluring.

"All I'm concerned about is business. I've retired from being a woman," she would say emphatically. And with a bold look she would drain a mug of beer in one breath.

How long did she continue her life as a woman art dealer?

It must have been six or seven years ago that she suddenly closed the business, returned the art works that she had on hand to the Katsuyama family, and declared that she was going to seclude herself in Kyoto.

After the war, my English teaching had kept me busy, and I had had fewer chances of talking at length with Ichiko. Mother had died just before Ichiko told me she was moving to Kyoto. Feeling sad about parting, Ichiko and I had a long talk after Mother's twenty-seventh-day mourning rites.

"Why have you decided to close the business, just when you have some good regular customers and your clerk has learned the business?" I asked.

We were in the room where Mother's photograph was displayed. As she sat facing me across the table, Ichiko fell into her old habit of plucking the top layer of her kimono where it covered her plump knees and glanced up at me through her eyelashes.

"Well, I thought it over quite a bit, and realized that, after all, this is a man's business. If Katsuyama were still alive—even if he were paralyzed and bed-ridden—the business could continue. But it's impossible for a woman to do it alone."

"Is that how it is? It's hard for an inexperienced person like me to understand what it's like."

After saying that, I looked over toward Mother's photograph and mentioned her comments on Katsuyama's character to Ichiko.

"Really? It was perceptive of her to say that. Of course she was talking about Father. . . . That's right, my own mother (she had died shortly after Katsuyama started providing for Ichiko) told me that when Father brought me into the main house, he temporarily lent her to the president of a trading company to get him to cover his campaign expenses. A bit simpler deal, probably, than Katsuyama's schemes. Maybe I put up with a man so much older than I was without feeling any distaste because somehow he reminded me of Father."

Ichiko sighed deeply and said, "Lately I've come to think that everything in the world, especially relationships between men and women, is like a game of blind man's buff. The person who is 'it', the demon, is blind-folded with a towel and can't see anything. Those who are free to run away—clapping their hands to attract the demon—can still see. So they shouldn't get caught. But each time someone does get caught. The mistake is in thinking you won't get caught. Don't you think fate is like that?

We brag that the demon won't catch us. But the louder we brag, the greater the chances are we might get caught by an even more vicious demon."

"You sound like you're talking about yourself. Why don't you tell me what you've been through?" I prompted. But Ichiko shook her head.

"It was nothing special . . . ," she said. "Even a fool like me feels like saying something philosophical after living in this world for over forty years. It probably seems funny to a smart person like you."

"I don't think it's funny at all. Compared to you, I'm like a child with middle-aged wrinkles on her face. I found your relationship with Mr. Katsuyama really intriguing. And your decision to close up the business and retire to Kyoto also seems to have a story behind it, so naturally I'm curious."

"Knowing the vanity of all things, and withdrawing from the world . . . ," Ichiko recited a line from a lute song popular in our childhood. "I'll probably tell you about it some time," she said. "Please wait about ten years."

The secret behind Ichiko's closing up her art dealership seemed to have had something to do with a man. But I didn't want to pry, so I changed the subject.

About a month after Ichiko closed her shop and went off to Kyoto, the body of Kenmochi Akira—an up-and-coming Japanese-style painter— was discovered unexpectedly on Mt. Zaō. He had disappeared on his way to India to join a climbing party that was headed for the Himalayas.

Kenmochi was unusual among contemporary artists in that he wasn't highly educated. A young artist who had risen from the position of apprentice to Takatori Kan'ichi, his name had only recently become known in artistic circles. In the world of Japanese painting, where the constrictions of the apprentice system still exist, Takatori and Kenmochi were more like master and servant than teacher and student. After struggling up this long road, Kenmochi was finally beginning to be recognized in his own right.

Takatori had never treated Kenmochi in any special way, but he began to favor him after Ichiko took notice of Kenmochi's paintings and invited him to her house. Takatori had attained his present position because the late Katsuyama, predicting his artistic development, had given him substantial financial backing. Takatori had always been attracted to Ichiko's lively femininity. Now, seeing her—a woman—promote Kenmochi, he began to think that he could exploit his position as Kenmochi's teacher.

By advancing Kenmochi, Takatori could help Ichiko's business and, at the same time, make her his own.

Ichiko's initial interest in Kenmochi's paintings was not based on her attraction to him as a man. Up to this point, she had quietly carried on Katsuyama's work by following in his footsteps. But now she was roused to test her own business abilities through this young artist, Kenmochi, whose paintings had a different air about them. Unlike the work of formal art school graduates, Kenmochi's paintings had a rare quality which preserved the rustic and simple traits of the farmers of northeastern Japan.

Naturally, Kenmochi was unaware of Ichiko's scheme to use him as material for speculation. He was overpowered by the charms of a mature woman, ten years older than himself and at the height of her attractiveness. As Ichiko grew to know him, however, she was repeatedly amazed at Kenmochi's simple genuineness, and her heart echoed a growing excitement. Ichiko felt that her body and soul were becoming transparent. Is this what being in love feels like, she wondered.

Just as she was turning sixteen, Ichiko was seduced by one of her older brother's friends. Ever since then, her sensual beauty had caused her to be constantly pursued by men, and she had been physically involved with several of them before becoming Katsuyama's mistress. As he had anticipated, even while he was using her as a decoy in his business, no rumors had ever linked her with the men who gathered at her house. No matter what others may have said about her, Ichiko felt that she was like a log in the area where man and woman are supposed to be truly intimate. She thought of herself as just not very interested in that sort of thing. In fact, she had decided that she would probably spend her days looking after her business and leading an enjoyable, interesting life. But she could tell, in her passion for Kenmochi, that she was losing her equilibrium. Emotionally, she shrank back in fear, while her body propelled her forward.

Kenmochi could not have been unaware of Ichiko's passionate feelings for him, and before long the two of them were caught up in an affair. Kenmochi behaved just like a frightened married woman in the days when adultery was still outlawed. He was terrified that Takatori would discover their secret. Kenmochi's timid behavior vexed the spirited Ichiko over and over again.

In fact, Takatori was furious when he sniffed out the truth. He fumed and threatened to spread the scandalous rumor that Ichiko, an art dealer, had schemed to thrust her lover into art circles; he would use this rumor to destroy completely Kenmochi's foothold in the art world. Kenmochi vowed that, even if he were maligned by Takatori and cast out of art circles, he would find another way to become recognized in his own right as long as their love endured. But Ichiko, being older, could not bear to see Kenmochi suffer such rejection.

In order to placate Takatori, Ichiko yielded to his physical demands. Takatori's domineering posture collapsed. Kenmochi agreed to end his relationship with Ichiko, and went so far as to decide to join a group of mountain climbers setting out for the Himalayas. Perhaps viewing the majesty of these high mountains that were, as yet, unknown to him would open up new horizons in his painting.

Ichiko resolved not to continue intimate relations with Takatori. So, she decided to close up her business and move to Kyoto. She hoped that Kenmochi, too, would build a new life. But her hopes were betrayed when Kenmochi took his own life in the snows of his native mountains without ever seeing the awesome, snow-covered Himalayas.

No one knew how, after parting from his companions in Singapore, he had found his way to the northeastern mountains of Japan. His teacher Takatori explained to reporters that Kenmochi had been confronted— and not for the first time—with an artistic block at a crucial moment and must have had a nervous breakdown. Mutual discretion made certain that the triangular love affair was not divulged. So, although there were rumors that Kenmochi had suffered disappointment in his love for Ichiko, even I had no idea at the time what the real situation was.

I heard the actual truth of the matter from Ichiko just two years ago when I went to Mt. Kōya to place my late mother's ashes in the inner temple. Ichiko wanted to join me, and we met in Osaka to make the pilgrimage to Mt. Kōya together.

The night before we entered the inner temple, we stayed over in the visitors' lodgings in one of the temples on the mountain. Ichiko brought out a small, unpainted wooden box from her travel bag and placed it on the shelf next to the box holding Mother's remains.

"Are you also dedicating some ashes?" I asked. "Whose?"

With a solemn expression on her face, Ichiko said, "The box holds a photograph and the ashes of the burned letters of an artist named Kenmochi—the one who committed suicide six years ago."

Then she told me the story I have related.

I finally understood the circumstances under which Ichiko had closed her art dealership and had gone into seclusion in Kyoto.

"There are some businesses in which women just can't be successful. Art dealers use people as dice. When problems between men and women get thrown into the gamble, there's nowhere to move," Ichiko said. "At that time, I wanted to kill my own desires so that Kenmochi could succeed. Instead, my rash interference killed him. I wanted to follow him and kill myself, but, as the years pass, here I am, still alive. I've even become the wife of a priest and am making money as a restaurant owner. . . . Sometimes, when I wonder what on earth I am, I feel like I'm something totally insubstantial, a mere shadow. No, no matter how many more years I live, I'm never going to fall in love with another man. I've decided that if that happens, rather than causing him unhappiness, I'm going to be the one to die."

At that moment, a deep smile etched Ichiko's face, a smile that conveyed a blend of resolution and sorrow. Only the smile of a woman who had walked life's path for close to fifty years could have combined these feelings.

Two years had passed since our pilgrimage. Recent reports confirmed the food at Ichiko's Buddhist-style vegetarian restaurant next to the main gate of a certain temple in Kyoto to be tasty and reasonably priced. Tourists from Tokyo often stopped by to dine at the restaurant on their way back from Sambō-in. The temple belonged to the Tendai sect, and its head priest, Mr. Kajita, was an intellectual who also lectured at a university.

I knew Ichiko felt guilty about Kenmochi's death. Still, I thought off and on that, through listening to Mr. Kajita's teachings about Buddhism and preparing Buddhist-style food morning and evening, Ichiko might, as she grew older, come to have a deeper understanding of the Buddhist concept of the vanity of all things. But that November night, when the telephone call came and I heard that Ichiko had left home, I felt apprehensive. I couldn't laugh in a carefree way like Kinu.

I had trouble sleeping, and spent the night haunted by one dream after another. Finally, as dawn ended the long, late-autumn night, I was fully awakened by the telephone in the hall. Kinu had stayed overnight and had arisen immediately to answer it. I heard her respond with one or two phrases, and then I heard footsteps rushing down the hall.

"Ma'am, are you awake?" I heard her say in a trembling voice. "The telephone call is from Kyoto. Miss Ichiko has committed suicide."

"I see. . . ," I said with a sigh and got up. The voice on the telephone was not Kajita's. It was a clear, young, male voice.

"This is Kajita's eldest son," the voice began. "Aunt Ichiko was found dead in a rocky crevice at a place called Gyokudō, in the mountains beyond Sanzen-in in Kitayama, north of Kyoto. There hasn't been an autopsy yet, but the police are saying it looks like suicide from an overdose of sleeping pills."

The young man's voice shook slightly as he spoke. His self-control must have collapsed as he reached the end of his report. When I realized this, his grief pierced my heart.

"When will you be able to come?" he said, regaining control of his voice.

"By today's train—this evening at the latest."

"Please do. Father says he would like you to see her face before she is cremated."

After I hung up the phone, I could hardly move. I stood there, barefoot on the cold wooden floor of the hallway.

"They say it's suicide. But why on earth . . . ?"

Kinu had slumped to the floor with her arms spread apart and gaped open-mouthed at me. Every year of her age showed in her posture, and, as I glanced at Kinu's clownish pose, I was reminded of a scene from my childhood—the lively clamor of playing blind man's buff. Bending over, with arms spread wide, looking like Kinu, the blindfolded person who is the demon chases the clapping children who veer away to the right and left. Kinu must have been thirteen or fourteen when she was sent to play this game with us. She undoubtedly wore the blindfold then.

But at that moment, it wasn't Kinu's appearance as the blindfolded demon that I was remembering. It was what Ichiko had said with such profound emotion when we talked at this house before she moved to Kyoto. She had said that we are all caught by our particular fate, just as if we were caught by the blindfolded demon. Yet she hadn't mentioned the affair with Kenmochi. At that time, Ichiko never wanted to come near the blind demon again, and she had prayed that she would never have another love affair filled with such darkness. It is likely that this desperate wish was granted until the year before last, when I saw her at Mt. Kōya. Now, knowing that Ichiko had suddenly taken her own life, I could only think that she had again been captured by the blind demon. What kind of haunting form could it have taken this time?

I remembered once meeting at Ichiko's house in Kyoto the beautiful, young boy who was Mr. Kajita's eldest son. Since that was already five or six years ago, that young boy must be a university student by now. Could he have been the blind demon who enticed Ichiko to her death? Recalling his voice as I had heard it over the telephone—its low clarity and stifled quaver, like the trembling of a brook—I stood there frozen to the floor.

Translated by Beth Cary

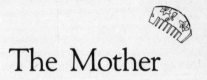

The Mother

Ōoka Shōhei

Outside Japan, Ōoka Shōhei (b. 1909) is known largely as the author of *Fires on the Plain* (*Nobi*, 1951; trans. 1957), one of the finest war novels to come out of the Second World War. But the range of his literary activities has been quite broad, covering historical novels, love stories, autobiographical pieces, biographical essays, literary criticism, travel sketches, and even detective fiction. A French major at Kyoto University, he started out as a scholar and translator specializing in Stendhal. In 1944 he was drafted into the army and was sent to the Philippines, where he eventually became a prisoner of war. *Memoirs of a POW* (*Furyoki*, 1948), which he wrote after returning to Japan, established his reputation as a novelist, a reputation that was further solidified with the publication of *Fires on the Plain* three years later. His war stories, however, are not so much commentaries on war and its atrocities as depictions of basic human nature *in extremis*. It was natural that, in time, he should begin writing a variety of stories which had a non-war setting but which equally probed into the innermost interiors of the human mind. In his book *The Art of the Modern Novel* (*Gendai shōsetsu sakuhō*, 1962) he wrote: "Writers' and critics' interests lie in digging deep into the human psyche and seeing if God or the subconscious or anything else that is transcendental can be uncovered there." Many of his literary works are attempts to do just that.

"The Mother of Dreams" (*Haha rokuya*, 1966) also shows Ōoka attempting to dig deep into the human mind, admittedly his own mind in this instance. Like Natsume Sōseki's "Ten Nights of Dream" (*Yume Jūya*, 1908; trans. 1969), it makes use of dreams to suggest what lies in the subconscious mind, but, unlike Sōseki, Ōoka structured the dreams around the Oedipus complex that made him at once love and fear his mother. It is the most imaginative story among a series of autobiographical pieces that include "Older Sister" (*Ane*, 1950), "Mother" (*Haha*, 1951), "Father" (*Chichi*, 1951), and "Aunt" (*Oba*, 1965).

THE MOTHER OF DREAMS
Haha rokuya

Ōoka Shōhei

The First Night

During the autumn when I was in fifth grade, I happened to develop a fever from some unknown cause and entered a suburban hospital. It was the first time in my life I had been away from my parents and slept by myself. The Western-style sickroom, with its white walls, its windows which opened and closed vertically, and its bed, was very novel, but at night I was unspeakably lonesome.

Once in a while friends came to visit me at the hospital, bringing eggs, fruits, and other presents of food. On her way to the dining room, my nurse would take my eggs out from beneath the side table without saying a word to me. It was very unpleasant. Around that time, I began to resent being treated like such a fool by adults.

I had visits from my mother every day. She would set out for the hospital after she had seen my father off to his job downtown and finished cleaning the house, so that by the time she arrived, it would be about eleven o'clock.

She would sit with her back to the bright window and feed me my lunch.

"How about some of this?" she would say. She'd stand up next to the bed so that her breast drew close to me. Mother was still young then and looked beautiful in a formal kimono with the obi tied up just under her breast. I was to remember later how maidenly she seemed.

Two younger brothers had been born, so such opportunities for me to talk together at length with my mother had disappeared. Father never did bother to visit me.

It made me happy that she bought a new book for me every day. I seem to remember how Mother looked as she crossed the square, clutching to her breast a book just purchased at the bookshop in front of the station. But since there is no way I could have seen that, it must be that I dreamed it; or, since I had imagined it that way so often, I ended up feeling as though I actually had seen it.

I read straight through the children's magazines and the Tachikawa Library of samurai stories. A relative of mine, who was a student, had told Mother about a newly published story magazine that was more sophisticated, and she bought me several issues.

There was a story in one of them which made a powerful impression on me. It told about a young boy who, unable to bear seeing the sun set, pursued it across the fields and hills. The sun went down rapidly, so the boy began to run. When the boy's pace had outstripped the rate of the earth's rotation, the sun slowly started to rise from the western sky. But when the boy, exhausted and contented, sat down on a stone beside the road, the sun at once began to go down again, while the ruddy glow of evening spread all around. Once again the boy stood up and broke into a run. The sun began to rise; the boy rested. The sun, as though attached to a weight, sank completely below the horizon.

The boy crossed the fields and hills and ran far away to the farthest end of the earth. "And no one knows where he went," concluded the melancholy tale.

I had a dream. There was something like a wart on the side of some heavy object about the size of the earth. I took it between my two fingers and tried to pick it up. Even though I realized I couldn't pick it up, I had to, and so I struggled.

I had that dream not long after I entered the hospital and was feverish much of the time. If it had occurred today, my illness would no doubt have been diagnosed as infantile tuberculosis. But I was hospitalized nearly three months with a disease no one could define.

An illustration in another children's magazine attracted my attention. It was the figure of some kind of flower spirit, wearing a crown of flowers, holding a lyre in one hand, and dancing on the grass. The outline of its body beneath the transparent robe was clearly drawn. I couldn't take my eyes from the part where its thighs joined.

I quickly read through the tale, but couldn't keep from repeatedly opening it up and gazing at just that one picture. As I was looking at the picture, my mother came in. I quickly laid it face down on top of the quilt on my chest, but doubtless could not hide my consternation. I didn't think of closing the magazine and putting it to one side.

"Try this," Mother said, peeling an apple for me, while the magazine just lay there like that. She passed me a dish and caught sight of the picture as she removed the magazine. She said nothing.

I had a dream. I was fleeing through the night, pursued by something dreadful. From the darkened sky ahead of me, some electrical wires were suspended, barely touching the ground, so I had to jump over them as though I were skipping rope. I writhed in agony, leaping over the wires one after another. They continued to come down, aiming at my feet as I fled.

I thought that the frightful thing that was hunting me down would also have to cross the electric wires. When I looked over my shoulder, I saw an area like the square in front of the railway station, with wires spreading out over it, stretching in the direction of the apparition. The apparition was hump-backed like an old woman and stood as though it were taking aim at me. Never taking its eyes off me, it moved only its legs, like a machine, and jumped over the wires one after the other.

I woke up. Right above me, visible in the dim light, the hospital ceiling had been stained by rain water oozing through a leak in the roof. It had definitely been my mother in the dream. Why should Mother have turned into such a dreadful old crone? Why did she chase me? Why should I have had such a dream? I agonized over it, completely at a loss.

The Second Night

In my dream I was on the verge of committing suicide. I didn't want to go on living longer than five more years in a world full of corruption. Twenty-three years were quite long enough. Although it had been my intention to kill myself when I reached that age, in my dream I was at the point of committing suicide at that moment.

As I stood atop a precipice, I commanded a view of the sea far below. The blue water was transparent. Clearly visible—almost painfully so— were the greenish rocks in the depths, which sketched a pattern of radiating stripes. I had to dive in.

But the water was too clear, and the green of the crags was too beautiful. An inlet had formed there. The mountains encircling the water were also green and perfectly still, as though watching over me. The ocean and the mountains were too beautiful; I hesitated to kill myself.

A boat which had taken me on board headed for the open sea. A single island floated like a battleship on the horizon. It was a small, outlying island, shaped like a right-angled triangle, like those which appear in examples of the Pythagorean theorem. The island was composed of red, yellow, and green rocks all joined together.

The rugged shapes and the irritating colors were intolerably unpleasant to me. Although I no longer had any intention of committing suicide, the island came rapidly closer.

The Third Night

My mother died when I was twenty-three. Mother's body was going to be placed in a plain wooden casket. When it was carried into the twelve-mat room in the back, my father said jokingly, "Well, let's try it out," climbed into the coffin and lay there on his back. "There—how's that?" he said. This offended me.

Father survived Mother by only five years. One of Mother's kimono was discovered among his possessions. Although all her mementoes were supposed to have been divided up when Mother died, that everyday kimono made of pongee was left. No one had been aware that Father had kept Mother's kimono.

I realized that that kimono was one which Mother had worn a long time ago when she had visited me at the hospital.

One day when I showed the kimono to Hanako she said, "I think I'll try it on," and began to undo her obi. Hanako's long underwear was of the fancy kind I'd never seen before. (Until then I'd never seen any but Mother's undergarments.) When Hanako put on Mother's plain pongee kimono over it and tied it with a rose-colored waist cord, she became beautiful.

"I'll be your mother," said Hanako, bringing her breast close to me. From that day on, I could not part from Hanako.

The Fourth Night

When I climbed to the top of a steep hill road, paved with broken stone, there was a golf links. Opposite the green-painted netting was the white club house, absolutely silent. There was no sign of anyone. Nor was there anybody on the wide lawn. There was only the wind blowing.

From this height, the ocean was visible. It was dark over the ocean, which was closed in by clouds and mist, but I could clearly see the whiteness of the spray from the black sea water striking the rocks on the shore. Because the spray was so far away, it looked like a frozen white line.

Then we kissed again at length. When I opened my eyes, I could see the ocean beyond the line of Hanako's cheek, and the white line which appeared to be frozen. I was looking at the sea now, but what was Hanako looking at, I wondered. Hanako had abandoned her former lover and run away with me to this seaside town.

I watched Hanako's face. She was looking downward. There was a frightening expression on her face, one I had never seen before. She was gazing at the ground where the rippling grass had sprung up in the reddish clay.

Hanako is going to die, I thought. It was a moment that passed as though in a dream.

The Fifth Night

I felt that I had to seek out Hanako. Although Hanako was already dead, in the dream I kept thinking that I mustn't let her die, that I must find where she was. So I hired a taxi in the dead of night.

I was seated slightly bent over in the taxi. Only its small meter lamp loomed up dimly.

"This is the place," the driver said to me, his facial features not clearly visible, and I had to get out. I was at a place that looked like a square in front of some rural train station. In between the rows of low houses, the only lights were two or three red paper lanterns at a sushi bar. The night was already far gone.

However, since Hanako was as destitute as my mother, it was unlikely that she would be living on a main street like this. She should have been living in some dirty side street, but since the driver had said that this was the place, I was obliged to get out.

I turned several dark corners, and knocked at the door of a house where all the lights had been extinguished.

"Is Hanako there?" I asked.

Responding to my voice, two or three stunted, shadowy forms tumbled out. I couldn't tell whether they were men or women.

"She's in the back," they said, all the while appearing to crawl about on the ground.

A low wooden roof ran along one side of the house, and under the eaves there lay some old timbers. The eaves hung down as far as my hips, apparently because the path I was walking on was raised above the level of the ground.

My feet could feel the softness of the soil. There was an indescribable odor. It was neither the smell of the low eaves, nor was it emanating from the moist earth. It rose instead from the drainage ditch that ran behind the house. Standing next to it, I could make out the current in the ditch in spite of the darkness. At the bottom of the ditch, pebbles, bottles, and even fragments of pottery were clearly visible. I could even observe how some sort of bluish-white slime was caught in the submerged objects and flowed in the direction of the current. It was from there that the unpleasant odor arose.

Above the opposite bank of the ditch a woman's face appeared, grinning. It was not Hanako, nor was it my mother. It was an old woman I had never seen before. She waited for me, still grinning.

She appeared to be lying on her back, as an invalid might. Her two arms, bent at the elbow, must have been extended from shoulder level. No doubt she had been buried in the ground like that. Her torso must have been immersed in the ditch. Although it must certainly have been cold and evil-smelling, the old woman, apparently oblivious to it, went on grinning.

I struggled to see my mother's body in the depths of the water, but nothing was there. There was only the fluttering of the bluish-white slime entangled with the pebbles, bottles, and broken bits of pottery.

I cried out and woke up.

The Sixth Night

I was in a mountain hotel, somewhere in a foreign country. The dining room was empty. Several waiters in white jackets were to be seen. From the window, I could see the plaza in front of the hotel. Many cars were parked there, and well-dressed foreigners, their arms linked together, were coming and going.

I had been brought along by Mother to this hotel. I was delighted that this sort of luxury was possible, but it felt a bit frightening at the same time.

However, it wasn't possible for me to dine with my mother. I was aware that she was now with a man in one of the hotel rooms.

The plaza before the hotel was a broad terrace which cut into the side of the mountain. It resembled the terrace of Assisi. Opposite the parapet, the Umbrian hills seemed to form a row of gently sloping peaks enclosing the narrow, rounded valley. The square was flooded with a strange light. It was like the dim, smooth glow during a solar eclipse.

When I looked up, it wasn't the sun which was in the sky. An ellipse, about three times the size of the setting sun, was suspended there instead. Enclosed within the ellipse was the Virgin Mary, her facial features indistinct, holding an equally indistinct Jesus in her arms.

From the ellipse, arrows of white light were shooting off into the four quarters of the sky. It was the reflection of this strange light which flooded the terrace. The end of the world was certainly coming, but people didn't realize it. Laughing, they passed to and fro on the square.

Mother came out. Was this really my mother? The skin of her face, calloused like an animal's paw, had countless deep wrinkles running all over it. She had on a black one-piece dress, such as a schoolmistress might wear, and walked as though pulling up her legs one at a time.

My mother raised her fist and shouted some sort of abuse. She was insulting the hotel guests who would not buy her. This indecent mother of mine had to be taken quickly from the hotel.

I ran down from the terrace. Below the stone wall it was level; large, broad-leafed trees grew luxuriantly there, also bathed with the same strange light. There was a rococo-style pavilion, where a small man, evidently a Frenchman, had spread out a blanket, on which were arranged some odds and ends which he was offering for sale.

Since I was sending off my trunk, I needed to buy a luggage tag.

"They're twenty francs apiece."

I searched my pocket, but had only ten francs, so I was unable to buy one of the smooth, unmarked brass tags. The fact was that we were destitute, so I could not run away and leave my mother behind.

Still in a dilemma, I gradually awoke.

I suffered greatly from my mother's continual appearance in my dreams as a strange old woman, and thought I would write down the story of these dreams.

Translated by Agatha Haun

Setouchi Harumi

Unlike most women writers of her generation Setouchi Harumi (b. 1922) has a college degree, but her life resembles theirs in that she too went through a period of wandering in her youth that later formed the basis of her literary works. After graduating from Tokyo Women's College, she married a scholar in Chinese history and wandered in northern China with him for several years during the war. The life was at times very hard both economically and emotionally for her, especially after her husband was conscripted and she was left alone with their infant daughter. They finally returned to Japan in 1946, but soon a different type of wandering started for Setouchi, for she fell in love with one of her husband's former students and left home all by herself. Although the affair was short-lived, it marked the beginning of a long period in which she tried to live her life to the full at any cost. Partly because of financial necessity, but mostly because her energy was irrepressible, she produced a number of novels and stories during this time, often drawing on her own romances with various men. "Lingering Affection" (*Miren*, 1963; trans. 1982), the story of a love triangle, is typical. In 1973 she surprised her friends and readers by becoming a Buddhist nun. She has, however, continued her activities as a novelist no less energetically than before. An articulate speaker, she also makes occasional appearances on television as a literary and social commentator.

"Pheasant" (*Kiji*, 1963) is an autobiographical story taking its material from the author's life with her husband, which ended in divorce in 1950. The title refers to the traditional Japanese belief that a pheasant is an especially affectionate bird towards its young. Its piercing cry has long been said to be a parent bird's anxious call for its child and has provided a metaphor for many poems of parental love. The two children in the story have the same name written in different characters. To distinguish one from the other, two different spellings—Rie and Riye—have been used in the following translation.

PHEASANT
Kiji

Setouchi Harumi

Whenever she had to carry a heavy, bulky load, Makiko would unconsciously hold it to her breast with both arms.

"Makiko, that posture of yours is strange. It doesn't show you at your best." Until Kuji pointed it out to her, Makiko had not herself been aware of this habit.

"Maybe so. But when I have something to carry, this is the most comfortable way to do it," she replied off-handedly. Then she looked up with a start.

"But, you know, this habit of mine started a long time ago, from holding Riye. You see, if you carry a load as if you're carrying a child, it's a lot lighter."

For a moment, Makiko eyed her body rather apprehensively. Her past had penetrated deep into this posture of hers—leaning back, with hips dropped down and abdomen protruding, legs outstretched, feet planted, and holding fast to her load. It gave Makiko a shiver to think that even now, more than ten years after she had been separated from her child, she could not rid herself of such a habit.

Even clearer, more definite evidence that Makiko had borne a child remained with her. Whenever she was in bed with a man, she would lie with her left breast down. It was a habit left over from the time she'd been sleeping with and breast-feeding her child.

"Look. See this white scar? My baby bit me once and my breast got infected. The scar is from when they lanced it. I didn't feed her from this breast after that, so that's why it has stayed firmer," Makiko explained as she pointed to the nipple of her right breast, which she had entrusted to the palm of Kuji's hand.

Those small breasts, which fit comfortably in the palm of a hand, differed in size, the right one from the left. In her girlhood, they had been some three times the size they were now. Only those two full breasts, swelling heavily against each other, had broken the childish line of her body, which had a charmless pole shape, like a wrung-out towel.

She started to go on about it to Kuji but shut her mouth instead, for the foolishness of talking about the lost fullness of one's breasts dawned on her.

"I bet they had a lot of milk."

"That's right. They were heavy, and painful."

The first time she offered a nipple to the infant Riye, Makiko was frustrated that the baby, whose sucking instinct had not yet awakened, was not about to move her lips and tongue. So she tried pressing down firmly on her hard, stiff breasts with her fingers. With a pleasantly resonant whoosh, pure white milk shot past Riye's face and across the next bed to the wall beyond, dousing it thoroughly.

Makiko's biological clock was well-regulated. She'd had her first period the spring she'd finished primary school, and now, even though she was nearing forty, she showed almost no signs of decline. Though she was slender in build, the curve of her pelvis was ample.

Within her first month in Beijing, to which she'd gone after her marriage, she became pregnant with Riye. Morning sickness, and the birth itself, were astonishingly easy on her. When Makiko started having labor pains, her husband, in a flurry, took her to the hospital in a foreign car. He returned home to fetch something they'd left behind, and while he was gone Makiko gave easy birth to her baby. The birth was so easy—like an animal's in fact—that it made Makiko feel ashamed.

It would seem that Makiko's body had been blessed with a greater abundance of maternal qualities than most women's. Even after she had separated from her husband, she got pregnant easily; and sooner than tell the man, Makiko just disposed of the matter herself. There was no hesitation on her part.

The first time she made love with Kuji, Makiko said as she nestled in his arms, "Do it so I won't get pregnant. I get pregnant very easily."

Just by saying that, she was able to feel completely at ease. It was a wonder that she'd only had the one child, Riye. Even though she wanted another, she wouldn't have one. When she was feeling sentimental she would say to Kuji that this was her only way of being faithful to Riye. In fact, however, it was hard to believe that it was simply loyalty to the child from whom she was separated that allowed Makiko to have abortions without a second thought. Rather, it was just not in her nature to hesitate over or reflect deeply on such things.

Kuji had one daughter by his wife. Once, in their literature club, Makiko had spoken with Kuji, who'd been in the club longer than she. He'd said: "My daughter reads your nursery stories, you know."

"And how old is the young lady?"

"She's a third-grader, named Rie."

"No! My girl's name is Riye, too!"

And with that brief conversation, their relationship began. Upon meeting this Kuji, whose daughter was the same age as the daughter she'd been separated from, and had the same name, it was as if Makiko's well-protected core had been broken in upon quite without ceremony. And thus she slipped into a relationship with Kuji. That they had passed some eight years together was due, perhaps, to Kuji's having touched some soft spot in Makiko at the very beginning.

When Makiko spoke about Riye she didn't show the kind of forced humility—to cover for pride and excessive love—that mothers usually show when they talk about their daughters. On the contrary, even though it was her own child, she talked about Riye in a polite, even formal, way. When Kuji laughed at this she said: "Well, after all, I only gave birth to the child. I don't do anything motherly for her at all. And besides, she is now the daughter of the Kusumoto family. She's not my child."

That was Makiko's excuse. She was the sort of person who, when she used the name of her ex-husband in conversation, never failed to call him "Mister."

"That child—in her looks she takes after Mr. Kusumoto. She's a real beauty. You know, it so happens I have a photograph of her sent to me by someone about a year and a half after the separation. And what do you suppose has happened to her? She's beginning to look exactly like me when I was a child—so much so that it makes me a little queasy. I'm really disappointed."

"A child's face changes all the time, you know. Do you have that photo with you?"

"Yes. Shall I show it to you?"

Makiko took a fading, card-sized photograph out of an empty sponge cake box into which assorted photos had been carelessly thrust until they were about to spill out. When she noticed that Kuji's mouth was twisting into a smile in spite of himself, she demanded:

"What are you laughing at? Well. . . ?"

Makiko herself was trying mightily to keep a smile from her face as she poked Kuji in the shoulder.

She said, "She looks like me, doesn't she? It's enough to make you sick. . . ."

There was meek Riye, her perfectly round face encircled by bobbed hair. Her eyes, wide open beneath the thick hyphens of her brows, were brimming with a childish indignation and she was chewing intently on her little lip. Probably just before the picture was taken she had been upset by something and had cried. In her eyes, which were fixed—angrily it seemed—on one spot, tears glistened. It was the dejection of a four-year-old child who had been abandoned by her mother.

One day, not too long afterwards, Kuji, who was visiting Makiko's room as usual, pulled a photograph out of his pocket and without a word placed it on Makiko's desk. It was of a young girl, ten or so years old, with her hair pulled back to expose a wide forehead. Her thin body was enfolded in a red-plum-print light kimono with a tuck at the shoulders and held closed with a waistband. The broad forehead, the large and laughing eyes, the nose too high for a child's, the thin shoulders, the skinny frame—these were all exactly Kuji's features in looks and build.

"She sure looks like you. It's strange. No matter how much of a child she is she looks so much like you. . . ."

Kuji replied, "Your daughter Riye must be this big by now, too."

Aha! So that's why he brought the picture here, Makiko thought to herself, dumbfounded. Of course, since Riye's picture was taken a number of years ago, when she was four, by now she must have grown into a girl much like this one.

"It's unbelievable that Riye should have grown this much. I can't imagine it," Makiko muttered darkly to herself as she stared hard into the photograph of Kuji's daughter. Hers was not the look of a mother who, seeing the face of a girl, recalls how her own child has grown up. Rather, with that glint in her eye, she was a woman who, seeing the face of her lover's daughter probes it for traces of the child's mother.

Gradually Makiko began to plead with Kuji to buy things that his Rie might like: girl's magazines, twenty-four-color crayons, a muffler, a music box. . . .

From time to time, a thank-you note written in a faltering hand would come from Rie. Makiko would give Kuji an irritated look that said she would not show him the letter, then she would turn aside, read the letter, and throw it away.

Makiko's solicitude for Rie seemed to be interpreted by Kuji as a kind of consolation for her inability to direct her maternal love straight at her own child. But to Makiko that was ridiculous. She never once entertained the notion that Rie could serve as a substitute for her own Riye. Rather, whenever she would arrange to buy gifts for Rie, she would inevitably have this unsettled feeling, as though something were rubbing her skin the wrong way, and she felt a secret hurt. She sent presents to Rie, and was especially apt to make the child the topic of her conversations with Kuji. She had already begun to dote single-mindedly on Kuji to the extent that life without him seemed unimaginable. Her actions, then, stemmed from nothing more than her efforts to anticipate Kuji's inner thoughts and fulfill his desires, however slight.

Makiko, who had quite indulged herself with men, found fulfillment in any situation by ceaseless, and free, love. It had much in common with the self-sacrificing love, born of ignorance, that is shown by prostitutes.

When Kuji first made Makiko's acquaintance, his fortunes were at a low ebb. The métier he had chosen as his life's work—literature—had not proven successful at all. He was earning practically nothing at it. His health was extremely poor, and on top of that he had a rare condition which was causing a proliferation of cataracts, adding to his general malaise the fear of losing his eyesight. Even as Makiko learned of one reason for Kuji's unhappiness, another was exposed; it was like peeling the layers from an onion. Nevertheless, with each new layer, Makiko's love was all the more aroused.

"Even if you go blind, that's all right. I'll just dash off any old piece of writing and earn some money. I'll take care of you and your family. You could dictate your writings, couldn't you? Even if it doesn't sell, write a good novel. . . ." Makiko really did believe in what she was saying.

Kuji was not the first man whom Makiko had loved in this self-sacrificing way. When she got engaged to her now ex-husband Kusumoto, after having met him through a match-maker, she decided she would try and strengthen her weak constitution before entering his home as a bride. She surprised everyone by launching abruptly and decisively into a month-long fast. And for the love of young Tashiro she abandoned her husband, Kusumoto, and their only child, Riye.

But whichever the man, the abundance of Makiko's love was overpowering, and he would mistake it for motherly love. However, as proof that her emotion was not maternal, Makiko would only release this boundless love to the one who was the object of her desire. Towards blood relations or other women she was, at best, perfunctory. Makiko's love sought to fulfill rather than be fulfilled. Most men were unable to take on her vast love; it flooded over them and they ended up being swept off their feet by its waves. In the end, men who were loved by Makiko all became unhappy.

Makiko herself could never face up to that inevitability. Her heart was truly in need.

About this time, Makiko turned forty. At last it seemed to dawn on her that her ill-starred fate turned fitfully on the axis of a paradox: her overly whorish personality had been forced to live in a body blessed beyond the ordinary with maternal capabilities.

On top of this realization, she noticed something else happening. Until now, she had almost never thought about Riye, even in dreams. But of late, the child seemed to float into her consciousness at the slightest provocation. Yet however diligently she tried to recollect, the memories she had of Riye, with whom she'd lived for only about four years after the child's birth, were completely uncovered down to the minutest detail in the course of only three evenings.

The Riye who appeared so seldom in dreams was always swaddled in a vivid red and green, maple-leaf patterned silk cloth. That cloth was from a half-jacket that Makiko had liked and often worn in her school days. When she was in Beijing, she tore it apart herself and sewed the pieces back together in her own style to make this unusual swaddling wrap. Onto the main part of the wrap, which was shaped like a bag and could completely enfold the child's body, she attached a triangular hood made of the same material. Only Riye's tiny face peeped heart-shaped from amid the maple leaves, which seemed to be ablaze. "How cute!" said Chinese housewives when they caught a glimpse of the bundle Makiko was holding.

In one dream, the riverside willows were in bud. The family—parents and child, with Riye being carried bundled up in her wrap—were taking a walk, as they had so often done, down a quiet lane on an evening permeated with the smell of frying oil. They were at a lake in the country— was it Lake Shi Sha? In another dream, Riye having grown ill, they bundled her all up in the swaddling wrap, and stood trembling under a tower gate which floated over them in what seemed to be a silhouette. They drove off in a foreign car, and dawn came.

In the number of years since the separation, Makiko had had so few dreams of Riye that she could enumerate all of them. At the time of the separation, Makiko had thought each night that she would like to see Riye in a dream, but she never did, and gradually stopped even thinking about her. Now, without any warning, Riye came to her three or four times in dreams.

In the dreams, Makiko's heart would begin to throb with longing. And yet after she woke up, more than by feelings of longing or joy, she was attacked by an oppressive and ominous foreboding that left her depressed for half a day.

Besides that one photograph kept in the bottom of the empty cake box and rarely brought out, Makiko had folded up and locked away in her heart two landscape scenes which also included Riye.

In one picture, the stone wall and moat of the Imperial Palace were arranged on the left, while on the right was a view of the whitewalled tower of the Diet Building and, in the distant foreground, waves of buildings undulated off toward the horizon. It looked to be a print of the scene around the Miyakezaka neighborhood.

The cherry trees lining the edge of the moat had shed all of their leaves, and beneath their bare branches walked Kusumoto, bundled up in an overcoat, and Makiko. Between the two of them walked little Riye, holding their hands. Riye would lift up her feet so that the two of them could swing her. To the casual observer, it would have looked like a close-knit family out on an amiable walk. But only Riye's bright voice rang out cheerfully; husband and wife wore hard expressions and avoided each other's eyes.

At that time, Makiko and her family had no home. It was just before their breakup, and the atmosphere between Makiko and her husband had grown chilly and threatening. They had been living at the house of a home-town acquaintance of theirs and had been allowed to stay until the end of the year. But now they were turned out and had nowhere to go. Kusumoto and Makiko had exhausted themselves in the war of nerves they were engaged in over whether or not they would separate, and they had neglected the most important matter at hand: that of finding a "nest." Just at that time, in the basement of the Diet Building, where Kusumoto worked, the barber shop closed for the New Year's holidays. Until the barber returned from his native village at the end of the recess, they were allowed, through some connections they had, to slip into the shop and take lodging there.

During the recess, the Diet Building itself was devoid of people. Yet in the basement there lived cleaning women, electricians, and office clerks. Well-fed rats would suddenly scurry across the corridors.

Behind a partition in the barber shop there was a small room with straw matting on the floor, and a sink for preparing food. As temporary sleeping quarters for a family of three, there was space enough.

There, for about ten days, Makiko and her family spent an odd vacation. Since, like it or not, facial expressions were reflected in the built-in mirror that filled one wall, Kusumoto and Makiko tried hard to make faces that, if only in the mirror, seemed harmonious. And there were times, too, when they took a bored Riye for a tour through the vast building.

Along the floors of the corridors, which were covered with bright red carpets, countless rooms were lined up one after another, decorated with velvet curtains, dazzling chandeliers, and splendid mahogany furniture. Waves of excitement surged through little Riye's breast as though she were exploring an enchanted castle in a fairy kingdom.

"Papa! Mama!"

Riye's voice carried down the endless hallways, and countless echoes came calling back. And the overly-excited Riye at times had little accidents on the carpet that was so thick it nearly buried her tiny shoes.

Trying always to avoid the tension that arose between them as soon as they spoke to each other, Makiko and Kusumoto had grown exhausted. They felt tempted to stay awhile in that unreal, fairy-tale land and give their frazzled nerves a rest.

And it was on a walk one day during that period that they came to the row of cherry trees at Miyakezaka. The Diet Building was towering distinctly against the clear and windless sky. Riye, who had been dangling between the two of them, suddenly put her feet down, and shaking free of Makiko's hand, raised her tiny arm and pointed at the Diet Building.

"Mama, that's my house! I can see my house!"

For the first time in a good many months, Kusumoto and Makiko laughed together.

The other scene in Makiko's heart was colored a much darker, grayer tone.

It was two months after the Miyakezaka incident. A cloudy sky, threatening snow, hung overhead.

On damp, low ground in Ogu there stood rows of tenement apartment buildings, rough and run-down, operated by the city of Tokyo. Makiko, Kusumoto, and Riye were sleeping in one room of a mere two-room apartment belonging to a friend who had just returned from the war. This place, too, was not very comfortable, as it was a temporary resting place under someone else's roof.

On this dreary scene, which recalled the deserted outskirts of some town, sleet fell for several days. Day by day, the damp, gloomy air—air which made people grow irritated at even the slightest provocation—grew heavier and closer.

On that morning, Kusumoto exploded in anger over some matter so trifling it hardly seemed to warrant the outburst. When she came to, Makiko found that she'd been hit in the right eye by the full force of Kusumoto's fist. Fresh blood was spurting from her eye, and she had been knocked down.

Riye threw her whole body at Kusumoto, and was beating on him.

When Makiko saw in a mirror how her face had swelled up in a lump, she finally made up her mind. After recovering for two nights at a friend's house two train stations away, Makiko returned to Ogu early in the morning. Kusumoto was still at home. Riye's smiling face popped into view in Makiko's one unbandaged eye.

Standing at the entrance, without any intention of going in, Makiko invited Kusumoto and Riye out to the front. That day, too, was cloudy; the sky was low.

"It's no good. Please let me go." It was the voice of one who'd been up all the previous night, thinking. Makiko's tone was dry.

"Well, haven't you just come back?"

"No, it won't work. I'm no good," Makiko replied.

"I won't let you have Riye."

Makiko didn't respond.

"If you're going to go, then go. Leave just the way you are."

"Mama!" Riye was about to run after her.

"Your mother is going to the hospital. You come back over here," Kusumoto said in a suddenly furious voice as he picked Riye up and held her.

"Take off that overcoat and get the hell out of here!"

Makiko took off the overcoat without looking at Kusumoto. She also threw off the muffler. As she put them down on a rock at the side of the road, she bowed, and silently walked away.

"Mama, see you again soon," Riye called out in a high voice.

Makiko turned around and waved, but she could not see for the tears in her eyes. The two electric tram car tracks, lead colored, stretched out before her, she did not know how far. Her coin purse had been in the pocket of that overcoat. Thinking she would just walk as far as her feet would carry her, she kept her pace. Her tears dried, and a cold light from the leaden-colored tram tracks was reflected in her eyes. It looked as though the tracks stretched on forever. Desolate suburban districts extended on either side of her.

So this is my road, she thought. Then she imagined she heard Riye's voice. Swallowing hard, she pulled up short. The wind pushed at her back. Putting on a mask-like expression, she started walking again. She did not look back.

Just as in a mother's heart her dead child never ages but stays forever the age it was at death, so the Riye Makiko kept in her heart was the four-year old child she'd been at their separation, and no matter how the years passed, she never grew older. The face that Makiko recalled was just a lonely phantom face, so like Riye's father, with his overly regular features—the face of the infant Riye when they were still living together.

Whenever Makiko saw a three- or four-year-old little girl, she would instinctively avert her glance. Nevertheless, even in that brief moment the child's face and clothing would be branded deeply into her eyes.

How could there be as many three- and four-year-old girls as this in the world, that such frightening numbers of them should appear at any time on any street corner, or should suddenly come dancing out in front of Makiko's eyes from behind something?! With coaxing, familiar smiles they would come twining around her, and would take hold of her with their brazen little hands.

Children were strangely attracted to Makiko. In the train, or wherever she visited, children, having sensed that she was a kindred spirit, would get in their eyes that knowing look, peculiar to the young, and would send her intimate winks.

Nevertheless, as she grew older Makiko developed a dislike for children. Unaccountably, whenever they came coaxing and twining around her, she reacted with an instinctive aversion, as though some disgusting animal had lunged out at her. She would get goose bumps.

And yet, in the palm of Makiko's hand there still remained—and enough to make her shiver—a pleasant memory of the plump, smooth wrists of a little girl, the feel of a slender, slippery back wet with soap bubbles, the sweet sensation of the nape of a neck so frail it could be strangled with just one hand. Even now, in the midst of her fantasies, the sensation lingered over stronger, clinging to her palm. Makiko had no desire to touch the actual body of a young child. To betray the memory that remained on her palm—what an unpleasant and dispiriting prospect that seemed to be. If by some chance these imaginary sensations came true, she had a premonition that, more than a disappointment, it would be a terrible nightmare.

Although Makiko made such a great sacrifice to join Tashiro, her affair with him came to a quick and pathetic end. Here was a young man, twenty-two years old, who had never known a woman's body. On his concept of ideal love, any adventure, any immorality could be painted. However, he had no way of understanding this lone, twenty-six-year-old married woman who had abandoned her husband and child, left her home, and had come to him with a desperate look on her face and nothing but the clothes on her back.

Hair in disarray, cheeks ravaged from crying, her dirty eye-patch slipping off—in this brooding, womanly face (she'd even neglected her lipstick) there was nothing of the refinement, the elegance, of the tranquil wife she'd been, her arms wrapped around her young daughter. In the vanity of his youth, Tashiro tried frantically to hide from her his depression and uneasiness in confronting a woman he found totally unfathomable.

The two gingerly exchanged their first embraces in a room in a small inn on a miserable street corner in Kyoto, far away from their home towns, and from Makiko's husband's family in Tokyo. Tashiro felt Makiko's breasts. Taken by the warm skin of his first woman, and by its softness, he squeezed them hard without meaning to, and said, trembling,

"Ah, they're so soft, as if they could melt away. . . ."

"No, silly. A young girl's breasts are supposed to be hard." As she was saying this in a gentle voice, Makiko suddenly, helplessly, burst into violent sobs. Fear and regret at having dragged such an innocent young man into this cruel predicament had already begun to spread out, heavy and dark, in her heart.

Her pity for Tashiro being bound up with what was left of her love for Riye, Makiko cried in confusion, no longer able to cope with the situation. Tashiro was flustered; the more reassuringly he pledged his love, the more Makiko's premonitions about the inauspiciousness of that love sent cold shivers running up her spine.

Many people asked Makiko about Riye, some out of curiosity, others out of politeness or sympathy. Some of them sympathized with Riye; others admired Makiko's determination and ability to take action. Still others remarked about Makiko's cold-heartedness. In all cases, however, their feelings toward Makiko were somewhat wide of the mark.

There were rumors that Kusumoto had taken as his second wife a kindly woman, who, having no children of her own was treating Riye to the blessings of being an only daughter. Makiko retold those rumors in answer to people's questions, and she did so with certainty, as if she herself had been an eye-witness to Riye's situation.

People who heard this invariably wondered how Makiko and Riye could both live in Tokyo and not see each other. Makiko's reply was formulaic:

"Seeing Riye wouldn't bring her back to me. And they are doing such a good job of raising her. I should refrain from making any trouble, don't you think?"

In the last ten years Makiko had never once tried to see Riye, neither had she felt any strong desire to do so. She had long ago decided that

Kusumoto would not let her have the child, but in point of fact, she could not remember ever having discussed with him where Riye would live. In any case, she had never risked her neck trying to get Riye. Taking advantage of Kusumoto's insistence that he would never let her have her daughter back, Makiko put herself in the position of having run away on her own. From then on she never once attempted, or even thought, to take Riye by force.

Through mutual acquaintances she would have news of Kusumoto from time to time. She found out that, by Kusumoto's choice, Riye had been attending the American School since kindergarten. Makiko thought that if she were at Riye's side she would certainly not permit such an education, and she was deeply concerned over it. But believing that she herself was not qualified to say anything, she hastily washed her hands of the matter, despite her uneasiness at the rumor.

For her part, if Makiko had had even the slightest will to see the growing Riye, she could have made opportunities to do so in secret. But for some reason Makiko did not feel any desire to see her grown child. She did not have the courage to get to the bottom of her resistance toward seeing Riye. She was, for whatever reason, running away from it.

When had she started running away?

For about a year after her separation from Riye, Makiko was tormented by visions of the child. In the street, in the theater, in the bus, she would begin sobbing uncontrollably, and would have to leave wherever she was. If, when she passed in front of a children's store or a shop specializing in infant needs, she glanced carelessly inside, she would physically experience a kind of seizure.

However, at some point—she could not clearly recall when it was—Makiko learned the skill of turning her eyes away from the cause of her pain, and she protected herself as much as possible, and with time, this skill improved. Before she knew it, she reached the point where, without any effort, she forgot what she had forgotten in order to forget.

Thus her mind was filled with nothing but the waves of actual, everyday living, waves that threatened to sweep her off her feet.

Though extremely rare, there were times when Makiko was afraid lest Riye would suddenly sit down next to her on a train or bus. This fantasy brought more fear than expectation. Perhaps for Makiko, who was not religious, her ultimate fear was of just that moment, at some point in the future, when she might run into Riye, by then a woman whom she would not recognize.

If she wished for anything, it was that she might once again see Riye as a baby girl, just as she'd been long ago when they parted. She wanted to confirm in that way the memory left behind in the palm of her hand.

There was a time, just once, about a year after she'd left Kusumoto's house, that she went to see Riye. At that time, Riye was being taken care of in the home of Kusumoto's elder brother-in-law, in a country village some miles away from their home town.

As she made her way to the isolated rural temple where this brother-in-law's family lived on just as they had during the wartime evacuation, Makiko's head was completely empty of thoughts. She had broken off the reckless love affair that had led her to abandon her home and Riye. After that she had been living the life of a poor woman alone, in Kyoto, where she had been staying ever since she ran off.

It wasn't even that she wondered what she'd do when she did meet Riye. It was just that, as though a flame had been lit, a strong desire to see Riye suddeny once flared up within her. She went there as if she were in a daydream.

She soon found the temple. There were no signs of people in the hushed precincts of early afternoon, and she stole smoothly toward the garden.

It was a time when the brother-in-law, who was a junior high school principal in town, and his older children, would all be off at school. His youngest daughter and Riye would certainly have stayed behind.

Even as she approached the temple, Makiko was keeping a careful eye out for Riye, now along the edge of the stream, now on the road leading through the fields in which rapeseed flowers bloomed in profusion.

She had guessed that Riye would be at the temple's detached cottage located in front of the pond in the back garden. Between the pond and the cottage stood a thick bamboo grove. Undetected by anyone, and trying to deaden the sound of her footsteps, Makiko slipped into the dark grove. The air was forest deep, and fish jumped in the pond.

Holding her breath, she edged step by step toward the greenery around the cottage. Then, from inside the white-papered sliding door came:

"Hey! Hey! Come on. Go outside and play."

It was an old woman's voice. Makiko recognized it as that of her former mother-in-law. She'd been kind to Makiko. Suddenly sentimental, Makiko heard voices raised in childish song:

"You, you—where are you, hey?!

In Higo province, hey!

Where in Higo province, hey?!

In Kumamoto, hey!"

They were the voices of two children. Struggling to keep up with a high and lively voice was a weak one that seemed to have no self-confidence.

The voices, intertwining, grew distant as they moved off through the parlor and out the other side of the cottage. Makiko was shaken. She crept out of the bamboo thicket, then walked across the artificial hillock and round behind the temple. Her stockings were torn when she crossed over a hedge. But she managed to jump down onto the road.

Riye's singing voice, that weak voice lacking in self-confidence, rang in Makiko's ears. She remembered that she had never made any serious effort to teach Riye words, let alone songs.

From Beijing to their home town, from their home town to Tokyo, Riye had been dragged from place to place just at the time when she would have been learning to talk. And since they always moved to a new area before she had had time to learn the speech of the old one, she was a lot later than most children in learning. On top of that, just at that time Makiko fell in love, her spirits soaring every day, and she had neither the time nor the patience to devote to talking with little Riye, who couldn't say much of anything. Riye was just beginning to take notice of the things around her, and there she was, for reasons she didn't understand, being bounced about for hours on her mother's back, her mother weeping all the while, or being suddenly and hysterically embraced, or going for half a day or more without even a word being said to her. Makiko had no memory of ever opening a picture book and showing it to Riye, no memory of ever teaching her a song. Rather, her only memories were of taking Riye along with her when she went to meet Tashiro, of Riye being squeezed between the two of them like a sandwich, of covering Riye's eyes and stealing kisses. and it was about that time that Riye, who had never had any trouble sleeping, took to crying for hours in the middle of the night, so that the only way for Makiko to get her to fall asleep was to put her on her back and walk her up and down the road in the deep, moonlit night.

Feeling as empty as if a spirit possession had just left her, Makiko made her way from the barley field to the rapeseed field, looking for the two children by following the sound of their singing voices.

Down the road that ran right between the barley field and the rapeseed field came the two girls singing, their hands joined together. Makiko approached them in a daze. At the sight of this strange woman, tears streaming down both her cheeks, the two girls were terrified and stood rooted to the spot. The next instant, the brother-in-law's daughter turned her back and ran for dear life, shouting in a loud voice. Riye just stood there as she was, motionless. Makiko knelt down in front of her and, unconsciously reaching for her hands, pulled her closer.

Riye remained expressionless, her face reflecting neither familiarity nor fear. She was wearing the sweater Makiko had been knitting up to the day she ran away. The cuffs of the sweater, which used to come right down to Riye's wrists, now only covered her plump arms halfway down. Hers was a pretty little face, one which had come to resemble Kusumoto's more than the face in the photograph, which had resembled Makiko's.

"Riye dear. . . ."

Makiko didn't know what to say next.

"Where's your Papa?" she asked, as it was the only topic the two of them had in common.

"In Tokyo," Riye replied, clearly and mechanically.

Drawn in further, Makiko asked, "Where's your Mama?" She could tell that she was fawning on the child.

"She died." Riye's voice did not falter. That voice sent infinite echoes through Makiko's head, silently penetrating and clearing it.

Even at that time, Makiko did not try to take Riye with her.

Kuji's daughter Rie, who had been a little third-grader just yesterday, grew up and became a college student. Throughout the long season of their love, Kuji had, from time to time, shown Makiko photographs of his daughter, and thus she had followed the course of Rie's growing-up. In that first photo, Makiko had seen a long, skinny neck and body, planted at the top of which was a head that looked disproportionately large. But as Rie grew, her body took on symmetry, and she developed into a long-legged, lissome young lady who resembled her father in her slightness of build. If, from her elementary school days, her face had filled out, her cheeks had softened, and the length of her nose had become less conspicuous, perhaps it was because hidden traces of her mother's looks had emerged in her face. Looked at in this way, the rich fullness of her lips and the roundness of her chin reflected nothing of her father Kuji's looks.

One day, Kuji came as usual to visit Makiko. As he was putting on his sash, he muttered, "My Rie, she's started. . . ."

"Huh? Started what?"

"Started *that*. . . ."

Having finished tying his sash, Kuji turned to face her. As she looked into his big eyes, which were filled with gentle love, his meaning at last dawned on her.

The age at which Rie reached womanhood was rather late. Makiko immediately reflected back to the time when she herself had reached that age, and she recalled the commonly held view that mother and daughter were alike in such female functions. The supposition that her daughter, her own flesh and blood, might have already become a woman called up a solemnity of emotion of a sort Makiko had not at all expected. It felt as though her own blood vessels had suddenly increased in size. It seemed to her as if the power of the flow of life was coursing through her body, raising a great sound.

Makiko was caught up in a hallucination, as though the sweet rapture she could remember once having felt surge all the way down her back were being brought to life again. It was the sensation she had had the first time Riye began to suck instinctively on her mother's nipple. The darling child had suddenly, and with surprising strength, started sucking on the teat. Almost insensibly she sucked the milk, which came hissing right out of the core of the stiff, hard breast. And the pleasure Makiko felt as the stiffness loosened and softened ran straight down her spine. As this tingling sweetness flowed down her back, a rapturous calm infused every cell of her body.

From out of the fog of that distant time nearly twenty years ago, these sensations revived her with deep vibrations like those of a pipe organ, and restored her sense of the profound blood ties she had with Riye, whom she had not seen in well over ten years.

After that conversation with Kuji, another three or four years passed. It became clear that Rie, who had grown up knowing nothing about the nature of her father's tie with Makiko, had at some point learned that the relationship was not a conventional one, not one of which her own mother had been a willing part. She no longer sent letters, and eventually even stopped sending New Year's cards.

Makiko remembered clearly that the last letter she'd received from Rie was a thank-you note for the formal, Japanese-style outfit Makiko had put together for her at New Year's during the girl's first year in high school. Since Makiko had put her heart into the gift, the letter that Rie wrote at that time had an unusually deep effect on her, and she read it through carefully.

The time she and Kuji together selected Rie's outfit at a clothing store in the Ginza was the only time that, through her own negligence, Makiko had projected Riye's image on that of Rie.

In Beijing, the first year after Riye's birth, the two of them had greeted the end of the war at a place down Xi-dan Lane. At that time, Kusumoto was in the army, having been drafted by the local authorities. Makiko was at her wits' end, busy with Riye, who had just had her first birthday. Kusumoto had changed universities before he got drafted, but the official notice of his new appointment had not arrived from Japan. Because of that, the salary from his new university position had not yet been paid. Not only did Makiko have no savings whatsoever, but communications with the homeland were all but non-existent. She begged the young maid servant, who'd been with them since Riye's birth, to stay on without pay. Leaving her in charge, Makiko made the rounds day after day, job-hunting under the blazing sun. The job that she finally found was as a clerk at a forwarding agency located along the Palace wall. Her first day on the job was the last day of the war.

Being in an overseas territory, and running up against so unexpected a turn of events as the end of the war, Makiko was shocked. When she realized what it all meant, she dashed out of the forwarding agency office, turned her back to the Palace wall, and fled frantically down the large street in front of the Xuan Wu Gate. The next instant, she was seized with the animal-like fear that violence might break out and she would be separated from Riye. She flew through the gate of her home and dashed over to Riye, who was in the garden. As usual, the maid was holding the baby in her arms. As she reached out and took Riye from the maid, Makiko sank weakly to the ground.

From the following day, Makiko began to sell off for cash such Japanese clothes as she had. This was the only way to earn living expenses until Kusumoto returned, and she did not know when that might be. She had six or seven trunks packed with kimono, which had been part of her trousseau. Almost all the kimono still had the basting in them, and her arms had never entered the sleeves.

The maid helped her to hang things all over the house as if they were giving them a summer airing. Makiko was reluctant to part with her clothes. Color suddenly flooded into the gloomy, Chinese-style rooms, their windows covered with lattice work. The silk, as it gathered the light, took on an iridescent shimmer. It was strangely brilliant. Even the baby Riye romped about, shrieking with delight as she crawled beneath the curtain of kimono.

"I shall buy one for you, too, Riye. When you grow up, you'll wear a little kimono at New Year's. And we'll put festival dolls out for you, and you'll get to wear a long-sleeved kimono."

Considering the urgency of the moment, when their very lives were in danger, it was hard to tell if these words sounded more like a prayer or empty nonsense.

From the time of Riye's birth, there had not been another moment in their lives when the two of them were blessed with pure joy as on that day.

When, at the Ginza clothing store, she saw spread out before her all the bright formal outfits for young girls, Makiko remembered, completely unexpectedly, that summer-airing day at the house down the lane in Beijing. The promise she had repeated while holding the innocent Riye in her arms came back to her as if it were yesterday.

"Oh, this is a nice one!" Makiko said without hesitation, as she pointed out a kimono with a bamboo design in five colors dyed over a white background. For all its brightness, this formal outfit had a great deal of dignity. The phantom face of Riye in her mind's eye took on, for the first time, the look of a beautiful young woman. Makiko rapturously pictured that face as it would look above this formal kimono. In that moment, she completely forgot about Kuji's Rie.

"Please take a look at the photograph of me in kimono. I look as if I'd suddenly become an adult! Mother says a girl is not a woman until she pays attention to the attractiveness of the hairline above her collar."

A photograph of Rie in her new formal outfit accompanied her last letter. In the lamplight, Makiko stared with unusual keenness into the photograph of the virginal, kimono-clad Rie, whose hips and shoulders were not yet fleshed out. By the time this girl became a college student, Makiko would have to give Kuji back to her. The idea did not come to Makiko all at once; rather, it had come floating up quietly into her heart. She had avoided facing it before, but she now saw that for some time, the day that she would part from Kuji had been written there in clear black letters.

One day around that time, Makiko went to a certain hospital in order to put together a report she'd been working on. She was writing an article on the subject of abortion.

The completely tiled operation room was some two hundred square feet, and was bewilderingly bright. The dazzling sunlight of late autumn afternoon penetrated, glittering, through glass windows on the south side, and stretched in a straight line toward the operating table.

The operating table, of the latest style, was set in the center of the room, and looked like a gigantic plate placed aslant. Facing the sunlight, the patient's pubic area was already exposed, like a pink eye. Her legs had been drawn apart, and the yellow skin on her flesh hung loosely. She was no longer young.

The patient's eyes were covered. The cheeks, visible beneath the blinders, were sunken, and a gold tooth sparkled from the slightly open mouth. As the anesthesia was being administered, the patient counted out numbers in a loud voice, like a child. Anyone could see she was a simple, honest person.

Makiko called to mind her own memory of that blank, uneasy sleep when consciousness fades. Above the patient before her eyes, Makiko had another vision of her own body in a wretched position, her legs held painfully apart with an ordinary operating room chair.

An oily sweat broke out all over Makiko's body. Regrets at having come crept upward from her feet, which had grown cold. Nonetheless, she remained as if riveted to the scene before her, quite unable to avert her eyes from the patient's body.

All of a sudden, a flesh-colored mass was pulled from the patient's insides. Looking like a sea anemone, that round, thick piece of flesh with its tight opening was the cervix. As dirty forceps were lined up in quick succession on the side table, blood began to flow from the cervix. It gushed out without stopping. The life blood that was being drained from this woman, with her dried up yellow skin, filled the discharge bowl in an instant. Makiko had a vision of a fetus—without will, without defined shape—wincing in the dark of the womb at the cold touch of the forceps, and trying to escape.

The inside of Makiko's mouth grew dry. The back of her head turned cold. For some time now, the patient, unconscious, had been moaning like a wild animal. To Makiko, it was Makiko herself screaming. Had she lived until now only so that she could receive this punishment? She overcame her desire to flee, and stood rooted to the spot. It wasn't that she had even a shred of curiosity. In place of the unconscious patient, Makiko was herself taking on all the pain that the patient was suffering, all the humiliating torture.

Amidst the clotting blood, a white thing that looked like chicken fat suddenly came out. It was a bit of the fetus.

In Makiko's vision, innumerable eyeless, noseless fetal phantoms lined up in jostling heaps like the gray tombstones at Adashino, making her want to scream out in terror. Just as people at their hour of death use their last bit of strength calling out for light, so Makiko called out for Riye. All of a sudden, Makiko could hear again, with heart-rending vividness, Riye's hearty first cry as it had echoed down through the morning gloom at the maternity hospital on that little lane in Beijing.

"These are the eyes," the doctor whispered.

The tips of the forceps held two tiny black things that looked like little sweet beans. And as her knees buckled and she collapsed, Makiko saw baby Riye, wings spreading out from her shoulders, soaring gently upwards and beckoning.

Translated by Robert Huey

Hirabayashi Taiko

In "The Goddess of Children" (*Kishimojin*, 1946; trans. 1952) Hirabayashi Taiko (1905–72) has her heroine say: "I have lived the whole breadth of a woman's life. From now on, I will apply that same energy to plumbing its depths." The comment could well be applied to the author's own life. Although Hirabayashi was born into a well-respected rural family, she moved to Tokyo on the day of her graduation from high school and embarked on a flamboyant life both as a woman and as a left-wing activist, eventually marrying one of her comrades. She made her literary debut in 1926 with an autobiographical piece that was among the prize-winners in a short story contest. Her career as a proletarian writer came to an abrupt end in 1937, when she and her husband were arrested and imprisoned for alleged unpatriotic activities. After a few months of life in prison, she contracted tuberculosis and had to spend the next eight years trying to recover from it. With the end of the war she resumed writing, but this time her thematic focus was on the liberation of the suppressed humanity within the individual rather than on the liberation of a particular social class. Reflecting her personal experience, her postwar stories often portrayed prisoners and hospital patients who show a strong will to live, and to live as fully as possible. "I Mean to Live" (*Watakushi wa ikiru*, 1947; trans. 1963) and "A Man's Life" (*Hito no inochi*, 1950; trans. 1961) are representative of such stories. Various illnesses hampered her creative activities in her later years. With great persistence, however, she continued to write stimulating stories, including "Secret" (*Himitsu*, 1967), which won her the Women's Literature Prize in 1968.

Many of Hirabayashi's postwar stories that feature women can be said to represent the author's attempt to "plumb the depths of womanhood." The most famous among them is "The Goddess of Children," which studies female sexuality in a small child. "A Woman to Call Mother" (*Haha to iu onna*, 1966) treats the same theme, except that the subject is an aged, dying woman.

A WOMAN TO CALL MOTHER
Haha to iu onna

Hirabayashi Taiko

A new patient had arrived in the three-person room. Although she was no longer young, her shoulders sloped smoothly and narrowed to a high waist. She had tied the sash of her kimono so that the ornamental knot rested ever so lightly on her hips. The effect was just right.

She brought her things bundled up in an elegant, arabesque-patterned cloth rather than in an overnight bag. Dangling the bundle, the taxi driver had tagged along all the way to the room. She started to tip him with a lissome motion of her hand and called to him.

"Say, driver, just a moment, please." Her speech had a touch of the way people used to hail rickshaw men in the old days.

The greeting she gave to the person in the next bed was every bit as brusque as a man's. That patient, a woman in her forties with a stomach polyp, had been feeling bored and hoping something would happen. She sized up the newcomer at once. "Uh-oh," she thought, "this person's going to be hard to get along with."

But, when the new patient spoke, she was remarkably candid. "Excuse me, please. I'm worse off than you girls are, you see. It's really an effort for me. Oh, it hurts—that hurts!" Lying down, she massaged her waist.

Her hair, cushioned on the pillow, had such a lustrous shine that it seemed as if it would melt. She had put it up tightly in a style that at first looked ordinary, but that on a closer inspection turned out to be an old-fashioned coiffure held in place with a Japanese comb. Her face was attractively slender—a delicate nose, raven eyelashes, and redness only in her camellia-colored lips. She must have been a striking beauty in her youth.

A nurse and a doctor came right away and gave her some sort of injection.

Part of her chest was exposed then, revealing skin that was rather dark. The two breasts had wizened like dried persimmons. They were too meager and sagged too much, so they failed as decorations for her narrow chest. As is often found among geisha who were delicately thin in their youth, her body was in a state of decline worse than its outward appearance suggested.

After the doctor left, the woman with the polyp said, "Let me guess. You must be someone who used to do this—." She went through the motions of playing a samisen.

"You're wrong," said the new patient, raising her slender head from the pillow and then letting it fall back because of the pain. The nurse was always coming in to check her pulse and take her blood pressure with the instrument that was left lying around in the room, so it seemed certain that her condition was serious.

Another nurse came and questioned her, writing down her replies on various forms. She answered wearily.

"So at the present time you are single?"

"That's. . . right." She could not even utter both words in a single breath.

"Well, then, the party accepting responsibility is your daughter?"

"That's. . . right."

"And your responsible party has consented, right?"

"Well. . . ." She gasped and with a wheezing laugh said, "No, she hasn't."

"Now that's a problem." The nurse tried to press the matter, but the patient turned over on her side.

"Mrs. Shida, someone who has not consented is no good as a party of responsibility. In the first place, you won't be able to get her to sign anything, right?"

"I don't need any responsible party. I paid the money into an account at the office in advance, so take just as much as you need."

"It's not the money!"

Even though the nurse was approaching middle age, the indifference in this woman's speech was making her impatient and irritated.

The nurse also knew from the results of the examination that this patient had little hope of recovery. So, if she did not take care of the matter of the person accepting responsibility now, the time would come sooner or later when she herself would be taken to task. Besides that, however, she just could not put up with such absurdity.

Shida closed her eyes, visibly annoyed. Cloudiness tinted her upper eyelids like thinly applied eyeshadow. Their skin was thin enough to show the movement of the eyeballs underneath.

"What a problem! At any rate, I'll try calling your daughter to come. And you with three daughters, too!" Muttering and looking at a document she had brought, the nurse left the room.

"Mrs. Shida, things are pretty difficult here when you don't get all of the forms taken care of. Let me help," the woman with the polyp offered. "Shall I telephone for you? I can use the one in the cafeteria."

This woman had supposedly gotten a polyp in her stomach, but that was just the explanation given to her by the doctor. The true nature of her disease must not have been very different from Shida's. There were extraordinary numbers of patients with stomach ulcers, polyps, intestinal inflammations, and so forth, at the clinic. Interestingly enough, even though it was a cancer clinic, there were almost never any cancer patients.

The woman with the polyp ran a little neighborhood pub in the lively old-downtown district. No matter when she telephoned her home, however, her husband never answered.

"He's playing around, you see. He's always off seeing women when I'm not there." She seemed resigned to this and had made it into a joke. Nevertheless, three times a day without fail, she could be seen tottering down the hall in her terry-cloth nightgown on her way to telephone him.

Shida did not ask the woman with the polyp to make a telephone call for her. She merely grumbled, "It's no use," and shut her eyes again.

That night, Shida lay groaning.

The next morning, the woman with the polyp and the third patient in the room, a girl who had come from the neighboring psychiatric clinic, went to pick up their breakfast trays. While they were in the corridor, the woman with the polyp whispered to her, "I don't like it. That woman may go earlier than they think. And just when there were only minor cases here, too. . . ."

The girl's face, however, showed no emotion at all. She had slashed her own rectum and lost her anal muscles as a result. Apparently, though, she was not affected by it as severely as had been anticipated. Happy to have more freedom here than in the psychiatric clinic, she would run about in the hall all day long.

The woman with the polyp spent all that day looking forward to the arrival of Shida's daughter. She was hoping to see, in that very room, the touching scene of an estranged parent and child meeting at long last. But the daughter did not come.

The same nurse returned in the evening. "I see your daughter didn't come. We have a problem here. What about changing to another party of responsibility?"

"It wouldn't do any good. There isn't anyone who'd do it."

"Why is that? They really are your children, aren't they?"
Wondering if her words had been too pointed, the nurse watched Shida's reaction closely.

"They won't come, even though they are." Shida spoke deliriously and closed her eyes.

She had eaten almost nothing since the previous day. A covered bowl of thin rice gruel had been on her table tray for a while, but the nurse came and left milk in its place. Shida reached out, took the milk, and drank about half of it, but she vomited it into a basin right away.

From then on, her eyes were closed more and more often.

The nurse in charge spoke to the other nurses in the office. "I might ask the police to get in touch with them. I don't know what reasons they have, but this is terrible, don't you think? Their own mother could die at any time, and yet. . . ."

Previously, there had been another such case. It had happened to the girl from the psychiatric clinic who was sharing Shida's room. A woman who might have been her mother or aunt—one couldn't tell—said to her, "I won't come anymore. Let the nurses take care of you from now on." The woman never came back, and even when the girl had surgery there were no relatives present.

Although similar, Shida's case was more emotionally charged. And yet, it concealed something strange and mysterious. Her daughters' failure to visit her seemed an indication that their emotions were too strong. It lacked the coldness of neglect based on an absence or inadequacy of feeling.

The next day, when the attending physician went out into the hall after his regular visit, he questioned the nurse accompanying him.

"No one from her family has come yet?"

"So it seems. But, apparently no one was living with her."

"They must really be on bad terms. Problems over dividing up her husband's estate or something?"

"I don't really know, but in the space for 'occupation' the form says 'founder, school of Japanese dance.' She doesn't seem to be someone with money problems. A dance teacher named Shida Ryūsuke used to appear a lot on television. She looks different now, but there's a rumor going around that it might be her."

"Cases like this are tough on me, too. The patient has more than the illness to contend with."

"Admissions says she'll go visit the daughter at home in a few days."

"Good idea. But it means a lot of extra trouble."

The daughter who was summoned did not come on the next day, either. They had the neighborhood policeman visit her on the day after that, but she still did not come.

Saturday and Sunday passed. In her off-duty hours on the following Monday afternoon, the nurse in charge of admissions went to a certain housing complex and visited the family into which Shida's daughter had married. The daughter, whose facial features closely resembled her mother the patient, appeared to be two or three years over thirty. Like her mother, the daughter had a figure as beautiful as a willow. When she sat on the tatami mat and bowed, her long, delicate hands moved with subtle expression. She was the beauty with a slender face that Shida must have been twenty or so years ago.

The nurse, in ordinary clothes for the occasion, put her message into gentle terms as she tried to gauge the feelings of her listener.

The daughter only said, "I see, I see. We appreciate all that you've done." She showed none of the black hatred toward her parent that the nurse had thought she might.

"Please do whatever you think is best. She is in your hands." The words were repeated over and over.

"You say she is in our hands, but all we can do is treat the illness. If no one comforts and encourages the patient for us, none of our treatment will do any good."

The daughter lowered her head. As she examined the the trim shape of her kimono, she seemed to be thinking about what to say.

"Well, . . . I don't think my mother wants any comforting from me." The words rang out one by one like raindrops on metal. And, like raindrops, they had a mechanical quality. There was no trace of emotion.

"Why might that be?"

There was no answer.

The nurse was a good-natured woman, but even she had become more than a little irritated.

"For our own information, could you tell me in general why you feel that way?"

"No, there isn't that much to tell. It's just that—I'm sorry, but my husband will be home at any minute, so I'd like to end this conversation now."

"All right, I understand. It can't be helped."

The nurse returned to the hospital feeling too put off for words.

From around that time, Shida seemed to be visited by partial lapses of consciousness. Her eyelids would gleam like stretched satin, and then she would suddenly open her eyes, stare at the ceiling, and, as if in ecstasy, say, "It was beautiful. It was so beautiful. . . ."

Once, the woman with the polyp tried to bring her out of it, saying, "What did you see? What kind of beautiful thing did you see, Mrs. Shida?" But, Shida was already inhabiting a body and mind in some dimension quite removed from the present world.

She gave an answer, "Aaaah—." Nevertheless, her eyelids remained retracted, and her eyes were glassy and lifeless, lying deep within the sockets that seemed to have been dug out of her skull.

After the people at the hospital had exhausted every possible means, it finally came about that Shida's daughter would visit the hospital on a certain day. The nurses in the office and the woman with the polyp awaited her all morning with feelings of eager anticipation.

Around two o'clock, the daughter arrived in the office with a visitor's pass. She was carrying a paper package the size of a small box. Having been directed to the semi-private room, she bowed gracefully and pushed open the door. The nurse who had visited the daughter came along with her from the office.

The woman made her way at once to the pillow that supported her mother's distinctive coiffure.

Without anyone asking her to, the woman with the polyp whispered into Shida's tiny, rounded ear, "Mrs. Shida, your daughter has come."

But the look in Shida's eyes neither lightened nor darkened.

The daughter nonetheless stared at her mother for about two minutes. Then she removed the wrapping from the paper package and placed a box containing ten cream puffs onto the table.

"I really appreciate everything you've done for her. I'm sorry it's been so much trouble. These aren't much, but please have them at tea time or whenever."

Just above the slender hips that looked exactly like her mother's, the daughter had tied her kimono with a quietly elegant obi. The thin cord holding the sash in place was low, so that the large ornamental knot swelled out at its base. From the way she carried herself, one could tell that she had been quite rigorously trained in dance by her mother.

Hardly had she made a deep and graceful bow, when she turned around without so much as a glance at her mother's face and started walking toward the door.

"Excuse me, ma'am! Surely you're not leaving already, are you?"

"Yes, I'm going home."

"But that's awful! Can't you see how awful you're being? Surely you didn't come just to pay a courtesy call to us!"

She said, "I'm sorry," but the determination in her walk as she left the room belied the modesty of her words.

The woman with the polyp cried for at least thirty minutes after the daughter left. Shida herself, however, kept her eyes lightly closed. Once in a while, she took hold of the spouted glass by her pillow with her slender, bamboo-like fingers and drank some water.

"Aren't you sad, Mrs. Shida?"

"Not at all."

That was all she said. Either because of pain or a lack of energy, she let her long hand, which lay out of the blanket, fall abruptly to the side of the bed. She closed her eyes again.

The woman with the polyp muttered, "You're almost strangers," but still she felt that the words were not enough. "You're worse than strangers."

Shida showed no reaction even to these words. But—and I have had such an experience—critically ill patients themselves do not sense the danger facing them as clearly as others can. Although they are nearing death, they are unaware of it until the very end, because they have within themselves a certain feeling, which they come to depend on, that gives them a false sense of vitality. When a hundred-watt lamp is switched off, it gives out no light. While it is on, however, it gives off one hundred watts of power. There is no in-between. A life that is about to extinguish itself completely at any moment still gives off its full hundred watts of power as long as it, too, is switched on.

Even so, once in a while there were instants in which Shida's mind appeared to separate itself from reality and go wandering into another world. Those instants gradually became more frequent.

A pleasant sensation like the feel of thin silk floated lightly around her. She had experienced this feeling in the past. It was the one that she used to know in her younger days when she lived life to its fullest: the touch of the air that her supple body brushed against while dancing.

Those were her days of suffering, when it seemed as if even that sweet air contained an aphrodisiac she could not resist. Dance was a writhing torment that overwhelmed the person she was then.

She danced in the style of the Miyama school, and there were many hopes pinned on her to become the foremost dancer in that tradition. The Miyama style, however, was not widely known in Tokyo, so Mr. Miyama of its head family was not able to establish a large institution. He had a tiny practice studio in Imagawabashi in the back part of what used to be a Matsuya department store. There he gave lessons to students who had come with him from Kyoto, as well as to a small number of their pupils.

Shida had received her first instruction in dance from one of the master's own students, a Miyama Ryūjaku, and at some point she had become one of Ryūjaku's lovers. Ryūjaku, however, was by nature prey to his own domineering emotions. On top of that, his profession required him to take on a large number of women students, so that he was continually involved with any number of women.

Only after she gave birth to a daughter did Shida completely realize that there was no hope of marrying Ryūjaku.

At that time she still had the inheritance from her father, who had been a cotton wholesaler in the Horidome district of Nihonbashi, so the revenge she wanted for being jilted did not include material compensation. Her hatred and resentment were all the purer and stronger as a result.

By nature, she did not like to shed tears over things, and she soon decided to make her opponent cry instead of crying herself. She knew what an important tool—an advertisement—a dancer's face is. So, although it was not a very original method, she threw sulfuric acid into Ryūjaku's face. It left a scar so bad that, every time Ryūjaku performed in public from then until he was an old man, he used a bamboo palette knife to smooth it over with paint and then put on his make-up over that.

She had achieved her revenge, but she still had a child to care for. It was a thorny path that she traveled on her own, away from the support of the school. For that reason, she strained to put every bit of the ability hidden within the depths of her body into her dancing.

She appeared as entertainment at many parties and wedding receptions, not to mention countless restaurants. She put up a sign on her house and took on students. Using her own last name for a stage name, she built up a circle of supporters, albeit tiny, that called itself the Shida Association.

The volunteer who worked the hardest for this organization was Yamakawa, the father of her second daughter. At that time, Yamakawa was still a college student living off his parents.

From the outset, she and Yamakawa were too incompatible to marry. Yamakawa's father took pride in having descended from the head retainer of a feudal lord in central Kyushu. At the time, he was administering a private school on that estate. The father attached great importance to social details. For her part, Shida was not of a mind to entrust her life to a younger man.

That was, however, the time of her greatest happiness, an era of fulfillment and self-confidence. It was also then that the true form of that brilliant celestial orb called "man" gradually began to appear to her without its dazzling radiance. Bracing herself, she began to think that men might be a far more worthless alloy of metals than she had expected.

Her dancing became more and more consummate as she developed such insights.

It was after the birth of the second child that her beauty appeared to have been burnished to its highest gloss. Her skin glowed like fine silk woven to a lustrous sheen. Her body was slender, but the muscles in her arms and legs had much firmness and strength in their response. The nerves connecting those agile muscles were coiled like springs inside the soft body that could bend like a bow.

Both male and female students began to abandon the unpopular Miyama style and turn to Shida. New pupils enrolled two or three at a time in her school, which was now completely separate and disowned by the Miyama tradition.

Shida herself had no inkling that a considerable number of the male students entered her school because they were attracted by the immoral reputation she had acquired. She was undoubtedly entangled in various secret love affairs. Of these lovers, only the name of a store-owner in Kiba became general knowledge. He had fathered her third daughter.

She never really had any interest in marrying this man, either. Even though she had three daughters to care for, she continued to spread the name of the tiny Shida school for more than twenty years after that time, with the help of her male and also her female students. Periodically her amorous reputation was gossiped about excessively—sometimes incorrectly, sometimes not—but those twenty or so years must have been the best part of her life.

She had planned to make Aki, her oldest daughter, into the successor of the Shida tradition, and as long as the girl had no really excellent marriage prospects, Shida intended to have her remain single. Nevertheless, when Aki was twenty-three, she fell in love with one of Shida's least-promising male pupils.

As might be expected, he was a college student.

Shida herself had never held any dislike for college students, who for her had an odor of raw freshness not unlike unripe vegetables. She also felt a vague regret at never having given birth to a boy. Whenever she saw a college student, maternal instincts surged irrationally within her.

However, she desperately opposed this love between the law student, who was the son of a district attorney, and her oldest daughter. She herself did not understand why she was so much against it. When she stood at the first crossroads of deciding whether or not to oppose it, she happened to choose opposition. From then on, she raced frantically down that path.

The daughter was deeply wounded—torn to shreds. She threw just as much strength into her resistance as her mother did into her opposition. She even thought of leaving home and marrying the man.

When Shida realized that, no matter what, she could not block their love, she resigned herself somewhat and suddenly quieted down. Then, for her daughter's sake, she tried as hard as she could to discover new merits in the law student she had opposed.

The process of discovering went too far. She was in contact with him about various matters, and in so doing she gradually began to feel weighed down by guilt. It was the same "pain of life" that she had felt so many times before.

By that time, with the intuition of his young manhood, he must have already perceived something. At the slightest encouragement from the student, Shida had a sudden change of heart and gave herself to him. She could not resist this weakness of hers, no matter what her age.

It was already too late by the time she realized the horror of what she had done. Her oldest daughter left home and, with much ceremony, married a man who worked at the head office of the Miyama school.

The love affair with the student proved to be transitory. Later she even cursed the stroke of fate that led her to stumble into it.

Fuyu, her second daughter, soon reached marital age. This time Shida prudently acted through a go-between.

After having seen what happened to her sister, however, this daughter lost all trust and respect for her mother. In any case, ever since learning the circumstances of her own birth, she had grown up arguing with her mother over all sorts of things. Shida for her part had only bitter feelings at the whole course of events, so she wanted to take care of Fuyu's wedding on her own and do it splendidly. Fuyu's wedding was to be Shida's way of shedding her bitterness once and for all.

With the wedding two months away, Shida went one day to a department store to buy some things she needed for herself. Then the idea of getting something for her daughter's future husband came to her. The store happened to have in stock Japanese formal trousers made of a hard-to-find silk from the Sendai area, so she bought a pair and sent them to him.

The gift signaled Shida's good intentions as a mother, but her daughter completely misunderstood it. She took it to mean that her mother had begun to do the same shameful thing to her that had been done to her sister. Showing no sign of open resistance, the daughter left home without saying a word. She had gotten in touch with both the go-between and her fiancé; only Shida stood isolated, separated from her.

With that, Shida's reputation in society sank completely out of sight. Students began leaving her one by one. Then Haru, her third daughter, ran away from home and turned to the oldest daughter for support. Eventually Haru married a high-school teacher.

Like images in a dream, the events of those mere four or five years appeared and rapidly followed each other to oblivion. Shida's illness developed after her isolation began.

The doctor who first discovered her illness had connections to the dance world, so he used the illness as an excuse to contact the oldest daughter and made every effort to bring about a reconciliation between her and her mother. But, it proved to be useless. Shida's characteristics had been passed down to the daughter without change, and the doctor was simply tossed back and forth between the two headstrong individuals. He could do no more than retreat.

Shida did not know the true nature of her disease, nor did she ever brood deep in her heart over her isolation. With manlike inner strength, she remained calm and told herself, "What will happen will happen." She lay in bed all alone in her once-beautiful house that had a practice studio built of cypress wood.

Wearing pure white *tabi* socks, she used to strike that highly polished floor with one foot, and it would ring out like a fine drum. But now, dust had piled up; even dead leaves lay on it, brought in from the garden by the wind. She had no complaints, however, because she had no regrets. A former student who lived in the neighborhood, now the middle-aged wife of a bookstore owner, came to her house and took care of the morning and evening meals and the opening and closing of the outside shutters for her.

Shida's outward appearance was pitiful, but within herself she had saved up a treasure trove of precious memories from her dazzling, golden past.

When she raised her hand out from under the blanket and gazed at it closely, she remembered times when the delicately shaped hand had achieved a slithering, reptilian effect that had made her dance movements ever more unearthly.

Because of her thinly built body, she excelled in very sad, forlorn dances that tended to abstraction, such as "Sumida River," rather than voluptuous, sensual ones. A person who looked up into her expressionless, madwoman's countenance would imagine a soul frozen through and through with sorrow and bitter grief. Even at such times, however, her body burned with an inner fire. During her life, she often acted like a willful child reaching for the food offering on the household altar. Those actions, too, were dreams that had passed forever. Just as she had lost her reputation, she had lost her daughters. The dishonor had also vanished. Nothing remained. And yet, she felt as if she owned a mountain of treasures. No one saw her off when, with nothing but a few things bundled up in an arabesque-patterned cloth, she was brought to the hospital.

During the next three or four days, Shida's condition worsened. She had violent spasms in which she vomited blood. As before, one hand lay outside the blanket; it hung limply off of the side of the bed. She continued to sleep that way night and day.

That hand, which in her prime had seemed to have its own eery, reptilian existence, now hung down like a lifeless hand crafted out of wood. The fingers dangled separately as if they had been tied onto it one by one.

The woman with the polyp said, "Still, there ought to be someone who'd pay her a visit. I wonder if she doesn't have any other relatives." But there was no one who would reply.

The nurses and the doctors had given up completely on the idea of any assistance from her family. They were now attending only to the disease.

Late one night Shida's pulse became irregular. The doctors and nurses rushed to treat her. After the commotion subsided a bit, the woman with the polyp went to Shida's bedside.

"You must want to see her—your daughter. Shall I call her for you?"

She should not have said it. For the first time, a teardrop, like a pearl, welled up in Shida's dark eyes.

The remains were taken to the hospital's mortuary room, but there was no one to keep the customary all-night vigil. The nurse in charge checked everywhere and finally found two women who said they were former students of Shida's. The two women took the corpse to the crematory.

Translated by Richard Dasher

The Working Woman

Abe Kōbō

More than most contemporary Japanese authors, Abe Kōbō enjoys an international fame that prevails both in socialist countries and in the Free World. Although some critics try to relate the un-Japanese quality of his works to the fact that he grew up in Manchuria, a significant part of it must be attributed to his absorption in modern Western philosophy (especially Nietzsche, Heidegger, and Jaspers) and literature (Dostoevsky, Rilke, and Kafka) during his youth. Equally important, the focus of his studies in post-secondary education was on natural science, most of which had been imported from the West. He began writing poetry and fiction when he was still a medical student at Tokyo University. His early stories were characterized by bold avant-garde techniques and left-wing political implications. Two of them, "The Red Cocoon" (*Akai mayu*, 1949; trans. 1966) and "The Wall—Mr. S. Karuma's Crime" (*Kabe—Esu Karuma-shi no hanzai*, 1951) won him high literary honors, but he did not gain wide public recognition until he wrote *The Woman in the Dunes* (*Suna no onna*, 1962; trans. 1964). Depicting an alienated schoolteacher forced to live with a village woman in a sand pit, the novel shows Abe's narrative art at its best. The alienation of modern man is also the main theme of Abe's subsequent novels, such as *The Face of Another* (*Tanin no kao*, 1964; trans. 1966), *The Ruined Map* (*Moetsukita chizu*, 1967; trans. 1969), and *The Box Man* (*Hako otoko*, 1973; trans. 1974). His other works include allegorical plays such as *Friends* (*Tomodachi*, 1967; trans. 1969) and science fiction such as *Inter Ice Age 4* (*Daiyon kanpyōki*, 1958; trans. 1970). His latest major work is a novel entitled *The Ark, S.S. Cherry* (*Hakobune Sakuramaru*, 1984), which describes a man preparing to escape, not from a flood, but from nuclear fallout, which he knows is approaching.

"Song of a Dead Girl" (*Shinda musume ga utatta*, 1954) is a product of Abe's early period, when he was a young political activist. It deals with the problem of low factory wages, a problem that persisted for many years before Japan's economic recovery in the 1960s. According to a 1954 almanac, the average monthly wage of a worker at a textile factory in March 1953 was 7,975 yen, as compared with 25,982 yen for an employee of a financial institution. An average Japanese household spent 20,544 yen for living expenses that same month.

SONG OF A DEAD GIRL
Shinda musume ga utatta. . .

Abe Kōbō

"Y ou fool, marriage now is out of the question!" said K. When he put it to me that way, I had to agree with him.

"Why didn't you write to me earlier?" K asked angrily. But it was K who had sent absolutely no response to my first letter. I didn't think that I was the one at fault.

Raising his voice, K finally shouted, "I wish you had run away!" This made me cry. K just didn't understand. If I had run away, I would have gotten lost.

"Go ahead and cry," said K, circling around me. "You didn't take care of yourself, so you can't understand my feelings one bit. I'll tell you one thing, though; a dog can't take his own life, but a person can. If you can't understand that much, just keep on whimpering like a dog."

I wondered if I really was whimpering like a dog, which worried me so much, I stopped automatically. After I had stopped crying, I looked up and saw that K had left, and in the place he had been sitting was a small bottle of sleeping pills.

I felt that K had turned into a bottle of sleeping pills and was telling me to go ahead and die. This thought calmed me and suddenly I did want to die. I started by taking ten tablets, but three or four minutes later became terribly frightened and gulped down the rest. Feeling as though I were a post being pounded by a mallet, I fell into a deep sleep.

When I regained consciousness I realized that I had become a spirit and was sitting next to my body.

The room still seemed to be square; everything, though, including my body, seemed to have shrunk slightly in size. I thought I looked rather endearing, with a troubled expression on my face, my left eye slightly open, and my right index finger against my collar. I stroked my face lightly for a while, then suddenly feeling very sad, I began to cry painfully. How I wished that K could hear my crying!

As I cried, I began to feel as if I were being watched. When I looked up, I noticed that there were four or five dead people walking behind me, trying to get out of the room through the open window. There was a student in uniform, a soldier with what seemed to be a piece of beef in place of a jaw, a man who was wearing a bloody shirt and who had lost his legs from the knees down, a skeleton-like tramp, and what appeared to be another soldier with his limbs connected to his body in random fashion, creating an ugly impression indeed. I wondered if these people had always watched my actions in this way. I called out to them before I knew what I was doing. They grew all the more flustered, however, and took off, pushing and shoving one another, without so much as a backward glance.

The realization that death wasn't the end of everything frightened me. Then I saw distant visions of my parents and sisters, with pale faces and empty stomachs, shivering even though it wasn't cold. They were waiting for the money that I was supposed to have sent them.

You are going to pay for your suicide! But it wasn't my fault, was it? I stroked the face of my dead body again. As I did so, the corpse seemed to smile faintly.

I climbed onto the window blind and peeked outside. I felt as though K were waiting for me at the corner. K, of course, wasn't there. Instead I saw cars and bicycles moving so quickly that they seemed to be flying. Not only were the vehicles moving abnormally fast, but people were moving at the speed cars usually traveled at. There were people standing and talking; everything about them had a bouncy quality and each mouth was moving like the lid on a pot of boiling water. I fell into despair. I couldn't escape even when I was alive; now there was absolutely no way to leave the room. I became frightened and ran over to my dead body. I began to feel as though I were in a small boat drifting out to sea.

The metropolis of Tokyo was like an ocean; there were limitless numbers of towns. These people and towns all looked identical, however, giving the impression that no matter how far you walked you remained where you had begun, making no progress at all. Wherever they are in Tokyo, people always lose their way.

That was why I got lost three times upon arriving in Tokyo ten days ago. This happened even though I had been walking according to the map. In looking endlessly for this bridge, I realized that it had houses beneath it rather than a river. After boarding a train, I found it would start to move backwards. At times, a single house would have two addresses. As a result of all the confusion, I succeeded in forgetting all the scenery I had passed by en route.

The incidents that have occurred since I arrived at this store, however, I couldn't forget even if I wanted to. When I first stood before the store, I believed that the true Tokyo could be found behind its doors. The store was quiet, as if it were uninhabited. The surrounding houses glittered, as if they were made of colored glass. The store in front of me was no less beautiful, with its gate surrounded by shining silver and a door painted blue. My chest was pounding, and I could feel tears of joy welling up in my eyes.

The owner of the shop was a tall, pale-faced man with bags under his eyes. He was like an old radio that produced strange sounds between sentences. When I showed him my letter of introduction, he replied, "I understand," in a kindly voice. He wanted me to put my signature seal on an empty sheet of paper. I replied that I didn't own one, whereupon he answered that he had expected as much and produced a seal with my name on it.

"Now you are just like my own child. You have a round red face, therefore your name will be Umeko. So, Umeko, what can you do?"

I answered politely that I could roller skate.

"Isn't it true that all the girls from your factory are rollerskaters?"

"Yes."

"However, we don't need any rollerskaters here. So, what else can you do?"

"I can clean."

"You can clean! Well. . . that's good. Girls who are good at cleaning are honest. They are helpful especially in early spring when the dry wind blows dust all over. Try and make the house as neat and tidy as possible."

"Yes sir."

"For some reason, all of your friends who came before you didn't like cleaning. They were more concerned with buying nice clothes or sending home money. So they all began to take customers. I never really got angry with them though. It was a question of their own free will. I had to let them have this independence of their own because, after listening to their reasons, I couldn't say that I really blamed them. By the way, do you know what I mean by taking customers?"

I looked down without replying.

"Don't you understand?"

I closed my eyes without letting out a single breath of air.

"So, I suppose that you do understand. Good! Even though you realize what it means, you'd like to work as a maid, and you don't want to take customers, right?"

"Yes."

"Very well, you like cleaning, so that is what you shall do. The best thing is always for a person to do what he or she enjoys. You must come from a very rich family."

"No, we are very poor."

"What! Your parents are poor and they are letting you amuse yourself like this? I don't understand it. They must care a great deal for you then, since they're willing to suffer for your happiness. Although they're poor they must not have to worry about where their next meal is coming from."

"No, they do have to worry."

"They do have to worry?! That makes it even more of a mystery to me. If they've been in that sort of money trouble, they must want you to send some money home. Or are they giving up eating to allow their daughter to pursue her own cleaning hobby? If you work as a maid there'll be little chance of your being able to send money home. As soon as I got your reply I sent 10,000 yen. As I promised, your salary is 5,000 yen, from that 2,200 will be deducted for food, 800 for space, 300 for your bed, and, as I couldn't possible allow you in the store with what you are wearing, there would be another 1,000 for clothes. The total comes to 4,300, leaving you only 700 for yourself. If you use that for spending money, then you'll have nothing extra. So what happens to the 10,000 that I lent you? Don't I ever get that back? Even though I know I'll be losing money, how would I. . . but no, I won't discuss that! I'm a man, I can't refuse someone who asks me for a favor. Anyway, I don't understand your reasoning at all. Those girls who take customers send two or three thousand yen home each month. Those girls, however, prefer playing around rather than cleaning. They end up spending their money on movies, games, cosmetics, or saving it up for marriage. Even then, I lend them 3,000 yen and tell them to send it home. I tell them that I can't stand people who forget what they owe their parents, and that they should make more money next month. I hate to think what their futures hold in store, when they get so lazy they can't even send money home! But they end up using all their money the next month again. Even so, I just keep on lending them money. I feel bad if they take customers to send money home and then can't do so. Life is so difficult!"

I started shaking and could hardly stay upright.

"Poor thing, the travelling has gotten to you."

The master took hold of my arm and, as if I were hanging on to him, led me to a small windowless room behind the kitchen.

That night, I considered running away and going back home. I wasn't afraid of the master, but rather of "my own free will." But the city was like an ocean and I would most likely get lost. No matter how much I swam, I wouldn't be able to reach the other shore. In the end, I would probably go under. Even if I did make it to the other shore, it might prove to be just another ocean. The city was ocean, the platforms were ocean, the trains were ocean, the factory was ocean, and probably even my house was ocean.

My father would most likely say, "That's a problem."

My mother would most likely say, "Shame on you!"

My father worked as a laborer and coughed from tuberculosis. But he only had work every four days or so. My mother worked in a textile factory, taking the oldest of my younger sisters with her. Then there were my three other younger sisters and brothers who, pale and swollen, squabbled continually. My father's income was about 2,300 yen per month. My mother and sister made 4,000 yen. That made a total of 6,300 yen. With the 2,000 yen I made from the factory work, that made it 8,300 yen for a family of seven to survive on.

First, we had to have my two brothers drop out of school. Then we started selling the things in our house one by one, but soon there was nothing left to be sold. When at last we had to sell even the sliding doors inside the house, the view was very fine; our house had become as open as an old woman's toothless mouth.

I recalled then what the supervisor had told me as I was leaving for home: if I wanted, he could find me a good job in Tokyo. This had prompted me to write to him. One week later, I received a letter of introduction from the supervisor and a 10,000-yen money order. My mother had bowed to the money order, placed it on the handmade family altar, and sat in front of it for an hour. When my father had reached out to touch the money order, my mother slapped his hand and glared at him. She had then gone running out to show it off to the neighbors. However, I was disappointed, for there was no reply to the letter I had written to K at the same time.

My father would probably ask, "Why couldn't you stick it out?"

My mother would probably ask, "You want to watch your parents die?"

And my sisters would probably look at me with their tired, hungry eyes as if I were something to eat.

The sea had flowed into my room from the city. I drowned myself in it of my own free will.

"But I wasn't the one to blame, was I?!" I continued stroking the face of my dead self.

"Umeko, Umeko," called Yoshiko hurriedly. But I wasn't able to answer.

"Umeko, aren't you in there? I'm coming in." Yoshiko seemed to open the door a crack, but in a flash she disappeared as she ran down the stairs. The master had just started up the stairs at the same moment. He didn't say anything, but spat at random on the floor of the room. He appeared to be quite angry. Then came the doctor, the police officer, and the undertaker. Despite his anger, the master was friendly to everyone, offering beer to all who came. However, once alone he made a frightening face, swore at everyone, and groaned as if he had a fever. "Hell, I won't let any country girl make fun of me. Just wait, I'll get to the truth of this matter. . ."

In spite of that, the master wrote a short note, printed in large letters, to my father and enclosed 50,000 yen. "That bitch!" he said. He slapped his hand down on the letter and took it to the post office himself. I thought that if I were to follow the letter, I would be able to find my way home, so I went along with the master to the post office and parted with him there.

I travelled with the letter the whole way, and arrived home three days later.

My house seemed to have grown even smaller and more insubstantial. Although it was daytime, my jobless father had been in bed. He was so thin that his paper-thin bedding seemed totally flat. His face was covered with wrinkles and if it hadn't been for his breathing I wouldn't have thought he was alive. "Father, I'll be able to meet you soon, won't I?" As I said this, he sighed and rolled over in bed.

Then the registered mail arrived. Without reading the letter, he first looked at the money order and began to shake. Then, as if he were drunk, he went running around the house laughing. After laughing for some thirty minutes, he at last read the letter. This time, still shaking, he fell onto his bed without attempting to rise again.

Around seven, my mother and sister, followed by my brothers, came in—all with blank looks on their faces.

My mother screamed when she saw the letter, but then, laying eyes on the money order, screamed all the louder. She hurriedly stuffed the money order into her belt and, with a desperate laughter, went around slapping my sisters on their heads.

"50,000 yen. . . How many rolls would that be? . . . Count them, Yoshibō . . . how many is it. . . 5,000. . . if we each ate one a day. . . Kimie, divide. . . ? 714. . . 714 days! Two years. Two each would make that one year."

"How about money for my medicine?" my father asked weakly. Mother stopped laughing, and glared sternly him. Coughing, my father said fretfully, "The poor thing, so she died. . . he must have been a hardhearted man. . . only 50,000."

"What, Father, you don't have a penny to your name and you talk so big. . . . Then why don't you go out and make 50,000? Well, go and make it! It's easy to say 'What a pity!' or to show how sorry you are. . . . That master has more real feeling. 50,000 yen is a lot of money. He is much kinder than her real parents. If you're so unhappy, bring 50,000 home sometime! Until you do, get lost! The grief you've put us through."

Mother took out the money order and waved it in the light from the weak bulb. Then she quickly put it away again and went running out of the house.

That night my mother and sister wrote a letter to the shop in Tokyo offering my sister's services as a token of their thanks. Father quietly cleaned his pipe with a twist of paper.

My mother reasoned that the sooner my sister left the better, so my sister prepared to leave the next morning. For the first time in a very long time, a good meal was set out before the family. The soup actually had some substance to it and there was enough for everyone. With a small bundle placed beside her, my little sister looked uneasy. She seemed about to burst out crying at any minute.

"Don't go!" I cried out, standing in front of her with my arms spread out. My sister, however, walked right through me as if I were nothing but air.

I wanted to recall where it was we had all started going under; and, upon reflection, it seemed to have started at the factory. I suddenly wanted to visit that factory.

It was night when I got there. The factory was at the bottom of a slope, and looked like a man curled up in a deep sleep. Even without getting an admission stamp, I was able to walk through the entrance gate. When I went to my dorm room all my former roommates were sound asleep. They were sleeping in such confined conditions that there was almost no space between the bodies. I lay down on top of them.

Someone whispered in my ear. It was Tanaka who had died of tuberculosis. "Yotchan, Mitchan, Kanae, Natchan—everyone is here!" said Tanaka. I was relieved.

In our room hung a loudspeaker as large as those used in sporting events. It started up at exactly four in the morning. It was a kind of music I had never heard anywhere else, so awful that no matter how tired or sleepy you were, you couldn't help waking up. It was entitled "Zoo," and people said it was something that the labor chief brought back from an exhibition in Tokyo.

Dawn finally came.

The "Zoo" started to play.

My chest started to pound. Sliding along the pitch-black hallway, everyone tried to be the first one out. They fumbled in the dark, struggling to get their roller skates on. Then they ran down a concrete road and lined up in front of the work place. The ten that got there first received soup tickets. I never was able to make it.

The spindles had 8000 revolutions. I pretended to thread while running back and forth between ten threaders. I felt as though I were whirling about on roller skates myself, but after a while my back began to hurt. There were indeed some who circled around too fast, colliding with the machines and hurting their hands.

At eight o'clock, the people in charge of our meals brought our boxed food for us to pass around and eat in turns. As usual, our supervisor timed us with a stop watch as we ate. The supervisor would always be carrying a stop watch, measuring even the time it took us to go to the bathroom, so he was thus given the nickname "Watch." The worst part was his timing how long we spent going to the toilet. If someone spent more than 28 seconds, he would say before everyone, "What a small hole you've got!" For that reason, we rushed as much as possible.

At two, our work was finished. We were soaked with sweat. Red-faced and breathing heavily we lined up and returned to where we lived. When, after reaching reached the entrance to our dorms, we took off our roller skates and placed one foot on the floor, the loudspeaker went off.

"Polish the halls, the mirror of your souls."

Then we had to bend over and, without touching our knees to the floor, proceed to the cafeteria while polishing the floors with waxing rags. This was stupid, so I stood up and watched. At the entrance, we were given a large plate with rice, and a small plate with boiled vegetables and a tiny bit of cuttlefish. We then walked to our seats. Those of us who were dead mingled right in with the living. When we reached our seats, Watch opened the doors of the alter, rang the bell, and said loudly, "Thank you for letting us save money while we work, and study while we work." After Watch had said this, we all repeated it in unison. It was still not time to eat, though. Watch had to write the menu for the day up on the blackboard.

TODAY'S MENU
   0.126 liters of rice
   0.11 liters of wheat
   50 grams of spinach in sesame oil
   8 grams of dried cuttlefish in soy sauce
   140 grams of sardine
TOTAL
   820 calories
   50 grams of protein

The above is 220% more nutritious than the average fare at other factories. . . .

Watch then turned to us and said, "Now, everyone, even though it says on your menu that you are being served sardines, you will find no sardines on your plate. Now, to you it may look as if there are no sardines on your plate, but there really are! That's because today we have a guest who is very important to our company. This guest is eating your sardines for you! For the guest to eat your sardines is the same as your eating the sardines. So, the sardines are there. You understand, don't you? So, then, Father and Mother, we thank you very much!"

"Father and Mother, we thank you very much!"

Watch started his stopwatch. Each of us who finished eating said, "Thank you for the food." Even the slowest finished in two and a half minutes.

While I pretended to be eating, I was thinking: Guests, guests and more guests! What kind of a guest would eat eighty persons' worth of sardines? Even if he took only two minutes per sardine, that would take about 150 minutes. I doubted that even a fisherman had ever eaten 80 sardines at one sitting. That guest must be a very fat person. . . .

Once the aluminum plates were returned and everyone had lined up in the hall, the loudspeaker went off in a sing-song tone: "It's class time! Laziness is the seed of sorrow! Polish your personality! Proof rather than words!" School then began immediately, but everything was exactly the same. Even though it was school, all it meant was that the dorm became a school. In the first hour we had home economics; everyone had to do their laundry. The speaker went on: "Wash it away, the dirt of your character! Be especially careful with the company hats."

The first half of the second hour was for cooking; we had to wash dishes and cut up the dinner vegetables. The last half was sewing; we had to mend our bedding.

The third period was moral education; we had to clean our rooms, toilet, and the bath. During this time the speaker announced a great number of maxims.

"Above all, perseverance. He who touches pitch shall be defiled therewith. Show respect toward your elders. The fast way up. Honesty first and honesty second. Blessed are those who smile."

The fourth period was physical education and we had to rollerskate in time to some music.

After dinner there was a free period. When I was alive, this was the time I always went to see K.

K was a movie technician at Kinema Theater and was the young man that I liked most. He had kept his hair short, was long-faced, wore thick glasses, and hardly ever smiled. He was the masculine type. He had let me watch movies for free, and because everyone longed for a white-collar boyfriend, they were all envious of me.

The bell rang and the speaker started up. "Everyone, this is your free time. Write to your parents back home. Calculate how much money you have saved. Read books and magazines to increase your cultural level. It's best not to go out, but those who do go out don't waste any money. Don't talk to outsiders. Temptation has you in its sights."

That day, having received a pass from Watch, I was on my way to meet K and had stopped to be searched by the guard. The loudspeaker was saying "Those who are late after watching a movie will be fined. For those who return 10 minutes later than eight o'clock, 20 yen; 20 minutes late, 30 yen; 30 minutes late, 50 yen." Then all at once, the loudspeaker changed its tone and began calling, "Miss M, Miss M, the factory manager wants to see you!" Prevented from leaving, I thought to myself, "My turn has finally come!" That month, there had been one person called up every day in this manner. Almost all were let go, vanishing without even returning to their rooms.

Disappointed, I turned back and found Watch waiting for me at the dorm entrance. He told me to hurry it up, and pushed me into the office. The factory manager was talking to a guest. The guest was a skinny young man wearing a fine suit of clothes. He was reading from a thick register, while the manager stood in front of him smiling. When the manager saw me, he continued to smile and with his chin gestured toward a chair in the corner. To the guest he said, "Well, the car has arrived and the president must be waiting."

The manager laid his hand on the guest's shoulder and went out with him. He didn't return for quite some time. Watch and I waited for some thirty minutes, and during that time Watch said, "That guest was from the bank. Banks are really something. For one thing, bankers' clothes are different. They look just like people from Tokyo. M, have you ever been to Tokyo?"

"No, I haven't."

"You haven't. . . . Yes, I can tell. You know at a glance a person who has washed his face with Tokyo water. Ha, ha! Would you like to go to Tokyo?"

"Yes, I'd like to, but I'm afraid of the delinquents."

"Delinquents? . . . Yes, you must watch out for them. But someone as dependable as yourself needn't worry; I'll guarantee that. I'm positive about it."

At that moment the factory manager walked in. As soon as he saw me, the expression on his face grew severe.

"Problems, problems! Thanks to overproduction, the price of our products keeps going down. The banks give excuses and won't lend us the money. At this rate, the company will go bankrupt!" He took a puff from his cigarette and spat, puffed and spat once again. After looking at me for a while, he said, "Are you wearing lipstick again, after you've been warned against it so many times?"

"I'm not wearing any."

"You're lying! Let's see," he said, and took out a piece of paper. "Wipe your lips with this!"

I rubbed my lips with the paper he gave me and handed it back to him. The manager held it up against the light to inspect it, but he found no lipstick.

"Why," he asked in a more natural tone of voice, "did you take money out of your savings?"

"My father got tuberculosis."

"Well, you seem to have bought some expensive shoes lately. Where did that money come from?"

"They're cheap shoes, and I got them as a gift."

"They were a gift? From whom? A guy, right? Well, is that something you should have done? Do you have your father's permission?" The manager spat. "No? Well, what's this all about? And your father's sick! What if something bad happens to you. How will I apologize to your parents? You're a real problem child! I just don't know what to do with you." He spat twice. "I hear that you talk too much at the committee meetings."

"I'm sorry sir."

"Since you've apologized like that, there is really nothing else for me to say. Ha, ha! I know very well that you are a tenderhearted girl. The reason I had you come here today wasn't to scold you. I know you're sweet, so I thought you would understand me and be on our side." The manager spat again.

And so, I was forced to sign my resignation papers. When I came out, Watch said smilingly, "That's great! Now you'll be able to look for work without worrying about anyone else—in Tokyo, for instance. You can get a job as a maid, learn home economics, send a lot of money back home, and get ready for marriage. Ha, ha! Looking back on it, factory work will seem foolish. Up until now you were in debt to the manager, so I didn't want to say this, but you're free now! Don't worry, just drop me a line. I'll take care of you anytime. Ha, ha! I'm the type that likes to take care of people. I really enjoy seeing the girls from the dorm, those I was in charge of, get ahead in the world."

You fool! You're the one who pushed me under!

I went over to Kinema Theater with the other girls. K had already left, but I was one of the dead so I wasn't able to ask where he had gone to. I sat in the midst of the crowd and watched the movie. There were twice as many dead as there were living, which made the theater overcrowded. If they were all to come alive again, I thought, the theater could really make a lot of money.

When I got back to the dorm, Hanae, who had worked in the factory four years, was sobbing. Tanaka said, "As usual, they're laying people off. They're planning to keep it up until the end of the month."

Oh, if only we were alive again! As this thought entered my mind, I suddenly felt like running around. When I started running, Yotchan, Mitchan, Kanae-chan, Natchan, and other dead workers I didn't even know came running along behind me.

There were twenty-two dead. We went bounding around the factory. We joined hands in a circle around the scary guard, all of us dancing and singing about him as he dozed. In the manager's room, we took turns leaping over the hat that the manager had left behind on his desk. We played around like this until morning. Maybe in her dream, Hanae could hear our voices.

Translated by Stuart A. Harrington

Ariyoshi Sawako

When Ariyoshi Sawako (1931–84) suddenly died in her sleep, Japan lost one of its most successful writers who combined literature with social criticism. Her bestselling novel *The Twilight Years* (*Kōkotsu no hito*, 1972; trans. 1984) had done a great deal to call public attention to the plight of senior citizens, and *Compound Pollution* (*Fukugō osen*, 1975), which had been serialized in a large daily newspaper, had aided the cause of environmentalists in a way nothing else could have. She also wrote novels on missile testing, on racial discrimination in the United States, and on many other social problems. Although her stories often lacked a tightly constructed plot, they seldom failed to convey the passion and intensity with which she took her stand on a given issue. And her stand was less political or ideological than humanitarian, a stand that appealed to a large segment of contemporary society.

Ariyoshi was a different type of writer when she made her literary debut in the mid-1950s, shortly after graduating from Tokyo Women's College. Her early stories, such as "Ballad" (*Jiuta*, 1956; trans. 1975) and "The Ink Stick" (*Sumi*, 1961; trans. 1975), depicted traditional Japanese artists struggling to survive in the rapidly changing modern society. Young Ariyoshi had a romantic longing for old Japan, partly because she had spent four years of her childhood in Java and learned about her own country through books. With the passage of time, however, her main interest shifted from traditional Japanese arts to traditional Japanese women, and she authored a series of novels on the latter subject. Best known among them are *The River Ki* (*Ki no kawa*, 1959; trans. 1979), which chronicles three generations of women from an illustrious rural family, and *The Doctor's Wife* (*Hanaoka Seishū no tsuma*, 1966; trans. 1978), which traces the life of an eighteenth-century woman who married the first Japanese physician trained in Western-type surgery. There is only a short distance from the study of women's problems to the study of social problems in general, and it did not take long for Ariyoshi to move from the former to the latter.

"The Tomoshibi" (*Tomoshibi*, 1961) is a story that comes from Ariyoshi's early period, but it includes many of the elements that constitute her later, more famous works. It is so titled because the setting is a Tokyo bar named The Tomoshibi (literally meaning "light"), the name suggesting something of the bar, its proprietress, and perhaps the author's concept of literature.

THE TOMOSHIBI
Tomoshibi

Ariyoshi Sawako

It was almost incredible that a small, quiet bar like The Tomoshibi should exist in the Ginza. Although it was located on an alley branching off a back street of Higashi Ginza, a noisy place where bars stood side by side in a row, it was still part of the Ginza. To the right, there was a large coffee shop, and to the left there was a well-known men's clothing store. The three shops across the street—a restaurant, a coffee shop, and an accessories store—were famous, and so, this one corner overflowed, with a true Ginza-like atmosphere, almost as if it were on the main street itself.

However, The Tomoshibi was inconspicuous in all respects. It was only natural that it wasn't noticeable during the day, since the bar opened at five in the afternoon; but in any case, since the frontage was narrow—only about six feet wide—it was overwhelmed by the imposing appearance of the neighboring stores on both sides. It didn't seem likely that there would be such a bar in a place like this.

There was a small lantern placed outside, above the door, and on this "The Tomoshibi" was written in quaint lettering. In the evening, even when it became both in name and in reality a *tomoshibi*, it did not shine very boldly.

When the night grew late and all the neighbors had closed shop, the street became silent. Even people looking for a place to drink would go right past it, not noticing that the street even had a bar.

The fact was, then, that the patrons of The Tomoshibi were an exceedingly limited group of regular customers. However, The Tomoshibi hadn't many of what one usually thinks of as "regular customers," the

241

type of people who gather together out of affection for the proprietress and barmaids.

There were few customers who came to The Tomoshibi every night; neither were there many stray customers who wandered in. Nevertheless, the bar was always filled to capacity, and although the popularity of the proprietress, who was called "Mama-san," might have helped a little, the patrons and the barmaids all knew the exact reason why.

It is true that the bar was small. In a space of about ninety square feet, there was a cramped restroom, a large refrigerator, a tiny counter behind which Mama-san and one barmaid could stand, and just enough chairs and tables for the other barmaid to entertain customers. Even with only the three of them, when none of the customers had showed up yet, a dry wind did not blow in the bar. Thus anyone who casually entered The Tomoshibi alone would be enveloped by a warm atmosphere, and immediately feel at home.

Here, no one felt like chasing away the blues by noisily badmouthing their superiors while under the influence; nor were there any customers who told vulgar jokes to first get into a state of mind sufficiently disillusioned to bring on a quick drunk.

"Hello there!" Mama-san greeted a customer who hadn't come for several months. Speaking as if he had come the day before yesterday, the customer asked, "It's been a while since I've seen the girl who used to work here—what's happened to her?"

"She got married," Mama-san replied quietly.

"Hmm, got married, huh?" The customer spoke as if he were surprised and impressed, and he looked around the bar once again.

"I see. . . . I guess if she were from this bar, a barmaid could really get married decently." As if he were quite convinced, he sipped his whiskey-on-the-rocks and sighed.

Mama-san and a barmaid known as Shizu-chan, who were seated quietly on chairs away from the counter, exchanged furtive smiles.

The girl, Eiko, who had been helping Mama-san behind the counter, had committed suicide about three weeks ago.

Any girl who decides to come to work in a bar has her own complex reasons. And, while she works, her life usually becomes even more complicated. Although she had found employment in a quiet bar like this, Eiko probably suffered from more hardships than the average person. It had looked as if she was confiding everything to Mama-san, and had been seeking her advice. Yet there was probably something she had not been able to confide, and maybe that had become unbearable. One night, she took some pills and died. Since she was a quiet girl, perfectly suited for The Tomoshibi, there had not been anything out of the ordinary in her conduct, and even the worldly-wise Mama-san had not noticed anything.

Since it was a whole day before the suicide was discovered, nothing could be done. There was no will, and her humble one-room apartment was left neatly in order. There was a savings passbook left for her younger brother, her only blood relative, but it certainly did not contain an extraordinary sum of money. That a young, nameless barmaid had died one night was such a small happening that it wouldn't even be mentioned in an obscure corner of a newspaper.

That is why Mama-san did not want to do anything that would cast a shadow on the memories of the customers who remembered Eiko.

"Is that so? She got married? Hmmm. . . ." The customer, perhaps because the alcohol had begun to take its effect, re-articulated his initial surprise, but Mama-san only commented gently, "Quite so, she got married."

"What kind of guy was he? Was he a customer here?"

"There's no use in being jealous. It's already too late." When Mama-san laughed in her sweet voice, the customer also gave a forced laugh, and at that point they ended the conversation.

"Another drink, please."

"Coming! Coming! Isn't it cold today?"

Although there were peanuts and smoked squid on the narrow counter, with the second glass of whiskey Mama-san provided some fresh cucumber with a dash of lemon, free of charge. The customer picked up a slice with his fingers, and while eating with a crunching sound, asked, "Did you choose all those paintings by yourself?" He was examining the inside of the bar again.

"Yes, but they're all reproductions!"

Several framed pictures, none of them any larger than fifteen square inches, were hung on the wall. Among these, two were Chagalls, one was a Miró, one was an oil painting by Takayama Uichi, and one was a woodblock print by Minami Keiko.

Those by Takayama and the Minami were originals, and those by

Chagall and Miró were lithographs, but Mama-san always said that they were replicas and didn't care to elaborate further.

Mama-san had bought them only because they were pictures that she had liked, and not because they were the works of famous artists. But if some customers didn't like the pictures, that was that, no matter what she said.

A picture in which lovers embraced on the roof of a small house in the moonlight. And a sweet, dream-like picture of a young girl singing, enveloped by a bird of fire. Next to the two Chagalls hung a surrealistic picture, with bright colors like a child's scribbles. It was the Miró. This was Mama-san's greatest pride, for she had thrown caution to the winds and bought it, although it was extremely expensive. Yet since the customers who came to the bar could barely appreciate the Chagalls, the Miró seemed even more incomprehensible to them.

However, when one looked at all of them, including the Takayama painting of greenery and butterflies, and the Minami woodblock print of autumn leaves and fish, even the Miró became part of a coherent whole which created a fairy tale-like, innocent, and happy atmosphere throughout the bar. Perhaps it was because of this atmosphere that customers were convinced that barmaids from this bar could become brides after all.

"Last night I had such a beautiful dream."

All of a sudden, Shizu-chan started to speak. Since it was a small bar, whatever anyone said could be overheard by everyone else, so there was no need to turn their heads. The good thing about this bar was the fact that both Mama-san and Shizu-chan had beautiful voices. Some customers said flatly that it was better just to listen to their voices when they started to speak, rather than to look at their faces.

"What kind of dream?" Mama-san responded in a leisurely tone.

"In my dream, I met a boy whom I had been extremely fond of when I was small."

"How incriminating!"

Because Shizu-chan had started to tell her story in such a passionate manner, one of the customers tried to tease her, but Mama-san waited patiently for her next words.

"This boy was the village headman's son. Since we were the children of tenant farmers, in spite of being in the same class at school, we didn't dare go near him. Even so, all the girls liked the young master. When he came close, I could hardly breathe!"

"It must have been your first love!"

"Yes, I guess it was. But it's been over ten years since I left the village. I've never had such a dream in all these years, so I wonder why I should have one now. Last night's dream just came out of the blue. It really surprised me!"

"Was the young master a child? Or had he grown up?"

"I'm not too sure. I'm not even sure whether I was a child or whether I was like I am now. . . ."

"Isn't that nice!"

"In any case, it was incredibly beautiful. There were birds of fire flying around us."

The Chagall painting had apparently made its way into Shizu-chan's dream. Yet while she was talking, she seemed to enter a dreamy state of mind once again. Even after she had finished talking, she remained staring into space as if entranced.

"I'll go home after one more drink. I think I'll go to sleep early tonight and dream of my first love, too."

Customers would be engulfed by the mood of the bar before they knew it. Shizu-chan was skillful at telling her life story in this fragmentary way, under the pretense of relating, for example, a story about her dreams. Since she differed from the many barmaids who allure customers by going over their sad life stories in great detail, from childhood to more recent hardships, there were quite a number of customers who came to the bar wanting to talk to her.

"And so, Shizu-chan, you haven't returned home ever since you came out to Tokyo?"

"No, even though my father and mother are there, and they've been asking me to come home soon."

"Don't you like the countryside?"

"That's not the point. There are many reasons why I have to stay in Tokyo."

"Is some man giving you a hard time, then?"

"No man would ever give me a hard time!"

Although she was replying seriously, it still sounded so funny that the customers would unexpectedly burst out laughing. It was probably because of Shizu-chan's natural virtue that nobody would think of teasing her by saying, "Would you like me to give you a hard time?"

Only Mama-san knew that Shizu-chan's parents had died when she was still a child, and that she was having a rough time of it at her aunt's, into whose family she had been adopted. When Shizu-chan said her parents were awaiting her return, only Mama-san sensed the truth behind the lie.

In the back streets of the Ginza, drunken men would usually spend their time speaking loudly and amorously of women, and drunken women would speak similarly of men. Yet in this bar, even if conversations of that type did get started, they never lasted very long. Strangely enough, though, conversations about pet dogs or cats would continue on and on endlessly.

There was a Siamese cat at The Tomoshibi. It was Mama-san's pet, and every day she carried it with her to work. It had a light gray, slender body, and its legs and the tip of its tail were dark sepia. Since it had a straight, shapely nose, Mama-san believed that it was a beautiful cat.

"Don't be ridiculous! Don't you know that the flatter a cat's nose is, the more attractive it's supposed to be?"

"Impossible! Cats or human beings, it's the same. The higher the nose is, the better."

"You're wrong!"

"Well then, please look carefully. Use your aesthetic sense to judge this. Here. . . ."

Mama-san picked up her beloved cat and thrust it out in front of the customer's nose.

"I still think it's funny. . . ."

If the customer should persist in this manner, things would get serious. In high spirits, Mama-san would refill the glass of whiskey and say, "Here, pull yourself together with this, and look carefully once again. Here Chika, Chika, make a nice face. . . ."

One might wonder whether the customer or Mama-san would be the first to give in, but it was the always the cat in question who, hating to stay still, got bored with trying to outstare the customer, yawned out loud, scratched Mama-san's hand, and jumped down. The area on top of the window above the heater was Chika's seat, and once she retreated there, she would not come out, no matter how one called or invited her.

"Mama-san, don't you like dogs?"

"I like them, but you can't keep a dog in a bar."

"I really like dogs. Even when I get home late after drinking, I always wake up at seven in the morning, since I have to take Hachirō out for a walk."

"Is his name Hachirō? How cute!"

"Is it an Akita?" Shizu-chan interrupted.

"How did you know?" the customer asked in surprise.

"Oh, it's just a lucky guess. I thought a name like Hachirō might be quite appropriate for an Akita."

With this boost to his spirits, the customer drew out a billfold from the inside pocket of his suit and, produced a photograph from it.

He was a customer who perfectly matched the proprietress and barmaids. The snapshot was of his dog.

"See, look, isn't he a handsome one?"

His eyes and mouth were certainly those of an Akita, but the line between the ears and the neck was rather questionable. Yet even so, Mama-san was charmed by the eyes and mouth and said, "How adorable! He looks like a fine, lively dog."

Her manner of praise was clever, but young Shizu-chan, who was peering over from the side, was too honest.

"Hmm, is this really an Akita?" she questioned in a loud voice.

"It's an Akita, all right. This dog's father, you know, has quite a pedigree."

"What about the mother?"

"Well, you see. . . ." he said regretfully, drinking up the remaining whiskey. "It's a case of 'a woman of humble birth marrying into royalty.' "

In other words, Hachirō was a mutt. However, if lineage were to be determined patrilineally, as in the imperial family, then without doubt he would be a descendent of the noble Akita breed.

Being quick with her wits, Mama-san said, "They were quite gallant parents, weren't they?" and saved the customer from his predicament.

With this, the customer regained his balance. Ordering a double-on-the-rocks, he began to speak in great detail of how Hachirō was such a fine dog that he didn't bring disgrace to his father's name.

Birds of a feather flock together, and that night as many as four dog-lovers had gathered there. Since each of them had to introduce the pedigree, name, personality, and distinguishing features of his pet, The Tomoshibi didn't close until quite late.

"Since it's late, Shizu-chan, I'll take you home," Mama-san said to Shizu-chan, who was waiting with her collar pulled up. Mama-san locked the door and stopped a taxi.

"Please take us first to Higashi Nakano, then Shibuya." No matter how tiring a night she might have had, her manner of speaking was always kind.

As the car along through the night streets, Shizu-chan started to giggle about something she remembered.

"What is it?"

"Oh, I was just thinking of the dog contest we had."

"Wasn't it funny—everyone thought his own was the best."

"But they were all mongrels!"

"That's why we didn't get into a fight."

Mama-san was smiling serenely, the purebred Siamese cat fast asleep on her lap. It was a conceited cat with a picky appetite. None of the customers who boasted about their half-breed dogs dared to show their antipathy towards Chika, because she was protected by Mama-san's goodness.

"You know, Shizu-chan. . . ."

"Yes?"

"If these late nights continue, we'll surely need a replacement for Eiko."

"I think so, too."

"Unless we find someone who will take turns with you working late, you'll get too tired. Do you know of anyone who would be good?"

"Well, I don't have too many friends, so. . . ."

After a while, Mama-san, looking out of the window, murmured, "What a fool Eiko was to die!"

Almost ready to cry herself, Shizu-chan said hurriedly to the taxi driver, "Oh, please stop here. That corner will be fine. Yes, right here."

Although Mama-san had taken her home on several occasions in the past, Shizu-chan would always get off by the main road and avoid being taken by car to the front of her house. Since there must have been some reason, Mama-san didn't insist on accompanying her any farther. She would quietly see Shizu-chan off, turning around in the taxi which had started to move, and would watch her figure disappear into the darkness. Small dirty houses stood clustered, side by side.

"Position for barmaid. A young person, with or without experience. The Tomoshibi."

Mama-san wrote this with a brush on a small piece of paper. For three days her routine was to put up the sign at night when leaving, and take it down before eight in the evening when the customers came. Three or four applicants came knocking at the door, despite the fact that it was such a tiny advertisement and for such an inconspicuous bar.

During the hours before her customers came, Mama-san held "interviews" in the bar, and when there were customers, in the coffee shop next door.

One girl was so young she seemed like a firm plum still attached to a branch. It appeared that she had come to the accessories store across the street and read the advertisement by chance. Her family was apparently well-off, and she had been casually thinking that she wanted to work. Mama-san shuddered at her naive boldness.

"When you discuss this matter with your parents, please make sure that you tell them I said this is not the sort of place you should be coming to."

"Oh, then there's no use in discussing it with them. Am I unqualified?"

In the eyes that asked "Am I unqualified?" shone fearless, youthful, as yet unblemished pride. Hoping that this child would be able to grow up just as she was, Mama-san gently smiled and nodded.

"Yes, you're unqualified."

"Oh, shucks!"

Since she stuck her tongue out and left without seeming too disappointed, Mama-san felt greatly relieved.

On another occasion, a sickly, tired woman came by.

"Why did you quit the other bar?"

"The proprietress scolded me too often. About not being lively and boisterous. She complained a lot, but how could I help it? After all, that's my nature!"

"That's true."

"But I have my own good customers. That's why the proprietress didn't want to let me go, but I don't like working under someone I have personality conflicts with."

Realizing quite clearly that she wouldn't get along with her either, Mama-san smiled and stood up.

"As you can see, our bar is rather small, isn't it? We don't need any more customers than we already have. If fate so ordains, I'll see you again."

It seemed as if the many layers of grime from the woman's harsh daily life were smeared across her coarse skin. Wishing she had the confidence to try and wash away this person's unhappiness at The Tomoshibi, Mama-san was sad that she couldn't hire her.

However, even if Mama-san invited this person to come and work at the bar, sooner or later she would leave of her own accord.

Mama-san had always hired the type of barmaids who would stay only at The Tomoshibi.

"Good evening!" a voice called cheerfully.

A figure dressed in bright colors entered the door, and the bar became crowded at once. It was the madam of one of the five largest bars in the Ginza.

"My, I haven't seen you for such a long time!"

Mama-san, in her usual manner, invited her in warmly. Mama-san's smile never changed according to whom she was talking. Some ten years ago, Madam and Mama-san had worked in the same bar. They both became independent in the same Ginza area around the same time. However, Madam had been quite a businesswoman. Therefore, after moving from place to place, her bar and her name had become so noted that any person who dealt with the Ginza could not have failed to hear of them.

"This bar hasn't changed at all!"

"I guess it's been two years since you last came."

"How I envy you! I suppose if you don't have to make alterations in the interior of your bar for two whole years, you don't have to spend much money. As for my place, since the customers are so demanding, we frequently have to change the wall hangings and the paintings. . . ."

It was probably because Madam had some good qualities that her constant complaining about her financial situation, as well as her total envy of this small bar, were not intolerably offensive. Drinkers are very honest with themselves, so unless the proprietress is somewhat good-natured, customers won't be attracted to the bar.

"I have something to talk with you about." Madam said suddenly in a low voice, pulling Mama-san out to the coffee shop next door.

"Don't you have an opening at your place?"

"Well, I am looking for someone right now, but there aren't very many people who would come to work at a bar like ours."

Madam took Mama-san's modesty seriously, and after firmly nodding, leaned forward.

"I know of a nice girl. . . . Will you take a look at her?"

"But isn't she one of the girls at your place?"

"That's true, but she won't last there. She's just too nice. I don't know what to do, because whenever a customer teases her even a little bit, she starts to cry. I tell her over and over again that unless you strike back when you're teased you can't survive in the Ginza, but it's completely useless. The girls at my place are always being offered positions at rival bars whenever I'm not paying close attention, except for that one. She's fairly popular with the customers, but she still has an inferiority complex. Touch upon that complex and she gets depressed. I just haven't any idea what to do!"

"What kind of inferiority complex?" Mama-san attempted to pursue the matter further, but Madam waved her hands dramatically and ignored the question.

"Well, in any case I'll tell her to stop by and see you after work, so take a look at her. She's the perfect girl for your place. It would be easy for me to fire her, but she's such a nice girl that I don't have the heart to kick her out. Do it for me, all right?"

Madam pulled out a one-thousand yen bill and picked up the check from the table in one swift move. Having finished her business, she hastily paid for the coffee and left.

Forced to accept the proposition, Mama-san returned to the bar. She didn't feel so badly after she remembered that Madam always behaved in the same way.

Since the two bars belonged to such different categories, they were not in competition with each other, and even if Madam tried to pass off a secondhand article that was of no use at her place, Mama-san would not be offended. On the contrary, she rather enjoyed going over in her mind what Madam had said, "She's such a nice girl that she can't work at my bar." That she was such a nice girl she was not even appropriate for the very best bar in the Ginza district certainly pleased Mama-san.

Therefore, when the night grew late and Momoko appeared—quietly opening the door and inquiring, "May I come in?"—Mama-san said almost by reflex, "Oh, I've heard all about you. Everything's all set. Please start working here from five tomorrow evening."

Shizu-chan seemed to take in Momoko's round face and lovely lips immediately, as well as the fact that her dark blue overcoat was very becoming.

Just before leaving for home, Shizu-chan asked nonchalantly, "Is the person who came by a little while ago working with us from tomorrow?" But Mama-san, who was busy getting ready to close up and go home, answered without going into great detail, "Yes, I'll introduce her to you tomorrow."

Mama-san was rather noisily occupied in the restroom.

"Shizu-chan."

"Yes?"

"It's quite late, so you can go home first."

"Are you sure it's all right?"

Shizu-chan wondered what Mama-san could be up to, but anxious to head for home just as soon as she could, she left straight away.

The next day, having been delayed by collecting bills, Shizu-chan arrived at the bar a little later than usual and found Mama-san cleaning here and there inside the bar with the new girl.

"Good morning!"

"Oh, good morning! This is Shizu-chan, and this is Momoko-chan."

Mama-san introduced them in an intimate manner, as if she were bringing together two of her children. Momoko bowed humbly, and Shizu-chan felt slightly embarrassed. Deep inside, she had received quite a shock.

Dimly aware of the fact that Madam, who was an old friend of Mama-san, had spoken to Mama-san about this matter, Shizu-chan had been worried about what kind of person was going to come. Yet unlike last night's impression of her, the minute she looked at Shizu-chan today, Shizu-chan was taken aback.

She's cross-eyed, Shizu-chan realized at once. To use a Japanese expression, her eyes were "London-Paris"—her right eye was focused on London, while her left eye looked towards Paris. Furthermore, one of her eyes was a bit too close to the other. Besides these, there were no other faults in her appearance.

When Momoko went to the restroom, and there were still no customers, Shizu-chan found her chance to speak. "Mama-san," she began.

Mama-san, in a low, yet sharp voice, said firmly, "Shizu-chan, the subject of her eyes is taboo." Since Shizu-chan was also a nice girl, she accepted this immediately. Something deep within moved her to tears.

Perhaps because there was one more person in the bar than before, thus making it more lively, many customers turned up that night. The regular customers quickly took notice of Momoko. But since, unlike Eiko, she stood further behind the counter than Mama-san and was occupied with diligently opening and closing the refrigerator door, they couldn't talk to her very much.

Very few customers came to this bar simply for the barmaids, however, so no one was very dissatisfied with her behavior. The Tomoshibi remained completely the same as it had been. The customers quietly sipped their drinks, and when once in a while they did say something, Mama-san would take up the conversation, with Shizu-chan in her carefree and easy-going manner joining in.

One customer did find something different from before. This man, who had been chugging his beer, returned from the restroom with a strange expression on his face and asked, "What happened to the mirror?"

"Oh, someone broke it," answered Mama-san.

"You must have had some rough customers!"

"We can get a new mirror, but it might be broken again. Besides, we really ought to be able to put up with the inconvenience."

Probably only Shizu-chan noticed that Mama-san, upon realizing the source of Momoko's inferiority complex, had taken her in only after removing the mirror from the restroom.

"Anyway, our customers aren't the type that have to feel guilty when they look at their drunken faces in the mirror," Mama-san said in her mellow voice.

"Right! That's right!"

This cheered the customers; there was no chance of them being put out by it. Although the type of customer who got drunk and became boisterous rarely came to The Tomoshibi, there were, among the regular customers, there were some young men who liked to sing quiet songs. However, once they started to get tipsy, they demanded that Mama-san and the girls sing, too. Mama-san would say, "No, I can't because I'm tone-deaf," and escape, refusing to sing under any circumstances. If one flattered Shizu-chan, though, telling her that she was good, she would sing a number of songs in her melodious voice. Since she made every popular song come out like an elementary school tune, her specialty had become nursery songs. Everyone was impressed by her specialty. Her singing was popular probably because it was most appropriate for the atmosphere of the bar. She could certainly not have been called very talented.

"Mama-san, wasn't Eiko-chan pretty good, too? Wasn't she?" With his eyes half closed as if trying to remember, a customer asked, "Didn't she go away to get married? Is she happy?"

"Yes, yes, she's very happy."

Shizu-chan began to sing:

> When she was fifteen Nanny got married
> Letters from home
> No longer came.

"In this present age, what do you think we lack the most and need the most?"

In one corner of the room there were customers discussing serious topics while drinking their whiskey.

"Hmmm, let's see, . . . how about dreams? As far as I'm concerned, right now that's what I lack the most and need the most."

"Well, I agree, but I don't call them 'dreams'."

"Then what are they?"

"Fairy tales."

"Hmm, fairy tales. I guess you're right."

While that conversation was going on, Shizu-chan was singing away in front of customers in another corner.

"Well, what do you think about being able to listen to nursery rhymes in a Ginza bar?"

"Now I'm beginning to understand why you said you wanted to come here."

Sometimes a dreadfully tone-deaf person in high spirits would sing along with Shizu-chan.

After four or five days, Momoko was in a state of total astonishment. She wondered if this, too, could possibly be a bar.

Some types of people aren't affected by hardships; Momoko was the type who wasn't affected by past experiences. Even though this was the fourth time she had found herself employed in a bar, she possessed naive qualities which made it seem as if she had only worked in a bar for the first time yesterday. Shizu-chan began to act as if she were Momoko's elder sister all the time, and on occasions when Mama-san wasn't present, she would ask, "Well, do you think you'll be able to handle working here?" and peer into Momoko's face.

"Yes, I look forward to coming to work. And also, it almost seems like this isn't a bar, but some other kind of place."

"Well, if it's not a bar, what is it?"

"A kindergarten!"

Shizu-chan almost fell out of her chair, laughing. Before very long, Mama-san returned and Shizu-chan presented her with this masterpiece. Mama-san was reminded of the fact that the Chagalls and the Miró, all hanging on the wall, were also childlike. Even the small, low chair in the corner was appropriate for a kindergarten, she thought.

Around Christmas and at the end of the year, The Tomoshibi was not affected by irregular waves of customers. Just as there were never times when the bar was full and customers couldn't come in, so there was never a day when there were absolutely no customers. Momoko was most grateful for the fact that she wasn't compelled to wear a fancy kimono just because it was Christmas or New Year's.

Mama-san casually wore lovely, unobtrusive things, but she did not force her pleasure in clothes on other people.

"Happy New Year!"

"We value your patronage and hope to see you again this year."

Early in the new year, one customer dashed in as soon as they opened the bar crying "Happy New Year!" Mama-san politely repeated her New Year's greetings, and without waiting for any prompting from him, asked, "Well?"

"They were born!"

"Well, that is an auspicious event indeed! How many of them?"

As usual, they were discussing dogs.

"Six. . . . I went out of my way to make sure that only purebreds got to her, but I failed again. Half of them are spotted. Even their faces are quite different from their mother's."

"That's probably the aftereffects of a previous mate."

"I've heard that's so. . . once you've made a mistake, you can't breed purebreds."

"But aren't the puppies cute?"

"Cute things are cute, even if they're mutts. There are too many of them, but I can't bring myself to give them away. My son also says that they're his children and loves them very much. It's a nice feeling."

As they spoke, another person who shared their interest wandered in, and leaning forward, commented, "Even though you may think they're mongrels, sometimes it happens that while you're rearing them, they become purebreds, just like one of their parents."

"Isn't that a miracle!"

"A miracle, indeed. In my experience, this is where the owner's character plays a great part!"

"I see. . . ."

"Yes, it's really true. Was it in Aesop that the ugly duckling became a white swan?"

"Wasn't that Hans Christian Andersen?"

"Whichever! In any case, things like that happen."

"So then, will you try to raise all six of them? A miracle might happen to at least one."

For a while after that, miracles were the topic of conversation. After those customers had gone their merry ways, and before the next wave of customers arrived, Momoko said, "Mama-san, miracles really do happen, don't they?" She started to speak very seriously.

When Shizu-chan asked "Have you ever seen one?" Momoko nodded in assent, saying, "My eyes are getting better!"

Momoko continued in front of her two listeners who were holding their breath.

"From when I was small, I was always teased about my eyes. As I got older, it was even harder to bear, and I was always crying. Since I could make better money in a bar than at other jobs, I was able to help my family, but the customers always mentioned my eyes. It was really painful."

Looking up suddenly, Momoko's eyes lost the correct balance between right and left, and one side inclined outwards.

"Ever since I came to this bar, nobody has commented on my eyes. In the beginning, I thought that you were purposely avoiding the subject. But even the customers didn't say anything. When I came to think of it, nobody seemed to even notice my eyes. On New Year's Day, I went to the mirror and was almost too scared to look—until then, I had always disliked large mirrors and had used a compact to do my makeup. Then, well, miraculously, my eyes were cured! I don't know why they got better, but I think that miracles do happen after all."

Mama-san, who had been listening attentively to Momoko's story, said, "Really? How wonderful!" She spoke with great feeling, placing her hand on Momoko's shoulder. Shizu-chan looked as if she were going to cry if she spoke, so she quickly turned her back to Momoko and said in a deliberately dry tone, "How wonderful!"

To the two of them, it did not seem as if the miracle Momoko had spoken about had taken place, but if that was what Momoko believed, then a miracle had definitely occurred.

"Hello there!"

Once again familiar customers were coming through the door.

"Welcome! Happy New Year!" Momoko greeted them cheerfully.

Translated by Keiko Nakamura

Hiraiwa Yumie

Hiraiwa Yumie (b. 1932) is one of the most successful authors of television drama in Japan today, although her activities, ranging from playwriting to traditional Japanese dance, cover such a wide field that it would do her no justice to single out any one of them. A graduate of Tokyo Women's College, she started out as a writer of popular historical fiction, and at age twenty-seven received the highest literary prize awarded for that genre. Although she married in 1960 and became a mother the following year, her writings expanded both in quantity and in scope, extending to detective fiction, juvenile literature, and short stories with modern settings. She also began writing scenarios for TV dramas, and a series she wrote in 1967–68 attained a Neilsen rating of 64.2%, thereby becoming the most popular drama in the history of television up until that time. She has authored many other popular TV dramas since. One of them, called the Hiraiwa Yumie Drama Series, has been among the longest lasting television programs of all time.

Hiraiwa's works frequently include the word "woman" in the title. This is because they almost always pursue the implications of being a woman and of living as one in Japan. "Lady of the Evening Faces" (*Yūgao no onna*) is taken from one such book, a collection of short stories called *Women of Japan* (*Nippon no onna*, 1979). The story's title alludes to one of the heroines of *The Tale of Genji* whose delicate, passive, fragile beauty is compared to a flower known as the "evening face," a kind of moonflower. Like that flower, which opens for just a couple of hours in the evening, the coy noblewoman dies after a fleeting love affair with Prince Genji. Her daughter, however, is stronger and survives the hardships of a motherless childhood until finally she comes under the prince's protection. Hiraiwa's story focuses more on the daughter: when it begins, the mother is already dead and the daughter is preparing for her hundredth-day memorial service (the common practice in Japan is to commemorate a person's death every seventh day for seven weeks after the funeral, followed by the hundredth-day service). The television drama "Lady of the Evening Faces" was broadcast on Fuji TV in April 1979, with Wakao Ayako playing the leading role.

LADY OF THE EVENING FACES
Yūgao no onna

Hiraiwa Yumie

Yabe Mieko had decided to observe her mother's hundredth-day-memorial service alone. As noon approached, the light of the sun had reached the middle of her mother's sitting room, which extended into a small garden on the south side of the house. In a corner of the room unbrightened by the sun, Mieko had placed an altar stand. On it she had arranged her mother's memorial tablet and a photograph taken a year before she died. The photograph showed her dressed for the New Year holiday in her finest clothes; she wore light makeup and, with her head tilted slightly, appeared self-conscious. She looked much younger than her fifty-three years. When she died, Mieko chose this photograph to place on the family altar because it had been taken by Matsumura Kazuo and also because she liked the way it made her mother look.

At the time of the forty-ninth-day memorial service, Mieko had set out two more altar stands and on them had placed a basket of flowers, some cakes, and in the center the Remy Martin brandy her mother had enjoyed. In this regard, the hundredth-day observance was more or less the same. The major difference was that on the forty-ninth day a number of people who had been associated with her mother had come to pay their respects.

As if it were quite natural, Matsumura Kazuo had sat beside Mieko and greeted the guests as the "husband" of the deceased. The guests, in turn, were aware that Yabe Kae had been his lover, and they accepted his filling this role. Most of the guests, taking a common-sense view, had given their tacit consent to the couple's immoral relationship. They even looked with favor on the love between Matsumura and Kae because it had lasted for nearly thirty years and because they knew that during her life, Kae had devoted herself to Matsumura far more than his own wife had. They were reassured, as well, that Matsumura, except for not marrying her, had amply rewarded Kae.

In fact, in the two years since Matsumura had retired from his position as an executive director of a large bank, the two had been, in everyone's eyes, a loving husband and wife entering their twilight years together. Every three days, at least, Matsumura came from his own house near Seijō Gakuen to Kae's house in Aoyama, cared for her small garden, and looked in as she instructed a few close friends in the art of Saga brocade weaving. The two occasionally went for a walk as far as the area around Yoyogi Park. In general, they seemed to be following a quiet, easy lifestyle appropriate for their later years.

People close to Kae, knowing that Matsumura Kazuo had a wife and children, took it for granted that his wife, as well, recognized Kae's position and sanctioned the relationship. Thus, they saw it as natural that, when Kae died suddenly of heart disease, Matsumura, who was the first to arrive, made all the funeral arrangements. Furthermore, they watched over him with concern, moved by the extent of his grief, which became more intense with each seventh-day memorial service.

The incident occurred in the midst of the forty-ninth day service. Suddenly two women rushed in from the garden and tried to drag Matsumura out.

"How dare you cheat on us this way!"

"You traitor!"

"You're inhuman!"

Their shouts were heard by everyone present, and the younger of the two women struck the altar, breaking it. In a daze, Mieko shielded her mother's mortuary tablet and photograph with her body. The younger woman then shoved her away from behind. The guests were in an uproar, and the priest fled without finishing his recitation of the sutras.

After this tempest had subsided, Mieko realized that the two women were Matsumura's legal wife and his daughter and that the man who had come in after them and led Matsumura away by force was his son. The forty-ninth-day service had become a shambles, and after that Matsumura did not visit the house in Aoyama. Instead, the son, Kunihiko, came with a lawyer and thoroughly cross-examined Mieko about the relations between her deceased mother and Matsumura.

"Mr. Matsumura was a friend of my deceased father. After Father died, he was kind to us in many ways."

Mieko said nothing more to the two men. In her opinion, the way Matsumura and Kae had chosen to associate with each other was not the concern of a third party. She had wanted to say that Matsumura had neither divorced his legal wife nor abandoned his family for Kae, and yet it had been Kae, rather than his wife, who had been devoted to him. No matter what reasons she might have offered, however, the odds were against her.

Mieko waited meekly as the days passed. Not a word came from Matsumura, not a single phone call. The hundredth-day service neared, and Mieko made up her mind. She wrote to each of her mother's acquaintances who had attended the earlier observances, asking them to refrain from coming on the hundredth day. She was sure those who had witnessed Matsumura's wife and children bursting in at the forty-ninth-day observance would understand completely. She also declined the services of the priest. He was the chief priest of the temple where the members of the Matsumura family were buried. Undoubtedly, he was relieved that his presence was not required.

Mieko assumed that Matsumura Kazuo would not come either, but during the morning of the hundredth day, a florist delivered a vase of flowers. No card was attached, but he said the order had come from Mr. Matsumura. Mieko held onto the faint hope that he might by some chance arrive. Although she felt lonely, her main thought was of how glad her mother would be if he were kind enough to pay a visit.

Mieko had decided on two in the afternoon as the time for the observance. Of course, she was not expecting anyone to come, so that was merely her own schedule. When the hour arrived, Matsumura had not appeared, and she realized that he would not, probably in deference to his family.

Mieko's mother, whom Matsumura had loved, was dead. Mieko was fond of him, but she was not his daughter. Matsumura was in his late sixties. It would be his wife and children who would look after him from now on, in his old age. Naturally, whatever his inclination might have been, he could not treat his family unkindly.

Mieko slowly got up from her seat on the floor and knelt before her mother's memorial tablet. She poured some of the brandy her mother had liked into a glass and, after looking for a moment at the photograph, placed the glass before it.

"It can't be helped, Mother. Mr. Matsumura does have a wife and children." Mieko was just thankful that his relationship with her mother had not been disclosed to his family any earlier. It was fortunate, at least, that Kae, while living, had not experienced any unpleasantness.

Three times Mieko lifted a pinch of powdered incense and dropped it in the burner; then she joined her hands reverently. At that moment, she heard footsteps in the garden.

"Excuse me, but the front entrance was closed." The young man lowered his head in apparent confusion as Mieko turned to look at him. He was a tall man, about the same age as Matsumura's son, but he was not the one who had led Matsumura away by force.

"I'm afraid I don't recall having met you." Mieko got up and went out to the veranda, where she knelt down again.

"My name is Ogata Hajime." He offered his calling card. It seemed he worked in the research division of a university pathology department.

"Are you a doctor?"

"Yes. Actually, I'm here at Mr. Matsumura's request. He won't be able to come today."

"Is he ill?"

"Yes, well, he's in the hospital."

"Which hospital? What's wrong with him?"

Ogata Hajime regarded Mieko with embarrassment and answered only her first question. "He's at a hospital in Izusan. May I come in?"

Mieko, who had been taken by surprise and had begun to stand, settled back down. "Please do," she said.

Ogata removed his shoes, passed in front of Mieko, and seated himself before the portrait of the deceased. Out of habit Mieko straightened the shoes he had taken off. She thought it curious that they were large shoes. Matsumura, who was of medium height and build, had small feet for a man. She did not know the shoe size of her father, who had died when she was a baby.

Coming to herself, Mieko went to the kitchen and made tea. When she returned, Ogata was still seated as before, his eyes fixed on Kae's photograph. Mieko offered him the cushion she had readied for Matsumura. He held himself stiffly at first, then changed position and sat cross-legged.

"Are you by yourself?" he asked, as he lifted his teacup.

"I thought I would keep today as a private remembrance. I didn't know Mr. Matsumura had been hospitalized." She inquired about his condition.

"It's come about gradually over the last month. First he injured his hip." Ogata lowered his gaze to the teacup. "When he returned home from the forty-ninth-day memorial service here, he apparently struck his hip in the entryway." His eyes, as he looked at Mieko, betrayed complex feelings. He seemed to know about the events of the forty-ninth day.

"It happened as he was struggling with Kunihiko, and he didn't think at the time that it was serious. It became quite painful later, though." Matsumura had seen a doctor, but afterward he became unable to stand on the hip.

"So he was hospitalized for that?"

The expression in Ogata's eyes darkened further. "The hospital in Izusan where he is now specializes in geriatric conditions."

"Geriatric conditions?"

Ogata turned his gaze toward Kae's photograph. "I think your mother's dying came as a considerable shock to Mr. Matsumura." Falteringly, he explained the sudden aging of Matsumura Kazuo. "In years he's still not that old, but there are many examples of men in whom retirement or a death in the family leads to such aging. Something which has been stretched tight until then suddenly loosens, and senility sets in."

Mieko was astonished. She simply could not believe that Matsumura had become senile. When she thought about it, though, she was reminded of his abstracted state immediately after her mother's funeral. Again and again she had seen him, his eyes filled with tears, gazing fixedly at Kae's photograph. Even when he spoke to someone, he seemed dazed, and he made no attempt to hide his beaten expression.

"Is his condition very bad?" Mieko asked, her voice unsteady.

"I can't say it's good, but it's not as if he doesn't understand anything at all. Actually, since several days ago, he's been obsessed with today's service for your mother. So much so that he asked me to come here."

"It was you who ordered the flowers, wasn't it?" The likelihood occurred to Mieko, and she lowered her head. "Is his family taking good care of him?"

"No, it seems none of them visits him." As if he himself were a member of the Matsumura family, Ogata added, "I just don't know what to make of it."

Mieko, however, could understand the family's anger. When Kae's existence had become known, Matsumura had been denounced as a traitor by his wife and children. How unpleasant it must have been for them to learn that he had sunk into senile confusion from the shock of his lover's death. Mrs. Matsumura and the children must have honestly felt that they did not even want to visit him, let alone care for him.

"Would it be all right for me to visit him?"

"Why not? I'm sure he'd be delighted." Ogata told her where the Izusan hospital was located and, soon afterward, went home.

Mieko wanted to go to the hospital right away to see Matsumura, but because of her job, she had to wait until the next Sunday. She worked in an office in a modern building in Toranomon, where for three years she had been private secretary to the Tokyo branch manager of an American soft drink company. Her boss, Michael Brown, was a native of Boston, once divorced and currently single, a young man much enamored of Japan. He was kind and cheerful, and Mieko found it easy to work for him. He had come to both Kae's wake and funeral, but Mieko had purposely not notified him of the subsequent services. Occasionally, on weekends after he had returned from business trips to New York, she would be kept busy with extra secretarial duties.

Saturday evening, on her way home, Mieko picked up the eel sushi she had ordered ahead of time from Matsumura's favorite sushi shop in Akasaka. She left home early on Sunday morning. Traveling by the local Odakyū and Izukyū lines was less expensive than taking the bullet train. An only daughter raised by a single mother is sensitive to such insignificant details.

From Atami, Mieko headed toward Izusan by bus. The hospital which Ogata Hajime had told her about was a much smaller, shabbier building than she had even imagined. All of the people being cared for there were elderly, which probably accounted for the impression the place gave of being a home for the aged rather than a hospital.

Matsumura Kazuo was brought in a wheelchair. He had aged completely during the mere month and a half during which they had not met. The vitality was gone from his eyes, and the strength had drained from every inch of his body. Even so, his face lit up with joy when he recognized Mieko. His words, however, were uncertain and rambling, as if he suffered a speech disorder. Just when Mieko thought he would call her by name, he cried out, "Kae!"

"He often calls out your mother's name, 'Kae, Kae!' many times a day." So the nurse taking care of Matsumura, Okamoto by name, told Mieko when she learned Kae's identity. She spoke as though she knew, in general, about the affairs of the Matsumura family. When asked, she informed Mieko that neither Mrs. Matsumura nor the children had even once come to the hospital since Matsumura had been admitted.

"The daughter's fiancé—or, anyway, the man who will become Mr. Matsumura's son-in-law—often comes and spends the whole day trying to talk with him, even though he doesn't understand much. Mr. Matsumura cheers up a lot, too, when he comes."

When noon came and Mieko set out the eel sushi she had brought, Matsumura wolfed it down. Watching his manner of eating, which could not be called anything other than "wolfing," she was unable to hold back her tears. The Matsumura she had known had been a well-groomed, respectable, reliable gentleman. He had possessed a dignified bearing as a bank executive, and wherever he went he was respected as such. When she had been with Matsumura, Mieko had overlooked the fact that she was his lover's daughter and had felt completely confident, accompanying him with a feeling of pride.

Now, however, he was dressed in a worn, dirty sweater and trousers that hung on him loosely, showing his sudden loss of weight. His unkempt hair had lost its sheen, and sparse stubble covered his chin. Mieko could hardly bear to look at him as he grasped his chopsticks with a hand like a withered tree branch and, mumbling, stuffed his mouth with food. Looking down, she poured his tea and carefully picked up the grains of rice he had dropped.

When he had finished his meal, Matsumura began napping like a child. Back in his bed, he wrapped himself up in his blanket and immediately began to snore.

"Generally, the family looks after a patient if the care needed is no more than this," the nurse said. Aside from dealing with his recurring incontinence and his inability to move his legs, Matsumura was a patient requiring little attention. The process of aging, however, was precipitate.

"Some men become confused when their wives die, but Mr. Matsumura is the first I've known to become senile after his mistress died. He really did love her, didn't he!" The nurse laughed coarsely even though she knew that Mieko was the said mistress's daughter.

While Matsumura was sleeping, Mieko thought she would pay her respects to the doctor who had visited her house. She thought he might have the day off, because it was Sunday, but she asked Miss Okamoto to see if he was in the hospital.

"Dr. Ogata?" The nurse puzzled over the question. "There's no doctor by that name here." She looked at the calling card Mieko held out and began to laugh.

"Oh, him. He's the one who's going to marry Mr. Matsumura's daughter."

Mieko was taken aback. It had not occurred to her that Ogata Hajime was the fiancé of Matsumura's daughter. Although it was clearly written on the calling card that he worked in a university pathology department, Mieko had jumped to conclusions and had taken for granted that he was a doctor connected with this hospital.

She found herself going into the hospital courtyard. Spring had come to Izusan earlier than to Tokyo, and the plum blossoms had already passed their prime. The sun was bright, and the sea was blue. She was standing there absentmindedly when footsteps approached. Just as she was thinking, it's those footsteps, Ogata said, "You showed up after all."

Mieko, not knowing what look she should assume, turned around reluctantly. Ogata wore a more relaxed expression than he had the time before.

"Mr. Matsumura seemed to recognize you," said Ogata. He ate a lot of eel sushi, didn't he?" Recently he added, he had been quite worried over Mr. Matsumura's loss of appetite.

"I. . ." Mieko could not suppress what she was thinking, and continued, "I'm such a scatterbrain. I thought you worked at this hospital." Although she had intended to laugh as though it were a joke, a note of reproachfulness could be heard in her words. She was flustered. "I had no idea you were Yōko's fiancé." Mieko knew the name of Matsumura's only daughter, who was two years older than Mieko. Matsumura had doted on this daughter.

"We became engaged in November of last year. It's an arranged marriage." Ogata spoke without reserve. "There's a danger of my being misunderstood if I say this, but it's Mr. Matsumura I'm fond of." His former pathology professor was a close friend of Matsumura's from high school and through that connection Ogata had come to know him.

"The professions of physician and banker are different, but I always had great admiration for his personal character or, should I say, his attitude toward life. And I always was a bother to him in one way or another."

Through this acquaintance he had met Matsumura's daughter Yōko and had gone on to become engaged to her. "Right after we got engaged, Mr. Matsumura confided in me about you." Matsumura had told Ogata about Kae, saying that he loved her more than his wife. He had entrusted his lover and her daughter, if anything should happen to him, to the man who would become his son-in-law, and Ogata had accepted.

"It may seem odd, but I knew Mr. Matsumura's character and understood that he couldn't help being as he was, so I assumed he was doing the only possible thing under the circumstances. In fact, when I asked him about what had happened, I was touched by your mother's love for him."

Mieko thought that must have been the time when Matsumura was manager of the Osaka branch. He had left his family in Tokyo and taken up his new appointment alone. The bullet train had not yet been constructed, and the special express train between Osaka and Tokyo took seven hours. That was seventeen or eighteen years before and, because of concern over the education of their son, who was in junior high school, and their daughter in elementary school, Mrs. Matsumura did not move from Tokyo. Moreover, she did not even try to go to Osaka on weekends to look after her husband. Her primary concern was for her own delicate constitution.

In Osaka, Matsumura caught a cold and then developed pneumonia. Although complications arose and his condition became quite serious, Mrs. Matsumura did not rush to his side. She too had caught cold and had a kidney inflammation. It was Yabe Kae who hurried to nurse him.

Mieko, who was in elementary school, stayed home with her grandmother, who was then still living. Mieko wanted to see her mother, and sometimes her grandmother took her to Osaka for the weekend. Her mother was completely worn out, but she looked deeply fulfilled. She hugged Mieko tightly. "I'm sorry, forgive me." She was in tears, but nevertheless she did not return to Tokyo with Mieko. Mieko surmised that it was then that her mother and Matsumura had become lovers.

That was not the only time Kae had devoted herself to Matsumura. Also during his stay in Osaka, he was told by a doctor that he had high blood pressure and possibly diabetes. Kae strove, using intensive diet therapy and Chinese medicine, for the recovery of Matsumura's health. The doctor was astounded by the results. From then until the present, Matsumura had maintained almost perfect health.

Mrs. Matsumura seemed to know nothing at all about that. She always thought her own health of greater importance than her husband's. In addition, she seemed the sort of woman who was incapable of using her own judgment in handling all the household affairs and anything having to do with the children, something about which Matsumura had often complained to Kae. She was the sort of wife who called her husband when he was involved in an important meeting to tell him that the maid had suddenly taken time off. When the children received poor grades in school, she hysterically found fault with him.

"My wife is angry with me because, she says, I'm too caught up in my work and don't help the children with their studies as well, but who is it I'm working for? I work like a dog to make a living for my family, for their future. Why can't she understand that? Besides, there are always times when a man has to forget his family and do his job. My wife, though, just doesn't seem to understand, no matter what I do."

Mieko also remembered Matsumura saying, as he relaxed in the living room of their house in Aoyama and ate Kae's home cooking, that he was sick and tired of it all. It occurred to her that if Mrs. Matsumura was the type who made things difficult for her husband, then Kae was the type who did everything she could for a man. The people around Matsumura, who knew both Kae and Mrs. Matsumura, also agreed on this point. Had Matsumura spoken about such things with his future son-in-law?

"I was acquainted with Mr. Matsumura for quite some time, but until I became engaged to Yōko, I knew nothing at all about his family. After our engagement, I gradually began to understand the significance of what he said. Now, since he's been afflicted by this aging phenomenon, I understand all the more."

Matsumura's wife and children did nothing but criticize him for having had another woman for so many years, but, Ogata continued, "They had no interest in considering why Mr. Matsumura had come to do such a thing. They didn't even want to hear about how helpful the other woman had been to him. I know how emotional a matter it must be for them, but it's a shame that they're so stubborn and disagreeable."

Ogata said he intended to dissolve his engagement to Yōko. "But, if I bring it up right now, they're likely to interpret it as a reaction to Mr. Matsumura's condition, and so I'm waiting for the right time. I don't want to be responsible for giving him any further shocks." After Ogata finished speaking, he looked refreshed. "Why don't we go to Mr. Matsumura's room? He's probably up now."

Studying Ogata's back as he walked ahead of her, Mieko felt mixed emotions. His explanation for breaking the engagement with Yōko seemed reasonable, but also selfish. However he might argue, in the end wasn't his real concern that marriage to the daughter of a man who had become senile would be burdensome?

Ogata's behavior that afternoon, however, was sufficient to clear away Mieko's doubts. Matsumura, having awakened from his nap, was overjoyed to see Ogata. His words were incoherent, but his facial expression became animated, and he listened to Ogata's conversation with continuous pleasure. Ogata, for his part, went on chatting about a wealth of topics, from one to the next, just as if he were talking to an ordinary person.

From the recent news he chose specialized economic and political topics, as well as talk of pro baseball, a favorite of Matsumura's, and the latest developments in his own field of pathology. Mieko, sitting with them, also found the conversation of unflagging interest. Matsumura listened earnestly to Ogata's conversation. He did not respond, but it was obvious from his appearance that he was satisfied with simply listening.

The afternoon waned, and visiting hours ended at five o'clock. "Well, I'll come again next week. You take care of yourself until then." When

Ogata said good-bye, Matsumura appeared sad. He whispered something in a voice too low to be understood and wheeled himself, alone, back to his hospital room.

"It's always like that when I leave. He seems so lonely. Even patients hospitalized with an illness from which they're expected to recover say the loneliness they feel when their visitors leave is unbearable. In Mr. Matsumura's case. . . ." Breaking off, Ogata was silent. This patient had no hope of leaving the hospital.

At Tokyo Station, Mieko parted from Ogata. They had returned by bullet train.

Mieko went to Izusan every Sunday. Occasionally, the visits became a heavy burden. The company for which she worked was foreign-owned, and consequently, the employees had a two-day weekend. For Mieko, however, now that her mother had died and she lived alone, one day of the weekend was taken up with housecleaning, laundry, and shopping for the week's supply of food, as well as with various other chores.

The deed to the Aoyama property had been transferred to Mieko some time before, but the house was still in her mother's name. With the future in mind, Kae had saved a considerable amount of money, and the inheritance from Mieko's father had been skillfully managed by Mr. Matsumura and had withstood the ill effects of inflation. The funds seemed sufficient for Mieko to pay the inheritance taxes without disposing of the house, but in settling the matter she had to go again and again to the ward office and the tax office.

Of course, there were times when she wanted to stay at home on Sunday, relaxing and simply doing nothing. The trip to Izusan inevitably took the whole day, but even so, she would rouse herself and set off.

Just as Matsumura had loved Kae, he had cared for her daughter. It was as though he took the place of the father Mieko had lost when she was young. She told herself that, in return for his kindness, she had to do all she could for Matsumura in his old age.

Ogata also, without fail, went to the hospital on Sunday. Invariably they met there and returned to Tokyo together on the bullet train. Mieko found this rather awkward. Apparently Ogata only had Sunday off, so Mieko even considered changing her day for visiting Izusan to Saturday. A sudden change from Sunday to Saturday, however, surely would have seemed contrived to him and in fact the errands she had to attend to on Saturday mornings had increased. She could only visit public offices and the bank at that time.

As a result, Mieko went to Izusan every Sunday, met Ogata, and on the way home, in the bullet train, they talked about themselves. Ogata's family operated a prominent, large hospital in Sendai, with his father as administrator and his brother as assistant administrator. He, the youngest child, had specialized in the unglamorous field of pathology because it appealed to him. It had also been decided that he would inherit all the assets his mother had brought to her marriage as the daughter of a wealthy Sendai family. Thus he could devote himself to his research, free of the worry of working for a living.

"Even though my monthly salary is enough for me to eat and live on, somehow my parents seem to think I'm incapable of earning a living." Ogata, as he said this, seemed just like the pampered son of a good family, a pleasant-natured young man with a strong sense of fairness.

Spring passed and soon the rainy season began. Quite naturally, Mieko grew close to Ogata. From parting at the station, they had gone to having dinner together and to visiting each other at home. Ogata lived in a small apartment in Takadanobaba. He had lived there since his student days; when his marriage arrangements were settled, he would receive money from Sendai and move to a proper apartment. His apartment building was fairly old, and the rooms had no baths. The public bath was far from his place and inconvenient, so he did not go frequently. Mieko would invite him to her house after they had returned and heat a bath for him. Then she began to cook him dinner and would serve him beer. He could not handle alcohol well, and when he drank, he often fell asleep. Before long, the two had become lovers.

That summer, Matsumura died quietly at the hospital in Izusan. "I've heard many cases of people who pass away like that with amazing quickness. They begin to age severely and, with their family unable to care for them, get put into that kind of hospital," Ogata reflected. "I feel sorry for all of us. Don't you? The way our health and strength can fail so suddenly."

In her position, Mieko could hardly attend Matsumura's wake or funeral, and thus her connection with the Matsumura family was completely severed. The same was true of Ogata. His engagement to Matsumura Yōko was broken, and instead, preparations for his marriage to Mieko were begun. Her relationship with the Matsumuras was kept secret from Ogata's parents in Sendai. The Ogata family members, who were somewhat disapproving of the match because Mieko had no close relatives, were not particularly opposed when they learned that she was the daughter of a middle-class family, her deceased father having been a man of some means who had been employed by the Ministry of Finance.

Most importantly, Ogata had already moved into Mieko's Aoyama home, and they were living as husband and wife. In the autumn, Mieko went to Sendai, where the marriage ceremony took place. The older brother of her deceased father, who came from Fukuoka to attend the ceremony, was Mieko's sole relative. In these days, however, people are in fact happier to be unencumbered by relatives.

The ceremony had taken place, but the couple's life hardly changed. They lived at Mieko's house in Aoyama, and Ogata commuted every day to his laboratory at the university. Mieko continued working as well. There was no need for her to stop; she was earning a larger salary than Ogata. Even though he was a doctor, the size of his salary as a pathologist working in a laboratory can well be imagined. He also had to buy books to use for his doctoral dissertation, and on many occasions he put some of his own money into his research. Mieko announced, soon after they were married, that it was fine if he used his income in this way, since her earnings were sufficient for them to live on. They had no housing expenses and could eat quite well on her salary. Ogata neither drank much nor gambled. In giving her all for her husband, Mieko had a reason for living. They received no assistance from Sendai, but as long as Mieko was working, they could get by financially.

An exhilarating year went by. Mieko got up at six in the morning, prepared breakfast, made their lunches, and before waking Ogata, took care of the housecleaning and laundry. In the evening, when she finished work, she rushed from the office, did her shopping at the supermarket, returned home, and made dinner. Except for one night a week, when he worked late, Ogata usually returned home at seven.

Mieko became unsociable even at the office. She was no longer invited by her co-workers to go out to dinner or tea, and she stopped accompanying the branch manager to movie previews on Friday evenings. When there were parties, she would give some excuse and not attend. Her company being financed by foreign capital, lively parties were held at every opportunity.

Before her marriage, Mieko used to attract much attention at these gatherings. The unmarried branch manager, Michael Brown, invariably served as her escort, and her chic evening dresses, as she stood beside him—he would be wearing a tuxedo or dinner jacket—were always admired. She dressed well, and she knew what flattered her. When she went shopping for a new evening dress, she was always in the company of Matsumura Kazuo. The exclusive Akasaka shops offered an assortment of the finest designer fashions from Europe. Matsumura took great pleasure in choosing from among them a dress which suited Mieko and in giving it to her as a present. Consequently, evening dresses in vogue that year were always hanging in her closet, and these, in fact, were enough to make Mieko the belle of the party.

Once she had married, Mieko had no choice but to reduce her clothing expenses. The cost of food was greater than when she had lived with her mother. Then, they had been satisfied with green tea poured over rice, but that would not do for Ogata. Although not on a regular basis, Matsumura used to give money to Kae quite frequently, and that too had helped the Yabe household's finances. Now that income had stopped.

Mieko was ashamed to go to a party in an old dress. Before her marriage she had thought nothing of wearing the same dress many times over with a change of accessories, but after the marriage she could only see this as a sorry alternative. When life had been comfortable, she had not noticed; now that she had to live on a budget, both she and her surroundings appeared meager and left her feeling anxious. There were the savings and stocks her mother had left her, but she did not want to live so extravagantly that she had to use them.

Mieko began to think that it would be good if Ogata occasionally showed some concern about this state of affairs. She would have been delighted with insignificant things like his bringing home some top-quality beef on payday or giving her special cakes or seasonal fruits, but he seemed to lack even that much thoughtfulness. Since he did not give her his salary, she thought he at least ought to give her his semi-annual bonus, saying, "Here, use this where you need it," but he was completely indifferent on this score.

It was not that Ogata was stingy. At the hospital he was, in fact, easily parted from his money. This was probably to be expected, since his entire salary became spending money. He boasted to his co-workers that his wife told him to do with his salary as he pleased. "You're lucky to have a good wife. Do you know what mine does? Every month, after she's snatched away my paycheck, she goes on and on about how little I make, how I'm no good for anything." Ogata listened in a fine humor to his co-workers' envious words. It was his practice, when the bonuses were distributed, to treat them at his own expense.

Ogata was imposing on Mieko the unmitigated spoiled nature of the youngest child in a family lacking for nothing. He was delighted and content with her self-sacrifice, but he failed to notice that she was beginning to feel dissatisfied. From his point of view, it was Mieko who had said it was all right if he did not give her his earnings for living expenses, and her mother had, in fact, lived half her life in devotion to one man.

In her second year of marriage, Mieko's birth control failed, and she had an abortion; afterward her health was greatly impaired. Physically she recovered in no time, but mentally she was devastated. She lost the expectation that she had cherished until then that some day she could stop working and have a baby. Their livelihood always weighed heavily on her shoulders, and what with her work at the office and her chores as a housewife, she had absolutely no free time.

Had she been single, she could have let the housework slide. She could easily have gone without doing the cleaning and laundry every day. She could also have eaten out and saved herself the time of preparing a meal and cleaning up afterward. She would also have been free, if she were single, to take time off, travel as she wished, and recoup mentally or to go to parties with her co-workers and enjoy herself as much as she desired. But now her life included something called "a husband," and she could not do as she wished. She gradually became exasperated, wondering just what that husband who had tied her down so was doing for her.

And yet Mieko could not go so far as to make demands. Why didn't she say the words, "We're having a hard time making ends meet, so please put in a little of your salary"? Her silence could only be ascribed to an uneasiness that, were she to put her discontent into words, her pride in the thought that until then she had sacrificed herself for her husband would be shattered.

In any event Mieko, in her second year of marriage, already felt worn out and driven into a corner, and began to look on her husband with the greatest distrust.

In June Michael Brown, the branch manager, was transferred to New York. The succeeding branch manager had already come to Japan, and a party was held both as a welcome for him and a farewell for Michael. Mieko could not fail to attend. She selected and wore the newest of her dresses. She had bought it all of three years before, but she had not had the energy to buy a new dress.

The party was a success, and Michael thanked her for her years as a most capable private secretary, danced with her, and kissed her good-bye several times. He was an extremely handsome man, often said to resemble Robert Redford, and his athletic build, as he neared forty, was attractively masculine. In contrast, the new branch manager was an extremely fat man who sported a short mustache. Inwardly Mieko was disappointed. Even though the branch manager changed, the fact that she was the manager's secretary did not.

One day after Michael had returned to New York, Henry, the new branch manager, called Mieko aside during the lunch break for a rare private conversation. He had already spent ten or so years in Japan, and any native whose speech was poor could have taken Japanese lessons from him.

"Yabe-san, when did you get married?"

"It will be two full years in autumn," Mieko answered unconcernedly.

"I hear you got married soon after your mother passed away."

"Yes, it must have been half a year later."

"Had you been seeing the man you married before she passed away?"

"No, I hadn't. . . ."

The corpulent branch manager, when he saw Mieko's suspicious look, shook with laughter. "Do you know that Michael was hopelessly in love with you?"

Mieko shook her head. "That's a poor joke."

"It's no joke. He was seriously disappointed." Henry said that in fact he had been asked for advice two years before, when Michael had come to New York on business.

"He said he'd taken quite a fancy to his Japanese secretary and wanted to marry her, but she and her mother had no one but each other, so he had hesitated to propose. Her mother had just died, though, and a chance had arisen. So I told him that in Japan, for a year after someone in the family has died, there can be no talk of happy events and that he should wait for a year. But, half a year later you got married."

Mieko tried to brush aside the conversation as the new branch manager's joke. Nevertheless, the idea that Michael had been about to propose to her lodged deep in her heart. Before she knew it, she was comparing Ogata and Michael. When she saw that in every respect—appearance, sex appeal, finances, status, and character—Michael was superior, Mieko's feeling toward Ogata became decisive. Perhaps because her love had cooled, she could not bear to think what a fool she had been. In spite of the fact that she had been sacrificing herself for Ogata because of love, because she loved him as her husband, how much thoughtfulness had he shown her in return?

"If you need money, why don't you just ask me for my paycheck? How can I tell if you don't say anything?" That was Ogata's reply when Mieko finally brought up the subject.

"Even if I don't put it into words, as long as we're husband and wife, you ought to know. You of all people, living on my salary for everyday expenses, should know." Mieko felt that a woman's self-sacrifice and loving care should be answered spontaneously by her man's even greater thoughtfulness and concern. At least the relationship between her mother and Matsumura, with which Mieko was most familiar, had been like that.

"That's because you don't know what marriage is," Ogata said in amazement. "What you're talking about is the relationship of a man and a woman who aren't married, at least a man and a woman who can't marry. What I mean is, a mistress or kept woman accepts 'give and take' as a matter of course."

Having been informed that this did not hold true for married couples, Mieko said no more. The one-sided service of a wife to her husband might be considered the natural course because love is there, but in Mieko's case that love had already disappeared. She now felt only the desire to be free.

"If you leave me, you'll be all by yourself. Don't you think you'll be sorry then, that you'll be lonely?" Until the end Ogata sought to change Mieko's mind, but she thought only of leaving him.

In autumn, just before their second wedding anniversary, Mieko became single again. She was indeed lonely, but she was free. From then on, she would be able to live just for herself.

She noticed that the men and women walking about town thinking the same way were surprisingly numerous. They all strutted triumphantly along the chasms of the city wearing the elegant expressions of the single nobility. Mieko left in the evening, and lost herself in their throng.

Translated by Patricia Lyons

THE TRANSLATORS

The translators of the stories in this anthology were all enrolled in Professor Makoto Ueda's course on "Images of Women in Modern Japanese Literature" at Stanford University. This course has been offered in alternate years over the past decade. Many of the translators have completed, or are working on, degree requirements for doctorates in Asian Languages at Stanford. Others have received B.A. and M.A. degrees and are now employed in various fields.

BETH CARY was Assistant Director of the Center for East Asian Studies at Stanford before assuming her current position as Assistant Director of the Japan Society of Northern California. CHIA-NING CHANG, Assistant Professor of Japanese, University of Hawaii, is doing research on modernist Japanese literary criticism in the Meiji-Taishō period. WEI-MING CHEN received her Ph.D. in Chinese literature and is now a free-lance translator/interpreter of Chinese and Japanese in the Bay Area. RICHARD DASHER, a Ph.D. candidate in linguistics, is language training supervisor for Japanese, Korean, and Tagalog at the U.S. State Department Foreign Service Institute. SARA DILLON is a Ph.D. candidate in Japanese literature at Stanford, and also a writer and poet.

MARK A. HARBISON is writing a dissertation on intertextuality in medieval Japanese poetics and is one of the translators of Professor Konishi Jinichi's *History of Japanese Literature*. He is also translating two recent novels by Ōe Kenzaburō. STUART HARRINGTON resides in Japan and is with International Interfaces, Limited, in Yokohama. AGATHA HAUN wrote her dissertation on prison literature in the Soviet Union and Japan. She is now doing research in Finland. CHRIS HEFTEL is a member of the Hawaii Law Bar and Vice-President of H & W Communications in Honolulu. ROBERT HUEY, now Assistant Professor of Japanese at the University of Hawaii, has written a book on medieval Japanese poetics and is now doing research for a book on poetry contests in the same period.

PATRICIA LYONS is writing a thesis on the agrarian poetry of Miyazawa Kenji. MARYELLEN TOMAN MORI, now a doctoral candidate at Harvard University, is doing research on the writer Okamoto Kanoko. KEIKO NAKAMURA teaches Japanese language and history, as well as Asian-American Studies, at Harvard University. KAREN KAYA SHIMIZU received her B.A. from the University of Southern California and her M.A. from Stanford. She is now with the First Hawaiian Bank in Honolulu.

Literature

ACTS OF WORSHIP   Seven Stories

Yukio Mishima / Translated by John Bester

These seven consistently interesting stories, each with its own distinctive atmosphere and mood, are a timely reminder of Mishima the consummate writer.

THE SHŌWA ANTHOLOGY
Modern Japanese Short Stories

Edited by Van C. Gessel / Tomone Matsumoto

These 25 superbly translated short stories offer rare and valuable insights into Japanese literature and society. All written in the Shōwa era (1926-1989).

THE HOUSE OF NIRE

Morio Kita / Translated by Dennis Keene

A comic novel that captures the essence of Japanese society while chronicling the lives of the Nire family and their involvement in the family-run mental hospital.

REQUIEM   A Novel

Shizuko Gō / Translated by Geraldine Harcourt

A best seller in Japanese, this moving requiem for war victims won the Akutagawa Prize and voiced the feelings of a generation of Japanese women.

A CAT, A MAN, AND TWO WOMEN

Jun'ichiro Tanizaki / Translataed by Paul McCarthy

Lightheartedness and comic realism distinguish this wonderful collection—a novella (the title story) and two shorter pieces. The eminent Tanizaki at his best.

CHILD OF FORTUNE   A Novel

Yūko Tsushima / Translated by Geraldine Harcourt

Awarded the Women's Literature Prize, *Child of Fortune* offers a penetrating look at a divorced mother's reluctant struggle against powerful, conformist social pressures.

DISCOVER JAPAN, VOLS. 1 AND 2
Words, Customs, and Concepts

The Japan Culture Institute

Essays and photographs illuminate 200 ideas and customs of Japan.

THE UNFETTERED MIND
Writings of the Zen Master to the Sword Master

Takuan Sōhō / Translated by William Scott Wilson

Philosophy as useful to today's corporate warriors as it was to seventeenth century samurai.

THE JAPANESE THROUGH AMERICAN EYES

Sheila K. Johnson

"Cogent...as skeptical of James Clavell's *Shogun* as it is of William Ouchi's *Theory Z*."—*Publisher's Weekly*

Available only in Japan.

BEYOND NATIONAL BORDERS
Reflections on Japan and the World

Kenichi Ohmae

"[Ohmae is Japan's] only management guru."—*Financial Times*

Available only in Japan.

THE COMPACT CULTURE
The Japanese Tradition of "Smaller is Better"

O-Young Lee / Translated by Robert N. Huey

A long history of skillfully reducing things and concepts to their essentials reveals the essence of the Japanese character and, in part, accounts for Japan's business success.

THE HIDDEN ORDER
Tokyo through the Twentieth Century

Yoshinobu Ashihara

"Mr. Ashihara shows how, without anybody planning it, Japanese architecture has come to express the vitality of Japanese life."
—*Daniel J. Boorstin*